What peopl

MW01681120

"The time to air out this content is ripe!"

– *Post News Diaper Rag*

"Some things never get old. While others most certainly do. Rochester reveals it all, unsparingly!"

– *A Wrinkle in Type*

"A comedy for the aged!"

– *The Fifth Dementia*

"So flush with adventure you'll want to take even longer in the commode!"

– *Constipatreon*

"In this long-awaited accomplishment of his underachieving life, #3 still manages to fall short. Again. Oh well. I don't need his money anyway. Is this thing still recording?"

– James P. Rochester Jr. II (his father)

"Rochester delivers internal buzz for the old and crotchety alike!"

– *Partzheimer's Digest*

"Get ready for a lot of romp and circumstance!"

– *The Still Life*

"It's good to see women put back in their places!"

– *Beyond 70*

"At last, a formidable challenge to insomnia—without medication."

– El Autor

Pill Record

Day	Name	Wake	Mid-Morn	Mid-Aft.	Eve
Mon					
Tues					
Wed					
Thur					
Fri					
Sat					
Sun					

AGENT BIGGLESBY

NOT DEAD YET

JAMES P. ROCHESTER JR. III

MARTHA ZACCHEUS MAGDALENA
VENTURA, CALIFORNIA

Published By:
Martha Zaccheus Magdalena, LLC

First Printing Edition, 2026
ISBN 978-0-9816195-1-4

Dedication

To all the little engines that run a little slow,
or get distracted and ground down by life,
or who prioritize taking care of others:

Rest and be assured.
God knows what He is brewing.

Your focus will soon return,
and you will find a time and a pace
that work. Don't rush it.

Author's Note

I would like to thank the handful of people who encouraged me and helped me bring this project to fruition. You know who you are, though probably not what you mean to me.

Most especially,
Mom, 1939-2023
y Papá, 1934-2023
who sometimes laughed at my jokes.

AGENT BIGGLESBY

NOT DEAD YET

JAMES P. ROCHESTER JR. III

CHAPTER ONE

Glorious Swansong

Long linoleum hallways. Buzzing fluorescent lights. The pungent smell of urine and hospital napalm, still prevalent in our pacific theatres of group demise. Welcome to Sunset View Senior Living & Dying Community. (They don't put the latter on the signs, of course.)

Endless beige walls seem to go on for kilometers, with sagging wooden handrails broken up by identical doors to identical rooms. Intensely shiny floors are embedded with red, yellow, and brown lines to guide even the most demented of patients and staff. It feels like 1970 but somehow it's already almost 2030.

In this eerily quiet setting, a masked figure in black prowls about. In a motion picture, tight close-ups could temporarily disguise the brittle old age of man and facility alike, but not for long. Angular limbs, shuffling feet, and shabby decor conspire too much to expose the façade. And sudden glares of pale translucent skin don't help either, peeking out from openings between his faded black ski mask, gloves, and jumpsuit from a time before the moon landing.

He abruptly stops before committing to the next corridor. The metal equipment in his backpack clinks and settles. He knows he doesn't pack it like he used to and worries someone might have heard him. Listening, he only hears canned laughter on a distant TV, and the flickering lights overhead. Our man rethinks his direction, not yet in life but in this hallway which ought to be more familiar.

Was it the other way? he tries to recall. Beads of sweat pool around his bushy white eyebrows. As he peers around the corner, he hears the tinny sounds of a movie playing from a cell phone propped up on a medicine cart. *The Godfather* (Coppola, 1972), he confirms.

Our man suddenly ducks back as a female nurse exits a room and moves her cart to the next one. The man looks again, eager to see her. She is young and beautiful, wearing the facility's burgundy scrubs, with blue latex gloves and colorful sneakers. She chews gum as she glances at her movie and prepares another pill cup.

Why does everyone look so young? our man ponders for the millionth time in four decades. Her beauty only intensifies as she gasps at Hollywood gunshots, car doors slamming, and a vehicle racing away.

"Oh, Fredo!" she laments. "That is so sad!" She looks around, wishing to share her pain with someone.

I'm here for you baby, our man wishes he could say. She clearly needs comforting. *And age is just a construct.* This was one of his key takeaways from a class on aging. *The other was...* He can't quite recall. Perhaps it will come back later. *She already had her chance,* he reminds himself. *And I have other plans tonight.*

A coughing resident calls out, "Have you finally come to make passionate love to me, Darling?"

Our man perks up, hopeful for *the poor old loser.*

The woman sighs and enters the room with his dosage. Our man cranes his neck to see but can only hear murmurs. To his credit, he wonders if he even heard right. He might only be reliving his own past. She had shut him down earlier with, "No, Sir. Just delivering your evening cocktail."

"What cruelty!" he had said. "For someone to joke like that in a place like this!"

The nurse returns to her cart. On her phone Michael Corleone says, "I know it was you, Fredo. You broke my heart." She needs a moment to collect herself.

Isn't that Godfather Two? wonders our man, confused *by what they're doing these days.* His mind wanders again. *Oh yes, the second was that it's important to die without regrets. You get in life what you have the courage to ask for.* And, *always be yourself!*

He had agreed with Freud from a very early age. *Suppression and repression are worse than cancer. Though ultimately throat cancer got Freud, maybe he should have cut back.* Our man waits to match his next move to the nurse's.

"Then will you please give me some hemlock already?" had been his answer to her rejection.

"Sorry, no hemlock for you!" had been her witty reply. This was a nod to her recent discovery of *Seinfeld* (David & Seinfeld, 1995). "Besides, you know we have to keep our numbers up. Accounts Receivable would be very sad if something were to happen to you."

"Your emotions show some bounds, Darling," he had despaired aloud. "But don't worry, I won't hold it against you when you change your mind. One has to make allowances for youthful rashes and discarding what is of ageless value."

She didn't call attention to his blurring of concepts. Nor did he try to explain to her how, in many a time and place, he had been rewarded and not shamed for voicing his wants and wishes openly and unabashedly. Many a woman had been willing to join his exciting rides in life. It had made him a gambler with a mantra of, *Always go for broken.*

This is his usual banter. Most female staff ignore it. Occasionally a newbie takes the time to visit Human Resources to request a reprimand or even dismemberment. ("From the community," she clarifies, to avoid her own write-up.)

The bases of female complaints have generally gone over his head, much like the flickering fluorescent above. It suddenly gives up and goes dark, which pulls him back to the present moment.

He notices the cart has moved and the nurse is entering her next room. He looks both ways and launches himself into the corridor, shuffling past her cart. He teeters around the next corner and makes it out of view, undetected.

The nurse returns to the hallway and instinct—or more likely odor—makes her look in the direction he went. Hearing nothing, she resumes her rounds.

Mere feet away, our man leans against a wall, sweating profusely. He raises his mask above his nose and catches his bad breath. To address it, he takes out a container of TicTacs and shakily pours a few onto his gloved hand. Only one then makes it up to his mouth. The others drop to the floor, bouncing loudly. He freezes in place.

Somewhere in the facility several TV monitors capture this ward's winning performance. Yet only an empty chair and a half-eaten bag of spicy pork rinds are there to appreciate it.

Our man sweeps his fallen TicTac comrades to the wall with his foot. He then eyes the elevator bank and hurries toward it. A loud DING sends him pivoting into a room.

The elevator doors open and two large, baby-faced, Asian-looking male Twins emerge. They wear the same burgundy scrubs of the facility. Their eyes are pasted to their cell phones as they walk, scroll, and guffaw in unison.

A wandering senior in a bathrobe pushes a walker nearby.

"Wrong floor, Mr. Downright!" says one of the Twins. "You need to go up, right? Mr. Downright?"

The confused senior returns a blank stare.

The Twins nod as if teachers begging for permission to move on. Mr. Downright finally nods and turns to the elevators.

"By the way," calls out the other Twin. "Have you seen Mr. B wandering around anywhere?"

The old man returns another long blank stare but nothing comes to mind.

Was he in politics? wonders our *oxygenarian* in the shadows.

"That's ok!" says the Twin, regretting the delay.

They continue their search. Downright returns to his original hallway, the elevator already forgotten.

"I'm not going to have any more of that, thank you!" yells a man from the bed far behind our ninja. Startled, our man turns and sees his eyes are closed, *perhaps he is dreaming*. He quickly assesses where to hide and opts for the bathroom instead of the other unoccupied bed.

A Twin pokes his head into the room but does not see the figure entering the bathroom. "Have no more of what, Mr. Eulogy?"

"You're not fooling me!" insists the resident.

"About what?" asks the Twin. He remembered to use an open-ended question rather than signal awareness of problems.

From his hiding spot, our man studies the Twin's face. *Samoan perhaps?* He hasn't quite figured out their features and has been told it is impolite or even aggressive to ask. *On some microbe level. Next, they'll have us washing our thoughts three times a day.*

"Don't play dumb with me!" barks Mr. Eulogy. "You're all trying to kill me!"

Our man in black is all ears. He has been increasingly worried that *it would be sad and ironic to die here of all places, murdered in this pathetic nursing home.*

"Pathetic Senior Living Community," corrects a female voice in his head.

"How exactly are we trying to kill you, Mr. Eulogy?" asks a Twin.

"Poison! There's poison in my food!"

Our man expects to hear words of shock and denial in some polished corporate dialect.

Instead the Twin answers, "Oh my, that's a very insensitive thing to say, Mr. Eulogy! It not only implies we are hired killers but that we are not very good at our jobs. I don't know how I feel about that." The Twin is pleased with himself for recognizing a *teachable moment*.

Both seniors are taken aback yet admire the honesty.

His brother chimes in, "Don't worry, Mr. Eulogy, no one here is going to force you to eat. You can just sign a waiver."

"A waiver for what?"

"To reduce our liability."

"Oh, nothing will stop your lying ability! Just keep it all away from me!"

"That's ok," assures the Twin. "Toxic media seep in one way or another."

Each elder man blinks with helplessness.

The Twins leave. "Have a good night, Mr. Eulogies!"

Our man shuffles back to the door. Mr. Eulogy notices him and wonders if he should be on his feet too. He chooses to relax instead since they're clearly after the other man first.

Our man sees the Twins walking toward the nurse's cart. In the opposite direction the elevator doors are still open, beckoning.

He makes a break for it. As he crosses the intersecting corridor, he sees Mr. Downright, lost. They lock eyes and Downright raises a hand for help. Our man feels torn.

Moments later, Downright stares out blankly from the elevator. Our man crouches behind him; he reaches around and taps the top button repeatedly and quite loudly. *Oops.*

The Twins stop and turn as if cats detecting prey.

Our man holds his breath in addition to his bladder, *which has been for quite a while now.*

The Twins' view of the elevator is Downright-obscured. His vacant smile suggests more of the same, so they wave and turn away.

Mercifully, the elevator doors glide shut. Our man relaxes his posture but not yet his bladder. "Maybe Filipino?" he wonders aloud.

Mr. Downright has a lucid moment. "Yes, plus something else."

As the elevator begins to rise, a Twin calls out, "Hey Ronda, any sign of Mr. B tonight?"

"Is that idiot missing again?!"

Our man is offended. "I am not missing. I am staying active, as recommended."

His cocky smile emerges and is matched by a bright flash of light. In the hallway below, a green fluorescent light saber has sparked back to life.

Chapter One Point Two

Contraband

On the seventh story rooftop, the air is cool and crisp. A door opens and our ninja emerges, his breath crystalizing. He immediately shields his neck with his hand. *Not another kink, I hope!* He grumbles about how often problems show up in his body. It could be from a whole night of sleeping in the wrong position or from a simple sneeze.

His thoughts are interrupted by a whiny male voice. "So, you thought you could get away with it?!"

Our man's heart defibrillates. He sighs with resignation and turns, hands uplifted, but not in prayer.

To his surprise his accuser is facing away, talking on his cell phone and vaping. He is the facility's lone security guard, skinny and pale, with a discount uniform several sizes too big. "What am I talking about?! I was on SpotMyDriveway and saw it all!"

To our man he only looks fourteen. *But that can't be right. Tattoos creep out of his collar and sleeves. You can't be fourteen and get those, can you? Aren't they permanent?* He remembers to duck behind the large air conditioning apparatus, conveniently placed for situations like this.

The other party must have said, "And?" The guard continues with, "And! That was not my truck in our driveway!"

Uh-oh, busted! thinks our man. He wants to hear it all but then remembers his own unauthorized plans for the evening. He scans the area below but no car awaits. He checks his watch and gives it a shake, wondering if it's even working.

"Repairman my foot! What's broken?" demands the guard. "Ok, other than the garbage disposal… And the light in the den! Fine but… Ok, and the dryer too! Well, how much is he charging?!"

And how is she paying? is what our man wants to know.

Down below, a beat-up sedan arrives and idles under some trees. Our man is pleased but concerned. *He better wait for me.*

"Hang on, hang on," interrupts the guard. He checks his phone for a text. "I'm sorry, Bubbles, I gotta go. The same idiot keeps going missing again."

Our man almost blurts out, "Can we all just take an IQ test and see who the real winners are in this organization?"

The guard hangs up, hits his vape, and throws his cell phone over the edge as if a spent cigarette. "No, man!" He looks down hoping to mark where it smash-lands but soon gives up and hurries into the building. His keys sway loudly from his belt. *I should get a siren. I'm a first responder too, you know!*

He almost plows Downright over as he emerges. "Whoa, what are you doing up here ol' fella? I bet you need to go down, right?"

"Yes, badly!" answers the poor guy. "I've been holding it for hours!"

"Well, I'm sorry you brought it up." The guard escorts him. "Here, let me let you down."

That's accurate! observes our man to himself. When the door closes, his muscle memory takes over. He executes precision moves from a prior lifetime. Except, his zipper won't budge. He tugs at it and contorts himself in different positions. He finally gets it open and brings out his rusty old equipment. First, a harness but he can't quite remember which end is up. He puts his legs through it and somehow gets it right.

Next, he cannot recall how to thread the line. He stirs up an old rhyme from cobwebs in his mind. *A rabbit and a weasel walk into a park. One hooks left while the other jukes right… I guess it has been a while.* He threads it as best he can. He then anchors the line to the HVAC equipment and gives it a tug. He seems satisfied but then second-guesses himself. *An extra knot or two wouldn't hurt.* He ties it twice more and pulls it tight with all his might.

Ready at last, he takes a deep breath, stands tall, and runs for the ledge. A sign reads, *Watch Your Step.* Before he reaches it, he trips and falls head-first into the gorge-like alley below.

To the amazement of the balding, mid-50s male driver in the car below, this headlong descent looks quite *bad-rumpus.* But to our hero it is quite terrifying and possibly the end.

Numerous thoughts occur to him as they would to anyone in such a seemingly slow-motion-event as this. Typical thoughts might be, *Do I have any regrets about my life? Should I ask God for mercy?* Yet for our senior it's more like, *Was I too picky? Should I have compromised my feminine ideal more?* He wishes he could leave a message for the facility director. *Do take me off the meal-count, Peaches. I shall be late henceforward.*

However, during what appears to be the final split-second of his life above earth, he manages to turn himself around. He jerks the brakes and experiences long, high bounces. His compressed cane goes flying from his pocket and explodes into full size upon contact. He realizes he used a bungee cord instead of a rope.

As he is kept in suspense high above the pavement, our man scans to see if any neighbors have noticed. Not a single porchlight comes on. Feeling safe to proceed, he releases more cord. He then falls to the ground and down to one knee, like a marvelous superhero with one fist to sidewalk. Not intentionally, of course. He steadies himself while catching his breath and scanning the perimeter. He spots the broken cell phone. Then his cane beyond that. And the idling car, venting its toxicity.

Instinct makes him look high into the night sky. A distant star seems to twinkle on and off. Timing himself to an off-moment, our man lunges into a roll. He bobbles his cane but recovers it. He checks again for the twinkling light in space. When it goes dark he makes another awkward roll and is disappointed to require a third one to finally reach the car.

He stands a bit dizzy, with leaves and debris clinging to him. He taps on the passenger window. It lowers and he confirms, "Al?"

The driver shuts off his Paul Simon (1986) song and says, "You can call me Alfred." He passes our man a large manila envelope.

Our man opens it, reviews the contents, and appears delighted. He then opens his fanny pack, which spills out used, balled up tissues. He counts out six twenty-dollar bills and offers them to the driver, who hesitates to touch them. He finally accepts them, turns on a light, and holds them up to it. He has no idea what to look for but it's standard practice at the Dollar Generator where he once worked. He finally says, "Ok, get in," and unlocks the door with the ease of a button.

Our man enthusiastically works to discard his gloves and jumpsuit. It's not easy. His pants get stuck about his ankles as he tries to shimmy out of them. He leans onto the car to avoid falling. As he untangles himself, he also removes his mask. "Free at last!" he loud-whispers.

His face revealed, it is high time to more properly introduce him. He is 84-year-old Herbert Bigglesby, former superspy, affectionately dubbed 0070 by friends' and enemies' dislike. There is some controversy about which side dubbed him 0070 first, but all agree it suits him well, like the old tuxedo he now straightens. He also fixes his bad combover. (Dear Reader, are there any good combovers? He'll look quite a bit better when he commits to baldness.) He then kicks away the last bit of jumpsuit and opens the car door.

"Mr. Bigglesby!" calls a harsh female voice.

He looks up. It's Mrs. Pearbottom, the *boss lady* of this facility. She is in her sixties, matronly and robust, wearing a kind of suit no one should wear, not even in Washington. Her once-exceptional beauty is presently concealed by a combination of neglect and intentionality. It wouldn't take much to restore this national treasure.

The Twins lag behind her, putting away their phones. They each notice the smashed electronic device on the ground and seem to want to stop and honor it or get it tended to.

Herbert locks the envelope under his arm and climbs into the passenger seat. "Do floor it, Alfred," he says coolly.

Mrs. Pearbottom blocks the car door from closing. "Stop, Mr. Bigglesby! You're not going anywhere!" She almost ends up on his lap as they struggle for the door.

"Quick! Close the window!" commands Herbert as he pushes the button repeatedly. It does not work.

"Her hand is there!" complains the driver, refusing to undo the window lock. "Besides, I need all the fresh air I can get." He turns away from Herbert and lowers his own window further.

Herbert continues his pathetic struggle. The Twins grab the door.

"Mrs. Pearbottom!" whines Herbert. "This is *my* life! Manage your own life and leave mine alone!"

The driver feels inspired to find a particular song by Billy Joel (1978) on his phone.

Herbert continues, "Driver, let's go! I'll pay double!"

Alfred shuts off the engine. "Sorry, Pal. Not happening."

Herbert huffs in disbelief. "I didn't say you could call me *Pal*."

Mrs. Pearbottom scolds him. "Mr. Bigglesby, this behavior is unacceptable! You still belong." To the Twins she commands, "Help me raise him up."

"I'm not dead yet!" Herbert grips the emergency brake and the handle over his door, trying not to budge.

The Twins extract Mrs. Pearbottom and she straightens out her outfit. Next, they yank on Herbert but he holds tight. "Don't get me wrong, Mrs. Pearbottom! Just carry on without me!"

She stares at him in disbelief. *How do I live here without you?* (Warren/Yearwood, 1997) she would like to sing. Yet she refrains from such a refrain, knowing the next one to sing will lose.

After a final effort, Herbert relaxes his arms, smiles, and announces, "Alright, then! This concludes our drill. Thank you all for participating." He winks at the driver and climbs out but keeps the door open. "I'm afraid, however, that I will have to recommend a FAIL since it's obvious I could easily have been this man's hostage tonight if I had not stalled for you to arrive."

The driver looks shifty. He hopes the old man's ludicrous hypothetical scenario will be taken for the clear conspiracy mongering that it is, with no basis in reality.

"Oh, stop this nonsense at once!" demands Mrs. Pearbottom, much to the driver's relief. He still wishes Herbert would close the door.

Herbert keeps up the ruse. "I do suppose I could throw in a few points but I really don't see how I can let you go."

The driver pleads, "Can I just go with a warning? I mean, I have other affairs—rides—to get to."

Mrs. Pearbottom regards him for a moment, wondering if he should be detained. Fortunately for him, she has enough to deal with tonight. She nods to a Twin, who closes the door. The sedan shrieks away before the door even catches.

They all watch him go, wondering.

Herbert looks up at the sky and shields his face. "Can we get out of satellite view?"

The Twins look up too but Mrs. Pearbottom is livid. "No! There is no satellite! And this is not a drill! Mr. Bigglesby, please hand over the contraband."

Herbert turns away and fiddles with his hearing aid. "Oh, no thank you, I can walk myself."

"I know you hear me perfectly well," insists Mrs. Pearbottom. She gestures for the Twins to grab him, which they do. "Give it here."

"No! It's mine!" Herbert tries to keep the prize out of reach, as if an actor being robbed of an Oscar during the Gollum Age of Hollywood (Academy of Motion Picture Arts and Sciences, 1963; Tolkien, 1993/Jackson, 2001).

The Twins hold on tighter as Mrs. Pearbottom tries to secure the envelope. "I won't!" insists Herbert. "You can't make me!"

On the contrary, the Twins force open his hands and Mrs. Pearbottom takes the package.

Herbert is deflated. "Oh, woman! Do let a grown man retain some dignity."

As Mrs. Pearbottom peruses the contents, Herbert worries some of his *contentments* might be misconstrued. Violations become so much clearer during execution than when only musing about them.

"Before you judge me, please know I have been taking your lectures on self-care quite seriously, and to heart."

Mrs. Pearbottom extracts vodka and cigars saying, "No, and… no." She hands them to the Twins who are delighted with their spoils. She continues, "Herbert, you know Dr. Hamstrung expressly forbade all manner of–"

"Yes, inhalants and blood thickeners!" fumes Herbert. "Really now, how is a lad of that age supposed to understand the true nutrients of life, beyond what he reads in textbooks? There's no diversity of thought in those tomes!"

Mrs. Pearbottom digs out a pair of concert tickets. "LA Phil?"

"Is he any good?" asks a Twin, trying to see the tickets. Both are interested.

"That's 4,000 kilometers from here!" complains Pearbottom.

"Distance is relative, Madame. We should see the Boston Pops while we still can."

"The Founding Fathers?" asks a Twin.

Herbert ignores them. "It's not like I'll be missed if I'm gone."

Any hope of denial by Mrs. Pearbottom goes unmet. She draws out the final item: a magazine entitled, *Brazen Biker Babes with Big*

Bazookas. The cover shows two sexy women in tight leather, armed with grenade launchers and machine guns.

"Trade!" and "Hey, I said it first!" comes from each Twin.

Mrs. Pearbottom's eyes narrow. Her remonstrating glance produces a shift in the Twins, who now condemn the contraband.

Herbert defends, "You shouldn't judge them by their lack of cover. Unlike the present company, I believe those ladies could protect me, and keep me warm to boot."

The Twins appreciate what appears to be a fine intellectual point, worthy of a college education.

Herbert pushes further. "Surely we can all appreciate the publisher's challenge in trying to garner interest in an obscure collection of poignant essays on the Marxist Feminist Ontological Ipso Facto 19th Century Post-Elizabethan Ideal without a little, shall we say, candy for the eyes?"

"And they wonder why diabetics go blind," retorts Mrs. Pearbottom. She has had enough and says so. "I have had enough! Get him inside, please."

Herbert dreads his fate. "I am to be burned with the steak!"

"Hardly."

"No, just puréed into the mush that poses for critical thinking these days. A no-salt intellectual diet. Why maintain blood pressure at all, I wonder?"

"Please remove him," orders Mrs. Pearbottom.

The Twins nudge him toward the door but Herbert pulls away. "Mrs. Pearbottom, with all due respect, may I have a word?"

After a moment she assents. The Twins stand down.

Herbert looks up at the blinking light and leads her under a tree. "Look, I know this isn't your dream assignment either–"

"Oh my!" she scoffs. "What do you pretend to know about my dreams?" In the space of a millisecond her mind flashes with a myriad of times doodling in her fifth and sixth years of schooling. She would draw images of elderly folks in wheelchairs, playing shuffleboard, or having physical therapy. Her very young self smiles with crooked yellow teeth.

"I believe I was in those dreams once," interrupts Herbert, his eyes sparkling.

"Goodness, how you flatter yourself."

"Defend your pride all you want," he says. "But worry not. I won't betray our long history together."

She turns to the Twins, afraid they heard and might believe him. "Nonsense! We do not have that kind of history together!"

"Of course not! Nevertheless, how am I to impress upon you to take my concerns more seriously? Why, even that driver could have been here to do me in."

Mrs. Pearbottom struggles not to explode. "You're blaming me for something you yourself arranged? Have you gone native?"

"Perhaps." Herbert gestures over her shoulder.

She turns. Endless billboards advertise personal injury lawyers who can help you pin your hopes and dreams on the backs of others. *Passive Income Now!* says one, *$6 Billion in New Settlements!* Or, *Strike the Empire Back! $9 Billion in Awards!* And, *There's No Shame in Being a Vampire-American! $12 Billion Jackpot!* These are just a few.

Herbert continues, "I simply believe my safety requires more than Harold and Claude over there."

"We can hear you," announces a Twin, looking up from his phone. "And I'm George."

"Oh, confound it!" barks Herbert. He knows their names but he will never tell them apart. He pulls Mrs. Pearbottom further away. "I just don't believe they are trustworthy. And on Mr. Eulogy's behalf, I'm going to report them to the Ombudsman for mental tampering."

"Mr. Eulogy?" She can't help a smile. She looks around to make sure she can speak freely. "I don't normally say this, but we all know he is quite out-of-it."

"So is your one security guard!" complains Herbert. "You really pick 'em from the bottom of the litter."

She stares at him. "Well, we are a second-chance facility."

Ouch. Herbert moves on. "Mrs. Pearbottom, surely you recall there have been literally hundreds if not thousands of people who have wanted to see me dead."

The Twins share a look and snort-giggle. Herbert and Mrs. Pearbottom move further away.

"And they had their chance," answers Mrs. Pearbottom. "Plus, your numbers are quite exaggerated, especially for the past fifteen years. Nobody cares anymore."

"That you know of!"

"Herbert, even before we announced your demise the whole world could see you slipping. I mean the spy world. Any remaining hatred or animosity was replaced by feelings of pity and good wishes."

"Pity? For me?"

"Your funeral was hardly even necessary. More of an excuse to get everybody together one last time."

"Except me, of course."

"Yes, well, that would have been awkward. But you were able to see it on closed circuit. Headquarters spared no expense! And the salmon was amazing."

Herbert stews on his negative memories.

Chapter One Minus Five Months

Forced Funeral

Let us now catch the reader up on how Herbert ended up being relegated to a quaint nursing home in a rural United State. A brief list of mishaps will suffice. Any resemblance to other secret meetings and proceedings with a bureaucrat citing reasons for a forced retirement should either be ignored or assumed spot on.

Here are the minutes and *secondings* of Herbert's dismissal, as posted online by a formerly gruntled employee who is now acting way out of line.

"First," begins the Committee Chair, "let us consider the grave gravity of the *femme fatale* incident. Picture this: At 30 thousand feet, a 79-year-old male agent sporting a tuxedo and chic eyewear bee-lines it toward our falling, flailing female asset who is on track to collide with the very Mother Earth herself. It was a typical situation in our world; that part is not unique. In fact, this male agent once did these things flawlessly and with his eyes wide open. But by 79 he was sometimes closing his eyes, or becoming distracted, and on this day he overshot the asset. Undeterred, the seemingly helpless damsel took charge and maneuvered herself toward him instead.

"Yet, just as their hands were about to clasp, our man bobbled it. Yes! He pulled his parachute cord too early and, from the woman's point of view, he seemed to fly upward, sadly waving goodbye. She was left to imprint her final mark on the Earth she loved so much as a dedicated Vegan.

"Folks, there is no need to suppress any emotions. It is perfectly proper to feel aghast, and a whole range of other things, given this shameful failure to adequately protect and cover our assets worldwide. It should be noted that, according to our sources, even the pursuing assassin, who now goes by the name of Rosie, by the way, found herself respectfully averting her eyes. It could be presumed she felt pity for our *Spy in the Sky* (cfr. Parsons, 1982) who so clearly demonstrated being past his prime, his bedtime, and his era of useful service.

"Yet that mishap did not suffice for the powers that were, or are, or are yet to be. (Eh-hem, Mrs. Banquet, are you feelin' me? You seem distracted by your phone... Thank you, much obliged.) Allow me to continue. This agent was then given yet another chance, due to claims of expertise in multiple areas. It was argued that he had several legs up on our newer agents and could guide them on proper footing in various locales.

"These videos I now present show our renowned agent at 81, on a Vespa 946 Dragon, still my personal favorite, trying to navigate the unapologetically narrow alleys of urban rural Italy. As you can see, he does not quite enjoy the mastery he once possessed. Did you see that? Let me rewind it. Here he *unwitfully* and with many witnesses plows over a free-range American couple, strolling their newish baby in a carriage. This kind of incident had never before been seen in our history, not even in our most unofficial reports, let alone official ones.

"Of course, no one disputes that our work, undertaken in the interest of National Defense, often involves unfortunate collateral damage. However, the death of a planned, chosen, and explicitly wanted baby made the story difficult to deny or bury. It created a public relations nightmare and the media took to it as if introducing an Olympic athlete from an abusive background followed by a coaching scandal. Garnering similar empathy, the public quickly learned that the parents of this child had struggled for decades to even conceive of conceiving, let alone to successfully have a child delivered safely across land and sea. Apparently, this formerly impossible, inconceivable, and surviving-against-all-odds kind of biological being was a modern miracle, an answer to many thoughts and prayers, and the fruit of hard work and pilgrimages to scientific shrines far and white.

"Our Ministry, of course, did the right, noble, and honorable things. We offered official apologies and even discounted outings to the heartbroken couple. To our detriment, however, they were very well-versed in the stagings of grief and legal sentiment.

"Yet instead of choosing to row the boat in our same direction, our increasing liability of an agent insisted the parents and child were clandestine operatives, commissioned to slow him down while he was pursued by ruthless killers. He maintained this hypothesis even when shown incontrovertible evidence that they truly were innocent civilians. He was then quoted in our national papers as saying, "All that fuss over a baby? Maybe they were better off having cats. They kept their cats alive much longer."

"Do let that sink in, my esteemed colleagues. He was somehow allowed to keep working here. To our shame, this man did not actually retire until physically impaired. These next videos show security footage of him at age 82, outside the palatial home of the Vile One himself, Dr. Henric Vilefinger. Apparently, our man was having difficulty throwing a hook to a mere second story balcony. It's a wonder the hook didn't hit him on the head each time.

"Per another asset, who was long in bed in that organization, we learned that a pack of Dobermanns soon came running for his blood. Our man was able to scramble over a garden wall, but at the cost of his hips which snapped like breadsticks, which is not surprising for a man of his age. Incidentally, has anyone tried the new restaurant on York and Sussex? Simply divine, especially the artisan bread. Anyway, such bone fractures can happen to any of us much sooner than at 82, just by miscalculating the geolocation of our chair.

"Fortunately, Dr. Vilefinger was a good sport about it and did not press charges. Yet somehow our man, still naive to his own obsolescence, managed to wrangle a consulting role for himself. What a wonderful idea it seemed, after all, to further reap the fruits of his decades of experience. Indeed, to harness his know-how from an entirely different century, nay, another planet! And so, we kept him on to offer his wildly inappropriate counsels to our newest and most impressionable young agents.

"As I understand it, in all fairness, his handler did try to dissuade him. He made it quite clear that fieldwork would no longer be about ingredients for nuclear recipes, nor about uncovering clandestine training camps. Perhaps he hoped our agency's turn toward *computery* and economic *spycraft* would be a sufficient turn-off to the Cold War veteran. Yet this unretiring man, increasingly impaired in wisdom and in strength, persisted and prevailed. And our colleague, *per se*, fully regrets caving against his own better judgment.

"Thus, even as a consultant this agent found ways to do harm. Here is footage of him meeting in a hospital cafeteria with a novice agent, whose real name is being kept under wraps. This is due to the sensitivity of his current mission, and also to help us save on insurance premiums by assigning the same Member ID to several similar agents. While this video has no audio, the then-trainee alleged our man counseled him to attempt to seduce the head of Personnel of all departments! Of a Beijing firm with close government ties. The purported goal was to discover torrid secrets, Asian laundering, and poorly clad situations, which could be exploited via *blankmail*, to not be offensive. And, rather than accept a reprimand, our man defended his misogynistic practice as a sound, routine strategy.

"Incidentally, perhaps the World Health Organization would do well to consider adding a diagnosis for him and his ilk. In contrast to the startle and flight response of posttraumatic stress disorder or PTSD, this man still detects opportunity in every spark, no matter how unfounded or inappropriate. It could be deemed a post-nomadic sex disorder, or PNSD, characterized by hasty approach rather than prudent caution, and imperviousness to the evidence of many mounting failures.

"Yet for decades now we have lived in this millennium, and it turned out the woman's government did not like the ruse. They complained vehemently to the point that our own PM has doubted whether to even continue funding our underappreciated world-saving services any further. Oddly, she would rather not have to explain so-called hush money, nor harassment, nor any other such things to journalists and the voting public."

The online minutes trail off after that. In that meeting it was not only decided to permanently retire the aged agent, but to do so in a way so irreversible that not even the best of writers and producers could ever reintroduce such a fallen character. Thus, the Ministry staged a splendid *faux* funeral for the man who now bears the awful responsibility and name of Herbert Bigglesby.

The story of his terminal demise was an easy sell. Anyone relevant already knew he was in the hospital for his new hip surgery, the kind everyone is getting these days. So the phrase, *died of complications*, was easy to propagate and proliferate. And the newly donned don Bigglesby was allowed to watch his own funeral, thanks to a droning drone high up above.

The event was, well, attended. Herbert's remains were hand-crafted and looked quite believable, with even his signature smirk and sharp black tuxedo in place. (By the way, it should be kept in mind that, thanks to skillful negotiation of a two-for-one pricing deal, a second dummy can be procured for another staffer, free of charge.)

Of course, his funeral was a socially obligatory affair. Every relative friend, enemy, villain, rival, and creditor received an invitation. Each had a chance to pay his or her final disrespects to the man who had done so much harm to enemies of the fee world.

One by one the guests approached his lifeless corpse. Some discreetly stabbed it, others used a thin veil for suffocation. A flamethrower was perhaps the hardest to conceal, but Security ignored it, pretending to be among the bribed and imbibed, and not wanting to get burned. Vilefinger himself could not resist sinking his cold finger-of-fame into each eye socket. One by one the guests were all satisfied of his terminal condition. They said farewell to the man who had often been hailed or denied as the most effective male superspy to ever frustrate the forces of evil and governance.

It was only shortly before his funeral that Herbert was so quickly and unceremoniously packed up, delivered, and admitted to Sunset View in rural America. While miserable about it overall, he was quietly pleased that his former colleague, now known as Mrs. Pearbottom, had been assigned there as well. Although he was more than a little chagrined to learn her presence was not that of a peer but in a paid leadership role, undoubtedly correcting for years of male supervision.

Settling in at Sunset View was not an easy affair for Herbert. Ever uncertain of his safety, he immediately began raising concerns. Mrs. Pearbottom would gently reassure him that every precaution was being taken.

Or *taken away*, was his perspective. Yet after months of doubt, he was relieved to hear that Dr. Vilefinger had suffered a stroke and was left incapacitated with vascular dementia. Yet his doubts had a way of creeping back, much like grass in the cracks of a sidewalk.

Herbert would have been much relieved if he could simply observe a typical day between Vilefinger and his loyal caretaker, Godfried. Most commonly, Vilefinger can be found wearing nothing more than a diaper and smearing his feces on a white canvas and calling himself an artiste. Many such canvases, all displayed with blue ribbons, now line his palace walls. (Windows are kept open at all times as a buffer to staff turnover.)

"Godfried!" cries out the dementia patient many times each day.

"Yes, your Vileness" answers Godfried, who turns down his music by Coldplay about formerly ruling the world (2008).

"I almost forgot! We must find and kill that annoying agent, Mr. Super Pants, I forget his name!"

"Yes, your Vileness. I will initiate Project Compassion right away."

Godfried places a call but quietly disconnects it before anyone answers. "Yes, I say, Godfried here. Listen to me carefully. Initiate Project Compassion. Oh yes, he's quite serious. With absolute rigor."

"Yes, absolute rigor!!!" calls out Vilefinger, who follows it with his evil laugh. He then returns to smearing his art. "*Frijoles, frijoles, they're good for your passion project*," he chants.

After some moments he calls out again, "Godfried!!!"

"Yes, your Vileness."

"I almost forgot! We must find and kill that annoying agent, Mr. Super Pants, I forget his name."

"Yes, your Vileness. I will initiate Project Compassion right away."

And so on, and so on.

Of course, Herbert is able to forget danger at times. But he cannot help wondering if, with all the budget cuts slicing through every department, who can really be watching the watchers?

CHAPTER ONE POINT THREE

Mrs. Pearbottom

The discussions that led to Herbert being confined at Sunset View occurred nearly a year ago, at the allegedly ripe old age of 83. He was given a very assuming name, especially of obsolescence.

To conclude with the renames of the day (Ivory, 1993), he was placed under the protection of Mrs. Lucretia Pearbottom. Despite his non-bridal yearnings, Herbert has appreciated her presence but has also tried to have contact with the outside world. People like him tend to imagine that obvious one-way trips like this and Mars can be somehow made roundtrip. Tonight, his seven-story dive into space has been his most elaborate venture yet, from a risky management perspective.

Let us now resume where we left off, with Herbert and Mrs. Pearbottom chatting under the night sky and the Twins catching up on their social media.

Herbert continues, "Mrs. Pearbottom, I realize you think I'm being overly cautious, but my gut has never failed me before. Outside of the bathroom, that is."

She tries to empathize. "Herbert, I do emmpathize. It must be very difficult to stop believing people are still out to get you after decades of that being the case."

"Ah, so it's paranoia, is it?" he scoffs. "Is that how I'm being regarded these days? As delusional?"

"Not at all!" denies Mrs. Pearbottom. "We don't use such terms anymore. They're officially offensive."

Herbert blinks repeatedly and can't help but nod in despair. "Goodness, you people disgust me!"

"Of course we discussed you. As with everyone in our care. We call it interdisciplinary collaboration. It helps dilute responsibility if there's a lawsuit." She then drops her official corporate tone. "Look, in all fairness, I realize you might not be entirely wrong about unfinished threats."

"Thank you! And to what do I owe this magnanimous concession?"

"It simply occurred to me, as a woman, that when the men at headquarters drew up a list of possible remaining enemies and unhealed wounds, they were likely only thinking about men. I doubt they even remotely considered women and children who might want to see you die a slow, painful, death. Not that I personally wish for your demise." She mumbles an additional word.

"*Anymore*? Did you just say *anymore*?"

"What? Don't be silly! If I did not want you here I would have had to declare a conflict of interest for this assignment, and I eschew such paperwork. Besides, I'm happy here. And I wish you could be too. Or were making the most of it."

"I see. You're actually content! We never did have the same ambitions."

"Oh, please. I've made peace with reality. It's time for others to save the world."

"I meant even in the past you seemed to settle."

"My choices were not from lack of ambition! I just knew what was needed for our work to thrive."

"And what was that?"

"Somebody had to have the humility to be there for you and the others. To pick up the phone when each of you would call in from the field demanding accommodations at obscene hours."

"You offered obscene accommodations? To whom?!"

"What? No! You sick man! I'm saying someone had to stay back. We couldn't all be running around, leaving a trail of bodies to be covered up, or hidden away, or denied any connection to."

"Truth be told, I was glad you stayed back. It was too risky for someone I actually cared about." He scans her face for any sign of appreciation but she offers none.

"Herbert, regardless of our differences, you can be quite sure I have only ever wished the best for you. I have accepted the past, the present, and the future. It's all part of my daily practice of loving-kindness meditation."

"Loving which medication?" Herbert adjusts his hearing aid.

"Never mind."

"No, listen. I think loving blindness is nonsense. I still prefer to keep the lights on."

She is exasperated. "I really should get you inside."

Herbert is not one to see a glass ceiling as half broken. "Your suite or mine, Lucretia?"

"Mr. Bigglesby, stop it!" she rebuffs. However, daylight would have revealed a warm blush on her face. Even the Twins look up from their screens for a moment but then feel turned off.

Now, Dear Reader, before your sinful thoughts wander, let us diffuse any potential rumors about any possible lurid history between Herbert and Mrs. Pearbottom. It must be made plain that, despite his many years of justifying everything for the Cause, from petty theft to grand larcenies and indecencies, Herbert never once soiled the linens with Ms. Cynthia Watson, *aka* Mrs. Lucretia Pearbottom. For some reason he always considered her to be out of bounds, and he bound himself to never complicate her life with his.

For her part, Mrs. Pearbottom had early on dismissed the possibility of agents ever being faithful or reliable folk. So in her 20s she had gone on to marry the wealthy and predictably Right Honorably Boring Bantor Brycemore of Brighton Slipping in Fame, Limited. Mr. Brycemore had been a good husband to her, by which she generally meant he was often absent from hearth and home, which provided her with a maximum of freedom by which to serve the world of espionage.

Yet, despite Mr. Brycemore's worldly and temporal success, he had failed to help her engender a human child. That was one side-hustle she had coveted in life and it eluded her.

At this stage of her life she is not about to give in to Herbert's silly and suggestive talk. He is clearly not serious, and what an insult! To pretend interest in so late and desperate a chapter of his life. Post-mortem, officially. Plus, he still chases trainees, and soon he'll be back in diapers. It's unthinkable! Isn't it?

Many women would probably also be asking him, "How can you be this advanced in years, and so close to death, and still not show a morsel of interest or concern in an afterlife or the meaning of it all?"

However, Mrs. Pearbottom is not one of those women. She herself has also maintained decades of living *in the now*. She prefers everything in its place, with problems and hiccups kept to a minimum, and any thoughts about other lives easily dismissed.

Herbert returns their focus to matters at hand. "All joking aside, I'd feel a lot safer if you got rid of those two knuckleheads and added more professional security."

Mrs. Pearbottom surprises him. "I'll tell you what. Let me see what I can do."

He barely knows what else to say since he expected further resistance. "Well, thank you."

Mrs. Pearbottom continues, "However, in exchange, I would like for you to stop denying the challenges of this stage of your life. I would like for you to indulge me and face up to them squarely."

"What are you talking about?"

"Herbert, it's not easy for anyone to lose their former way of life and abilities, much less the role you once played in the world."

"Once? More like thousands of times!"

"Yes," she amends. "And it must be very difficult to no longer be able to come and go as you please."

"Who is spreading these false rumors? I come and go just fine. Even with the marginal excuse for food they serve here."

"See? That's even more on your plate you're dealing with. So will you please start talking to Dr. Bentiron about it?"

"Dr. Bentiron?" Herbert can't believe she is serious. "Do you seriously believe that *child* knows anything? He probably recites the Eight Platitudes. Eat right, daily exercise, sleep hygiene— "

"The doctor may not have all the answers, but everyone has something to offer. Some nuggets of wisdom, if given a chance. And just because your career is now… *complete* does not mean your whole life is over. There are just so many other interesting things to do beyond working."

"Like what, arts and crafts? Origami? I don't fold for anyone!"

"I am not saying you should do things other people enjoy. And I'm no therapist. But even I can see you need to find some new interests. Now that you have passed along the baton."

"That baton, as you call it, was stolen from me! Violently. It's red with blood, *Baton Rouge!* And those hobbies are all fluff! For people whose whole lives have been on hold anyway, like waiting for American jury duty, endlessly talking nonsense."

Mrs. Pearbottom ignores the objections. "I believe the doctor will say you're grappling with the early stages of grief, marked by denial and bargaining and thinking that somehow everything can still be put right. But deep down even you must realize that the evil empires have moved on from having any interest in you."

"Sure, officially! That's what they want us to believe!"

Mrs. Pearbottom grows exasperated. "Well if you think you're in so much danger then why are you out here prancing around and risking this kind of attention?" She can't help looking up at a possible satellite now and then pretending she didn't.

"Aha! Even you just looked!"

"No, I didn't!" she denies.

"Yes, you did! And the risks I take should simply serve to underscore how unsafe I feel here. Look at this place!"

He points to the entrance, where a lot of I's are missing from the large decrepit sign for Sunset View Senior Living Community. He also points at the broken phone. "And that! None of this is serious."

In her hesitation, the mundaneness of it all makes him stop and concede. "But maybe you're right. This is what my life has come to." To himself he adds, *Here I am, being lectured about being obsolete by a jaded old woman who has the gall to deny this place is a warehouse!* Yet his own logic catches him off-guard. "Maybe I do need to be like you and adapt. Make the best of it."

She offers a sad smile and a shrug of surrender.

Herbert suddenly rekindles his rebellion. "No! I will not! Mrs. Pearbottom, you might be ok waiting for death to find you playing bingo. But I would prefer to be out and about when it comes a-knockin'."

Mrs. Pearbottom gets angry. "I said I'll see what I can do. Now, either move inside or these gentlemen will carry you there."

Herbert regards her, then the Twins. They put away their phones and get ready to sweep him off his feet, possibly injuring him in the process. He nods.

"Thank you, Mrs. Pearbottom. I believe you've made your point. I will work on my Stages of Grief. And adjusting to life here. Maybe I'll even make some friends."

"Or just tune out and drool," suggests Michael. "Don't let anyone tell you how to do you."

"Thanks, George."

"I'm Michael," corrects the Twin.

"Fine. And I'll stop asking so many questions. Just take life and death as they come, batteries included."

The Twins look at each other, barely suppressing snort-guffaws.

Herbert wonders, *South American, maybe?* He relaxes and walks back to the building, not even bothering to shield his face from the satellite. In fact, he even looks up, smiles, and takes a bow.

***

Many miles above, a label on a satellite reads, *For Official Use Only*. Smiling emoji stickers were added by playful staff. As Herbert had suspected, he is being watched. The satellite's camera suddenly zooms in on Earth, in particular the USA, and most specifically on Herbert's smiling face. It does not capture Mrs. Pearbottom's face because she shields it as if from the noonday sun.

Somewhere across the ocean, in a shabby apartment, a sitcom plays in Polish. A cracked smartphone screen suddenly buzzes to life. An app shows Herbert's smiling face, frozen before his bow. A progress bar says "ANALYZING" and then "98% MATCH."

The phone is precariously balanced on the edge of a kitchen sink. An older woman, Rosie, enters hurriedly. She cuts the flame from her boiling pasta, picks up the pot without gloves, and turns to the sink. She bumps her phone into the colander just as she pours hot water and pasta into it. She retrieves her phone, annoyed but indifferent to her flesh burning. She rinses the phone under the tap, dries it with a towel, and wonders when she's going to remember to delete her old work apps.

It's funny how time flies when you're not on the run, or hunting people down, or extracting information, or killing them softly without words (Flacks, 1973).

Behind her, on a yellowing fridge, a retirement to-do list shows many tasks crossed out. However, "delete work apps" has been skipped for months or even years. *Letting go is hard to do.*

***

Picking up where we left off under the night sky, Herbert reaches the Sunset entrance just as the security guard springs outside, ready for action.

Herbert can't help his sarcasm. "Oh good, you're here! Now we're safe!" He enters the building.

The guard dismisses him and looks for signs of threat.

Mrs. Pearbottom points to the broken phone. "It's over there."

The guard feigns indifference and continues scanning for danger. *An IED could be masked in as little as a piece of litter,* he tells himself. *I would have been great in Afghanistan, if only my mom had let me sign up like Joey's mom.*

When everyone else is indoors, the guard collects his phone and inspects it. He then checks the perimeter one last time. When convinced that all is well, he tries to enter the building but finds himself locked out. He shakes the doors and bangs on them like Fred Flintstone calling for Wilma (Hanna & Barbera, 1960–1966). It could take a while.

CHAPTER TWO POINT OH

Senior Sentence

In the large community lounge, the hum of voices and television initially blend together. Seniors sit alone or in clusters among couches and tables. Some watch a sitcom, others have hunches over their games of chess and chance.

Herbert, still dressed in his wrinkled tuxedo, strides into the lounge and cracks open a can of sparkling water from a cart. He makes a face, unimpressed by its warmth. Mrs. Pearbottom and the Twins follow behind him, heading to another part of the facility.

"Downright, gross!" yells Senior Rita, a Guatemalan 80-something, looking over her glasses.

Everyone turns. In a corner Mr. Downright has dropped his pants and seated himself on a chair ready to do his business as a sole proprietor. He looks up, alarmed by the unexpected attention. "What is everyone doing in my bathroom?"

Mrs. Pearbottom instructs the Twins, "Will you help him to his room, please?"

"Of course," answers George, rushing over. "Mr. Downright naughty! Let's go potty on the rooftop!" He helps him raise his trousers.

Downright sad and bewildered, says, "But the man upstairs said to come down here."

"I'm sure he did," assures George, leading him out.

Michael addresses the others in song. "Folks, this can happen to anyone. So please say, *Take me up! Before you go-go. And I'll be there when you hit that call button*" (Wham!, 1984).

After he also leaves, Senior Rita notices Herbert's attire. "What are you all dressed up for?"

"My funeral." Herbert settles into a recliner and sees what they are watching. "*Golden Girls* again?!" (Witt et al., 1985-1992).

Jake Kimble, a brawny, former frat boy, now in his 70s, defends the choice. "You're kidding, right? Blanche still gets me so hot."

Herbert recoils. "Spare us the imagery, Jake."

Jake retorts with loud kissing smacks. Herbert shuffles to the TV and flips the channel to something more his style: an adrenaline-pumping Stallone movie.

"Hey, others were watching that!" Jake shoots up to his feet and presses buttons on the ineffective remote.

"Indeed," responds Herbert, who blocks the receiver. "And I am their Liberator." He uses a book to block the shiny remote sensor so it will continue to not receive signals. Then he returns to his seat.

Jake tries to let it go. He can see his peers do appear more engaged; even the drooling ones are now wiping their mouths. However, unable to bear it any longer, Jake suddenly runs over, removes the book, and uses the remote to switch the channel back. His show immediately gives way to a commercial for Senior Acuity Insurance as he returns to his seat.

A spokeswoman asks, "Do you still have all your wits about you? Have you checked up on them lately?"

"They're tested daily around here," responds Herbert.

The commercial proceeds. "When your sanity strays far from home, we'll be there for you and your loved ones."

Herbert shuffles to the TV and searches for his action movie again. He blocks the sensor with another book and turns to Jake. "If you change it again I'll give you a free colonoscopy. With my cane. Unlubricated. On the house. Which then has a seven-story drop."

Shocked expressions fill the room. Rita raises her brow. "Language?"

"Plain English," quips Herbert. He returns to his seat.

Jake is incensed. "Are you threatening me? He threatened me!"

Herbert ignores him. Jake feigns another attempt to go change the channel. Herbert jumps up, only to realize Jake has played him. He sits back down. Then Jake runs and changes the channel back to *Golden Girls*. Herbert extends his cane, gives chase, and swings at Jake who runs away.

When finally cornered, Jakes puts his hands over his head to block Herbert's pathetic blows. They are mostly already being blocked by furniture and walls.

Jake grabs at the cane but is unsuccessful. "Help! I'm being assaulted! Get me a lawyer! Immediately!"

"Just give me the remote," insists Herbert.

"No! I won't! Help! Someone record this!"

Various seniors take out flip phones and look over their bifocals to try to understand if they have a camera.

Another checks her watch and jots the time down in a small memo book with a pencil. A neighbor looks at her and she responds, "I'm recording what I see."

Other seniors manage to restrain Herbert. He pushes buttons on his watch as if it might shoot a lethal dart, or release a sedative gas, or at least play a lullaby.

Those were the days, he often thinks. But nothing happens and he gives up. "Oh, damn this retirement!"

The seniors give him space. He tries to yank off his watch but can't break the plastic band. He finally undoes the clasp and throws the watch across the room, where it merely clinks against the wall.

Mrs. Pearbottom storms in. "What is going on in here?"

Jake blurts out, "Herbert assaulted me and even changed the channel!" He tests his neck for lawsuit potential. "We were peacefully watching TV."

"No, he had them watching, *Golden Girls*!"

Mrs. Pearbottom stops Jake before he can reply. "Alright, that's enough! I expect both of you to apologize."

"What is this, third grade?" Herbert protests. "Besides, I was being assertive, like you taught us in the Best Version of You class!"

"Correction," declares Jake. "Your behavior was not *assertive*. It fits the *aggressive* paradigm, and also the definition of *bullying*. At least I paid attention."

Mrs. Pearbottom motions for Herbert to bite his lip. "Apologize now or I'm cutting off everyone's BenGay for a week."

A collective groan erupts. Seniors back away. Jake eventually turns to Herbert. "Fine. We're all adults. I'll go first."

As a lady should, thinks Herbert.

Mrs. Pearbottom thanks Jake for stepping up. Jake continues, "Herbert, I apologize."

Herbert matches the sentiment. "And I'm sorry too, Jake."

Mrs. Pearbottom sighs with relief but it's premature.

Herbert clarifies, "I'm sorry you're such a wanker, Jake. Jake Wanker. Now there's a good not-so-secret agent name for you."

"Mr. Bigglesby!" scolds Mrs. Pearbottom, exasperated.

Herbert concedes, "Alright! Mr. Kimble, I am terribly sorry to have interrupted your selection of riveting entertainment."

Mrs. Pearbottom accepts it. "Thank you! Fortunately, it's time for the news and then we can all call it a day."

She changes the channel to *Wolf News*, a cartoon with dogs in suits. A Husky with a microphone interviews a Pitbull with bandages on his face, outside an apartment building. A video insert in the corner shows the same Pitbull receiving medical attention earlier.

The now-bandaged Pitbull is mid-story. "I was just out for a jog and then out of nowhere this aggressive cat stops running in front of me, turns around, and starts clawing at me for no reason."

The Husky shares a brilliant hypothesis. "As an unprovoked aggressor, the cat has probably had behavioral problems since the litter. Back to you, Bob."

In the studio, a German Shepherd named Bob clarifies, "Thanks, Leonard. And for the record, we did try to reach the cat for commentary a full 30 seconds before this broadcast but have yet to hear a response, thus confirming his guilt."

Jake is restless. "Oh, change it already! That's not news."

Herbert smirks. "Maybe it should be. He just happened to be jogging behind a cat?"

Jake defends the dog. "You heard what he said! The attack was unprovoked!"

Mrs. Pearbottom changes the channel to *MNN, The Misleading News Network*.

"Ah, now we're talking!" opines Jake.

Everyone settles down. A serious woman anchor turns to the camera. "Up tonight: A Nashville animal hospital welcomes a three-headed chimpanzee. They're calling her Lara, Mo, and Girly, but you can make suggestions and text to vote! Then, custody officers and inmates working it out through improv, trust falls, and cash apps. And finally, an elderly woman conned out of her final million."

"Idiot," mutters Herbert without an ounce of sympathy. Disapproving looks turn his way. He defends himself, "What? Some people deserve to be scammed."

Senior Rita and others hush him.

The anchor continues. "Patsy Taiken, an 83-year-old resident of Residue, Nevada, had just inherited a family fortune when she received a call from a unique health plan organization."

On the screen, Patsy Taiken sits on a sofa being interviewed. She looks old, naive, and heartbroken. "They said I won free healthcare for the rest of my life! All I had to do was attend a few tedious talks on a cruise. So, I thought, what's not to like and trust about that?"

Images on the TV have Patsy walking her dog, doing yoga in the park, and watering ugly plants.

Herbert nods in disbelief. "A million reasons, Darling. To not be the catch of the day, for one."

"*Carpe Diem*!" Jake calls out, patting Herbert on the shoulder and trying to be friendly. "As they say."

Herbert isn't having it. "No, Sir! No one says that for that. It's seize the–"

"Bull by the horns!" says Jake. "I know 'em all, Big Fella!"

Herbert looks to the ceiling. "Lord, I was never a praying mantis, but can I please just eat this one?"

Neighbors are horrified. In contrast, Mrs. Pearbottom can't help looking impressed. "Well, aren't you a model of piety and trust in the Lord?"

"No, no! A hypocrite I am not. I've never pretended to be something I'm not, Peaches."

"It's Pearbottom to you! I mean, Mrs. Pearbottom." She directs everyone's gaze to the TV. "Let's listen."

Patsy appears to be politely waiting for them and now continues her interview. "How was I supposed to know there was something shady going on? There were no warnings like we get with the coffee being hot, or floors being wet. I was not even warned I might be scammed!"

Herbert feigns indignation. "What an outrage!"

People can't tell if he's kidding or not but definitely agree.

The news cuts from Patsy back to the anchor. "For other seniors like Patty—Patsies—we asked the FBI to explain."

Herbert appears delighted. "Oh good, let's hear the obvious."

Mrs. Pearbottom signals for him to *quit it.* He gestures zipping his lips and dropping the key into his drawers. He dances a little to help them land right. She tries not to mind him.

An FBI spokesman speaks. "Unfortunately, crimes committed in international waters are very difficult or even impossible to persecute."

"Let alone prosecute," corrects Herbert.

Even the anchor is tired of this topic so she says, "He offered us a number of tips for seniors, but our time, patience, and attention span are all limited. So please check out our ad-filled website and find yourself a great deal!"

"Poorer," adds Herbert.

The anchor continues, "While finding out what the ideal deal is for you this hopping shopping season!"

Herbert asks, "Why do they bother offering all this so-called help? You can't help the helpless."

"It doesn't mean we don't try," responds Mrs. Pearbottom. Herbert's and others look shocked but she ignores them. A staffer brings her papers to sign, which distract her from the TV.

A reporter who looks 15 turns to face the camera. "Next, in international news, check out this inappropriate footage of a man being killed by a Balinese Tiger. Not exactly Hello Kitty, Grandma."

We see shocking footage of a dead man being dragged about by a tiger. Senior Rita and others can't bear to watch.

Herbert becomes nostalgic. "I once made passionate love to a Balinese Crown Princess while saving her nation from nuclear devastation."

Seniors cone their ears with their hands to block out Herbert and hear the TV better.

Jake asks, "Was that *before* or *after* you dismantled your thirteenth underwater planetary imploder?"

Herbert wishes his eyes could shoot laser beams but alas. He wonders, *why did I risk so much for such ungrateful idiots?*

Mrs. Pearbottom looks up from her paperwork to see the worst of the tiger footage as it chews a dismembered leg. "Goodness! We don't need that in our dreams." She turns the TV off. "Off to bed everyone!"

The seniors stand and return chairs and cushions to their places.

Herbert comments, "I'll take that dream any day over memories of having my skin peeled off."

"What health plan offers that?" asks Senior Rita.

Herbert ignores her and throws his empty can into a regular trash instead of the recycle container next to it.

Jake is annoyed. "Seriously? You're not going to recycle that?"

"I recycled your mom."

"You're a sick man, Herbert." Jake storms out.

The others continue arranging chairs.

Mrs. Pearbottom addresses Herbert. "Mr. Bigglesby, if you keep fighting everyone and everything, it's only going to delay your making peace with, and ever enjoying, this potentially wonderful stage in your life. I do hope you'll reflect a little."

"Oh, I reflect a lot! People just don't like what they see in me."

She doesn't push it. Another senior steps up. It's Bob, who carries himself like a retired pastor. His t-shirt says, *Turn Lives Around: Boycott Drugs!* and shows cockroaches lying on their backs. He says, "Herb, I'd like to tell you a story. My mother didn't exactly know how to love me–"

"Go figure."

"But I'm sure your own mother didn't hate you the way you might think. Nor did she really believe you were utterly worthless and unlovable."

Herbert does not want to hear it. "Why are you telling me your life story?"

Bob continues but looks mostly at Senior Rita, hoping she'll be impressed. "I just think there's no shame in still yearning for, or in providing exotic, I mean, erotic, female attention, completely free of taboos and inhibitions. Eros is part of the human experience."

"So is error," comments Mrs. Pearbottom, to no one in particular.

Senior Rita takes no notice of Bob as she fluffs pillows and suddenly exclaims, "Oh look, a kitten!"

Bob is disappointed. Herbert can't resist needling him. "Ok, *Lonesome Dove!*" (Wittliff & Wincer, 1989). "But while you were yearning, I was churning."

"Just not with child support," remarks Mrs. Pearbottom.

Herbert turns and she shrugs her shoulders; she couldn't resist. "No, no," begins Herbert. "Do not spread false rumors about me. I may have broken a few hearts along the way, but I do not have any offspring."

"That you know of," she answers.

"Oh, I think I would know."

"But why would you know? Do you keep in touch with all your… liaisons?"

"No, but those people find you. Gold diggers, all." To Herbert it's all quite obvious. His views on relationships, parenting, and family have not changed in all his adult years.

He turns to exit but stops short due to an irrepressible urge to justify himself. "And for the record, Mrs. Pearbottom, I have never judged anyone for prioritizing their own hopes and dreams. I myself never wanted children or grandchildren, and didn't see such a life as compatible with my own, so I avoided it. But I was supportive of anyone who did prioritize that, and I feel terrible for anyone who pursued it and could not achieve it, as if cheated by life itself. Maybe those things just don't fit a to-do list. Who knows. But I do think my single-mindedness, and keeping out of other people's way, spared them from problems. If anything, my life is a testimony to giving myself wholeheartedly to something I *value*, as they say. And it largely worked out for me, until recently."

"Are you finished?" asks the facility director, eager to shield herself from Herbert's ability to still wound her after so many years.

"Hardly! You sit in judgment of me, but I'm the one who still thinks life holds some promise. Why have you given up?"

Mrs. Pearbottom cannot stand this man just now. "I only meant, finished for tonight?"

Herbert sighs, "Oh yes, very well." He exits.

Senior Rita follows Herbert. "You gave your life to a thing? What kind of thing? I hated my husband's snoring, but I miss it now. And his stupid look." She extends her lips like a fish.

Surrendering for the night, Mrs. Pearbottom cuts off the lights and exits.

Chapter One Minus Three Months

Prey, for Peace

At this time, the reader must be made aware of an odd night several months earlier, on a cold Thursday evening in March.

Among a sea of state-of-the-art workstations for officially non-existent espionage, a stout mid-50s Bolivian woman in uniform empties wastepaper baskets. Most people have gone home for the night. As the woman cleans, she occasionally glances at a conscience-free analyst whom we'll call Paulie. This acne-covered young man cannot help but occasionally eye her as well, as he tries to hack into a forbidden database. He nearly leaps from his chair upon hearing, "Good night, Paulie" from a colleague headed for the door.

Paulie quickly changes his screen to a website offering Pink Wednesday Deals on things like bikes and burkas to help bring breast awareness to the fore. He ineffectively covers his screen with his hand, as if time spent perusing e-bikes is his only betrayal.

"Oh, please ignore this, Frank! Pink Wednesday coming up."

"Your secret is good with me," replies his tired colleague. He wouldn't dream of stopping and filing a report. "Don't *stray* too late!" He turns and almost bowls over the cleaning woman and her cart. "Oh, I'm sorry, I didn't see you there."

She smiles and watches him go. "They never do." She speaks with her head down to avoid security cameras taking any interest. "It is like I am invisible! Which has made me successful, but I am tired to feel so insignificant."

"Uh-huh," mutters Paulie, not paying attention. As he types and maneuvers his mouse, he suddenly gasps with delight. The cleaning woman notices but contains her joy from anyone monitoring the monitors. Likewise, Paulie catches himself and returns to an overworked and underpaid expression.

Paulie's screen shows a pop-up with his colleague's name on it: "Frank Lincoln Col. Wilson, are you seriously wishing to access the *Ultra-Secret List of Ultra-Secret Retirement Facilities for As Yet Unmurdered Agents?*"

He draws a breath, confirms the panning cameras are turned away, and clicks on the *hells yeah* button.

Immediately we see profiles of elderly agents with photos, names, and addresses. Paulie scrolls through several of them until he stops on a picture of dummy Herbert in his coffin.

Paulie says, "Bingo… player," and the cleaning woman looks over. The profile reads, Current Alias: Herbert Bigglesby. Location: Sunset View Senior Living Community.

***

Ironically, at the very same moment, in a land far away, our friend Jake Kimble also calls out the word, "Bingo!" and, "What are the chances? Two wins in a row!"

Herbert rolls his eyes as Jake steps up to collect his prize in the community room.

"Ooh, a hair transplant service!" boasts Jake, admiring his prize.

"Maybe they'll throw in some testicles too," suggests Herbert.

Back in the tech-farm, Paulie jots down Herbert's address on a Post-it note. Before he can look up, the cleaning woman is by his side, emptying his wastepaper basket. Her eyes lock onto the screen and she seethes with pure hate for the deceased man in the photo.

Then her lips curl with satisfaction. Paulie is quick to move the Post-it out of reach when she tries to grab it.

Annoyed, the cleaning woman digs into her apron and produces a Pokémon card, which she puts on Paulie's desk. The analyst looks around nervously as it is not ideal to have this kind of exchange occur openly and in real time. However, *a single card was never the deal* and indignation tramples his instinct for self-preservation. He turns off his screen and taps his desk with two fingers, feigning enough resolve that the woman produces a second card.

Paulie reaches for it but the woman pulls it back. Her other hand beckons for the prized address and the analyst makes a quick exchange of it. Each examines their loot and is satisfied.

The cleaning woman takes a black bowler hat from the side of her cleaning cart and hides the Post-it note in the inner rim. She now proudly dons the hat and continues emptying baskets into her barrel. She has a lighter bounce in her heavy step.

CHAPTER THREE

Staying Fit

Back at Sunset View, Herbert is delighted to learn Mrs. Pearbottom has held true to her promise. She announces the sudden departure of the Twins, allegedly due to health reasons.

Herbert feels his voice has been heard and strives to buck his retirement less. He plays tennis, eats more of his meals, and even tries to make light conversation without bringing up world-saving events from his life.

Of course, the high points of Herbert's week are his physical therapy visits, or more specifically, visits to E. Claire Voyant, a young provider-in-training. She is quite beautiful and no-nonsense, in her early 20s, with a slightly perfect yoga build.

Just before Claire joined the staff a few months prior, Herbert had been ready to declare his hips a trouble-free zone. Then Ms. E. Claire stormed into his life and his inflammations returned with a passion in this otherwise sterile environment.

Claire shares her PT office with Olga Gargledu, an ugly bear of a physical therapist. She might have other qualities if one takes the trouble to get to know her, but few do. She is in her 60s and has a thick Eastern European accent. Herbert typically avoids looking at her but today, at this very moment, he can't help it. He hears what sounds like the breaking of bones on a frail 90-something female patient of hers. The victim appears not to mind since this is the only warm physical touch she ever gets. Olga finishes up and packs her things while the angular woman limps out.

Caution: this next image cannot be taken back. Herbert wears tiny 1970s polyester shorts, with his pasty white legs glaring to the eye. Claire wears blue latex gloves as she works on his leg. Herbert likes what she is doing, perhaps a little too much.

"I have to say, Ms. E. Claire, the rest of me is hoping for an equal opportunity."

This piques Olga's interest. "I can help, perhaps after hours."

"No! I mean, no thank you, Olga." Herbert is annoyed that she would interfere with his playful banter. He continues, "Claire, my whole body could truly benefit from your touch."

Claire smiles innocently, as if her own unfiltered and senile grandfather were flirting with her. "Well, I'm afraid this is the only part we're working on today."

She gets an A in boundaries, thinks Herbert.

Olga vies for his attention by dropping a heavy rubber weight on the floor. Herbert turns to look but flinches when Olga bends over to get it. He refocuses on Claire.

"Ms. E. Claire, you still haven't told me what the E in your name stands for? Might it be Easy?"

"No, not really."

"Emily? Encore?"

"To be honest," she says, "my parents couldn't decide. They said time would tell. Like my destiny. I think I have important work to do somewhere one day, maybe in Egypt."

"Or Elkhart?" offers Olga, thinking she's helpful.

Herbert frowns and leans closer to Claire. "I appreciate a woman who is open to adventure."

Claire is oblivious. "Well, that's it for today." She packs up her belongings.

Herbert tries again. "You know, Claire, your hands should be FDA-recommended."

"And your mouth should be HIPAA compliant," quips Mrs. Pearbottom, who stops by the open door. "Times have changed, Mr. Bigglesby. We can't have you scaring away our physical therapists too."

"Oh, I'm not going anywhere!" replies Olga.

Herbert shrugs at Pearbottom. "I tried."

Claire chimes in, "Me neither! Don't be silly. Being here is like giving back to my great, great-grandfather and other Veterans of the Great War."

Herbert looks devastated. "That's not the war you think it is."

Mrs. Pearbottom smiles and leaves.

Claire continues, "The truth is, Mr. Bigglesby, you fill a very important void in my life."

"Well, I'm pleased to hear it," says Herbert. "I too have a healing touch I would love to share."

"Oh, that's so cute."

"Say, my room, tonight, 10 PM?"

She appears truly bummed. "I'm so bummed. "I can't."

"I'm free!" announces Olga. "And I need to perform six hundred hours of continuing education for my license." She reaches up high to put away a water bottle, hoping Herbert will find her stretch sexy.

It's a stretch, he thinks. "Tomorrow then!"

Claire is sorry. "Sorry, I'm all booked. But please do some low impact skating or biking like we talked about."

Olga jumps in. "I can teach you those activities. And you can practice your healing touch on me."

"I'm not into miracles," responds Herbert. To Claire he offers, "Friday?"

Claire is apologetic. "Ooh, P-T-O. Personal time off."

"Then Saturday, after tea!"

"Good night!" Claire pats Herbert on the head and exits.

He looks injured. To add further insult, Olga drops her scarf and bends over to get it. Herbert recoils at the sight of her largesse. She winks at him before straightening. He shields his eyes with his hands.

"Let me guess, there's an abundance where that comes from. But surely you have to abide by a professional code of ethics?"

"Fortunately, you are not my client."

"I think the spirit of the law applies here."

"You can run, Mr. Bigglesby, but hiding from Olga? Not possible!"

She gives him a final suggestive eyebrow before exiting. Herbert checks for a cyanide pill in his ring. The secret compartment is empty. Undeterred, he taps it over his mouth for any remaining particles. He even licks his pinky and tries for residue. *Nothing.*

Chapter Four

Favorite Past Times

In the quiet of his bathroom, Herbert opens the medicine cabinet. He wears a silk bathrobe over silk pajamas. Numerous medications face him. These include: *Bore-a-zombie-ide*: lowers blood pressure. *Booz-a-lac*: helps liver function. *Herpes-Slurpee*: reduces inappropriate thirsts. He opens and takes two of each, throwing them back dry, *like a man, Jake.*

He shifts his gaze to an old Chipstick tube. He can't help but smile. *Such good memories.* He applies it, then twists the tube further till a steel spike emerges. A younger Herbert speaks in his memory, "My lips are so dry, do you mind if I moisten them?"

In a rich oak and mahogany library, a South American man in an identical silk robe holds a gun to the back of Herbert's much younger head. The man answers with a thick Spanish accent, "Not at all. It is important to die *con-fortably.*"

Young Herbert moistens his lips with his then-new Chipstick. Then suddenly, with catlike precision, he delivers the spike into the man's neck. Blood spurts everywhere.

"Ahh! What is this?" the man calls out, fearing he has mere seconds to live.

Herbert cleans the spike and retracts it into the tube.

The man laments, "Oh, your tiny little prick!"

"I beg your pardon!" answers Herbert. His indignation quickly shifts to empathy as the man drops to his knees, his life fading away. "I'm afraid I have no balm to ease your pain, *Enrique. Lo siento*!"

Herbert is puzzled as the man recalls his childhood faith. "Father, I have been a sinful man. I make no excuses. Please accept me even now." The man passes away, his hands folded together.

***

Back in the present day, Herbert exits his bathroom. He fluffs up a pillow and gets into bed. Not yet tired, he stares up at the ceiling. As he waits for sleep he recalls a sexy female Russian accent.

"Oh please, I am insulted!" she says. "What kind of a man uses lip balm after intimacy but not before?"

The younger Herbert is sitting up in a hotel room bed, smoking a cigarette. He applies his Chipstick. His solid-framed lover stands at the foot of the bed, tying a belt over her puffy fur coat. She then picks up her silencer-enhanced weapon.

"I do not do this easily," she explains. "It pains me to have to eliminate you, my KGB-assigned lover. I could have envisioned so much more with you."

"Then what is your hurry, Fair One? What is one more hour? Grant me a final semblance of the true love that could have been."

To herself she says, *I weaken, unable to resist the charm and allure of this most attractive and desirable man.* To Herbert she confesses, "Oh, we do do away with love in this job." She undoes her coat.

Modern Herbert smiles at her approaching memory. He puckers his lips and applies his old Chipstick, which nicks him. "Ow!"

"*Darlink*, no!" complains the woman in his memory. Blood spurts from her neck as she leans over him. She turns to grab her gun but it's too far away now. As she falls, she grasps the bed linens to slow her descent, soaking them in blood. She collapses.

Like so many strong but disappointed women, she is able to lift her head and express reflections that come too late in life. "You are such a man! And it is not your fault. No! I am an idiot female! It was foolish for me to think this could be real, despite our murderous and cheating lifestyles, and the inability to delay the gratification."

Young Herbert holds her by the shoulders. "Oh, my little Tolstoya, I had no idea you wanted me for yourself! I assumed you were only in it for the adventure, the fine hotels and travel, and the hushed *abortabotamies*."

"*Nyet*! I am forsaken. Now there will never be any cute *sheeldren* for us! They would have been so *milyy*. Which in my language means *cute*."

Modern Herbert turns pensive. "Yes, they probably would have been *milyy*."

The young woman continues, "Today I die of heartbreak, not puncture in neck. I have deceived myself! Thus, I deserve this *beater* ending."

While Younger Herbert's face shows pain of loss, modern day Herbert turns skeptical. *I doubt it would have worked out. We would have argued. She would have missed her career.* Who knows?

CHAPTER FIVE

Skating on Thinning Ice

With the gym door closed, Herbert glides surprisingly effortlessly on his 1979 Sears roller-skates, doing the kinds of tricks one would expect from a much younger man at Venice Beach or in Central Park. He wears a helmet, knee- and elbow pads, gloves, and even goggles like a Red Baron. He glides along the walls and between treadmills, ellipticals, and stationary bikes.

Yet the moment the door handle is touched from outside, he feigns stumbling and ineptitude. People enter and he looks over from his embarrassing wall-hugging position, hoping to see Claire. But alas, it's Mrs. Pearbottom showing the facility to what appear to be the same Twins as before. Except these have dyed their hair blonde. They eye skateboards in a corner, wishing they could ride.

"And this is our recreation room," announces Mrs. Pearbottom proudly, as if oblivious to the current state of this wreck room. "Ah, Mr. Bigglesby, say hello to our newest staff members."

Herbert releases the wall. He lifts his goggles and squints, looking confused. "I thought you both left," he says.

"Mr. Bigglesby!" scolds a horrified Mrs. Pearbottom.

The Twins exchange a giggle identical to that of their predecessors. If this were a movie, the same actors could be cast. On a tight budget all four could be the same person.

Mrs. Pearbottom introduces, "This is Mr. Wayne Jacoby here, and Woldecott Hammers there."

"We're onboarding!" says Woldecott.

"Except not," laments Wayne with a look at the skateboards. "May we?"

"Certainly not!" answers Mrs. Pearbottom.

Herbert isn't having it either. "Madam, I'm confused. I've known George and Michael here for months."

"I'm afraid you are mistaken." She then uses a tense side voice. "Herbert, please do not imply all people of a certain race look alike." She re-includes the newbies and says, "These new young men are completely new to our facility, and have no connection to any of the employees you might have seen here before."

"Nice to meet you, Mr. Bigglesby," says Wayne.

"We're so excited to be here," agrees Woldecott.

"And what became of their predecessors?" inquires Herbert.

Mrs. Pearbottom explains, "I'm afraid they suddenly became terminally ill. Apparently due to some congenital problem."

Herbert is disturbed but then relieved. "Well, fortunately, no genital problems in my lineage."

Mrs. Pearbottom tries to cover it quickly with, "A hazard of hiring twins, I guess." She immediately regrets her words, and her intolerant opinion as well. "I retract my statement. It was thoughtless and harmful. We sent flowers, of course."

Herbert softens toward the Twins. "Pardon me for being a little slow to welcome you. I'm sure you'll fit right in here." *The standards are very low.* He does not say that last part aloud.

"Thank you! We're here for anything you might need," answers Wayne.

"Yeah!" adds Woldecott. "Call out, like if you need help with anything, no matter how embarrassing or disgusting. We expect the worst from you."

"Like if you mess up your underwear, or can't go or something," clarifies Wayne. "We got you."

"*Enema! Enema!*" sings Woldecott in the style of Edward Van Halen's 1984 hit.

Herbert attempts another aside with Mrs. Pearbottom. "And you're sure they passed background checks?"

"Yes, with flying colors. And color blindness too, of course."

"Did you put them through a mental detector?"

"Oh, hush!" she chastises him.

"I just hope they're competent."

"Please, Herbert! Relax. And do stop profiling."

Mrs. Pearbottom assures the Twins that the tour and all manner of propriety will resume soon. She then finishes with Herbert.

"I thought you would appreciate this change. And since when are we lowly support staff not all interchangeable to you?"

"I never said you were interchangeable," Herbert objects. "I've always regarded your services as particularly invaluable and irreplaceable, Peaches."

Mrs. Pearbottom is caught off-guard, not only by his acknowledgement but also by his use of a nickname. She shakes both off and says, "We need to continue our tour. Good day, Mr. Bigglesby." She leads the Twins out.

"Nice to meet you!" says Wayne cheerily.

"Buh-bye!" calls out Woldecott, perhaps once having been a flight attendant.

On an aircraft carrier, thinks Herbert.

As the door slowly closes, Herbert is startled to see a thick human form mopping the hallway in a bowler hat. He narrows his eyes as he strains to see the face in the shrinking crack.

As if perceiving Herbert's gaze, the figure suddenly looks up and makes unintended eye contact. She is the same cleaning woman the Reader met elsewhere. Herbert's breath stops as he tries to recall why she looks familiar. The woman smiles involuntarily, a social reflex. She turns away to prevent Herbert seeing her face darken with venom.

Herbert tries to downplay his alarm over the bowler hat. *It's fashion! A fashion style!* he tells himself. *Anyone can have a hat like that.*

He shuffles to the door for a second look. When he opens it, the woman is GONE. *I mustn't be paranoid*, he reminds himself. *Some people just look like other people.* He slowly resumes skating, away from his fears and concerns.

CHAPTER SIX

Volley for Servitude

The next day, the sun is out, the clouds are puffy, and the sky is blue. A fading poster in a patio area proclaims, *It's a beautiful day to still be alive!*

Herbert and Senior Bob come out to the tennis court. Bob's T-shirt says, *Get CrossFit* and has a logo for *God's Gym*, which consists of a crown of thorns encircling Jesus who carries a cross. Herbert is dressed in tiny white shorts and a classic tennis sweater. The men and their fabrics stretch, with some bones creaking and popping.

Behind an outdoor bar, Woldecott prepares a fizzy water. He brings it on a tray to Herbert and says, "It's important to stay hydrated, Sir. Like, a lot today."

Herbert hesitates but recalls, *I'm supposed to go with the flow. But boy do these boys look shady. Though not talented enough to hurt a fly.* He says, "Thank you," and reaches for the glass but Bob scoops it up first.

"Too slow, Herbert!" he chuckles, and downs the cool water in one long guzzle.

Woldecott's eyes widen for the briefest of seconds.

Herbert is annoyed, his mouth suddenly feeling very dry.

Bob chides him. "I hope you do better than that on the court, *Herbster*!" He puts down the empty glass and heads to the far side.

Soon Bob serves the ball and the game begins. It whizzes past Herbert out of bounds, which makes Herbert smile. Bob serves again and Herbert easily returns it. It's an easy shot for Bob to play, but he suddenly stops and the ball bounces past him.

Herbert smirks. "You shouldn't talk the talk if you can't show up, *Bobster*." He turns and positions himself to receive the next serve but, when he looks up, he sees Bob clutching his chest.

Then Bob collapses. Wayne rushes to him, calling for the AED machine, and begins quality CPR. Woldecott rushes in with an automated defibrillator device.

Herbert is wary. "Are we making a training video?" He scans for a film crew but there is none.

Everyone watches, stunned. Eventually, an ambulance can be heard approaching.

Not much later, paramedics take their turns at resuscitation. Bob does not return to us. Herbert studies the Twins' faces for any sign of complicity in what occurred. Their steely facades show nothing.

Some onlookers can't believe this is happening and say so.

Herbert, however, can and does believe it. *Volley. Set. Mismatch,* he thinks. *That was meant for me!*

He scans for the glass and sees it. He moves to get it but the paramedics rush by, carrying Bob, dead on a gurney.

When Herbert can continue the glass has DISAPPEARED. He looks in all directions. The Twins are gone too.

Throughout these events, Jake has been lying shirtless and hairy on a deck chair, holding a 1970s tanning reflector. He calls over to Herbert. "Don't be too hard on yourself, *Herbster*. It happens all the time around here."

Herbert is not so sure.

Chapter Seven

Doctor Bentiron

In a psychiatry office high on the seventh floor, an agitated Herbert searches for cameras and listening devices. His eyes blink as if punctuating every thought.

A seeming *tween* in a lab coat sits behind a large desk, checking his phone whenever Herbert isn't looking. He is Dr. Bentiron, not yet 30, physically fit, no history of original thought, adorned with long hair and a two-day stubble.

After 18 minutes of legal disclaimers, he had opened the session to Herbert's perspectives, saying he is happy to let the patient "express his wildest dreams, fantasies, and fears verbally, physically, and even through dance, if he so chooses."

Herbert now gets close to Bentiron's ear and whispers, "That was no accident."

"Why are you whispering?"

Herbert scribbles on a pad, "I don't feel safe here."

Dr. Bentiron scribbles back. "All allegations were dropped."

Herbert has no idea what he is talking about and presses forward in a low voice. "Someone is trying to kill me and I don't know whom to trust. Mrs. Pearbottom said she got rid of George and Michael, but no offense, the two new ones look just like them, except for dyed hair. And they forgot the eyebrows."

Dr. Bentiron is horrified. "How can you tell?"

"Black eyebrows don't go on a blonde head. It's unnatural," Herbert scoffs. "And it's not just that. The other day I saw a new, though rather old, cleaning lady who looks just like someone who used to try to kill me a lot. For decades, really."

"Oh, Herbert."

"Don't *Oh Herbert* me! I'm not imagining these things. Something is going on here, my good boy. Or Doctor."

"Herb," says Bentiron, a buddy when you need one. "Herbie! Have a seat. We all know retirement has been hard on you."

"Oh, don't give me that malarkey, Junior!" Herbert sits down and speaks loud and clear to whoever may have bugged this office. "Ok, listen, whomever you are."

Dr. Bentiron points to his own name placard. "Dr. Bentiron."

Herbert dismisses him and continues for unseen listeners. "I am not here to talk about my general hopelessness, or my complete and utter despair, as I enter my final years, without any meaning or purpose in my life."

The young doctor looks surprised. "Why are we here, then?"

"I am here to talk about an obvious murder that was clearly meant for me! I know you people hear me, and I know you are after me. And you should be, because I am now after you! And I will find you, whomever you are, and it won't be pretty! In fact, it will be very ugly."

Dr. Bentiron is concerned. "My goodness! A little anger and self-expression are good *Herbster*, but–"

"Don't call me that, you pimple-faced prick!"

"Don't you mean, *Quack*?"

"You may certainly add that!"

"Mr. Bigglesby, can we just focus on pure logic first? Let's review the facts. Forensics examined the glass and did an autopsy. They found no evidence of foul play."

Herbert is ready to argue point for point. "No, they were given *a* glass, but not the actual glass, which disappeared moments after the incident. Plus, some poisons don't even leave a suspicious trace. On the flipside, nothing racial intended, what we do know for certain is that someone who has worked here, for less than a week, offered me a drink, which was then swallowed, by someone who died moments after drinking it."

"Of a heart attack!" recalls Dr. Bentiron. "On a tennis court! At a senior living community! Or frankly, dying community. Though worth investing in."

"But he only got off two serves!" counters Herbert. "I do see the optics, Doctor. How it seems completely open and shut. But it was a murder and not an accident. Those Twins are working for someone and I intend to find out for whom."

"That's interesting," observes Bentiron. Herbert eases up, finally feeling heard. The doctor continues, "I never know when to use *who* or *whom*, but that sounded right."

Herbert's muscles tighten. Dr. Bentiron sees it and tries to sound empathic. "Herbert, I realize it's hard to separate happenings that happen so close together in time. Yet a first rule in science is, *correlation does not imply causation*. I mean, just look at where we are! People and food expire here all the time."

Herbert looks away dismissively. He walks over to the window and confesses, "Perhaps you're right. Frankly, Doctor, I've been wanting to expire myself."

The doctor looks nervous.

As Herbert gazes at the alley with dumpsters below, his view spins with vertigo (Hitchcock, 1958). Suddenly he slams the desk and regains his balance. "This changes everything, Doctor."

"Good! I mean, about not wanting to die anymore." Dr. Bentiron looks down at the alley. "I don't know why a depressing nursing home would be this tall."

"Senior Living Community," corrects Herbert.

"Of course."

Herbert continues. "Doctor, the help I need isn't about perspective, or having happy thoughts. It's about security."

"Were you anal attentive as a child?"

"Only at church. With everybody facing forward. But don't you mean *retentive*?"

"That too."

"Doc, I need to know who's after me and why. And we need to do something about it."

"Yes, I think that's right!"

"Then you'll help me?"

"What? No! I'm talking about *who's* after you and not *whom*. But then is that *who's* with an apostrophe or *whose* with an 'e' at the end?"

Herbert struggles to not kill *this idiot*. He continues, "And you know what's hardest about it all?"

"Good, don't hold back. Get it all out."

Herbert deflates. "Never mind." He does not want to keep talking but then can't help it. "I gave my whole life to you-know-whom and here they are leaving me high and dry like a sitting duck. Quack!"

Dr. Bentiron can't tell if Herbert just called him a duck or was quoting one. As an enlightened person, however, he chooses not to be offended since it is within his personal autonomy to do so. He makes a mental note to bring it up as a small victory in his supervision this week.

Herbert continues. "I can't believe our agency has ignored me like this! Despite all the concerns I've raised! Where is the loyalty? I'm not some teacher or prison guard to be betrayed by my union!"

"Is that an important value for you?"

"Betrayal? Dryness?"

"No, loyalty."

"I don't really think of *no loyalty* as a value. It's more like a problem. For me, at least, but I'm old-stool."

"School? Never mind, flexibility is important."

Herbert grows suspicious as a new idea forms. "Wait, do you think I might just need to relax and trust headquarters more?"

"Maybe. What do you think?"

"You don't want to know."

"Touché." Dr. Bentiron checks an email. "Well, at least know that you're safe, if that's what you're worried about."

"I see. By the way, on a completely different note: Are you and Mrs. Pearbottom an item? I won't judge. But she does have a thing for the younger ones."

Dr. Bentiron tries to hide his shock. "Can we stay professional here? I understand you're alarmed, and I hardly think you're crazy, if that's any consolation."

"Why, thank you!"

"Of course! Your feelings of insecurity and betrayal make sense to me. Many people in our line of work end up bitter, depressed, and questioning if they really accomplished anything with their lives."

"Bitter about the job?" asks Herbert. "I have no regrets about that. I mean, world peace is world peace. Now, can we get back to Bob being poisoned and me being in danger, or at least about you and Peaches getting it on?"

"Toxicity really pulls at you!" says Bentiron. "Have you ever noticed that?"

Herbert is almost in despair. "What are you talking about now?"

The doctor takes a deep breath and tries to get the session back on track. "Herbert, I'm trying to meet you where you're at."

Herbert looks around. "I'm here in your office. Where are you at? Is this a hologram?"

"I wish. But let's get back to your own troublesome reflections."

"Good. Let's." Herbert relaxes.

"So, when did you first begin to question everything you did in your former career? And how exactly did you live with it at the time? I mean, for every one disaster averted, weren't three more created?"

Herbert can't believe what he is hearing. "Whom do you work for again?"

Dr. Bentiron looks at his watch; he needs to move this meeting along. "Mr. Bigglesby, in my professional opinion, I believe you're showing symptoms of PTSD. Our friend Bob died unexpectedly, and your survival instincts flared up, which used to be appropriate and necessary. But now they are overreactions, though it's great that you don't want to die anymore. So, here's what we're going to do. I'm going to write you a prescription for something to help you relax, play some golf…"

"And help me sleep while my enemies slit my throat?"

"Yes, sleep is important–wait, no! Mr. Bigglesby, I don't want to use words like *paranoid* or *delusional.* Nor recommend antipsychotics just yet. But you might be having difficulty with reality testing, if you know what I mean."

"Are you serious? Calling a murder a murder *is* accepting reality! And decent grounds for concern. Why won't you help me?"

"Because…" Dr. Bentiron hesitates to say what he is thinking. He then does so in a low voice. "Because as important as you were earlier in life, it's sadly quite likely that the only people who care if you're alive or not are in Accounts Receivable."

Herbert is dumbfounded by the bluntness. Which is all he can think to say at the moment. So, he does. "I have to say, Doctor, I am quite dumbfounded by your bluntness."

"I thought you'd say that," answers the doctor. "And then you did. And I heard it. Look, I am sorry. I get that you're in a tough place. But instead of dwelling on whom you know that might still be out to get you, and instead of overlooking their advanced years and deficiencies, I suggest you focus on savoring your good memories while you still have access to them."

Herbert is shocked yet again. "First off, it's *who* you know, not *whom.* And what do you mean, *while I still have access to them*? Is headquarters going to have my memories erased?"

"Oh dear." Dr. Bentiron laughs and jots something on his pad. "What kind of powers do you think we have?"

"Stop! Erase that! I do not believe you have the power to erase my memories."

"Good. But as a point of education, your condition is not exceptional. Cognitive decline is normative at your age. You will soon have the experience of knowing you know some things but no longer be able to retrieve them. It'll be on the tip of your tongue but be completely blank."

"I see. So, I should stop trying to create new memories and just be nostalgic till I'm a raving drooling idiot?"

"Even then, keep it up."

"And how exactly will my memory go?" Herbert scans the office like he has never been here before. "Like, what was for breakfast? And who are you, again?"

"See? That's exactly my point. I'm Dr. Bentiron. Your psychiatrist. You're a resident at Sunset View Senior Living Community Center, Regional Division USA. Wait, what are you doing?"

Herbert has stood up and is examining Dr. Bentiron's degrees on the wall. "I'm trying to see if you're actually a part of the intelligence community."

Herbert takes down one of the degrees to study it. Dr. Bentiron jumps out of his chair. "I can assure you–"

"Assurance? Like a third-party payor? I've been assured all sorts of coverage and left out naked in the wind."

He puts the degree back on the wall but crooked, which annoys Bentiron.

"But maybe you're right," Herbert continues. "Maybe I should just accept what's coming. What difference does it make if I live much longer or just move along now?"

"That's not what I'm saying," insists Bentiron loudly, as if worried about being misquoted in a postmortem review. As he speaks he tries to make his crooked degree look more on the level. "Herbert, you may still have another 15 years, for all we don't know. In fact," He then tries to lighten things up with a TV voice. "Your mission, and I do hope you choose to accept it, is to work on adjusting to this phase of your life and not comparing it to the past."

"Oh, I see! But then why preserve my life at all? Other than to make a killing, so to speak."

"You have a very cynical attitude, Herbert. I didn't go to medical school to run a business. As long as there is a viable, non-dependent, fully formed human life, I'm all about it."

"Oh, I wasn't criticizing. I'm just saying maybe I've seen enough, heard enough, and done enough. Maybe I should cash out my chips. It's just hard to do it alone."

"Are you suggesting doctor-assisted–"

"Shhh! Nothing so crude. We'd have a gentle euphemism. Like, Librarian-assisted… demise."

"L-A-D? L-O-L!"

"What are you spelling?"

"Sorry. Never mind. Let's get back on track."

"Good idea! Train tracks!"

"No! Herbert, you mustn't conclude I recommended harming yourself. By the way, we did recall your cyanide diapers, right?" He jots himself a note.

"Yes, I can't even wiz my way to oblivion now." Herbert is not about to admit he still has a trick or two up his pant legs.

Dr. Bentiron glances at a clock. Herbert notices.

"Is it time to end it?"

"I'm afraid so."

"Then we agree! I'd rather go soon before they get another chance to do me in."

"Herbert, please! Look, we've covered a lot of topics today. Can you summarize your takeaways?"

"Fine. Yes. Focus on the good times."

"Exactly! No one can take those from you."

"He thinks the thinks that remind him of the good days. And perhaps of even better days?" (cfr. Chumbawamba, 1997).

"That's the spirit. Gee, let's end on a good note."

"That's not necessary."

"Humor me. Tell me again about your time with Ms. Vesuvius."

Herbert becomes mischievous. "Oh, she was quite the flytrap! Her scientist professor astronaut thing was…" he savors a memory.

"I had never seen such a great body of work! But, you know, it's her personality I miss most."

"See, aren't you feeling better already?"

"If by happy you mean sad."

"Yes! Mental health is the bomb." He takes to scribbling on his prescription pad. "Ok, so I'm going to add *Cycloticklefest.* Let me know if it has any side effects before I dole it out to my private cash-paying clients."

"Do you smoke it in groups?"

"Mr. Bigglesby, this is serious medicine," lectures Bentiron. "At least until a recall happens."

Herbert remembers another concern. "While you're writing, Doc, I'm also having a little trouble going. Not coming, mind you."

"I got you. We all *gotta* go sometime. No offense!" He keeps writing, then pauses. "*I* before *E* except after *C*."

Herbert explains. "In the loo I went from reading a one-page flier, to a pamphlet, to a *Reader's Digest* all in one go. But now it's more like *War and Peace*" in there (Tolstoy, 1878/1993).

Dr. Bentiron is still writing. "It can be."

"That's a book. Never mind." Herbert can't help but test another title. "*Crime and Punishment?*" (Dostoyevsky, 1866/2006).

"Some people do believe in *karma*."

Herbert goes to the window. "You know, statistically, white men *can* jump."

"Ok!" Dr. Bentiron suppresses his alarm but his voice cracks. "Please don't!" Then he plays it cool, imitating a teacher he once had. "Look, who am I to judge? It's ultimately your choice."

Herbert didn't expect that. "Where's Dr. Bentiron? I may come to respect you yet, young man."

"Thank you. The only thing I ask is that if you do decide to… *unledge* yourself, that you wait till I'm not here or on duty."

"*Unledge* myself? Never mind the respect comment. But I do think I'm ready to take your advice about joining a bridge club."

"Oh, good!" responds Bentiron.

"Is there one that frequents the Golden Gate?"

"Herbert, please! Live in the now!"

Bentiron's exasperation improves Herbert's mood. "Why? It's so fun to muse about ultimate departures. People have done so since time immemorial. But don't worry, Medicine Man, I still plan to make the most of this life and go out with a laugh."

"Yay!" responds Dr. Bentiron. "I'm glad. Life still has so much to offer someone like you." He should have stopped there but errs by going into specifics. "Like bingo, and boneless chicken, and friendship in the Day Room."

Herbert has a mischievous grin. "That's not what I'm talking about." He inches closer. "We only live once and there are so many things to try. I'm guessing you're… try-sexual?"

Dr. Bentiron is intrigued but is too aware of surveillance devices.

Herbert continues, "What about having our own little psycho-tickle-fest right here?" His smile is reminiscent of Jack Nicholson's in *The Shining* (Kubrick, 1980).

Dr. Bentiron swallows the saliva that has been collecting in his mouth. He tugs at the fabric in his moist armpits.

For a brief, satisfying second, Herbert pictures himself tickling Dr. Bentiron, who laughs. He breaks away and shrieks about the office like a child who *does* and *does not* want to be caught. Like a true cat-and-mouse event, it does not end well for Bentiron. Herbert eventually takes hold of him and throws him out the window. The young man swims in the air, no longer laughing, and wondering where he went wrong despite years of top-notch programs.

Dr. Bentiron interrupts Herbert's fantasy. "Mr. Bigglesby, I'm going to need to transfer you to a colleague."

"But why? I feel so understood!"

"I'm afraid we're done for today."

"Then no catharsis for me."

The doctor gives Herbert a silent *no* while thinking, *Maybe a straitjacket*. He recalls another Nicholson movie he never took quite seriously enough (Forman, 1976).

Chapter Eight

Reunion

The moon rushes across the night sky, as often seen in time-lapse photography. Herbert cannot sleep and sits propped up on his bed trying to read a book called *Chicken Sold for the Soup*. He cannot concentrate. He still has his day clothes on beneath his robe, ready to spring or fall into action.

He looks at his door, where he earlier jammed a chair up under the handle. He gets up, picks up the large hunting knife from his nightstand, and tests the door handle for the eighth time; it's still locked. He returns to bed, closes his eyes, and breathes deeply.

Moments later the door handle moves ever so slightly. Herbert's eyes shoot open as he jumps to his feet, knife in hand. He shuffles to the door, knocks the chair out of the way, and flings the door wide open ready to slice up whomever he finds there.

An empty hallway stretches out in either direction, with green fluorescent lights buzzing overhead. Herbert checks both directions for any movement. *Nothing. Maybe I am losing it,* he worries.

He retreats into his room, locks the door again, and resigns himself to calling it a night. He takes off his robe and begins to unbutton his shirt. Then he decisively rebuttons it. *Paranoid or not, this is not where I go down.*

Using his knife, he cuts into his mattress and retrieves another old leather fanny pack. He explores the contents, laying them out on his desk: several old credit cards and gift cards; modest amounts of cash in Canadian, American, UK, and other currencies; various passports; and a Chipstick with all spike and no balm.

He reaches further into his mattress and pulls out an empty PanAm (1927-1991) duffel bag. He packs it with his tuxedo, badly polished shoes, slippers, pajamas, and the bathrobe he just removed.

Entering the bathroom he adds toiletries, medications, and a portable blood pressure cuff and monitor. He hesitates to pack adult diapers but then adds a few as well, though one drops out without his noticing.

Returning back to his room he decides to take a number of books he can't part with. The weight of his bag grows heavy. When he attempts to lift it, something in his back protests sharply, making him grimace. He looks at his watch.

It's almost morning. A session with Ms. E. Claire wouldn't hurt. But I cannot stay here, he decides. He collects his things, opens his door, and departs as stealthily as he can, which is not a lot. His bag bangs the walls once or twice.

If this were a movie, the camera would not move from his open door. After a moment, Mr. Downright lost again, shuffles past with his walker. He then backtracks and enters. He does his business in the bathroom and emerges in a pajama top and diapers. He climbs into bed and shuts off the bedside lamp for what may be the last time in his life.

The Bolivian cleaning woman quietly rolls in with her large trash barrel. She gently closes the door, making sure no one saw her. It's pitch black now except for a sliver of moonlight from the window. She listens to Downright heavy breathing and watches his chest rise and fall. She then puts her bowler hat aside and makes sure her hair is tied back as if for sport.

Next, she approaches the bed and takes hold of both of the man's hands with just one of hers, in blue latex gloves. She covers his mouth with the other. His eyes shoot open in alarm as he starts gasping for air. She begins a well-rehearsed speech.

"My name is Olivia Martinez… de Jorge Pincez Flores… de Tejunga, for short."

The man relaxes and even seems to smile. She lets him speak. "Is that you, Princess?" He tries to caress her face.

"Gross! No! My name is—Get down!"

"I'm always down! Right, babe?"

"Silence!"

In her imagination this becomes a music video with Downright squirming slow-motion as she covers his lips plus a version of *Take My Breath Away* (Berlin, 1986).

"*All of this commotion / crossing every ocean / just for today!*" In the video she is younger, seated on a Bolivian Airways flight and staring out the window.

Next, she wears goggles in a make-shift chemistry lab in a small apartment kitchen. *"I tried every lotion / and settled on my potion / knowing I won't hesitate."*

She finishes a concoction and uses an eye dropper to soak the liquid into bits of bread she broke earlier. She places them on the window ledge of her 20th story project apartment in Chicago. *"Take my bread away!"*

In the alley below, a dead pigeon lands in a pile of other dead ones. Some birds are startled and take flight. A few, like future inmates, then wander up to see if they can try some.

Back in Herbert's room, the lethal cleaner now known as *Olivia* stares out at the moon. She looks like many a pop star, reflecting on hopeless sorrow. She sings, "*And now before day / it's time you slip away.*"

In the darkness, Downright's ghost eases out from the bed and floats past her, his face still unseen by her. He ascends into the sky until lost in the moonlit clouds.

The song ends and Olivia resumes the mundane parts of her job. If she had stayed by the window she would see Downright's ghost briefly descend from the clouds. He hovers, looks around confused, then flies away more decisively.

Olivia removes the bed's top sheet and throws it in her bin. The pungent smell of urine makes her cover her nose. She then turns on the lamp and immediately realizes her mistake.

Oops! But this is Downright. Shocking! she thinks. *And he was trying to tell me but I did not listen. Why do I never listen? What is wrong with me?*

She then shifts from self-loathing to having a new respect for her intended prey. *How is that old man still so clever?*

During the above termination, Herbert went and took the spare bed in Mr. Eulogy's room. The old man was snoring soundly. The weight of his bag and stress seemed to slide right off, letting him fall fast asleep before he could even think, *Boy am I dead.*

Still in Herbert's assigned room, Olivia lays her trash barrel onto its side. She drags her tired old body out of bed and into the barrel. When she stands it up, the man's feet are sticking out. She can only bend one of his knees; the other is already stiff with *rigor mortis.* She removes the lampshade and arranges it on the protruding foot; *the tassels add a nice touch.*

She then collects trash from the bathroom to help conceal her body of evidence. Lastly, she dons her bowler hat and exits to continue her unfinished search and her trash removal service.

***

At the crack of dawn, a showered and high-spirited Herbert, wearing a 1970s red track suit, shuffles into the physical therapy room. He wears his fanny pack and carries the heavy duffle bag, trying not to hurt himself. No one else is there yet.

However, he sees Claire's bag and deposits his next to hers. He rehearses saying, "*Bonne soirée*, my little É. Claire Voyant. I suppose you foresaw this day would come?"

An ominous security camera hums from a corner in the ceiling. A monitor in another room records Herbert sitting on the padded table, his legs swinging like a child's. He soon leans down on one elbow. Then he unzips the top of his tracksuit and adjusts his position, negotiating between pain and pizzazz.

Under a back door, a small rubber tube is inserted into the room. A valve is then turned on next door and a faint, sinister *hisssss commencccces.*

While trying to look sexy, Herbert suddenly cocks his head, detecting a tangy *something* in the air. His eyes narrow, but it's too late. The room begins to blur. The lights soften while objects widen in haze. Herbert struggles against his own increasing heaviness. He blinks furiously to stay awake. He seeks firm footing on the floor but then hugs the table as he falls.

The back door opens and a large female silhouette enters, wearing the familiar burgundy scrubs. "Ah, Olga," Herbert greets, his words slurred. "Have you seen Claire?"

The woman has her back turned as she prepares something on the counter. A faint metallic tick-tick-tick-tick on a cymbal starts up. *Whole Lotta Olga*, thinks Herbert (cfr. AC/DC 1977).

"Eh-hem!" responds the woman. Her pitch is higher than expected, an unnatural falsetto. "Claire couldn't make it today." She snort-giggles. "But we'll get cracking in a moment."

Herbert asks pointedly, "Isn't that her bag?" Even as the words leave his mouth, reality hits him like a hip fracture. *This is not Olga but a stranger! And yet,* "You seem familiar," he says. "Have we met?"

"Many times, actually." The woman turns to face him. She is Rosie, from the Polish apartment. Her lips curl into a grin, revealing her sharp platinum dentures embedded with diamonds. "But I didn't go by Rosie back then."

"Roseyback who?"

"No, I'm just Rosie."

"To be sure." Herbert sighs with vindication. "Wait! So then I'm not yet crazy. Just in danger for my life is all!"

"Very much so," responds Rosie, who lunges in attack.

Herbert stumbles backwards. He manages to grab and swing a small pink dumbbell, which he connects to Rosie's face, sending her dentures flying across the room. (They conveniently land in a glass of clear orange liquid next to a bottle labeled BreathTorch. It looks like an advertisement for mouthwash as bubbles stream from embarrassing food particles trapped in the dentures.) Herbert's momentum sends him crashing to the floor with a grunt.

Rosie pauses, deciding whether to retrieve her dentures or pounce on Herbert. She opts for the pricey dentures. Her fingers sizzle in the acid-like wash but she feels no pain.

While on the floor, Herbert grabs a long physical therapy hook and yanks Rosie's ankle, making her crash to the floor as well.

Not wasting a *second* second, Herbert drops the long hook, climbs to his feet with the help of a cabinet, and topples it onto Rosie, shattering the glass. He then adds a barrage of PT equipment on top of her as well: dumbbells, rubber balls, yoga blocks, all while keeping her pinned down beneath the wreckage.

Upstairs in her office, Mrs. Pearbottom maintains a carefully balanced yoga pose. Her face is serene, her clothes athletic, but not aesthetic. She listens to a song, *Meditate, Good Times!* (cfr. Kool & the Gang, 1980).

Muffled thuds and shattering glass from below interrupt her poise. Additional heavy objects crash against walls. Her balance falters. Annoyed, she uses her desk phone to make inquiries.

In the background, her large bed can be seen through an open door. There may or may not be a young man sleeping there. Mrs. Pearbottom dials extension after extension but no one answers.

Down in the PT room, Herbert struggles to keep Rosie contained in her cabinet position. "I knew Vilefinger was still active," he says. "That's who sent you, right?"

She struggles to grab the PT hook Herbert discarded but can't quite reach it. "You know better than to ask that!" she admonishes. "It's a KICA violation."

"Oh, please. Honor among the death-inducers?"

Rosie finally grasps the question mark tool and studies it. "I like this."

Herbert asks, "Why haven't you retired yet? I thought the Vile One took care of his own."

"Vile Fibber? Oops. Whatever. I'm retired. But what a joke! I never could make meetings end."

A forceful kick opens the front door wide and it bangs against the wall. Herbert and Rosie look. Olivia strides in, her bowler hat perched on her head. She looks serious and tired.

"I knew it!" reacts Herbert.

Rosie also has a positive response. "Hi there! I haven't seen you in ages!"

Olivia tries to stay focused. However, she takes in all that is Rosie and wants to launch into another music video. *Hey soul sister / I thought you were a mister / I must have missed something you did* (cfr. Train, 2009). But she knows it's not a good time to ask.

Herbert assures Olivia, "Don't worry about KICA. I figured it out on my own."

Olivia wonders if Rosie violated the code but doesn't ask. Instead, she holds her hat and flings it like the lethal frisbee that it is. This book could end here but it won't.

In the millisecond that counts, Rosie yanks Herbert to the floor with her long hook. Foam mats break his fall instead of his bones, thus giving our story more time to unfold.

Olivia looks at Rosie with annoyance for her accidentally saving him. Rosie looks ashamed, like the first time she accidentally broke someone's neck in training.

The flying guillotine ricochets off several walls with showers of sparks before it returns to sender. On the way it impales into Rosie's forehead. This is due to her characteristically bad timing when it comes to standing up for something. She blinks for a moment as she looks around, unclear about where it went or why everyone is staring at her.

"*Pendeja!*" snarls Olivia in Spanish, storming toward her. "That hat is not for you!"

"I never said it was!" answers Rosie. She doesn't flinch as Olivia tries to yank it free. The hat is deeply wedged. Rosie shows mixed feelings, annoyed by the animosity but also craving Olivia's approval.

Herbert, meanwhile, grabs his flee bag to go. Just then, the Twins rush in, ready to help. Herbert greets them with, "Well, better late than never! Take care of these ladies, will you?"

The boys hesitate so he adds, "Be quick about it and I won't file a complaint with Personnel."

The Twins exchange a glance and guffaw. Without a word, they each pull out their weapons of choice from who knows where: a pair of nunchucks and a bo staff.

Herbert's smile vanishes. "Or maybe I'll just move along. Tootles!" He shuffles to the door using his bag as a shield.

Behind him, the Twins provide an elaborate display of skills. Nunchucks whirl through the air with swishing sounds, while the bo staff spins in flawless twirls. Their movements are precise. It's as if they are auditioning for *Beijing's Got Talent*. Their act builds up to a dramatic crescendo but is interrupted by a DING! on their phones.

Each stops and reaches for his iClone. Texts read, Now casting for *Dancing with the Throwing Stars!*

Wayne is impressed. "How do they even know?"

They both click the button labeled, *Apply Yourself Later*. They notice Herbert has left and they follow. The women are still busy undoing the impalement.

Moments later, Herbert bursts into the community's institutional kitchen. He frantically rifles through his duffle bag for his knife. "Come on, come on!" he mutters, pulling out socks, toothpaste, and outdated maps.

When he looks toward the door, he notices a wide array of knives on the counter next to him; even a meat cleaver. He's relieved, but then something else catches his attention.

A trash container next to a giant freezer is overflowing with chocolate pudding cups. The freezer door is also ajar. Herbert pulls it open and gasps as a chill runs down his spine.

Covered in a glossy sheen of frozen pudding is his favorite physical therapist. "Oh, my sweet, sweet E. Claire," Herbert laments. His mind reels with flashbacks and fantasies. Here are but a few examples:

Herbert recalls Claire's warm smile the first time they met, her hand extended in confidence.

Next, Herbert basks in Claire's gentle but firm touch as she works on his leg.

In another fantasy, Herbert is the one in burgundy scrubs. His fingers inch their way up Claire's spandex-covered leg.

She smiles and says, "I wholeheartedly consent to this unconscionable departure from ethical and responsible treatment, my unbelievably skilled and power-imbalanced healer."

Next, the two of them stand arm in arm dressed for a tango. They stride into a casino. The image freezes like a VHS on pause; even Herbert's mind can't allow such a big departure from reality.

The tape rewinds and plays again. It's not a casino; it's Bingo Night at Sunset. Jake and other seniors pat Herbert on the back for nabbing the hot young PT.

In the background, a decked out Olga fumes. She declares a somber, "Bingo," and holds up her winning card.

Herbert is suddenly jerked back to the present by a muffled, "Mmmmm! Mmmmm!" He peers deeper into the freezer.

"Olga?" he asks, incredulous. She is indeed back there, bound and squirming. Her eyes plead for help; her groans repeat, "Mmmmm!" and "Mmmmm's!"

Just then, Herbert is startled to see Claire's eyes open. She licks away chocolate from her blue lips and asks, "Is she gone?" She speaks with surprising clarity for someone believed to be dead just moments before.

"You're alive?" asks Herbert, as if unconvinced. A thousand other questions flood his mind but only one other escapes. "What happened?"

"I have a disorder," she admits through chattering teeth. She shifts her position, causing frozen chocolate to crack. "I was doing something I can't control, when this… *person* brought in Olga, all tied up. She shoved us both in here. I didn't know what to do, so I just froze."

"Mmmm!!!" mmms Olga, eager to be freed already.

Herbert starts to free Claire but the sound of a metallic THUNK! interrupts him. A throwing star has embedded itself into the freezer door, just inches from his face. He turns and sees the Twins by the door, grinning as they twirl their weapons.

Claire still believes they are fellow staffers and says, "No, stop! He's helping us!"

Herbert shoves her back into the freezer. "Stay put, Pudding." He closes the door, grabs knives from the well-appointed counter, and sends them spinning toward the Twins.

One sinks into Wayne's shoulder and another into Woldecott's thigh. They look inconvenienced, not fazed. Herbert goes into rapid-fire mode, peppering them and the wall. With anyone else it would be a short-lived circus act. Some knives fall with clickety clacks.

Upstairs, Mrs. Pearbottom hangs up her phone in frustration. "Why is no one answering?"

The muffled clattering of knives echoes faintly from below. Mrs. Pearbottom rushes to her walk-in closet and puts on sneakers. She then rifles through her matronly suits and finds her AK-47. She shoves the weapon into a golf bag emblazoned with a future film sponsor's logo. She carefully arranges the clubs so as to obscure her weapon. Satisfied, she slings the bag over her shoulder and exits with determination.

Down in the kitchen, Rosie enters and immediately retreats. She uses the door to absorb the knives thrown by Herbert. She wears a headscarf as a bandage and adjusts her appearance using a compact mirror she carries. She wiggles her dentures, which still feel a bit askew. *Just three more payments*, she recalls.

She peers around the door at precisely the wrong moment and is impaled in the forehead again. She sighs with resignation. "Gosh darn it," she mutters.

Olivia yanks Rosie to safety in the hall. Her bowler hat is dented, but she wears it with defiant pride. The knives stop and Olivia checks the suddenly quiet kitchen.

She enters and scans the room like a security camera, even humming. Herbert is nowhere to be seen. The Twins pull knives from their limbs like hikers removing cockleburs from shoelaces. Olivia chooses one of the exits.

Down the hall, Herbert limps into the recreation room, his breath panting, and his pants heavy with sweat. *Though luckily not urine*, he acknowledges. He scans for options and his eyes land on his Sears roller skates.

Moments later, Herbert bursts through the community entrance doors in his roller skates. He clatters across the brief pavement and thump-thumps across the grass until he makes it to the street. It's an uphill battle as he struggles not to backslide.

Olivia emerges from the building with an old-school scooter and gives chase. A chin strap holds her dented hat in place. She allows a tiny smile as the wind rushes across her face.

A brief flashback to childhood recalls her riding a large toy truck down a hill, her hair flowing in the breeze. Shaking off that memory, her adult face tightens as she tracks her target like a hawk.

Next, the Twins come running outside with skateboards from the rec room. They spot Herbert and Olivia and run across the grass and up the steep hill, also inclined to join the chase.

Rosie emerges from the building next, holding her favorite PT tool with the long hook. Herbert's scent draws her attention like a bloodhound. She sees a woman's bike leaning against the wall, complete with a wicker basket and bell.

She yanks the bike away from the wall and runs with it, intending to mount it in motion. Suddenly she falls head over heels over it, and the bike over her. A strong U-lock is on the front wheel. She grabs it to rip it apart but then remembers something.

Earlier in the kitchen, while putting Olga into the freezer, Rosie had noticed and taken Olga's lanyard with keys, ignoring the pleas from her tape-covered mouth.

Rosie now patiently finds the correct key and undoes the lock. She is about to toss it on the ground but sees a NO LOITERING sign. Instead, she puts the lock in her basket. She runs with the bike and this time successfully mounts it and pedals hard.

In the kitchen, Mrs. Pearbottom arrives and quickly assesses the damage. She holds her golf bag at an upward angle as if an AK-47 might be hidden in it, which it is. The bag is nearly empty of clubs now. Another one slides out and falls to the floor.

Amid the mess she notices the empty pudding cups by the trash can and leading to the freezer. She sees the embedded throwing star too. She approaches carefully and opens the freezer door as if expecting a raptor. Instead, she finds her young PT, shivering.

"Claire?" she asks, though not really doubting her eyes. "You must be freezing!" She pulls her out.

"Mrs. P-P-Pearbottom! I'm-m-m s-s-so glad you're here!" She sees the golf bag. "Are y-y-you w-w-working in your r-r-rounds?"

"Not quite." Mrs. Pearbottom puts the bag down in a way that still conceals the weapon. "What happened here?"

"Some l-l-lady shoved us in there!" begins Claire.

"Us?" asks Mrs. Pearbottom. She looks and sees Olga squirming in the back. "Oh, my!"

She removes various frozen foods and pulls Olga out.

Claire continues. "Mr. Bigglesby came by too. But then Wayne and Woldy showed up and he shoved us back inside and said to wait. I didn't understand it. It sounded like they were dropping a lot of things out here." She looks around and forms a hypothesis. "Maybe knives?"

"Possibly." Mrs. Pearbottom selects a knife and cuts away their ropes. "Tell me more about the woman."

Olga is still too dazed to answer.

Claire says, "I don't know… but she had these metal teeth… and diamond grillz!"

Olga finally takes in the room. "What a mess!"

Mrs. Pearbottom thinks fast about how to keep them quiet without resorting to ice. She says, "Well, I'm glad you're safe. But you're not going to like what she did to your office."

Claire is ready to cry. "But we're just PTs. How can there be so much hate for what we do?"

"Maybe she had a bad experience somewhere," reasons Olga.

"It's a crazy world right now," says Mrs. Pearbottom. "Let's not alarm our residents. The police should be here soon. Maybe take some time off until we understand what happened."

Olga is quick to downplay it. "Oh, I will not cower in the fear because of unhappy customers."

"Very well, Olga. Just, please don't mention these knives or the state of your office to anyone."

"My lips are cemented."

"Me too," agrees Claire, "but I want to go see it!"

"Just don't touch anything," asks Mrs. Pearbottom as they exit to the hall.

Outside, a few seniors have gathered. Several point to the distant, disappearing chase. Some hold golf clubs.

Mrs. Pearbottom emerges from the building with her weapon still concealed in the bag. "Stay calm, everyone. The police are on their way." She sees the Twins in the distance.

Senior Rita asks, "What is happening, Mrs. Pearbottom?"

"We had an intruder, and as you can see, some of our staff took off after them."

"What did they want?" asks Jake.

Mrs. Pearbottom pretends to be thrilled that they collected her golf clubs. "You found them! I was so worried they stole them!

They're my *Quantas Ultraslim 3000s*" [Or another brand that would like to endorse a film].

"They were scattered in the hallway," answers Jake. "And by the way, those are some fine clubs."

"I wouldn't use anything less," she insists. "I'm too serious about my sport."

"Was it an inside job?" asks Senior Rita. "Employees just don't know how to go away quietly anymore."

Mrs. Pearbottom nods. "I'll let the police figure all that out."

Suddenly the security guard yells and points from the rooftop, "There they go!"

Everyone looks up to him for once. He points to where they were already looking before he distracted them. "See them?"

Mrs. Pearbottom gestures for the guard to *cut it.* He fails to understand the universal neck-cutting gesture so she uses her words.

"The police are on their way! Please, come down!"

"I can't hear you! Let me come down!" The guard goes inside.

As the chase is no longer visible, Mrs. Pearbottom says, "That's all we're going to see for tonight. Let's get back inside now, please."

Her seniors obey and head into the building just as Dr. Bentiron fights his way out. He reaches Mrs. Pearbottom and asks, tucking his shirt, "What's going on?"

"Took you long enough." She turns and ushers people inside.

Dr. Bentiron has no idea what is going on, or what he did wrong, or even what day it is. "I'm not even on duty," he defends to the air.

***

For those interested in keeping up with the chase, Herbert reaches the top of the hill and faces a steep downhill street. He looks back at his entourage, dons his goggles, and lunges forward. He tucks in as if skiing, like Gregory Peck in *Spellbound* (Hitchcock, 1945), with various unexpected backgrounds whizzing by as he heads to a quaint main street.

The Twins make it over the hump and drop onto their skateboards. They gain speed as they dodge potholes and cars while shooting Uzis.

Olivia expertly mounts her scooter for the downhill race, keeping a low center of gravity. Herbert would have said her extended rump looks a bit like the ass of nine.

Rosie soon follows on her bike, extending her hook-like lance ready to bring Herbert to his downfall.

Skating fast, Herbert sometimes leaves the ground, dodges cars, does corkscrews, or performs other feats. He even flies through the front of a parked AmazEx delivery truck (assuming an acquisition), which punts a package through the air and onto someone's porch.

If you were in that package, you would hear a familiar electronic bleat from inside the home, and a man calling out, "Honey, your package is at the door!"

His Honey then answers from a saltwater bath and says, "Return it, please! It was supposed to be here two minutes ago and I don't need it anymore!"

The husband comes outside looking for the package and sees Herbert and the hitman parade. His immediate reaction is to say, "Cool!" He then runs into his garage and emerges on a sail-cart, joining the cold-blooded pursuit.

While skating, Herbert takes out his cell phone and tries to find P's emergency number. This is admittedly hard to do while maintaining his physical balance and that of life in general.

The Twins continue shooting at him from their skateboards. While they were never very fond of him, today they miss him terribly. In fact, on either side of the street, porch lights explode as the Twins whiz by. It would be hard to believe except something similar occurred when they were training for moments like this.

Once upon a farm, paper targets of humans were attached to hay bales, with an old red barn far behind. The Twins would shoot their Uzis, holding them quite straight. Yet the targets, the hay, and the barn would go unmolested. *Crickets.* Instead, sparks could be seen, and ricochets heard, from the rusty metal silos off to the right and to the left of them. Noticing this, the Twins would stop and adjust their footing. Then they would continue to achieve more of the same. They are better at screenplay and dancing than murder.

Returning to our current pursuit, Herbert is still in the lead. He reaches P's voicemail, which is disguised by the *bee-dee-beep* of a "non-working number."

He patiently waits to speak while skating madly. Rosie's hook creeps into close proximity to his legs, trying to nab them. Herbert somehow manages to stay ahead, curving around objects.

Not that P's voicemail greeting uses foul language, but a very long beep finally occurs. Herbert puts the phone to his face and says, "Hello there, Chap, I do wish you would pick up. I could have been hacked earlier, thanks to your staff! And I still might be, so I'll be quick. I'm a little shocked-not-shocked by my new assignment, highly anticipated but apparently only by me. I had specifically been promised I would not be on the receiving end of endless *pepperwork*, so to speak, but somehow someone let some be sent my way. And now another company's *foremen,* though two are ladies, are trying to bury me. Do call me back, Darling, though I've obviously been called back already. We'll need to discuss title and compensation."

While weaving in and out of his message, Herbert also ducks and dodges harm. Rosie is still closest, followed by the Twins, Olivia, and the Sail-Kart Guy with the lackluster marriage.

In perfect sync, the Twins eject their ammo magazines and insert new ones to miss again with. Olivia and SKG dodge their empty bouncing cartridges.

SKG slowly edges past all the pursuers and even past Herbert himself as if it were just a race. Olivia and the other assassins share a confused look about who this man might be. None can help wondering if he might be the prophesized One in the ancient lore.

Now, as is common among people who inhabit this kind of world, the entire troop is soon headed for railroad tracks. And yes, a hot, steaming, heavy iron, prior-century train burning Pennsylvania coal, and churning out rich black smoke, approaches in the distance, perhaps on its way to Hogwarts or the North Pole or Istanbul. The steam whistle blows and the wheels churn like meat grinders, which leads Herbert to feel disoriented on this murderous express (Christie, 1934). As he regains his balance, he remembers he was mid-message. "Oh dear, is this thing still recording?!"

While a collision seems inevitable, the tracks suddenly curve and the train now runs parallel to the chase instead of at odds with it. Herbert gets a new idea for his escape.

"Oh, never mind, I have a train to catch!" he yells into his phone. He pockets the device and gropes for the caboose, hoping to get away with it.

The train only seems to taunt him, remaining just out of reach like so many plans and wishes in the Reader's life.

With a final energetic lunge, Herbert manages to grab the handrail. He gets bedraggled a bit, as he hangs on for still-valued life. His skates throw sparks at every metal-to-metal contact. Finally, he manages to hoist enough of himself up onto the back gate and pauses as the train helps him high-tail it out of there.

His pursuers fail to adequately navigate the perpendicular railroad ties and they fall down hard. Put another way, they wipe out, bite the dust, eat dirt, etc.

Only Sail-Kart Guy rides on, gliding along the smooth pavement. He holds up a selfie-cam and says, "If you haven't hit the like and subscribe button, please do so now and leave a comment below!"

The four frustrated would-be *Herbivores* get up and dust themselves off. They quickly notice imperfections in each other and dust those off as well.

However, the train suddenly SCREETCHES to a complete stop. They turn with renewed hope. It has arrived at a station where commuters get often on.

In a middle compartment, Herbert has already sat down with a wet martini in hand. He appears tranquil but checks his watch and thinks, *These frequent stops are untenable. An express track would have been wise if they expect people to actually use this thing* (cfr. Los Angeles Metro).

The doors finally close and he realizes his phone has been vibrating. The caller ID says *Peaches* but he refuses to answer. He notices and deletes numerous texts piling up from her.

Running along the outside, Olivia spots Herbert. They even make brief eye contact, but he pretends not to notice.

The train starts to move. Olivia hurries and jumps into a gap between compartments. The other three follow her but, judging from their faces, it's more out of obligation than personal interest.

Scanning the other side of the tracks, Herbert spots a shiny new Aston Martin parked between Funeral Arrangements by Lynch and an ice cream parlor called *The Creamatorium.*

As four unlikely commuters move between compartments, a bird atop a flag pole watches an old-timer shuffle into the ice cream shop. He soon emerges eating a Divine Mercy Sundae.

In the blink of an eyelid, Herbert is gone and the Aston Martin too. The ice cream missed the trash can and the bird flies down.

As the train chugs along, Olivia and friends search for Herbert. Rosie suddenly turns back as if hooked on a feeling but more likely a scent (Blue Suede, 1974).

The Aston Martin and the train move further and further apart in perpendicular directions. If one is travelling at 128 kph and the other at 96, will they ever meet again?

CHAPTER NINE

Running on MP

A phone rings in *SpyTone*, cutting through the silent darkness. It glows in a wicker basket of 40 or so others. A hairy old hand searches for the culprit and pulls it out. The caller ID says *Peaches*.

"Have you any idea what time it is?" asks P.

"Yes, we now have clocks here," responds Mrs. Pearbottom. "I don't know why some people imagine otherwise."

P lights a lamp and sits up in his plush bed, wearing turquoise silk pajamas. His wife turns away from the light.

Mrs. Pearbottom is at her desk, uploading security footage. "I'm afraid Herbert was compromised."

"Oh dear, I almost feared as much. Was it Dr. Bentiron?"

"No, assassins. Why Dr. Bentiron?"

"Never mind. Where is he now?"

"Home, I suppose. He only works on Tuesdays and Fridays." She looks back at her empty bed.

"Not Bentiron! Herbert. Where is Herbert?"

"Oh, yes, of course. He fled the facility. I'm having a slight bit of trouble reaching him. Perhaps we can add his phone to the tracking plan? I'll pay for it."

"Oh, nonsense."

"But Sir, I am responsible. I was inexcusably delayed in protecting him so I will tender my resignation in the morning."

"Stop it. Just prepare yourself for an intolerable number of tedious online trainings to complete."

"Thank you, Sir." She blocks the mouthpiece and gags. She imagines asking in a cockney accent, *Can I have some more, please?* (Lean, 1968).

P continues. "Do you know who is behind it? And have you sent us the footage?"

"I'm uploading it as we speak." She freezes the video on Olivia helping Rosie remove the knife from her forehead. "I hate to say it, but Herbert may have been right. Dr. Vilefinger does seem to be involved."

"Not you too! Why the devil do you say that?"

"There's something familiar about two of the attackers."

"There were two?"

"Actually, four. And maybe a fifth, but I think he was just a bystander with a YouTube channel–"

"I can't believe it!"

"It's to be expected these days. But I don't think he's involved."

"I don't mean that! Our paranoid delusional friend was right?"

"With all due respect, Sir. Language?"

P sighs. "Sorry, I suppose my AI filter is off." He notices his wife trying to tell him something. She holds up her watch and he says to Mrs. Pearbottom, "Well, they do say even a broken clock is right twice a day."

His wife frowns and buries her face in her pillow.

Mrs. Pearbottom answers, "Now we'll never hear the end of it."

"Unless they got him. There's always that possibility."

"Oh, no, please don't say that, Sir. It's all my fault."

"Now, now! Which is the best time to admit fault. And you have. So now just find him and bring him in, dead or alive. I mean, alive! And put all your other affairs aside."

"That won't be a problem, Sir." She looks at her empty bed.

P notices a voicemail. "Oh goodness, it appears he tried to call."

"Well, he's ignoring my calls and texts."

"I'll try to reach him. *Au Revoir.*"

"We'll find him, Sir."

"Yes, give him time. He'll come around."

P hangs up. His wife suggests, "Next time make it a real funeral."

"She's kidding!" P calls out to the walls. "We love all people. Just a little morbid humor from time to time. It gets us through the day! Or night, as it were."

He cuts off the light. "We're all sleeping now. Goodnight!"

***

The Aston Martin winds its way through rural country roads. Herbert's face is pure concentration but not necessarily on the road. He can't help recalling things people have been saying to him.

Mrs. Pearbottom: "The whole world could see you were slipping. Any remaining hatred or animosity was replaced by feelings of pity and good wishes. The whole spy world could see you slipping and frankly felt pity."

P: "I'm afraid we need to cut all ties with you."

Mrs. Pearbottom: "Please, Herbert! Relax. And do stop profiling."

Dr. Bentiron: "As important as you were earlier in life, it's sadly quite likely that the only people who care if you're alive or not are in Accounts Receivable."

Herbert himself: "Mrs. Pearbottom, surely you recall, there have literally been hundreds if not thousands of people who have wanted to see me dead."

Mrs. Pearbottom: "And that's not even counting women and children."

Herbert's phone vibrates. The screen says *UrineMan.* He eventually answers, "So, I finally merit your attention?"

P is in his kitchen looking for a snack in his PJs and bathrobe. "I'm so sorry, Herbert."

"I don't even know if I should be speaking to you."

"Well thank you then, for allowing me this chance to apologize. I truly am terribly sorry." P checks a date on a food package and throws it away.

Herbert is wary. "Apologize for what, exactly?"

P is caught off guard and throws away a foul-smelling leftover. "Well… for… having trivialized your concerns. You deserve better."

"You're quite right, I do! I gave my life to this company, and when I ask for a decent review based on actual incidents I saw with my own eyes, you treated me like a senile old fool."

"You're definitely no fool. And I accept your remonstrance. I'll say it clearly. We were wrong and you were right. And I'm glad you were able to take care of yourself."

"Well, no one else was going to."

P wants to get past these preliminaries. "Herbert, I know you're angry but I am now more than officially worried about you. Are you safe? Where are you?"

Herbert looks out his window (on the right side, of course). The Aston Martin moves slowly through a long busy parking lot of a 7-Eleven and other stores. Drivers are doing the slowest possible job of parking and unparking.

"I'm not ready to disclose specifics. Let's just say I'm going through a lot right now."

"I understand. I'm here whenever you want to talk about it."

"I have no intention of talking about it. I'll get to the other side of it soon."

"I'm sure you will." P keeps checking for something edible.

Brakes are slammed, a collision narrowly avoided. "If you idiots ever learn to drive!" yells Herbert.

P is taken aback. He fumbles and drops a plate that shatters. "Goodness! I'm not normally such a butterfingers."

"No, apparently just with me! And my life, all shattered! Just because you and that woman you put here with me refused to believe that you-know-which-finger wasn't out of the pie yet."

"I see!" answers P. He turns to what is sadly a dark and empty oven and countertop.

Herbert continues. "How am I supposed to have any confidence in you, or in your local director, who keeps calling, by the way, but I'm not talking to her!"

"Look, Herbert, I do understand. We've ruined your confidence in us. But please tell me about the actual attack. I have the security footage right here and I can recognize two of your four attackers."

"Congratulations! And did she tell you she hired three of them? They are on her payroll!"

"Oh dear, I'll be sure to review her hiring practices and bring it up in her annual."

"Did she mention the tennis incident? That play was meant for me!"

"No, she only mentioned someone, Downright, missing."

"That's a Downright lie! He's always lost. She's completely unreliable! And I was right. The one I feared is behind it all! And who knows whom else."

"Hummus? I didn't think of that." P opens a small container.

"Yes, whom else. Why is everyone commenting on my diction?"

"I have no interest in your diction." P tastes the hummus and grimaces. "Something is not right." He checks for a date on it.

"Precisely! The Vial is not as cracked up as we were told!"

"Oh, long expired!" P throws the hummus in the trash.

"No, someone only wanted us to think so."

"Herbert, I can confirm Henric Vilefinger is alive but quite incapacitated."

"That only used to matter! Leaders like that are propped up everywhere these days. They're somebody's bread and butter."

"Good thinking." P finds bread but no butter. Then peanut butter, but only enough to be disappointed by how little remains.

The bread is crumbly. He scrapes peanut butter with a long spoon. "I'm going to get to the bottom of this. And I'm not going to rest till I'm satisfied." He eats the little he collects.

Herbert is serious. "Good, because if not, you'll never hear from me again."

P chews quietly. It's not bad. And a good source of protein.

Herbert grows impatient. "Hello? Are you still there?"

"Oh yes, I was just wondering if that was a promise."

"No, it was not! You will always hear from me, just like the Revenue Agency! But at least I know you are who you say you are."

"Indeed." P finds a round cracker and eats it. "Herbert, do you remember when we first met?"

"Oh please, I don't have time to, P!" He shifts uncomfortably.

"Just hear me out and then find a bathroom. We were both so young at the academy, enjoying one of our first lunches together in the commissary. You turned to me and said–"

Herbert picks up the story. "Yes, I knew your name but little else. And when I noticed that smug McGill coming our way, I didn't care for him to sit anywhere near us."

"Correct!" continues P. "So, you turned to me, saying, Well, he cannot be that much of a fool, Percy. Oh, no, probably not a complete idiot, Percy. Not a total and utter moron, Percy."

Herbert enjoys the recollection. "Yes, and I went on just long enough for him to be standing there, hoping we would invite him to sit down. As I predicted, he tried to correct me saying, "Excuse me, but I believe you are mispronouncing that word. It's French, *per se*."

P takes over. "At which point you looked at me, and I'll never forget your expression, or his immediately afterward, when you said, with a French accent, My goodness, *Perceval!* Have I been mispronouncing your name all this time, *Per Se*?"

"Well, he did leave us alone after that. *Per se*."

"Yes, for these fifty-six years," confirms P.

"So maybe he's behind this!"

"Except that he's dead. Truly dead. Not dummy-fake-cover dead. Anyway, my point is that people have at times underestimated you, and I apologize for falling into that lot this time."

"I appreciate it," says Herbert. "Now, I know you can't answer this directly but… might your Secretary be involved?"

"Goodness, no. The whole Cabinet believed your funeral was real. Even the ones who signed the approvals. They hear a good thing and move along."

Herbert pauses, unsure if that was an insult. "Then your director must have been flipped. Perhaps by that young, so-called doctor. He seems to show up more than part-time lately."

"What? Is no one safe with her?"

"At last, you understand me."

"Yes, but I disagree. Whatever questionable judgment she shows in her own time, her loyalty remains impregnable."

"I don't know, Sir. Even Peter Piper pecked a few too many pickled peppers. She was nowhere to be seen when I was highly sought after."

"Oh, yes! She did apologize, by the way. For being late. She said she felt terrible."

"Oh, I'm so sorry! It must have been awful for her. I suppose she sent thoughts and prayers."

"Well, you don't have to be sarcastic about it."

"Or maybe I do! For my own sanity, or whatever is left of it. There's no such thing as being slightly late to a thing like that."

"Oh poppycock. You know she's fond of you. Regrettably, we all just gave in to a kind of *Kumbaya*, assuming everyone had grown up and moved on" (Gordon, 1926).

"Not me! I knew this was coming and you all called me *paranoid*. I was laughed at, behind my back and even to my face."

"Herbert, once again, I apologize. Profusely!" He closes the fridge. "Your safety is now my topmost priority. We will find out whoever is behind this. And get ahead of it. But while you're in the middle of it, perhaps you could manage to lie low for a few days? Take a little *vacay*, as they say?"

"Sure, and just trust you people?"

"I realize mistrust can be very confusing."

"Darn right she is! How can she even sleep at night?"

"Herbert, Mrs. Pearbottom is not going to let any more harm come to you."

"Just the same, I'll be handling my own affairs from now on. Starting with ending this call. I can't risk you tracing it." Herbert abruptly ends the call.

"But it's a cell phone! Of course, we can trace–" P realizes he hung up. "Oh, never mind." He revisits the crackers; it was premature to put them away.

The Aston Martin arrives at a BestRestTurnHere Hotel. The façade and Herbert's disappointment are both reflected in the right-side window. It's not the kind of accommodation he was accustomed to for half a century.

Herbert climbs out and thanks the Uber driver, who takes off like a Band-Aid, high-pitched squeal and all.

"Brilliant." The driver left an unfinished Slurpee on the pavement. Herbert tries to kick it but needs a second chance. It regrettably soaks his shoe.

Chapter Ten

Loss Leaders

A toilet flushes. Herbert enters his hotel room from the bathroom, wearing his silk bathrobe and pajamas. He assesses his room for safety. The blinds are closed. The door is locked and blocked by a chair. He finds the small but heavy room safe and positions it to further block his door. He then leans on his bed and catches his breath from that exertion.

Next, he opens his fanny pack and checks the contents. It's all as it should be. He is not quite sure what more to prepare. His mind revisits threats from the past.

He recalls the Russian female spy saying, "You are such a man! And I am an idiot female!"

He wonders about the South American businessman who agreed, "It is important to die *con-fortably*."

But my problems are from the living, he counters. He lies down.

Mrs. Pearbottom creeps into his mind. "That's ridiculous," she had said. "Who would still want to kill you?"

He also recalls his funeral, and the minister inviting mourners to pay their final disrespects. Even fact-checkers had tested his dummy self but he had withstood them all.

Little by little he finally drifts off to sleep.

***

Elsewhere in the world, several heavy older men in white towels sit in a steam lodge, mid-conversation. Some are fully Inuit, others only partially, and some not at all.

Waller Flinkenstein sits in the middle of a profound observation. "It sounds pretty brazen to me. I wouldn't entertain profit sharing."

A person of paleness enters, only his silhouette visible in the steam. Everyone watches in silence as P makes it over to them. He blows off some steam, and melts the sudden ice with, "Uh-oh, a troublemaker in our mist!"

Flinkenstein is welcoming. "Hello, Percival!"

"Greetings, Flick. Tony. Felix." He sits and relaxes.

Tony Bandito brings him in on their topic. "Percy, listen to this. Flick's *associates* object to being called *goons*. Apparently, the new acceptable term is, *muscle workers*. Can you believe it? *Muscle workers*."

P shows resignation. "I can't keep up. Next we'll hear about *pole workers* and it won't be during election season."

"Unless someone's caught tampering with one," adds Flick.

Tony observes, "If I was coming up today, I think I'd think twice before choosing the underworld. Or the legit side! Don't get me wrong, each still has a lot to offer. But the risk-to-rewards ratio is becoming a bit… *meh*."

"Unelected office seems to be the way to go," opines Flick. "At least for my grandkids."

"Depends how little they want to accomplish," says P.

Others concur with that wisdom.

P continues, "Say, not to change the subject, or to sound callous about the no-longer-alive. Is that how they say it?"

"Who cares?" asks Flick.

"Good point. Are any of you aware of a possible mark put on a man who may or may not go by the name of Herbert Bigglesby?"

The men try to hold back laughter and guffaws, but like in church, this makes it louder. Someone even passes gas. "Sorry!"

"More like *Bigglesbeen*!" declares Flinkenstein, which provokes additional suppressed laughter through the nose.

"*Double-Oh-Syphilis!*" adds Tony. "I'm grateful my daughter got out of that business but fast."

P blows more steam. "Because they might have *missed*. Not that anybody here would miss him."

Flick nods his head. "Percival, I think I speak for the lot of us when I say that that ship has long since sunk. No disrespect, but he was a pompous, egotistical, delusional prick, and nobody in their right mind would spend another second trying to find, let alone eliminate, his senile self. Plus, he's dead anyway, of course."

"Of course," acknowledges P.

Tony says, "Keep in mind, Percival, that for anyone to want to hurt him, he'd have to pose some kind of threat *outside* of your organization. I mean, by the end he was only doing harm inside it. Though I'm pretty sure he was the last to know."

Flick doesn't want P to feel too badly and says, "I did like his funeral, though. It was very tasteful."

"Yes, good food," concurs a large Alaskan native, Felix Culpa. "Very classy."

"Lotta other places cutting costs," says Tony. "But it should not be at a man's funeral, real or otherwise. He served his people to the best of his ability and you did him proud."

Flinkenstein finishes checking something on his phone and shares it with his neighbor in shock. "P, not to pry, but can't your people afford something better than a two-star for such an all-star? I mean, not that he's alive and on the run or anything, but please."

The chorus agrees. "Gotta treat your people with dignity."

"Save your money with the newer guys," advises Tony. "Fly them economy, Motel Fresh; they don't expect more. But not with your legends."

"Good point," comes from all around. "Respect."

"Gentlemen of the Underworld," begins P, "I can neither confirm nor deny his existence, or location, or standard of living, should he have need of one. But as to your comments, we are lucky to still get mileage reimbursed."

"That is no way to treat people. It's inhuman."

P does not want to lose any more threads in his being here today. "Nevertheless, can you think of anyone who might still be bitter, bothered, or butthurt enough to order a hit on him?"

"No one in their right mind," answers Tony.

"Ah, then it could be Vilefinger," concludes P.

"Oh, please!" declares Flinkenstein. "How bad is your intelligence? Henric couldn't find the open end of a cannon if he put his whole head into it, let alone his vile member."

"Thank you for being so frank, Flick." P swirls steam around with his hand. "We will all be mist one day."

Tony confesses, "I'm sorry it's come down to this, Percival. But sadly, no one cares about your guy anymore. And we do way more harm with videos and misinformation. I don't need nuclear devices or fentanyl."

"But those are still good if you're ever short," offers Felix.

"True that," says Flick.

"Felix, how about Arthur Riviera? Is he still sore?" asks P.

"Rat bastard!" coughs Felix. "Drove us all out while he got his. Though I got his too. And I don't mean his diseases."

***

For the benefit of the Reader, let us momentarily be a snowflake on a windowsill in Alaska, observing the aforementioned mogul.

Arthur Riviera is a skinny Filipino man in his 80s, based in Anchorage. He sits wrapped in a fuzzy brown bathrobe with a hood pulled tight around his face. He wears huge sunglasses and smokes a long pipe. He bobs his head to Run DMC's *Peter Piper* (1986) or other early '80s rap music.

Sitting around an indoor fire, he is surrounded by several native 400-pound women, fully covered by seal fur except for their eyes. All are gently bopping to the music.

A heavy, armed man sits by the door checking his coat for fleas. He finds one and tries to kill it but it's not easy. It keeps resurrecting.

A snowy breeze whistles through the room, sending shivers down some spines.

"Can't we get insulation?" asks a young hot woman.

Riviera lashes out with surprising passion. "This is a story of betrayal! I will not have another Miss Four-Chin!"

Nearly everyone reacts in fear and trepidation. That old wound is best avoided. But the young one is without daunt.

"Or maybe you can just hire a good mason."

"Masons are no longer free!" complains Riviera.

The older women watch to see if the naive young dummy will open her mouth again. *She still thinks she has options in life.*

She emptily says, "I'm just saying!"

"Your betrayal will not have some Felix Culpa to blame. No, you will stray from intentional ignorance, ambition, and ingratitude."

The young woman couches her words in epic wisdom. "Not so, my King. Yet just as the wind runs free, so too my attention spans."

Riviera does not like the sound of that, whatever it means. Violence crosses his mind, like the slaying of so many artic foxes for their fur. Or perhaps he can feed her to a pack of woolly dogs. But he knows he didn't get this far by being some hothead. Plus, his other women are wrinkly in the light. Soon 80 straight days of merciless daylight will be upon them. He reproves her gently instead.

"Bridled is the mouth of whosoever desires a long life. As your elders have so achieved."

The young one looks at all the stern faces. "Ew, please! I got places to go! A career and body to unfold."

Riviera takes a drag from his pipe. "I can see your life heading South, my Penguin. Will you perchance remember your master? The generous Lord who found you, and fed you, and fed you again? Who made of you what you are?"

The young one knows not to push her luck any further today. "Of course, my handsome Moose." She reminds herself of what her mother said a few weeks ago. *Juneau dreams can't be rushed, Child. And even if Artie did lose everything from Calgary to Fairbanks in just a few short years, it's worth biting your time.*

Riviera leans forward, hoping for a dramatic effect. "There is a reason I am respected as master of these lands, between here and Shishmaref! Not one ounce of vodka or penicillin arrives that does not first pass through one of my troubadour gladiators, as I like to call them. I came up with that. Troubadour gladiators."

He gestures to the henchman with the fleas, who accommodates his boss by playing a ditty on his lute. *"Master of these lands! / Master of these lands! / We can't get things even second-hand / without askin' Riviera! / We're all askin' Riviera! / Alaskan Riviera."*

His boss approves. "Luters always bring home the goods."

The singer recalls his fondling memories. "You should have seen our Lutist colony! Before Packer and them went to jail."

***

Now that these substantial characters have been introduced, let us return to P's steamy Q's in the sauna.

"So, you don't think Riviera still harbors any kind of grudge against him for turning Ms. Four-Chin away?"

"Oh, please!" Felix objects to that characterization of events. "I was the one who wooed her away from Artie, not him. I cramped his style with my little Four-Chin Cookie." He becomes increasingly nostalgic as if sharing his experience of hope at a meeting. "She has improved so many things in my life, pound for pound. So, if Riviera has a beef with anyone from the old days it's with me. Your guy is truly irrelevant, as it pertains."

"Very well, then!" concludes P. "I am quite satisfied. I'm happy to know none of you are behind this alleged assault that probably never even happened, officially."

"Of course," answers Flick.

Felix wasn't done boasting. Plus, he has a business to promote. "By the way, my babe moved on from modeling to remodeling. Her company does kitchens and bathrooms." He produces her business cards (from who knows where) and hands them out. "She got the itch during a photo shoot for plus-sized baths." (Let the Reader imagine that photo shoot in their own time.) "Turns out she's good at it and they put a lot of other folks *outta da bidness*. P, maybe you can put in a word with your director when she's ready to fix up her nursing home."

"Senior Living Community," the others correct.

P accepts the card. "Of course, Felix, I'm happy to obligate her." He stands and makes a final request. "Regarding Bigglesby, do remain solid chaps and let me know if you hear anything?"

Flinkenstein is all manners. "Of course! And we didn't mean to offend. It's just so rich! Like that anyone under 90 would care a whit about The Great Bigsby. Still, I'll make some calls for you."

"You're a doll, Flick. Thank you so much."

"More like a pin cushion," Flick admits.

P leaves but then his towel comes flying back into the room. Two of them instinctively catch it.

"Please don't let them charge me for that. I can't expense it!"

Realizing what it is, they drop it immediately. "Ew!"

CHAPTER ELEVEN

A Senior's Moment

In his hotel room the next morning, Herbert is sound asleep.

Downstairs, hotel staff finish setting up a breakfast buffet in a large dining room. Elderly people trickle in; they are lively and enthused, wearing colorful sporty outfits.

In Herbert's room, his phone suddenly vibrates. He wakes with a start and scans for danger. Everything is just as he left it, with a chair still jammed under the door handle.

He reads the text from P. *"Sorry, chap, the entire underworld denies involvement. They wish you well in your retirement. Low life!"*

As Herbert frowns, another text clarifies, *"Sorry, lie low!"*

Herbert texts back, *"Not good enough!"* and, *"Forget it@!"* He did not mean the @ sign. He finishes with, *"I don't trust you!!!"* and he adds poop emojis and a unicorn. He puts the phone down and gets up to use the facility.

Following his internal business, Herbert descends to the hotel dining room in his bathrobe and slippers. He is initially taken aback by the presence of many seniors, dressed and ready to go. They are all chatty as they load up on trays of unhealthy food.

A quick scan of the room reveals posters for the second coming of the *Too Soon to Die Convention*. Signs point to Convention Shuttles, though a prankster has made one say *Convention Shuffles.*

With just coffee and a muffin, Herbert looks for a place to sit; it's crowded. His gaze lands on a young woman's welcoming smile.

"You can sit here if you like," she offers. She has a fresh, innocent look and her table has seats for three more. She barely looks 18 but wears a business suit.

"Thank you." Herbert makes his way over, charmed.

"Are you here for the convention?" she asks.

He shares a secret. "I'm more partial to the unconventional."

"That's clever! Me too."

She pulls out the chair next to her. Herbert is thrilled and hurries to occupy it.

"Oh, sorry, this is for my Nana. Nana, look what I found you!"

Her grandmother arrives with her tray. She is unfair-looking and in her 90s. Herbert is disheartened but the older woman is ahead of him in disregard.

"I've told you already, I don't need your meddlin', Maudlin."

Herbert is offended. "Madam, I am not interested either, but I would hardly call the possibility *maudlin*."

"No, I'm Maudlin," explains the younger one. "Just Maude, really. And this is Allison."

Herbert puts down his tray and extends his hand. "Ah, bond… age!" He points at each. "Just bondage. A familial tie." He sits down opposite Maude. "Are you her caregiver?"

"Hardly." Allison bites into a sausage and studies a brochure.

Maude keeps it light. "We're just two gals out for some fun."

"I see. Let me start over." He extends his hand again. "Bigglesby, Herbert Bigglesby. A pleasure."

Maude shakes his hand. Allison only waves. "I expect they'll pray upon us again. Lay hands?"

Herbert winces in disbelief. *And they call me paranoid?*

Maude replies, "I'm so ready for it."

Herbert realizes they are serious. "Do they have security?"

"Very funny," says Maude. "Nana, I can't wait!"

Allison looks at Herbert. "You're going to miss the shuttle."

"Oh, I'm not here for that," he answers.

"Why not? You should come!" pleads Maude. She hands him the flier. "Go get changed!" she urges.

"But I like the way I am," he quips. The flier has images of clouds and a dove and he reads it aloud. *"Retire in Style with Eternal Dividends. Journey with Us for All You're Worth."* Herbert cannot contain his distaste. *"Grow exponentially in your grasp of the truth of things."* He looks up. "What do they charge for this malarkey?"

"Oh, please don't be crass," chides Allison.

"Next, they'll say, *True riches are there for the taking."*

"But they are!" says Maude. "We should hold nothing back. What other investment yields thirty, sixty, a hundred-fold?"

Herbert is horrified. "A carwash? Laundromat? Food truck? Sweetheart, you can't trust these people. They reach into your purse while smiling and stabbing you in the pelvis."

Allison looks Herbert over like a medic. "I don't see the blood."

Herbert checks his torso, arms, and legs. "Where?"

"My goodness," continues Allison. "You know, there are treatments for PTSD. My brother was a recluse for 40 years after Vietnam. Then he had three months of cognitive processing therapy and *voila!* Now he takes his grandchildren to Magic Fountain."

"Good for him, but I have no fear of crowds, I assure you. They even make me feel safer."

"Then join us!" encourages Maude. "It'll be crowded for sure, and with enough healing for anyone open to it."

"I'm a bit hard of healing" confesses Herbert. "And I couldn't bear to watch nice ladies like you being taken in by these charlatans."

Allison checks her watch. "Well, we unenlightened tools better get to our shuttle. It was… *interesting* to meet you."

The women stand and Herbert gets up too. "I hope you'll be careful. With everything you've saved up. Don't let them take it."

Maude asks again. "If it's about cost, please, be our guest, Mr. Bigglesby. I can't explain it now, but you'll understand why later."

Herbert can barely resist her pretty face. "I wish I could. I have some very important work to do today. Life and death, really."

"That's what I'm talking about, too!" counters Maude. She leans in conspiratorially. "Our meeting here today is no coincidence. We can't just lie low while the enemy takes charge."

A long shrill bell DINGS, whether anyone else hears it or not. Suddenly, Herbert is in a boxing ring, in his tuxedo, as the referee. He ducks to avoid a wild swing by a faceless boxer.

Maude cheers from the side, "Come on, Herbert! Take charge!"

Herbert turns to her and gets socked in the face, which contorts in slow motion.

Back in the cafeteria he asks, "Who sent you?"

"Someone who wants you alive," answers Maude.

"Oh, he does, does he?"

"Evil must not be allowed to triumph."

Allison pulls Maude. "We need to go, Dear."

Herbert follows. "Did he give you a password?"

Allison turns. "The shuttle leaves in four minutes."

"No, that wouldn't be it."

"Hurry," says Maude. "Higher P's got your back."

"There's no way I have enough time to change."

"Never say never. Live each day like it's your last!"

A woman after my own heart, thinks Herbert. "I'll be quick. But only in this matter, not later on."

Maude is disturbed. Herbert shuffles to the elevator.

A song similar to Cake's *Comfort Eagle* (2001) starts up. *"We are writing / a prescription / We are gilding the lily / We are trading on ignorance / And soothing all our coughers."*

While it might require a stretch, or just for the buses to be running late, Herbert grooms himself quickly. He shaves off his combover, then showers and dresses. He soon looks dashing and debonair in his tuxedo. As a final touch he dons sunglasses.

In front of the hotel, crowded shuttle buses have been departing. One remains unloaded, with an ambulance beside it and a line of seniors waiting. Herbert arrives and joins Maude and Allison.

"Yay, you made it!" cheers Maude.

"Of course!" Herbert tries for a hug. Maude keeps it minimal and directs Herbert's hands away from her lower back.

Paramedics carry the ailing person to the ambulance and the boarding begins.

"Well, that was certainly convenient," says Herbert. He leans over, "And hopefully not too obvious."

Maude is enthused with his newly budding faith. "Only to those who have eyes to see," she replies.

CHAPTER TWELVE

Bustling Over

The convention center is buzzing with activity as the buses arrive and unload. Thousands of seniors mill about.

Inside, Herbert, Maude, and Allison check in at one of many registration tables and receive lanyards with badges. Herbert gazes at the numerous booths promoting surgeries, dental products, walking shoes, foot creams, pharmaceuticals, and more. It's very loud.

Herbert pops out his hearing aids and all noise stops for him briefly, then resumes quietly and warbled, as if underwater. "That's better!" he yells.

The women smile politely.

A certain booth catches his eye and too loudly he suggests, "I think we should divide and conquer for a while! Do some recon!"

Others look over but say nothing. They also have hearing aids. Herbert gestures for Maude not to follow him as he departs.

"Ok," she agrees. "But be back for the first talk. It's in 10 minutes!" She gestures *ten* with her hands.

Herbert nods but may or may not have understood. He stops at a booth for arch supports and turns to make sure Maude isn't following him. Then he bee-lines to his real target: a booth marked, *Victoria's Secretions*. An older male attendant hands him a pair of wide-bottomed stringy lingerie to examine. Herbert feels the silky fabric and the absorbent padding, impressed.

From across the room, Olivia spies on him disapprovingly. She wears her bowler hat and pretends to evaluate silky blouses at a booth promoting *Precious Fabrics.* The table displays investment literature, seeming more like a bank than for clothing. She hides behind a prospectus when Herbert peers through lingerie scanning for threats.

Herbert is loud in addressing the attendant. "My good man, have you seen anyone suspicious in here?"

"Only my wife," answers the salesman without missing a beat. "She says they're very comfortable when she isn't too busy checking my phone or hiding GPS trackers in my stuff."

Herbert does not understand most of what he said. Regarding the lingerie he says, "It feels nice. I like 'em dry. Stirred and shaken, butt not wet." He gives the item back saying, "Maybe I'll get a pair when I'm old."

The attendant holds back an obvious question as Herbert leaves.

At the Precious Fabrics booth, a short male attendant sees Olivia, apparently distracted from the merchandise.

"You do not like *zhis*?" he asks. He is Danny, mid-50s, Austrian accent. He has a low stature and lower self-esteem, plus a severe limp. He resembles Claude Rains from Hitchcock's, *Notorious* (1946). He uses a cane and chews on Milk Duds.

Olivia suddenly realizes she was asked a question. "What? Oh, uh…" She smells the fabric and winces. "Too much chemical smell."

Danny looks alarmed and whiffs it himself. "*Das ist* not normal."

He makes angry eye contact with his big brawny worker, Gunther, who arranges cashmeres. He wears burlap overalls to contrast the finely woven threads on display.

Danny continues, "I mean, we certainly do not use *zeh* toxic radioactive chemicals and *zhen* double down on *zeh* final solu– pardon, *pharmaceutical* solutions."

In the awkward silence, they can't help glancing at the rows of booths hawking relief in plastic bottles.

Danny has a thought. "Oh, I know what! Silly Danny Rysin! *Zhis* is because I packed *zhem* so close to *zeh* engine of my car. In *zeh* rear. Perhaps I should not drive *zeh* itsy bitsy Spyder." He looks at her, hoping she is impressed. "*Zeh* Porsche Spyder." He pops another Milk Dud into his mouth and offers her some.

Olivia is dismissive. "No thanks, and I don't like that ride. For a rear engine I like a classic Beetle."

Danny is delighted. "Ah, *zhose* were amazing. For *zeh* ordinary folks kind-of-*vagon*. Anyway, what is important today is not purchasing any one fabric. You are here in time for a major investment opportunity." He beckons her to lean in.

"Just say it from there," she counters.

"Fine... fabrics."

"Fine fabrics?"

"No!!! *Precious* fabrics. Gold is dead! Dead! Caput! And *zeh* other precious metals: Dead! But, *voila*!"

He gestures at the literature on his table. Brochures proclaim, "Gold is Dead. Dead! Dead! Forget precious metals. Invest in precious fabrics."

Olivia smiles, "Seriously? You don't think gold will bounce back in another quarter or two?" She's quite certain he must be kidding.

"*Nein!* Not in our lifetime. Certainly not in your Papa's." Danny can't help looking around. "Might he be here with you, and have trillions, per chance?"

Olivia becomes incensed. "Why? Isn't my fortune good enough? Why does it always have to be some rich daddy's money?"

"*Nein!* I apologize! *Zeh* fathers are irrelevant! Deadbeaters. I never even met mine. We get by without *zhem*!"

She looks at him, wondering. "Well, I personally miss having mine. He was murdered. Anyway, it was not here but there."

Danny straightens fabric. "Mine was neither here nor *zhere*. He couldn't bother with us. Can you imagine?"

Olivia is dismissive and shifts back to investment talk. "Well, you watch, the mines will produce. Then, *kah-ching*."

She moves on and Danny is left dumbfounded and possibly in love. Gunther discreetly checks for a foul odor in other samples but cannot detect anything.

"I smelled it too, from a mile away!" says Rosie.

They turn to see her reading one of their information sheets. She wears a grey business suit and sunglasses.

"We will work on *zhat*." He offers a silk scarf. "But feel *zhis*, Sir."

Rosie frowns, lowers her glasses. "I am not a Sir. And I'm just looking." She turns and peruses other goods.

"My mistake, Madame!" apologizes Danny, still holding out hope and a scarf. "I am very sorry! But please, feel *zhis* fabric of *zeh* future."

Rosie nods. "I'm afraid I don't feel too good. But you do need to do something about that odor." She can't help a look of disgust.

Danny worries she might vomit. "Was it something you ate?"

He discreetly gestures for Gunther to bring something, *quickly!* His assistant misunderstands and offers random objects. "No, *Dummkopf!* A receptacle!" Danny mimics hacking into a bucket.

Gunther has no imagination. Danny tries a rhyme.

"Sounds like… *tuck it!*" and he tucks in his shirt.

Gunther is embarrassed; he won't say it out loud.

Rosie intervenes, "I'm not sick. And I do not need a *bucket*."

"Ah!" exclaims Gunther, embarrassed. "Next time."

Danny is impressed by Rosie.

She lowers her glasses. "The thing is, I look good, and I smell good." The men are shocked by her *chutzpah* and she continues, "But to me, these two are the same." She caresses a silk shirt in one hand and rubs the course burlap tablecloth with the other. "I just don't feel a difference."

Danny is skeptical while Gunther has the wisdom to ask, "Did somebody hurt your feeling?"

"Many times," she replies, appreciating the question.

Gunther is empathic but cannot think of anything else to say. He has used up his words for the day.

Danny offers Rosie his Milk Duds. She is enthusiastic.

"Ah, yes! I taste good too." She accepts a handful and pops them into her mouth.

"Are you pulling my leg?" asks Danny.

Rosie looks at his lower half as if buying a horse. "No. They would snap right off. And his are too strong," she says about Gunther. The latter is flattered. "But why are we talking about legs? Are these returns accurate?" She waves a prospectus.

Danny doesn't know whether to be offended or close a deal. "Of course, *zhey* are accurate, what do you *zhink* we are doing here, trying to cheat *zeh* world? And for what, to fund *zeh* Fourth *Reich*?"

Gunther is shocked by Danny's *bravado* and feels exposed. He casually picks up a pinwheel toy called Swapstic8, which looks like two swastikas laid over each other at an angle to make eight crooked arms. They have a jar of them on the table, free in exchange for a mere email address. Promotional lines on the jar read, *Fourth time is a charm!* and, *This time we mean business!*

Gunther blows through his Swapstic8 absent-mindedly, making it twirl. Rosie is immediately turned off and he reconsiders his politics. He returns it to the jar and sets out more fabrics. At some point Rosie takes another look at him and he blushes, but she would deny she ever looked.

Across the room, Herbert stands between two competing morgue booths. One banner says, *Flat Line U.L.C.* The logo has a single EKG beat followed by a long flat line. A subheading reads, *Rated Best Morgue in Town!* The *morgue-ist* corners him with a hearty, "Hello, young man!"

Herbert pretends to adjust his hearing aids but they are not even in his ears. He happily hears things warbled. The man continues, "Sir, when you prepay your morgue expenses, it takes a real load off your loved ones."

Herbert looks at his literature while a female competitor vies for his attention. "He's only out to profit from your losses, Hon! You don't want to do business with him." The woman is about the same age as the man. Her signage says, *There's Morgue to Death.*

"Oh, sure!" scoffs the man. "She's a regular charity over there."

"How long were you married?" asks Herbert, stopping them both in their tracks.

"Two decades," answers the man.

"Twenty-two years, four months, and seventeen days," specifies the woman. She then makes her pitch. "With my prepaid plan you get Emergency Room services too if needed, so you're covered either way. And unlike *Flat Line* over there, we don't discriminate based on our own ideas about *who* or *what* you call a Loved One. You can even include a significant vehicle in your grave if you so choose."

"I'm not buying today, but I'll think about it!" replies Herbert. He turns to go. "Probably not even that." That last part came out louder than he knows.

At a dental booth, Olivia sees Herbert and blocks her face with a brochure. Rosie takes a genuine interest in the same booth.

The morgue man blocks Herbert's path. "Sir, we have very reasonable plans. No money down and zero percent interest!"

"Good! That's where I'm at with it too!" replies Herbert.

Both *morgue-ists* hold up fake smiles until Herbert is out of earshot. The ex-husband still thinks he can offer advice.

"Do you not see what you did there?!"

Danny perks up across the room. *Nazi?*

The morgue man continues. "Don't come in with your lower prices when you don't even know if he's buying."

The woman turns away. "You're dead to me, Harold." She greets oldcomers browsing her wares.

***

By the convention hall entrance, Mrs. Pearbottom, Jake, Senior Rita, and others from Sunset View arrive. Claire and Olga push wheelchairs, dressed in their usual burgundy scrubs.

Jake cannot contain his enthusiasm. "This is amazing! I can't believe you planned this outing and didn't say a word of it till this morning!"

Sure, that's what I did, thinks Mrs. Pearbottom as she scans the room. *Planned it for months.* Aloud she says, "I figured it's nice to have a few non-emergency surprises once in a while."

Senior Rita looks distressed. "I don't see any slot machines. You said there'd be slot machines. Oh!" She sees them and hurries off.

The seniors spread out to various booths. Mrs. Pearbottom calls out, "Please remember, the bus leaves at three thirty, on the dot!"

Elsewhere in the room, Herbert stands alone. Olivia moves in and readies her hat. Before she can reach him, he turns and addresses a man promoting natural laxatives.

"My good man, are you able to fill this?" He digs out his prescription from Dr. Bentiron.

The sales representative won't take it. "I'm afraid not, but our natural solvents, cereals, and solutions may be a more organic way to go."

"Are you praising bran again?" Herbert leans in to see the price list on the counter. "Good nursing home that intestinal product's expensive!"

"Not if you think about it in bulk."

Herbert makes a face we might all make in that situation. "And why would I want to do that?"

Before the man can answer, Herbert is rescued by a sexy young woman in a cute sailor outfit. She greets him with, "Oh my, don't you look dapper! Are you ready to sail away?"

Herbert is delighted. "Perfect timing, young lady! I didn't want to listen to that guy anymore!"

She laughs at Herbert's frankness and volume. "My pleasure!" She pulls him away, arm in arm, to an area with tables. She is Rebecca Holmeslyce, in her early 20s. Olivia's eyes spin headwear at her.

Herbert re-applies his hearing aids. "Hold on, I don't want to miss a thing you say."

She is flattered. He looks her up and down and says, "Though I didn't think they allowed smoking in here."

"Who's smoking? Oh!" She smiles and puts a flier in his hand. "Um, here!" She speaks like a fifth grader chosen to read announcements over the intercom. "You've worked hard in life," she continues. "Join us for a free legacy giveaway cruise and make free healthcare a reality for all."

To Herbert, her words echo in slow motion and he hears a piercing metal DING.

He finds himself refereeing the boxing match again. A long red towel is spread across the floor this time, like a carpet. Rebecca crouches ringside, ready to pull it out from under Herbert's feet, *if only he'll just step on it.* He does at times step on it, but also moves off too quickly for her to yank it. Eventually he turns and winks at her, which annoys her that he was doing it on purpose.

When Herbert turns to Rebecca again, she is now wearing the red towel and nothing else. He does a double-take. Each struggles to hold it together, respectively. Her movements beckon with a lonely, pouty expression. He tries to focus on the fight but can't help looking back and calling out, "What a knockout!"

This coincides with a massive punch behind Herbert's back and one of the fighters goes down. The crowd goes wild, which makes Herbert turn to see what happened. He kneels by the vanquished one and counts to ten. He then lifts the winner's arm in victory.

When he spots Rebecca again, she is back in her sailor uniform. "Please say you'll come!"

Herbert snaps out of his fantasy and takes in the convention hall. "Sorry, did you say, free cruise? And free healthcare for all?"

"I sure did!" Rebecca answers, her smile beaming.

"I think my new hips have come in!" Herbert can't believe his luck. He didn't care about senior scams before, but this woman might be offering the kind of chance he needs to get away and enjoy a return to his good life again.

"That's almost what we always say!" she answers. "*Ad mausoleum,* really. About our *ship* coming in. Please say you'll come. I really need this job!" She makes a cute facial expression.

Olivia watches from nearby, still disgusted.

Herbert pretends to resist Rebecca's charms. "I don't know. Am I just some piece of prime angus beef and muscle to you, so you can reach your numbers?"

"Not at all!" defends Rebecca.

"More like ground chuck," says a male voice. It's Jake Kimble.

Herbert is caught off guard. "Jake! What are you doing here?" Herbert scans the room, recalling his life was in danger the last time he was around Sunset people. Yet he also tries to look relaxed. "Is Mrs. Pearbottom here?"

"Very funny!" answers Jake. "He must want you to think we're just randomly bumping into each other, as if he's not part of the kind of senior community your great-grandparents could be living in."

Herbert is clearly annoyed but Rebecca makes him smile. "No they couldn't; they're dead." She then produces more fliers. "Is the whole community here? I bet you all need a free getaway cruise!"

Jake accepts one. "Please, do say more!"

Herbert pulls Rebecca aside for a moment. "Darling, people at the nursing home are not what you're looking for. They're struggling, financially *and* mentally."

Jake winks at Rebecca, encouraging her to humor the old man.

She humors both. "We have something for every situation!"

Herbert needs to exclude himself from the peasant company. "Truth be told, I was only there to get an inside look at the profit potential. Undercover, so to speak."

Rebecca likes the sound of that but Jake treats it as Herbert's usual nonsense. Then he remembers Herbert was MIA. "Hey, where did you disappear to last night?" To Rebecca he explains, "We got vandalized yesterday!"

"That's terrible!" She mimics the concern of a manager. "Is everyone ok, question mark? I mean."

"Yes, no one was harmed," Jake explains. "And they didn't even really take anything. Herbert, what do you think they were there after?"

"It's hard to say." In his mind he adds, I only know what I'm here after, you dimwit! Low wattage. Check engine light. Bank with insufficient funds!

Jake continues. "Actually, one person is still—Downright—missing. For longer than usual."

"He's always wandering off," dismisses Herbert.

"Well, I hope you find him!" declares Rebecca. "The more the merrier on our cruise."

Herbert hints, "Thanks for stopping by, Jake. I do hope you enjoy the conference."

"Oh right! You need to woo. Woo-hoo. Be careful, Miss. He's secretly a secret agent."

A flicker of concern passes over Rebecca's face but she smiles as if it was obviously a joke.

Somewhere, a loud CRACK occurs, as if a heavy tree branch snapped and fell. In Herbert's mind he has happily broken Jake's neck and stands over his body. Yet even in his imagination this pulls something in his back and he stretches in pain. "Mmmh!"

Jake continues, "Oops, I probably wasn't supposed to say that. Though he's probably told you already. Like fifty times. Just let him down gently, Miss. Brittle ego like his clavicle."

"Oh, don't be silly!" answers Rebecca. "To me you are both strong powerful men, still in your prime… lending ability, to those in need! I don't even see things like old age, or veins, or lack of skin color. I just see men bravely facing life and looking for ways to put your years of hard work into helping others like me to achieve the goods of this world."

"Brilliantly said," opines Herbert confident he got most of it. He tries to stand tall and sexy. "I believe I have just the kinds of pounds you're looking for."

His gut spills over his belt and he realizes that came out wrong. "Or dollars! And Euros. Whatever currency, really." He sucks it in.

"Maybe that was it!" surmises Jake. "They came to kidnap you!" He winks at Rebecca. "For all his trillions."

"It wouldn't be the first time," answers Herbert. "Which is why I did not wait around to be a sitting duck, no quack you."

Rebecca smiles, unsure what to say next and afraid to offend.

Herbert worries she might be discouraged from pursuing him as a patsy so he attempts a fix. "Not that there aren't some great cat and mouse relationships in history, Miss…?"

"Holmeslyce. Rebecca Holmeslyce."

"And I don't mean Tom and Jerry," finishes Herbert.

Jake takes and kisses her hand. "What a beautiful name for a beautiful woman. But I'd better not crowd you two. I'll let Mrs. Pearbottom know I saw you, Herbert."

"I'm sure you will," he answers. "Though maybe let her enjoy her day for five minutes before she has to see you?"

Jake nods and departs. Herbert notices Maude coming, looking for someone. He turns his back and continues with Rebecca.

"Luckily, Ms. Holmeslyce, we don't all go senile and demented and impotent like that Jake. Now, how do I say this, my perfectly mature and age-of-consent Sales Lady? Are you looking for billions or mere millions?"

She reacts with mock shock. "Slow down there, Mr…"

"Bigglesby, Herbert Bigglesby. Though the ladies just call me Mr. Big."

"Ok, Mr. Big, but–"

"No, no! Not that part." He flexes his glutes as best he can.

Rebecca looks concerned. "I think you may have me a little wrong, Mr. Big. I don't really see you as the gazillionaire you probably are. Nor myself as someone willing to do just about anything to win your favors."

"Of course not!" answers Herbert. "Though I wouldn't judge you if you did. Even if you were the kind who takes advantage of people like me, and by whatever means necessary. Which you obviously wouldn't, but I would have no objection. Not one scruple or anything to get in the way."

"I appreciate that! Because I'm not just about numbers and business. Even though I might be really good at it. I like to think of myself more as an enlightened wanderer. I pursue deep, meaningful relationships, for however long they last, since we never really know what might take our attention next."

"You are wise! Not a child by any means. In your mid-twenties, I suppose?" He can't quite tell her legal age.

"Something like that," she answers. "You see, for me, solving world problems like universal access to healthcare is important. But it's also really just a bonus in my day."

"Mine too!" shares Herbert. "And I'm sorry if I offended you by speaking of money and charm as things I can just throw around to manipulate people like you, the financially dependent."

"Has your will been finalized?"

"It's flexible, like me."

She adjusts his collar. "You're so responsive to opportunity. I think we're on the same page about what really matters in life."

"And death, probably!" says Herbert, wishing he could adjust her clothing as well. *Ok, maybe a little.*

She bats his hand away when he tries. Olivia watches, disgusted by the flirtation.

Rebecca continues, "I have to say, I am very intrigued with you as a person, Mr. Bigglesby. Is it ok if we leave the tedious financial talk to my bosses?"

"As you wish, Ms. Holmeslyce. Perhaps we can meet for a glass of wine later and discuss this cruise of yours?"

"So. Much. Fun." She taps him with every word.

"And if you really do need a second or third income, I could start you on some moonlit work. After hours, perhaps?"

"Oh, that is very generous of you. It makes me feel safe and practically at home with you."

"That's a great place to be!" answers Herbert. "Perhaps I can tuck you in tonight. Or after lunch?"

Rebecca dodges with, "Let's get you onto that cruise first! Then what happens on offshore waters stays on offshore waters."

DING! Herbert finds himself in the boxing ring again. The fighters hear the bell and separate, but Herbert-as-referee wishes they wouldn't. "No, don't go!"

"I'm sorry but I must," answers Rebecca, back in the conference exhibit area. She touches Herbert's arm one final time and walks away with her sexy gait, leaving him wanting more.

"You're leaving me wanting more!" He cries out, clutching a tablecloth unconsciously like John Ritter.

She acknowledges him with a wink before blending into the crowd, if that is even possible for Rebecca. She fights the urge to vomit and then resumes her toothy sales persona.

Herbert snaps out of the warm glow and scans for signs of danger. Olivia, Rosie, and the Twins hide behind people, places, and things but he fails to see them. His gaze lands on Senior Rita at a slot machine. She pushes a button and the wheels spin. When they stop, images line up of colored pills, adult diapers, a walker, and BeSure.

For her male neighbor, a siren goes off with bright red lights to announce his win. Pills shoot out and he uses his hat to catch as many as he can. Senior Rita tries to be happy for him but clearly has thoughts of *life just not being fair.*

Olivia makes her way toward Herbert from behind. However, he sees Mrs. Pearbottom approaching and ducks out of view. Olivia also sees her and stops short, hiding behind a column.

Mrs. Pearbottom arrives and scans the area, wondering where Herbert just went.

Two young female Irish musicians rush by her. One carries a guitar case and says, "Sorry to be cutting it this close. Same plan we talked about?"

"Yes," answers the other. "*Balm in Gilead.* What kept you?"

Underneath a covered table, Herbert's eyes go wide with alarm. *Where is Gilead?* he wonders. He parts the tablecloth and peers out, delighted to find a pair of sexy female legs. Between them he sees the two musicians reach and enter the Main Hall.

A sign at that entrance reads, *Reap Eternal Dividends* with Dr. Uvenerate Singleton! Another says, *Don't Miss Our Fish Fry, 7:30 pm*!

As the female legs walk away, Herbert is impressed to learn they belong to Mrs. Pearbottom. He climbs out from underneath the table, just as Olivia crawls under it from behind.

Maude startles Herbert. "There you are! Our talk is in three minutes."

"Listen, there's something big going on. A bomb."

"What?" Maude is skeptical. "Here?"

"I'm not sure. I overheard two women planning it, probably lesbians. They said it would happen in Gilead, wherever that is, but it could be code for here for all we know."

Maude smiles. "Oh no, you're not leaving, Buster! Let's go."

"How can you be so calm? We need to evacuate!"

"Mr. Bigglesby, this is what we're here for."

Herbert is impressed and calls it out. "I'm... impressed! How are you so steady?"

"I'm not! I'm so pumped I'm shaking! I've been waiting for this for months and it's finally showtime!"

"I had despaired of new recruits but your attitude is quite inspiring. Ok, let me get to P first."

"The bathrooms are just over there but you have to hurry."

Across the way, Danny from Precious Fabrics limps into the men's room with his cane.

"Good idea," opines Herbert. "You wait here."

Herbert shuffles across. She checks her watch and chases after him. "Can you wait? I really don't want to miss it!"

Herbert is pleasantly surprised. "I see! Is this why they call you Gen X?"

"Why?" She is confused.

"Later I'm all yours but not just here and now." He gestures for her to wait and enters the men's room. "Be patient."

Maude's face dawns with realization. She is overwhelmed with conflicted feelings about trying to help this old man.

Olivia watches from under the table. Rosie notices her and feels indignation on her behalf. *We shouldn't work under the tables anymore.*

In the restroom, Danny fills a low urinal. He quietly sings, "If ever a *viz*, a *viz zhere vas, zeh* Whizzer is one, is one because, because, because, because... because of *zeh* wonderful *viz* he do, vah-dah-dah-vah-dah-dah-dah" (cfr. Arlen & Harburg, 1939).

Suddenly a large, long, oblong shadow like the Goodyear Blimp looms over Danny. Other men finish up quickly and leave. Danny looks over and sees a clown with a blimp balloon and smaller round ones for sale. The shy clown changes his mind and exits, revealing Herbert using a urinal from a long distance. Danny turns back and finishes his business saying, "*Zhat* must be some whizzer."

Herbert realizes he is being addressed. "I'm sorry, at my age we don't really have private parts anymore."

Danny flushes, zips, and then washes his hands. "I can honor your needs. Come see *zeh* revolution in fabrics at my booth."

Herbert continues gushing. "I may be a while."

"I don't mean *zhis* moment. Take your time." Danny exits.

Left alone, Herbert takes out his cell phone with his free hand. His urination slows, then resumes at full force.

Three beeps rise in pitch, followed by a familiar recording of a British-Indian female voice. "You have reached an unlisted number. You have reached an unlisted number."

In the background of the recording, children argue. A little girl says, "Give it back, Nicholas!"

"No! You weren't using it!" answers a boy.

The girl yells, "Mommy!!!"

Finally, in a New Jersey accent, the woman yells, "Stop it already, I'm working!" Then with her composed British-Indian accent she continues, "Please record your message," followed by a long beep.

Herbert talks fast. "Listen, P, it's Doub… ling Over in Pain, here. The eagles have *rendezvoused.* I repeat, the eagles have *rendezvoused.* And something really big has emerged. *Yuge.*" He looks around, the room still clear. "But I only have this one moment, while I'm taking care of my private business, shall we say? Sorry if you can hear what I'm doing, there's just no other time to call. Anyway, we need to stop a bomb. Yes, a bomb, as in, *kaboom.* It's going to be set off in a place called Gilead. Gil-ee-ad. I suspect it's code. I have no idea where it is, or what it means, or who's behind it, or under it, or anything beside it. But I'm all over it."

His flow diminishes. "I'll update you more later when I have more time. My time is very, very limited right now. I only have just this one moment while I'm doing who knows what in here. No need to picture anything."

His flow increases. "Just please, decode Gilead and get it evacuated as soon as possible. They sounded Irish, by the way. Two ladies, probably lesbians."

Outside the bathroom, Maude can hear every word. She wrings her hands. She is now quite conflicted about having brought this man to this conference.

Keeping an eye on her and the bathroom, Olivia and Rosie have not moved.

Herbert continues. "And by the way, unlike with some people, you can have full confidence in me that I'll do whatever it takes to save lives. Even if I have to resort to methods that now bring down harsh judgment but are proven to be effective. Though traditionally, the Irish don't report anything. And if they do, you can just reassign me to Boston or something."

Maude is horrified. She tries to drown out Herbert's voice by singing, "*We must love all God's children, yes we must…*" to the tune of, *She'll be Coming 'Round the Mountain* (Traditional folk song, n.d.). "*No matter how disgusting, yes we must!*"

Finally, she is relieved to hear his urinal flush. A moment later a sink runs, followed by the automated towel dispenser, and a tear. Herbert emerges, wiping the last bit of moisture from his hands onto his clothes. His phone is pressed to his cheek with his shoulder. He looks at Maude and says, "Anyway, I have to go, P," and hangs up.

"I thought you just went," complains Maude.

"Not without you! So, are you ready to move in, together?"

Maude is flustered yet again.

Herbert smiles. "Do they not teach that old co-ed raiding joke anymore? *Let's move in! Together!* Never mind. Though I did recently give up my residence. I'm a completely free agent again."

She nods and leads him into the auditorium, quietly resuming, "*We must love all God's children, yes we must…*"

Olivia watches, steel-eyed. She climbs out from under the table as Rosie rushes past her.

CHAPTER THIRTEEN

Cult·ivation

Herbert and Maude stand in the back, taking in the lecture hall. It's standing room only. Or perhaps walker-room only.

"There they are," points out Herbert. The two Irish musicians are on stage. Maude smiles agreeably. She scans for Allison while Herbert scans her. "You're quite the cool, calm cat," he says.

She ignores him, which he also considers very professional and nearly comments on it aloud.

The singer begins the bittersweet spiritual, "*There is a balm in Gilead…*" (Walker et al., 1909).

Herbert stops short, unsure he heard right. The audience erupts in applause. Maude immediately forgets her distress for the joy that enters her soul.

The singer continues, *"to make the wounded whole / There is a balm in Gilead / to heal the sin-sick soul."*

An embarrassed Herbert imagines a quiet DING. In his mind, he and the fighters in the ring stop and turn to the bell for clarification. The singer steadies it with her hand and says, "Sorry folks, we didn't literally mean we'd start with a bang. Carry on!" The boxers resume.

In the auditorium, the singers continue as well. *"Sometimes I feel discouraged / and deep I feel the pain / in prayers the Holy Spirit / revives my soul again…"*

Herbert smiles with relief. *It's nice to be wrong once in a great while,* he admits to himself. He takes out his phone and spells out a text: "*Sorry, premature evacuation.*" He hits *send* and immediately regrets it. He types another: "*No bomb! Everything working as it should.*"

Maude still scans the crowd for Allison. Herbert looks up from his phone and locates Mrs. Pearbottom and her seniors across the room. Claire and Olga are there too. He smiles, hoping Claire will turn and wave. Instead, Mrs. Pearbottom does and makes eye contact with him. He looks away, sullen, pretending not to notice. Mrs. Pearbottom stays on him like a teacher until he finally looks and mouths, "What?" like a seventh grader.

Pearbottom puts a hand to her heart and silently says, "I'm sorry." Herbert chooses to stay angry and composes another text.

The song proceeds. *"If you can't pray like Peter / if you can't be like Paul / go home and tell your neighbor / he died to save us all…"*

Maude spots Allison and heads to her section. It takes a moment for Herbert to notice and he shuffles to catch up. They squeeze into the two empty seats Allison kept for them.

"I was worried you were going to miss your favorite."

"I know, I love this one," answers Maude. She closes her eyes and enjoys the music. It's a much-needed break from the stress and agony that is Herbert Bigglesby.

Herbert watches her and comments, "You've really committed to this cover. I am quite impressed."

"Oh, I'd like any cover of this song," she answers.

Herbert thinks, *Atta girl, your lips are sealed!* He remembers he was mid-text and takes out his reading glasses. Trying to focus, he moves his phone closer and farther from his face. Thus far it reads, *Any nudes on who is after me?* He deletes *nudes* and types *news* but the autocorrect keeps changing it back.

Allison leans over. "Oh, put that away! You young people."

Herbert responds, "I'm almost..." but, rather than explain, he hits send and pockets the phone. He then casually scans around. His gaze lands on a sinister-looking Armenian man in a suit, waiting beside the stage. He is in his 40s, with a goatee, which is facial hair. When the man looks up, his fans smile and vie for his attention. He responds with a wave. Herbert comments too loudly, "Ah, that must be the Scammer in Chief."

Maude and others fight back their annoyance. She explains, "His name is Dr. Singleton. This conference is his brainchild. We are all but clay; please stop resisting the molder."

Herbert nods, recalling loose associations. "Cash is clay. Stings like a bee" (cfr. M. Ali, 1942-2016).

Maude has no idea what he is talking about. The song winds down and receives a warm round of applause.

***

Later, Dr. Singleton is mid-speech on stage. Maude and Allison listen attentively. Herbert mostly looks at Maude, who listens beautifully. She gently redirects his gaze to the speaker.

"And so I say," continues Dr. Singleton, "do not invest in treasures on earth, where rust and moth consume, and thieves break in and steal."

"No!" blurts out Herbert. "Just leave the front door open instead. And put some cookies out too."

He receives dark looks from the people around him. He scans the room again and lands on Mrs. Pearbottom, who listens but also monitors the room discreetly. She suddenly turns to Herbert as if feeling his gaze. He ducks behind his brochure for *Christopher Colonoscopy*, which has a cartoon of Columbus on a ship holding up a spyglass to two moons overlapping like buttocks.

Meanwhile, at other rear exits, the Twins enter in sync. Dressed in dark suits and sunglasses, they could be taken for Not-So Secret

Service. At another door, Olivia enters holding a *grande* coffee with the name *Olympia* written in Sharpie. She sees Mrs. Pearbottom and dons sunglasses in case she doesn't stand out enough already.

Dr. Singleton uses long dramatic pauses; he could have played Gandalf or Professor Snape in other fine literature (cfr. Tolkien, 1993/Jackson 2001; Rowling 1997/Columbus 2002). "And when you give..."

Herbert can't resist filling the gaps. "Or give in, rather?"

"Oh, shush!" demands Allison.

The speaker repeats, "And when you give, do not let your left hand know what your right hand is doing."

Maude suddenly startles. She removes Herbert's hand from her knee and puts it on his own lap. He looks equally shocked at the offending hand. He places his other hand on top of it, then holds a lecturing finger over the offending hand to convey a warning.

Dr. Singleton wipes NBA-level sweat from his brow. "Ladies and gentlemen, allow me to be really real with you. With y'all. I know the trials and tribulations many of you are going through."

Faces soften. Olivia squeezes herself into the aisle two rows behind Herbert where there is a conveniently empty seat. Only one row blocks her from him.

Mrs. Pearbottom notices this with alarm. She dead-stares at Herbert until he finally meets her gaze. She rubs her chin with her thumb and forefinger, subtly pointing over her own shoulder. Herbert looks at the rows behind her but she nods testily, wishing he would look over his own shoulder. Herbert struggles to understand, then wipes his mouth supposing crumbs or fluid could be lodged there. Maude reassures Herbert that his face is fine and urges him to focus on the talk. Mrs. Pearbottom is exasperated. Olivia can't help but smile a little.

Mrs. Pearbottom texts a message to someone named *Problem Child*. She types, *"danger!"* and then, *"2 rows behind you!!!"*

Herbert does not notice the loud BOINGS from his phone, or its vibrating with each message, though his neighbors hear and judge.

Dr. Singleton continues building his case. "And as you know, so many of our children are being derailed in life…"

The Twins and Olivia take an unexpected interest. This may apply to them. *Work can wait, after all.*

"Never before have so many people graduated with useless degrees, and yet be saddled with so much debt."

Herbert can't help asking, "Don't tell me this guy also raises from the debt?"

Maude almost slaps his arm. Olivia wishes she would too.

"Please, Mr. B."

He nods and presses his lips together like a fifth grader promising to be good.

Dr. Singleton laments, "And even with higher education, we see myriads and myriads of people living without any real purpose in life, other than seeking comfort, or revenge, or amusing themselves with selfies and mindless entertainment."

Well isn't he judgmental, opines Olivia internally, defensive of her boys. She looks around to see if others might also object but she only sees heads bobbing in agreement. Except Mrs. Pearbottom, who is not listening and types another text.

Oblivious to everything, Herbert lifts his phone to frame a selfie but is really trying to photograph Maude. People behind him get annoyed and lean to see the speaker better.

Herbert shifts his position and accidentally frames Olivia's face while he isn't looking. When he checks it, his screen is covered by Mrs. Pearbottom's latest text, which arrives with another BOING.

Annoyed, Herbert slides the notification away without reading it. Olivia covers her face with a brochure for discount flights to Bolivia. Herbert successfully frames Maude and tells her to smile. She complies and he snaps a picture.

"Ok, now listen to the talk, please," she requests.

Herbert lowers his phone, hurt by her lack of playfulness. "I don't think you have to be this convincing."

Dr. Singleton shifts to a new topic. "As parents and citizens, you all know that addictions are at an all-time high."

Herbert guffaws, "Oh, and the man does comedy! An all-time high for drug addictions! Let's give it to him." He claps alone.

This brings more angry looks and hushes. Maude is mortified. Behind them, Olivia deliberately spills the rest of her coffee onto the two people in front of her.

"Oh no! I'm so sorry!" she loud-whispers, wiping at them with an inadequate napkin.

Her victims try not to be upset. "It's Ok," they say. "It's only coffee, no big deal." They find tissues in their pockets but not enough to absorb the mess. They leave for the bathroom saying, "We forgive you."

Olivia pretends to appreciate their understanding.

From across the aisle, Mrs. Pearbottom sees the commotion and doesn't like the newly empty seats behind Herbert. She also sees the Twins moving to occupy them. She prepares her signature series Schoellhammer PewPewK, engraved with her prior initials. This weapon has in-graved several people.

Dr. Singleton is on a roll. "And I am not just talking about addiction to street drugs, and porn, and video games. Or nicotine, and medications, or gambling. I am talking about any and all forms of powerlessness. And codependence. We are all in need! We must recognize our weaknesses and appeal to a Higher Power."

Maude looks at Herbert, hoping he will listen and learn. Unfortunately, he is too busy framing another selfie of himself and her. This time it's from a lower angle, bothering no one. He achieves a perfect date shot but, before he snaps it, Jake photobombs it with his arms raised high up in praise in the background. Herbert turns and looks at him in disbelief.

Jake smiles and waves with the peace signal. Senior Rita also smiles and waves, seated next to Jake. Herbert acknowledges her with a half-smile and quarter-wave of his hand. He then notices Mrs. Pearbottom's empty seat and looks around to see where she went.

In the row behind Herbert, the Twins slide into the two empty seats. They attend to the speaker in all seriousness.

"With so many of our children at risk of fentanyl and other poisonings," Dr. Singleton says, "the situation has become quite brutal and unconscionable."

The Twins agree, disturbed by the state of the world, even as they prepare cords to strangle Herbert.

From the back wall, Mrs. Pearbottom watches Olivia and the Twins. She has her weapon discreetly at the ready. She sees Rosie re-enter the room, this time closer to Herbert.

Dr. Singleton startles them all. "Excuse me! Please! Just hold it right there!"

Rosie pauses and takes a step back. Olivia lowers her sunglasses. Mrs. Pearbottom holds her breath.

Dr. Singleton continues. "What I need for you to know, unseen woman, unseen man, is that I see you."

The four assassins and Mrs. Pearbottom can't tell if he's being literal or not. The Twins look at each other.

The speaker relieves their doubts. "I am not being literal. I truly admire all the sacrifices so many of you have made, especially mothers. And fathers. And workers. Who committed yourselves to being there. Even if imperfectly so."

Listeners try not to tear up, finally acknowledged for their years of silent suffering. Herbert and the Twins don't speak this language and look around with mild curiosity.

Dr. Singleton continues. "And I genuinely lament the loss of your own childhoods, which got way too serious, and much too stressful, far too soon in life. You are not alone anymore."

Olivia tries not to be moved away from her purpose but can't help it. She produces a tissue from inside her hat. She then wipes her eyes and nose with it and Rosie does something similar but blames her allergies. Mrs. Pearbottom pushes away any emotion.

Herbert can't take all the melodrama but keeps his voice down. "What the hell is he talking about?"

"Not now." Maude is too moved to explain.

About to strangle Herbert, the Twins wind their cords tight. Mrs. Pearbottom approaches from outside their peripheral vision.

Dr. Singleton doesn't let up. "And please don't ever say you don't have a family. You do have a family. All you need to do is acknowledge it!"

Olivia almost breaks up. Woldecott raises his cord to strike but his mother places her hand on his shoulder. Both Twins lower their arms until further notice.

Mrs. Pearbottom sees the "at-ease" and backs away to the wall. She notices Rosie engaged in the talk.

Herbert grows restless. "This guy is so full of it! If we weren't so busy with other more important things I would want to stop his little cult."

People around Herbert would love for him to go work on his other more pressing things just now. *Anything.*

Maude puts her hand on his forearm. "Mr. Bigglesby, you might not be right about this one."

Herbert is delighted by her touch. "Ok, Sweetheart." He covers her hand with his own and relaxes; she allows it as a pacifier.

Dr. Singleton continues. "As Mother Teresa of Calcutta once said, people can be surrounded by others, even family, and yet be drowning in loneliness. I might add, scattered apart in fragmentation. As a society we lack unity, despite so much uniformity. And no less dire is the financial situation of many people."

This jolts Herbert. "I knew it!" He lowers his voice. "Here comes his *Sermon on the Amount!*"

"Oh, shush!" Allison cannot take much more of him. Yet she and others begrudgingly remember to work on their loving-kindness mantras. Some even consciously make allowances for Herbert's age and weakened filter. Others can't help expecting self-control.

Dr. Singleton moves into problem-solving. "But enough lamenting! Let's talk about solutions. What our children need today are skills! And jobs! And competence. If Martin Luther King were alive today, I believe he would tell young people, of every tribe and tongue, to stop lecturing their elders. And to stop saying they have a dream. If only they could just say, *I have a job!*"

Herbert is in line with that one, as is every parent in the room. Younger people look offended.

Dr. Singleton continues, "Unfortunately, our debt-inducing universities are not achieving this. Nor are they advancing the sciences at the rate they could be. Instead, they and their journals are slowing progress. Like poorly run tech companies, they pit talented people against each other. They incentivize individual success, not that of science. Researchers face intense pressure to be unique and original rather than humbly row the boat of replication or adding to another's work. And newer researchers are too worried about housing and making a name for themselves. What reward is there for improving or disseminating another doctor's cure? They have their own books to write, and tenure to secure. Our system fails to nurture seedlings. Practical concerns make them fall by the wayside. Creative ideas are abandoned out of concern for sheer survival. Instead, what we need are institutions of higher *earning*, where deeper solutions can flourish, free from political, personal, or other obstacles."

"Amen to that!" calls out an untethered academic.

"Thank you!" acknowledges Dr. Singleton. "Now, I know I may seem a bit long-winded and unconvincing to some."

Herbert nods in agreement.

"Therefore, in honor of our tradition, I would like to hear a word from one of our counter-sponsors. Can I get a naysayer to read a message? Is there an unbeliever in the house?"

Many hands shoot up. Herbert looks and they all point down at him. The Twins block their faces with brochures.

Dr. Singleton addresses Herbert. "Ah, Sir. Would you do us the horror?"

"Nothing like a spotlight to draw out enemy fire," he whispers to Maude.

She encourages him, "Don't worry, Higher P has got you."

Herbert looks around. "Is he here?"

"Of course!"

Dr. Singleton urges Herbert, "Please come up, Sir. I promise not to challenge or offend your worldview."

Herbert overcomes his hesitation and shuffles up to the front with his mischievous grin. "You may challenge my worldviews all you want. After all, we are all here to understand the truth of things."

Dr. Singleton is delighted that he actually read his brochure. He recalls working really hard on that tagline. "Please everyone, make him feel at home."

Several seniors pass gas and the crowd applauds while Herbert approaches the podium. He reaches it and scans the room, smiling. The Twins hide behind their brochures. Rosie shuts her gleaming mouth behind a flier for *Unbeatable Dental Coverage.*

Herbert dons his reading glasses and orients himself to the page in front of him. "Let's see. A reading from *The Book of Nonsense.*" He smiles and lowers his guard. "Quite." He continues aloud, *"Are you tired of having people clinging onto you for dear life? Or angling for your inheritance?"*

Impressed, he stops and looks over at Maude, who smiles like an angel. She is hopeful again.

Olivia, however, does not like what Herbert just read.

Sensing something, the Twins and Rosie peek out from behind their brochures but are not sure of what Herbert just said.

Mrs. Pearbottom stands watchful in the back.

Herbert continues. "Or perhaps you've had colleagues betray you, planning things behind your back?" Herbert can't believe his luck. He attempts eye contact with Mrs. Pearbottom but she averts his gaze. He continues but stumbles over the next word. "Wash? Wash your parasites away with Bondilax. Sticky people may exist in your life, but their wellbeing is not your problem."

Olivia grows in murderous resolve.

Herbert keeps reading. "Bondilax is the answer to rigid bonds that lock people into lifestyles they don't want. And it's made with real Teflon! So, sign up today and watch your dependents cease to matter. Now available in gummies."

Herbert looks up at the crowd, pleasantly surprised by his message. Everyone is quiet, unsure how to react.

A single person claps, hoping to attract his attention. It works until he recognizes it's Olga.

He then turns to Dr. Singleton, who appears to be waiting for his judgment of the reading. Herbert renders it with a smile. "Well, that was unexpectedly sensible."

Dr. Singleton laughs and his followers applaud. A triumphant Herbert leaves the stage.

"Well done! Thank you, Sir!" commends Dr. Singleton as he returns to the podium. "We believe it's important to be able to articulate other points of view even if we don't share them."

Olivia mutters darkly, "How democratic."

Herbert thinks it's foolish too, but takes it as a win.

Olivia taps the Twins, who discreetly tighten their cords. She then tests the rim of her hat with a finger. Disappointed, she takes out a Rockford file and quickly improves its edge.

As Herbert approaches his row, Mrs. Pearbottom rushes to intercept him. He sees her coming and veers to the side, hoping to blend in with the audience by the wall.

Olivia, the Twins, and Rosie watch but do not yet move.

Herbert demands of Mrs. Pearbottom when she arrives, "Are you here to finish me off?"

"Hardly!"

"We have this situation completely under control without you."

"Who's *we*?"

Herbert indicates the two women he came with. "Agents Maude and Allison over there."

Mrs. Pearbottom studies them and would laugh at Herbert if there were more time and less hurt between them. "Herbert, they're real attendees!"

"Oh they fooled me too, at first. The young one plays her cover like nobody's business."

Mrs. Pearbottom regards him with pity; *he really has slipped.*

"And the old one plays crotchety Royal quite well."

"Herbert, your enemies are here and closing in on you. Look!" She points to the empty seats where Olivia and the Twins were moments ago. "Oh dear, they've moved." She scans for them but it's wall-to-wall seniors.

Herbert turns suspicious. "How would they even know I'm here unless you brought them to try again? And how did you even know I'd be here?" He gestures at Maude and Allison. "Did they betray me as well?"

Mrs. Pearbottom reaches into Herbert's breast pocket. He reacts, "Hey, Lady! Don't get handsy on me!"

Others turn as she produces his cell phone. "You led me here!"

People assume it's just another husband being busted for something and they lose interest.

Herbert pockets his phone. "Oh, I don't think so. This thing could have put a man on the moon. It wouldn't betray my whereabouts. My privacy matters to these companies."

"Herbert, look at me!" She takes him by the arms but he looks away like a child. She is no longer the indifferent director with a job to do. "My dear. Old. Friend. Whether you forgive me or not, I am not letting them get to you again."

Herbert still refuses eye contact. "Platitudes."

Out of the corner of her eye, Mrs. Pearbottom sees the assassins. "Look! There they are." She indicates the back wall. The four killers are spaced out, yet focused.

Herbert sees them and instinctively ducks, but then realizes they are occupied with the talk. "Are they just here for the conference? Maybe you're the paranoid one!"

"I don't think so." Mrs. Pearbottom gestures for him to look again. The killers have moved closer but stand still, like in the game,

Red Light, Green Light, One, Two, Three. They are never actually seen moving and seem completely attentive to the speaker.

Mrs. Pearbottom appeals to Herbert. "Look, I know they almost got you and I should resign after this. I just want you to know I am truly very sorry. I should have listened and I do hope you can eventually forgive me."

Herbert still won't even look at her. "And how do you explain your downright incompetence?"

She assumes he knows more than he does. "How do you know about that? Never mind, I won't dissemble. Fortunately you weren't there when he took your bed and got himself nixed."

"Wait, Downright? He's dead?! In my place? At your place?"

Oops. "Look, I don't want to only pretend to come clean, like the murdering hat thrower. Our footage shows that when you went to Mr. Eulogy's room, Downright then took your bed, and then the Bad Hatter strangled him. How did you know not to be there?"

"A better question is, How do you still show your face?"

"Fair enough." Now Mrs. Pearbottom does not know where to look. *He is completely justified in his anger and feelings of betrayal.* She conveys contriteness and promises to resign when the current threat has passed.

Herbert resists but she sees some thawing. He finally speaks. "Well, luckily I trusted my gut and wasn't some sleeping beauty."

Dr. Singleton gets louder. "Ok, folks, now let's talk about some positives, like about how we are all getting *fruct* in this life."

Herbert and Mrs. Pearbottom are surprised to hear that and turn to listen. Herbert adjusts his hearing aids.

"That's right, I said we're all getting *fruct.* Which may sound irreverent, but hear me out. As you know, our dear Leader himself said this life would not be easy, and that suffering is to be expected, even persecution. Yet he also said that in the midst of it all, it's important to bear fruit, to not bury our talents out of fear. Or complacency. But rather, to be active and show profit from our endeavors."

Herbert feels vindicated. "I knew it. We should stop this guy from scamming people."

Mrs. Pearbottom is incredulous. "Wait, you suddenly care about seniors?"

"No! Not most. Just some." He gestures at Maude and Allison. "Even if they aren't with us, they certainly don't deserve to be taken in by all this nonsense."

Mrs. Pearbottom is impressed but downplays it.

Dr. Singleton continues, "Yet to be fruitful, the grain of wheat must die or it remains a single grain. Thus, we cannot prioritize self-preservation."

"I can!" yells Herbert, drawing even the attention of his assassins. Neighbors *shush* him. To Mrs. Pearbottom he adds, "It certainly seemed like a good idea last night." She sighs.

The speaker continues unfazed. "Nor is it by our own cleverness or even diligence that we bear this profound fruit. No, instead of centuries of worrying about whether we are *justified,* let us let go of foolish plans and prepare to be *fructified*!" He looks around slowly. "Happy are the truly *fruct*, who surrender to His will."

"Surrender?" Herbert assures his neighbors, "I have never been one to surrender."

Her head bowed, Mrs. Pearbottom remains embarrassed.

Olivia appears torn; she wants to hurry up and complete her mission but also wants to hear more.

The Twins and Rosie are less divided. They are enjoying the talk but on a lighter level.

"Are you saying *any* life can be fruitful? That it's not too late?" Heads turn. Olivia couldn't resist asking.

"Thank you!" responds Dr. Singleton. "That is correct! It takes almost nothing to tap into the offer that is extended."

"So act now!" declares Herbert, mimicking a radio announcer.

Singleton explains, "Why not benefit from the fact that you are getting *fruct* anyway, by the minute sometimes, whether you want it or not? Fortunately, no one can truly block the Master's fruit from rising up in them."

Olivia is having a profound spiritual moment and Dr. Singleton can see it. "Let's help her out, everyone! Say it with me. *Let us all be fructified! Together!*"

Hands go up in prayer as people chant, "Let us all be fructified. Together!"

A few wonder if that last word was an instruction or meant to be repeated. Yet for Olivia, that is the only part she can accept right now. She raises her hands and repeats, "Together!"

Dr. Singleton looks up to heaven. "I am being *fruct* for thy greater glory!"

People repeat, "I am being *fruct* for thy greater glory!"

"Because it's the only way we can ever see straight!" continues the preacher. "Our healthy, wealthy, successful friends cannot see what they do not think they need! We are blessed in our neediness, in our helplessness, and in our ability to accept the comfort that is offered. Blessed are the cleaned-out of modern heart disease, for you can see Him everywhere!"

People chant back, "We see Him everywhere!"

Dr. Singleton adds, "My friends–no—We are a family! Please acknowledge that we are all one family!"

"We are all one family!" roars the crowd.

Olivia is not ready to go there. The Twins and Rosie stay quiet too, though Rosie is getting tempted.

"A family that bears fruit!" insists Dr. Singleton.

"A family that bears fruit!" chants the crowd.

Olivia looks at Herbert, trying to maintain a full hatred.

"Deep down you know it's true!" insists Singleton. "You must no longer live in anxiety, nor feed your hatred! We are all one ridiculous family!"

Olivia looks at Herbert again. He tracks a fly in the air, oblivious to all the emotion in the room. His childlike demeanor is difficult to hate in this moment. She finally drops her tense shoulders and chimes in, "Ok! Yes! Fine! We are all one ridiculous family!" She repeats it in Spanish, "*Una familia ridícula*!"

Rosie joins in now. "Me too! I want to be *fruitified*!" Her hands go up like at a concert. The Twins put their hands in the air too. Rosie adds, "I have been so *fruct,* over and over!"

Dr. Singleton beckons, "And we must pray for those who contribute to our being so *fruct*! Pray for them, lest our anger turn to fire and destroys us from within."

He wipes his brow with a small towel. "Now, I realize some of you are still in doubt, and that's Ok. But who does not know they have been repeatedly taken advantage of? We all know it! We all stand in lines! And submit forms! That we then find out! Are the wrong ones! Or need some anal detail we missed!"

Olivia calls out, "Yes!!! We all get *fruct!* All the time!"

"We make phone call after phone call, and get put on hold for hours, and nothing gets resolved. Then we hear, *How else can I not help you today?"*

"They deny our needs!" people yell. "And waste our time! Our lives don't matter to them!

Dr. Singleton continues, "They don't value your days, hours, or minutes of remaining sanity! After years of paying through the nose! For their denials, hassles, and holds! And limitations! Imitations of concern! But we are not deaf! And we are not defeated!"

"We are not deaf! And we are not defeated!" answers the crowd.

Herbert can't make out what they are saying. He adjusts his hearing aids one more time.

The leader adds, "Our barren deserts are flowering!"

The people resound with, "Our barren deserts are flowering!"

"And our fruits shall endure!"

"Our fruits shall endure!"

"Now imagine even more words about how bad things have gotten!"

Herbert observes, "He does not even need to say them!"

"I do not even need to say them!"

People chant, "Things are rotten! Really rotten!"

"But we are fruity!" says the Doctor.

"We are fruity!" echoes the people.

"And the future is like cotton!"

Familiar ones respond, "There's just no stoppin' us, y'all."

Dr. Singleton drives it home, "Because there is no stopping the power of family! And forgiveness! And *fructification* for all!"

His followers answer in unison. "We must connect! No matter how annoying! Not by wifi but in person! With everyone enjoyin'!"

The Twins are blown away. "Not by wifi? Is that even possible?"

Dr. Singleton hears it. "You might not even think it possible! But it is! We can all connect, responsibly! Turn to your neighbor and say, *Burden me with your being!*"

People turn to their sides, hesitant yet hopeful: Twin to Twin. Maude to Allison. Herbert to Pearbottom, but she opts to stay in work mode, her hand on her weapon and eyes scanning the crowd. Herbert feels rejected.

"Say it!" encourages Dr. Singleton.

People comply. "Burden me with your being!"

Herbert wants to be partnered too, not for this particular Cause but for a female hug or two. He sees Claire still alone and shuffles toward her as if wading through water. Pearbottom regrets her hesitation and follows.

Singleton continues. "Be not proud! Say it loud! You are not too much for me!"

People holler, "You are not too much for me!"

Herbert reaches Claire but it's too late, she has now partnered with a good-looking young man her own age. The kind that keeps a job and provides a comfortable home, and who is willing to raise as many kids as God sends. She seems fulfilled, which makes Herbert a little sad but also happy for her.

Seeing her own chance, Olga rushes to Herbert. He sees her coming, panics, and dodges. This results in Mrs. Pearbottom being inadvertently swept up into Olga's embrace. She startles as if a new lifeguard clutched by someone who might accidentally drown her.

"I take you as you are!" cries out Singleton, who is then echoed by all. He goes even further, adding, "And I welcome you with all your baggage!"

Herbert scowls at what he considers to be *too much. It's extreme. Hyperbole. Of all the things to say, Baggage?! Who does he think–* As he turns, he finds himself face to face with Olivia. Time stops. He expects all remaining hell to break looser. Milliseconds feel like millennia.

Olivia seems about to either cry or sloppily murder someone. She then opens her arms for a hug but Herbert flinches, stumbling backwards. She catches him by the forearms, not letting him fall. She makes direct eye contact and says, "I forgive you!... I take you as you are!... And I welcome you, with all your baggage... Dad!"

Herbert's eyes go wide with shock and disbelief. "Daaaddd???"

Mrs. Pearbottom turns, as do others, stunned.

DING! A sharp bell sounds loudly and clearly. In Herbert's mind we are back in the boxing ring. He is struck by a glove-covered fist and collapses to the mat in slow motion.

Olivia climbs through the ropes, rushes to him, and holds his head like in a *Pietá*, on her knees.

Mrs. Pearbottom watches from outside the ring, baffled yet envious of Olivia having an irrevocable bond with him.

Herbert struggles to stay conscious. "I don't… I can't… You're my… offspring?"

Olivia nods and tries to say what was once a well-rehearsed speech. "My name is… Olivia Martinez… de Jorge Pincez Flores… de Tejunga Martinez-again. You… You killed my stepfather! But I no longer want you to prepare to die" (cfr. Reiner, 1987/Goldman, 1973).

"I did? You are? You don't?" gasps Herbert, still not sure he is safe. "Why not?" Mrs. Pearbottom wants more reassurance too.

Olivia answers, "I mean, prepare for Jesus, maybe, but not for me. I want you to live forever!"

Herbert frets, wondering if she means live forever starting today or more like just prepare and get to know Jesus and be ready for eventual demise.

The Twins watch from a corner of the ropes, holding Herbert's water bottle and towel on either side of a walker with a seat on it.

Olivia continues, "All I know is I do not hate you anymore, *Papi.* I no longer want you to die a slow, painful death. *Tu eres mio.*" She brings his head to her abundant bosom. "Kids! Come say hi to your *Tata! Tu abuelito!*"

The Twins run over, ever-obedient to mom. They kneel in a warm group hug. Somewhere a song by the Carter Family (1935) asks, *Can the Circle Be Unbroken?*

Herbert remains smothered against Olivia's bosom, wondering when she will release him. Pearbottom looks on, feeling left out but also unsure of what she even wants in life.

Olga comments, "This is so not what I was expecting from this conference."

Rosie concurs. "It's definitely better than I thought."

Herbert had not noticed Rosie till now. He frets.

Olga reacts too and taps Claire. "Look, freezer lady!" They re-freeze in fear.

Rosie wrings her hands, afraid to be causing that reaction. "Yes, that was me! I'm so sorry! I don't deserve your forgiveness, but I still ask it. Can you forgive me, or maybe one day if not today?"

Herbert and others are speechless.

Olivia is annoyed. "I'm sure they forgive you, Hon. Why don't you just run along back to Romania?"

"Poland." She then insists of her three victims, "Can you? Each of you? Forgive me?" She looks at Claire and Olga. "Especially you two. I really had no business hurting you."

The PTs look at her in awe but Herbert is bothered. "Being shoved in a freezer for 20 minutes is one thing, but being hunted for decades, that was serious." He turns to Olivia. "And that goes for you too… *Daughter.*"

Olivia is caught off guard and is remorseful at first.

"I'm sorry, *Papi*."

Rosie is too. "I'm sorry too, Mr. Bigglesby. But I realize it's probably too little, too late, so I will go now."

"No, please stay!" insists Claire. "At least, I forgive you."

"I do too!" confirms Olga.

Rosie smiles, her teeth gleaming. "Really?"

Olivia regains her composure. "I mean, I *want* to forgive you, Dad, but it's a process."

Herbert remembers to ask, "By the way, which of you were in my room last night?"

Olivia looks away. "Can't we just focus on the future?"

Herbert scans their faces. "One of you helped Mr. Downright call it a night." He is partly using code to avoid explaining murder to Claire and Olga.

Rosie is shocked he would discuss this in front of outsiders. You don't ask these questions in polite company. And snitching is against all manner of decorum.

Olivia finally confesses. "That was me, Dad. I thought he was you at the time."

Herbert is offended. "I hope it was pitch black! You confused him for me?"

"It was a dark night of my soul, *Papi*. I'll never do it again."

"I see. Apparently I'm not the only one who has… disappointed family?"

"No, you're right, Daddy. I was naughty."

He is not yet comfortable being called *Daddy*. "It's Ok… *Daughter*. I think you're right that we all just need to move on and *live in the now*, as they say."

"Good! We were all just busy surviving. I had to put food on the table but now it's different."

"Then it's all out of your system?" asks Herbert.

"I think so. Yes. Dr. Singleton made a lot of sense. I don't want to go on like that. I'd rather be a family."

Herbert replies, "Well, I won't stay mad if this really is the end of it."

Mrs. Pearbottom is incredulous. "So that's it?"

"Why not?" Herbert is having a moment of lucidity. Or at least no longer wants to be hunted. "I probably would have made similar choices if I had been in her shoes and they had fit. People do all sorts of things when they are strapped for cash. With two little killers to feed."

Neither Claire or Olga takes that literally.

"Let's all just start over, shall we?" Herbert opens his arms for a group hug.

Mrs. Pearbottom still can't believe it. Olivia moves in, then her boys and Rosie. Herbert reaches to pull Claire in. She joins but moves his overly friendly hand up from her lower back. Olga shimmies closer to Herbert but he blocks her with a Twin.

"Thank you for accepting me," blubbers Rosie.

Mrs. Pearbottom remains in utter skepticism. "So, are you all just *Kumbaya* now?" (Gordon, 1926).

The Twins try to include her. "Hey, get in here! We're so sorry we ruined your kitchen!"

Rosie adds, "And the PT room. Can you also forgive us?"

Mrs. Pearbottom has a much harder time overlooking decades of animosity, topped off now by a physical assault on her facility. It seems surreal to be discussing forgiveness and bygones. "Um, let me think about it. That is the best I can do for now. And we'll have to see what the insurance covers."

"Of course," answers Rosie, "I'm ready to pay for my share of any damage."

Herbert softens toward Mrs. Pearbottom. "That is very kind of you, Peaches."

She looks at him. "You know, I think I'm the only one who has not yet been forgiven."

Before Herbert can answer, Dr. Singleton draws their attention to the podium. "Ladies and gentlemen!"

"Ah, back to the *scam-athalon*," says Herbert, dodging Mrs. Pearbottom's implied question.

She understands, *it's not easy. No, I'll just have to wait* (Holland et al., 1966).

Singleton proceeds, "Ladies and gentlemen, in case anyone was expecting some form of financial solicitation today, I encourage you to save your money and direct it toward the people in your lives who matter most to you."

Herbert doesn't believe him.

Mrs. Pearbottom smiles. "It looks like your assumption might not be confirmed today, Mr. Bigglesby."

Singleton continues, "So please seek out some refreshments together. Take the time to bond, just bond."

Rosie suddenly looks triggered, as if possessed. She bares her metal and diamond teeth, salivating. Her eyes lock onto Herbert's. He becomes poised for battle and they assess each other as if silverbacks in election season; violence can erupt at any moment.

Olivia takes Herbert's hand and brings it to her abundant cheek. He initially flinches. "It's Ok, I'm here for you, Daddy."

Rosie snaps out of it and takes a deep breath, bringing her hands together harmlessly.

Herbert pulls his own hand from Olivia's fleshy cheek.

***

Moments later they are all on line to buy coffee in person. Herbert is going to pay cash and counts what coins he has as if 1975.

Maude and Allison stop by. "I hope you see how wrong you were about Dr. Singleton," says the younger one.

"I suppose I was," admits Herbert. "By the way, I was thrilled to realize we don't actually work for the same… company."

"I think I was less confused about that," replies Maude.

"Which frees us up in a lot of ways," continues Hebert. "In fact, I think it's time I introduce you to my family."

Maude is horrified. How can a man misread my lack of interest this badly? Is there a diagnosis for that?

Herbert points them out. "This is Olivia, and her boys..." He can't recall their names.

"Wayne and Woldecott," fills in their mother.

Maude is overwhelmed and trying not to faint. "Oh my! Hi everyone! It's too bad I need to go. Away. Anywhere! My work here is… I'm done here."

Allison is surprised. "You don't want to stay for the other talks?"

"No Nana, I think I've had enough! Good news, I mean, for a year. Or maybe a lifetime, who knows?"

"But what's the hurry?" asks Herbert. "I was just beginning to consider new perspectives."

"Good! Keep at it!" encourages Maude. "Without me! I was just an instrument. An envelope, to be thrown away. But you're well on your way! Not because of your age. I'm on my way too, maybe to a cloister." She leaves. "Goodbye, everyone! Keep being enlightened!"

Allison makes an excuse for her and follows. "Poor thing probably had too much excitement."

Herbert watches them go. Maude never looks back. He is then startled to find all eyes on him. *Is this really happening?* he wonders. *What a motley crew. Hopefully it's all a big mistake.* His shoulders sag under the weight of it all.

Olivia can read his rejection and it hurts. "I know this is all happening fast, Papa. We'll figure it out."

Herbert manages a smile. "I'm sure we will." *Whenever there's a will people find a way*, he thinks.

As if reading his mind, Olivia answers and makes him put away his coins. "And we don't care about your money, Dad. We all want you alive."

Chapter Fourteen

Unplanned

Outside the convention center, the Twins and Rosie feed ducks on a stream. Herbert, Olivia, and Mrs. Pearbottom enjoy coffee and pastries on a picnic table.

Olivia is mid-story. "And that was when my mother said her husband found you both together, and that you stabbed him with your lipstick. Which, I didn't judge about that. Then you left us."

"Not that I doubt your story," begins Herbert. "On how you came to be. But I'm not even sure I was in Bolivia that year."

"Oh, you were," confirms Mrs. Pearbottom.

Herbert is not pleased with her encyclopedic memory.

Mrs. Pearbottom adds, "The only part I'm struggling with is that after a single sermon, you're ready to forgive him all that… lousiness toward you?"

"Oh, I didn't say he was lazy," clarifies Olivia. "And I can handle a man who putters around. It's better than gambling, making more babies, and going to prison."

Herbert chimes in, "People do change, Mrs. Pearbottom."

"And that was more than a sermon," says Olivia. "I see a whole new vision for my life. And I didn't expect it. I did not even know I was on the wrong path. But now I feel like an exhausted and broken *burro* who is finally free to put down her heavy and unjust *joke*."

Herbert agrees with the sentiment. "Yes, there is cruel humor in life. And how is your mother? Is it Dolores?"

"No, Conchita."

"Of course! Conchita. Is she well?"

"She's, well…"

"Oh, good! I'm glad."

"No, I mean, she died."

"Oh! *Lo siento.*"

Herbert and Mrs. Pearbottom show sympathetic surprise. They spare her *clichés* about what that must be like for her.

"Were you close?" asks Mrs. Pearbottom.

"Not really. She thought I took too much after the men in her life. But she really did love you, *Papi.* She said you gave great back rubs. With coconut butter mushroom seed oil wax lotion." Her face grows dark again. "So, when she died I had no choice. I swore to *mi mismo* that I would find and kill the slick-fingered man, who executed her husband and ruined our already impossible lives."

"Your poor mother," says Mrs. Pearbottom. "To have such a thoughtless, selfish, inconsiderate man inflict so much irreparable damage. And then completely disappear on you."

Herbert doubts Mrs. Pearbottom's loyalty again.

Olivia defends Herbert. "It's too bad my mother was so unfaithful herself, and my stepfather too, and my no-good husband. So many people choose smallness but my *papa* is going to be a giant. It's not too late. We'll get through this, *Papi!*" She takes his hands.

Herbert smiles nervously.

Mrs. Pearbottom asks, "So, then you left Bolivia?"

"Yes, as soon as I could. We began our search of him."

"And we all know how you made ends meet," says Herbert.

"Yes! At the sausage factory. I had to make the meats end. I was twisting and turning and cutting. It made me ready for anything. Then I got odder jobs."

Most instinctively look at her bowler hat.

"For Vilefinger?"

"Among others. Under the tables," confesses Olivia.

"The world can be quite degrading to women," validates Mrs. Pearbottom while looking at Herbert.

He ignores the dig. "How is your Vile old boss these days?"

"I don't really keep in touch," answers Olivia. "It's a, *Don't call me I'll call you* situation, but he never does, not even at Christmas. But I'm grateful. He first made me the first offer; I could not refuse it. It was more money and health coverage than I could have *imaginated*."

Herbert nods and looks past the donuts, his eyes beginning to glaze with fatigue. "This is a lot to take in."

"Just do little bites." Olivia uses her hat to cut segments.

Herbert tastes one to be polite. "Mmm, not bad."

Mrs. Pearbottom raises a concern. "Herbert, I am not at all sure what to report back to headquarters about all this."

Herbert wipes his mouth. "Olivia, please don't take this the wrong way. Would you be offended if I insisted on a paternity test?"

"I don't know," she responds. She sips her coffee and then more decidedly says, "Would you be offended if I kill you and leave your body in the stream?"

"Probably." Herbert is not sure if that was a joke.

Mrs. Pearbottom considers aloud, "You know, a test like that might be redundant." Herbert likes her reasoning until she adds, "He has clearly failed at paternity."

"I'm not sure you're helping here, Peaches. Perhaps you should go check on your residents?"

She assures Olivia, "Of course he'll do it! For everyone's peace of mind."

"Thank you for answering for me, Director Pearbottom."

Olivia is not one for delays. "Good, let's do it." She bags the pastries and calls out, "Boys! We are leaving!"

The Twins come running like kids. Rosie follows, unsure.

Herbert is shocked. "Wait, now? Today?"

"Or you'll be gone tomorrow!" answers Olivia. "I saw a truck. We can do it here."

Mrs. Pearbottom smiles at Herbert. "Check, mate."

"Surely you have seniors to go tend to?"

Mrs. Pearbottom looks at her watch, "No, we're good! As the locals say."

Woldecott arrives panting. "Grampa, can we get some ice cream?"

Herbert can't believe he's being called Grampa, and asked for spending money. This really is new for him. Nevertheless, he takes out his wallet and gives Woldecott a crisp dollar bill.

The boys feel pity. "Oh, that's ok, grandpa."

Herbert is embarrassed and quickly makes it a twenty. Wayne grabs it and runs. "Thanks, Grampa!"

Woldecott chases him. "Stop! He gave it to me!"

"To buy us both ice-cream, not just you!"

Olivia sighs happily. "Those boys."

Rosie keeps her distance. She's not sure where she fits in all of this. Olivia offers her the pastries and Rosie takes a croissant.

"Rosie, where do you fit in all of this?" voices Mrs. Pearbottom. "For whom were you trying to kill Herbert?"

Rosie is embarrassed to have her mouth full. She is also not accustomed to anyone asking or caring what she thinks, or how she feels, or why she does what she does. She swallows and says, "I wasn't working for anyone."

"Right, don't tell us," confirms Herbert. "KICA confidentiality and all that. But unofficially?"

"No one. Just me." Some food is trapped in her grillz and she discreetly works on freeing it.

Herbert and Mrs. Pearbottom do not believe her.

Olivia grows defensive. "Why does she have to be working for someone? Because of her gender? She can't be independent?"

"I don't have a problem with that," answers Herbert. You are free to hunt down whomever, so long as I'm no longer concerned."

"It just seems like an odd thing to finance yourself," says Mrs. Pearbottom.

Rosie is about to explain but Olivia grows hot. "You don't gotta explain yourself, Rosie! To nobody! Your reasons only need to make sense to you."

Rosie is eager to talk. "I don't know, looking for Mr. Herbert has just been a habit. It's what I know. No employer, no contract. Just years of doing it."

Herbert feels some commonality. "I can understand that! Were you forced to retire too?"

"Yes!" exclaims Rosie, feeling the camaraderie. "I was caught completely from my guard. I expected to die working so I never made plans for *after*. Then I had to figure out how to live, what to do with me. I tried gardening, but it's so boring and everything dies."

"It's very hard to stop doing what we know," says Herbert.

"But I will! I'm not going to kill you anymore."

"Well, thank you."

Mrs. Pearbottom is doubtful. "So, this... experience, today's sermon... is motivating you to stop and change?"

Olivia doesn't like her skepticism but Herbert answers first. "Why not? It's nice to be less hunted for a change."

Mrs. Pearbottom explains, "I'm just not sure I'm ready to let my own guard down just yet."

Rosie answers before Olivia. "Of course not! You should take whatever time you need."

"Thank you," says Mrs. Pearbottom. "But how is this supposed to work now? You each have decades of experience tracking, hunting, killing, and you have all the ingrained habits and routines that come with that. How can you just stop?"

Olivia is too irritated to speak. "Like you expected with Pops?"

Rosie breaks it down for her. "You raise some good points. Habits do not change easily." Her head tilts as she thinks. "But yes! It's logical. Since I now see that killing Mr. Herbert is no longer compatible with my goals and values, I must stop it. No excuses. I have a whole new worldview now."

"You go, Girl!" praises Olivia. "She's obviously been working on herself! As have I. And I think we could all use some self-improvement."

Mrs. Pearbottom recoils.

Herbert raises a point. "But how do we know you won't backslide? Either of you could have a relapse, and try and kill me in the night."

"Oh, no, *Papi*!" assures Olivia.

Rosie is more thoughtful. "That's valid," she answers. "I should probably have a sponsor. Go to meetings."

Olivia agrees. "Is there such a thing? I think I'm ready to deal with my hurting people."

Herbert approves. "That would certainly make my life more manageable."

They look at him judgmentally.

"What, I'm being supportive. And Mrs. Pearbottom, here's what you can tell headquarters. 'It turns out some of us don't like being forced to retire, especially when we've been correct about people still trying to kill us, for reasons we might not even anticipate, and we were right anyway. But seeing as how certain parties no longer wish to harm our exemplary servant Herbert, everyone can now just relax and enjoy life.'"

Olivia adds a caveat. "At least until Thanksgiving."

They look at her quizzically.

"That was a joke, people! I'm kidding! I can't wait to have holidays together. Like our independence day, *seis de agosto*."

Herbert had not pictured so far ahead and becomes depressed. "Well, how do we get this DNA test done?"

***

An RV is parked outside the convention center. The letters IM-RATLD are emblazoned on its side. They stand for, *Identity & Mobile*

Roots Ancestry Testing Lab, Decentralized. They originally wanted IM-REL8D but someone already had the trademark.

A long line of potential relatives waits in line. Among them are Herbert, Olivia, the Twins, Rosie, and Mrs. Pearbottom. The latter looks like a not-so-secret agent as she scans for trouble.

The RV door bursts open. A euphoric man bounces out and down the rickety aluminum steps. He pats Herbert on the back and says, "These people are good, fella! Very good!"

He is followed by an angry, tattooed woman with her candy-eating daughter. "Wait up, Tanner! Genes aren't the whole story!"

"Oh?" he responds, "Now it's *Tanner* again? Not those other names you used for me?"

Herbert wants to hear more but his own party is ushered in.

Once inside he is asked to fill out numerous forms on several clipboards. He is stumped by the first question and confers with Mrs. Pearbottom. "For last name do I use the prior or my current one?"

"Bigglesby. But don't worry, only your DNA matters."

When the forms are complete, the Technician uses cotton swabs to collect saliva samples from Herbert, Olivia, and the Twins. Then they wait. And wait.

They try to amuse themselves with magazines, phones, entire books, whole series of books, and finally, by racing insects around an improvised track.

Herbert eventually concludes, "I think they may be afraid to give us the bad news." He stands up, hoping all will follow.

The Twins stand but none of the women do. Herbert assumes Olivia is sad as she continues reading her magazine. "At least we tried. And I must say, it was quite… *special* to have this… time of… at least *imagining* being a long-separated family that has finally been united. But sadly, life often disappoints us, young Lady."

Olivia doesn't look up from reading. "*Tranquilo, Papi*, just wait."

The males sit back down.

Olivia adds, "And no one expects you to suddenly just love me or any of us, out of the blue. It takes time. We have to be realistic."

Herbert and the Twins look at each other but say nothing. On a computer screen the results start to arrive.

The Technician says, "Ok, here we go." He sits and reads from the screen. "Herbert and Olivia... ready?"

"Yes!" she answers and makes sure Herbert is ready too.

The Technician announces, "You're… related!"

"I knew it!" exclaims Olivia. "I love you so much, *Papi!* Do you love me? How much? Do you truly love your little baby girl with all your heart? Can you even think of spending another whole day without me by your side? Or even an hour?"

Herbert doesn't have words. "I… Wow. This a game changer."

Mrs. Pearbottom can't hide her smile. "Mostly just way fewer games."

Herbert is exhausted. "What happened to taking some time, Daughter?"

"You're right, I know! I'm getting ahead of myself."

Rosie reassures her, "Don't beat yourself up, Hon. You have been longing for a father all your life. It's ok to have emotions."

"You are right about that, thank you." They hug.

The Technician continues. "Herbert and the Twins…" Herbert can't believe he's reading what is obvious. The boys hold their breath. "Related!"

"Yes!" says Wayne with a fist pull.

Woldecott is more pensive. "This is so trippy! To go from years and years of trying to find you and kill you, to now having you come watch our games and performances."

The Technician would love to inquire about the meaning of hunting and killing but the line outside is very long and he can't possibly stop and listen to every family's unique story.

Herbert gets up and shuffles to the door. "I'm sorry, I think I need a nap."

"Please wait, Sir. There's more still coming." The Technician reads additional results. "Ms. Rosie… you are *not* related."

"You tested her?" Herbert is annoyed.

Rosie is pleased and smiles shyly at Olivia. "I'm fine with that."

Olivia plays it neutral, unsure of what she wants in life beyond a father right now.

Rosie understands, *no pressure.* All is played in the blink of an eye.

The Technician continues reading his screen. "Mr. Bigglesby, you also matched with some other people in our database. I'll just serve it up to go."

The group expects to receive a single page but, once the printer starts, it spews out page after page of a very long list.

Herbert is nonchalant at first but grows uncomfortable and even sits back down. Mrs. Pearbottom is also surprised by the quantity.

The Technician explains, "We have a very extensive database."

"How much was it?" asks Wayne.

No one honors the question. Woldecott concludes, "It must be a trade secret."

Wayne sighs. "We're not even in this line of business."

Mrs. Pearbottom is sympathetic to Herbert. "A game-change indeed, Mr. Bigglesby. You may need help making room for all this."

The Technician staples the thick list together. Olivia grabs it before Herbert can. "Don't worry, Papa. My boys are really good at computers. We'll help you find each and every one of my brothers, sisters, cousins, and more."

Mrs. Pearbottom can't help a smirk.

Herbert looks depressed. He takes a deep breath and thinks, *When first it was displayed / I was mortified / Now I doubt you'll kill me / if I'm by your side.*

Somewhere a liked song by Gloria Gaynor (1978) starts up. The Cake version is worth adhering to as well (1996).

CHAPTER FIFTEEN

Fruit of the Loophole

The conference concluded, seniors are boarding buses. They hold overstuffed goodie bags. Some suck on lollipops promising memory enhancement, which could be a self-fulfilling prophecy; they will likely recall paying a lot for something so dubious.

Herbert stands waiting with Olivia, the Twins, and Rosie. Behind them are Mrs. Pearbottom, Claire, Olga, Senior Rita, Jake, and the other residents. The bus has yet to open its doors and welcome them.

Olivia speaks. "*Papi*, I'm still sad that you never checked in on mom while she was alive."

Herbert is defensive. "I know it seems rude, but if I had made contact it would have put her in mortal danger."

"Not if you had married her. It would not have been immoral then."

Mrs. Pearbottom comments, "I don't know if rude is the right word for a multi-decade neglect."

Herbert turns, "Excuse us, Peaches, this is a family conversation."

Ouch. Mrs. Pearbottom is taken aback but realizes he is not wrong. She bites her lip and checks in with her other seniors.

Olivia continues, "You could have taken us with you. And your agency would have protected us."

Herbert sees it differently. "I don't think I had that choice. They would have killed you both to get to me."

Olivia accepts his reasoning until he ruins it.

"Plus, I was living a very busy life."

Her face darkens. "How, giving more back rubs?"

Mrs. Pearbottom gives her an *attagirl* nod.

Herbert is still not quite sure what to call Olivia. "Uh, *daughter*, please. Try to imagine the positions your mother and I were in."

"Ew!" All the women react with distaste.

"Certainly not!" declares Mrs. Pearbottom.

Herbert continues with Olivia. "I realize it's hard to understand what was required in my work. Your mother had access to very valuable information and I wasn't going to give your stepfather a massage to get it."

Wayne only catches the last part. "Why not, Grampa?"

"I... We had a lot of judgment back then."

"Ok, stop!" pleads Olivia. "If we're going to make it as a family, we have to leave the past in the past. I have forgiven you… *Daddy*, and I want to build something special with you. For all of us. In some quiet place."

Herbert worries. "Quiet? How quiet? Why quiet?"

Rosie is almost too afraid to ask, "Will there be room for me there? I have nobody in my life. Only vegetables."

"Like Mrs. Pearbottom!" quips Herbert.

She turns and slaps his arm. "Oh hush, Herbert!"

Olivia jumps between them. "Don't hit my *Papa*!"

Herbert is delighted by her defense. After a brief stare-down, Mrs. Pearbottom turns away and resumes speaking to her vegetables.

"Rosie," begins Olivia. "You are welcome to be part of whatever this is. We're a modern blended family."

Herbert hates that expression and it's evident on his face, as if gnats landed in his mouth. He checks the bus door: it's still closed.

Rosie keeps selling. "I don't take up much space. And maybe I could raise some rabbits, or sheep, and we could live off the fat of the lamb."

Herbert cocks his head as he tries to recall something similar (Steinbeck, 1937). The women think he objects to Rosie having skin in the game (Demme, 1991).

Just then he sees Rebecca pitching her cruise to more prospects. *She is quite the looker,* he can't help thinking. He stands tall to appear sexy but then coughs.

Olivia positions herself to block Herbert's view. "*Papa*, tell Rosie to not even worry about it. Our house is her house."

"Huh? Sure. As you wish." He tries to see past her.

Olivia reacts vehemently. "We're right here, *Papi*! It's time to focus on us for a change."

"What?" Herbert snaps out of it.

Olivia rants in Spanish about having made a bad call in expecting more from this *disgusting old slick-fingered misogynist sperm imposer.*

The bus door finally opens. A senior with a walker can't quite navigate the steps and falls. We hear a lot of plastic and metal clacking as others try to help him. *This is going to take a while.*

Woldecott watches soccer on his phone. Someone scores a goal and he yells, "Yes!" Then he says, "Hey, *Grampa*! You could referee our matches!"

Alarmed, Herbert turns to Olivia, "Don't they have a father?"

"Yes, but he's in prison again," she answers. "For like 300 years. Till his execution. Unless the Stupid reform happens."

"What kind of stupid reform?" asks Herbert.

"There's a referendum about people with a low IQ. If they decide the person was too stupid at the time of the crime then they can't have a long sentence anymore."

Herbert has no words. *Great, that's my son-in-law.* He checks on the bus but still no progress there. "What were his crimes?" he asks.

"I've done worse," answers Olivia.

Herbert appreciates her attitude. "Is it ok to ask his name?"

"Wrong. But I really don't want to talk about him."

Herbert is annoyed and Woldecott sees it. "Jesus S. Wrong," he clarifies, sounding like he has a Spanish accent.

"That's what I've always thought," answers Herbert. "Given all the chaos in the world."

The Twins are blown away. "Wait, you've heard of him?"

Herbert tries not to laugh. "I think everyone has."

The Twins have never felt so proud. "We're his kids! Our names are Wrong too."

"I had assumed they were," replies Herbert.

Again, the Twins could not be more impressed. "Then why didn't you run when we showed up at Sunset?"

"I don't know. Actually, I do know." Herbert indicates Mrs. Pearbottom. "These people had me believing I was paranoid. But I knew I was right."

"And I know I'm Wrong!" answers Wayne.

"Yo, me too!" laughs Woldecott.

Olivia beams with pride. "My two Wrongs can make anything right!"

Her mind flashes to a video commercial with music reminiscent of AC/DC (1976). Olivia stares into the camera like a gangster and sings, "*Do you need sanitizing deeds done for the price of soil? / Perhaps you don't know whom to contract with? / My Two Wrongs can make it right.*"

The video cuts to the Twins, very young, doing martial arts and throwing knives and stars at inhuman dummies.

"Call today for a free consultation," says Olivia in the video. "Discreet. No traces left behind."

The ad ends with pallbearers carrying several caskets. "Ask about our group rates, too."

***

The bus line nudges forward. Herbert pulls away. "I'm sorry, this is moving awfully fast."

"But we've only gone like a foot in an hour," objects Wayne.

"What I mean is, I don't know if I can suddenly be a father and a grandfather. Or have a son-in-law in prison. This is all so foreign to me."

Mrs. Pearbottom looks empathic.

Olivia assures him, "But *Papi*, give it time! We all just have to *bond, just bond*!"

Rosie's eyes narrow and her jaw clamps tense. Herbert is alarmed. They make eye contact. Then Rosie breaks it with a smile.

Herbert relaxes and resumes breathing. Still, he wants to get out of this situation, this pressure, this loss of independence. He fixes his gaze on Rebecca, still selling her cruise to seniors.

Noticing him, she holds up her flier and flashes a nice smile.

DING! A shrill bell rings and Herbert is back in the boxing ring. Rebecca stands at the ropes as if the rail of a ship, with blue skies and lovely white clouds. "Tickets, please!" she says.

Herbert as referee gives her his ticket. She is delighted and gazes into his eyes. The sun sets behind her, her beauty all aglow.

The name of the cruise line is *Island Industries* and a song starts up, reminiscent of Kenny Rogers and Dolly Parton (1983). Rebecca and crew members are suddenly dancing and singing, "*Island Industries / That is who we are / Whether near or far / You won't even barf / Come and try our cruise / We'll fix all your blues / Island Industries.*"

The dancers hold up spyglasses while swaying their attractive bodies. *"Let's all spy on each other!"*

Back in line for the bus, Herbert puts his hands together and addresses his kin. "Listen, uh... *family*! I think we need to put a pause in this... *pause*. And take some time to absorb it all. Yes! Having a family is a big responsibility. It's not trivial. So, I think we should let it sink in before we do anything hasty."

He can't help another glance at Rebecca. She talks to another male, which bothers Herbert. He continues, "We can revisit this topic later when I can give it my full attention. But first, I have one final critical mission I need to *compete*. Or, complete."

His family looks at him askance.

"Mrs. Pearbottom knows what I'm talking about. Senior scams are out of control right now and we must stop them."

A surprised Mrs. Pearbottom turns to them. She has no idea what he is talking about.

Olivia calls out, "Daddy, you're lying! They don't even trust you with a motorized wheelchair, let alone a mission! And you don't owe them nothing! Not after that awful fake funeral they gave you. With your rubber dummy?"

Mrs. Pearbottom is offended. "That was no low-budget affair, Dear. Mahogany casket, embroidered silk lining–"

"Only your family cares about you!" insists Olivia. "Us! Not your *former employer*. Or your government. Or any healthcare system. They all *use* you and then they spit you out, *Papi*! Don't you see it?"

Herbert appeals to Mrs. Pearbottom non-verbally. She attempts to help. "Herbert, you really do need to stop so much activity and get some rest."

It's not what he wanted. "On the contrary, I am fine!" he declares. "And fit for duty!" He stands tall and turns to Olivia. "*Child*, it breaks my heart–"

"Oh, Daddy! It's ok!"

He repeats, "It breaks my heart that every day millions of seniors are being scammed out of their life's savings. I can't just sit back and ignore them!"

Mrs. Pearbottom and Olivia are confused. "You have before!"

Olivia becomes shrill. "You don't gotta care about those people! We are your mission now. Your family is your lifetime of adventure!"

Herbert looks for oxygen and spots Rebecca's hairline receding into the crowd.

"Excuse me!" Rosie's voice cracks and she clears her throat. Everyone turns to her, surprised. "Mr. Bigglesby, I believe you are mistaken. Dr. Singleton is *not* a scam. Sorry–No! I am not sorry! My therapist has me working on expressing my views more. That man is not a phony, just let him be."

Olivia is supportive. "I agree, Rosie! She's right, *Papi,* and we should pick a church to go to as a family."

Herbert is discombobulated. "A what? Look, I don't care about this preacher right now. There are other bigger scams going on right now, under our noses. I need to pick one."

The Twins look at each other and snort-giggle, pretending to pick their noses.

"I agree!" declares Rosie, enthused. "I'm itching to bust something up. Did you meet the smelly fabrics people? *Pew!*" She pinches her nose, not only for emphasis but because the same awful smell has arrived. She turns to find the source and sees Danny and Gunther loading a van with racks of clothing. "See?" Rosie points. "They're so sus!"

"Yeah, sus!" declares Wayne.

"No!" counters Olivia, blocking Herbert's view. "You don't gotta have no other mission right now! Just us!"

Herbert is already dismissive of that concern. "Suspicious clothing? I'm talking about big stuff!"

"I'm sure they have all sizes," says Wayne.

Olivia clutches Herbert by the lapels. "*Papa,* stop protecting strangers! Care about us for a change. We need time together!"

Herbert looks into her eyes. "Try to understand... my… *Child.* Look!" He points at the many seniors accepting Rebecca's fliers. "Look how naive and helpless they are! She must be interrogated, broken down till she reveals all and we put her boss behind bars!"

Mrs. Pearbottom nods. "Herbert, our superiors will never approve of this. The whole point is moot."

"Well, I don't approve of them! And I'm a free agent now. I am not being put under a rest again!"

Olivia startles. "You got arrested? Father in heaven, what is it with the men in my life? Why they all get caught?"

Mrs. Pearbottom clarifies. "Not that kind of a rest, Dear. Herbert needs to stay, ok?"

"A *staycation*!" supplies Woldecott.

"Plus we need to fix up our home because of some recent destructive events."

Rosie looks away, ashamed.

"Lucretia, please!" begs Herbert. "I need something real to do! Look at what the outdoors did for their Roosevelt. My savanna is foiling international crime!"

Olivia fears she's losing him. "You are not leaving me again, *Papi!* Or any of us!" She holds up the DNA list.

Whether anyone else actually sees it or not, just then Olivia breaks out into a music video with her Twins backing her. They lip-sync a song close to one by Cake (1998). "*I need your Army 'round me / I need your Naval clutch / I need your Airmen fighting / a great deal.*"

In the music video, Olivia becomes a barefoot child holding a dirty broken doll, avoiding shattered glass in a bombed-out Bolivian village. Planes, tanks, and ships blow up her country.

In contrast, a younger Herbert parasails off the coast of shiny wealthy Monaco with a sexy Persian woman.

Olivia sings, *"You tell me that you'll raise me well / you tell me you'll coach my games / but whenever I participate / you're off flirting with the moms who make concessions."*

Back on the bus line, Olivia lectures Herbert. "What do you think I don't understand, *Dad*? That even *now,* when we have a chance to start over and make up for the past, you're going to run out on us again?"

"He's not going anywhere!" insists Mrs. Pearbottom. "This whole conversation is ludicrous!"

"Run out?" asks Herbert. "No one is running out." Everyone looks at him in disbelief. "Running out of time, maybe. What are two weeks? We can pick up being a family after that."

Olivia mutters a stream of choice words in Spanish about the undependability of men and her own foolishness in thinking Herbert would ever change.

Mrs. Pearbottom puts her foot down after scratching an itch. "This cannot happen, Herbert! And stop torturing your daughter. Let others carry the baton already."

"The baton? *Le baton rouge!*" he pronounces with a thick slow accent. "Red from being violently taken from me!"

Not that again. Mrs. Pearbottom despairs of reaching reason with him. Olivia is in tears. Herbert is too annoyed for words. Rosie still watches Danny and Gunther loading up.

The Twins confer with their mother and produce a suggestion. "Uh, *Grampa*?" begins Woldecott.

"Do you also wish to lecture me?" asks Herbert.

"No, but we have an idea," answers Wayne.

Woldecott cuts right to it. "What if we come with?"

"*Come with*?" asks Herbert. "Is that like *forthwith*? Or wait, you want to accompany me on my secret, secret mission?"

Rosie wonders if she is welcome in the proposal.

Mrs. Pearbottom is shocked and frustrated. *It's an obvious no!*

Wayne responds, "Totally! We can help you take down the evil, dirty, awful, smelly, bad guys!"

"And Mom's still pretty handy with her hat," adds Woldecott.

Olivia wipes a tear. "I'm just not ready to lose you again, *Papa*."

Herbert looks at her, then at the boys, and then at Mrs. Pearbottom. He notices beautiful Claire as she waits in line with Olga. He searches out Rebecca one more time and sees her chatting with the last person he would ever want on Earth: *Jake Kimble! Ew! And his shirt is unbuttoned. He's trying to look sexy, disgusting!*

Herbert takes a breath and makes a proposal: "I might regret this but, how would you all like to experience a free cruise?"

Mrs. Pearbottom protests, "Herbert, you're not hearing me!"

The Twins do fist pulls. "*Yesolutely*! It's all-you-can-eat, right?"

"I'm sure! But you're going to have to work for it."

Olivia is delighted. "No problem! My two Wrongs will make everything right!"

"What kind of work?" asks Woldecott.

"Computery stuff, that sort of thing." Herbert looks around to ensure privacy and then conspires with them. "I need you to create magazine covers and articles that make it look like I went from modest wealth in the 1970s to becoming a billionaire and trillionaire over the past 40 years."

"More like 50." Mrs. Pearbottom couldn't help it.

"Fine! Can you Boys do that for me? On the information superhighway?"

"The which?" The Twins are genuinely thrown.

Their hipster mother clarifies, "The interwebs."

"Oh! Easy peasy. No zits squeezy!"

"Wonderful!" says Herbert. "Make me a CD-ROM of stories about all my major exploits."

Olivia's face goes dark. Woldecott jumps in.

"Grampa, why do they have to be seedy?"

Olivia is proud yet alarmed that he knows what that is.

Herbert clarifies, "A CD-ROM is a kind of disk. I can still say disk, can't I?"

Olivia smiles. "Oh! Those old things." The boys smile too but are unsure what any of it means.

Herbert continues explaining his plan. "I need to look incredibly rich so people will want to scam me out of billions."

For the Twins something still isn't clicking. Herbert asks their mother, "Well, do they know about space age technology or not?"

The boys are offended he would even question that part of their being, their existence, their very make-up.

"They can get it done," confirms Olivia. "Let me translate. Can you boys pound the web with Granpapi's fake fo-sho rick-rolling success (Astley, 1987) for the past nickel in time?"

"Oh, that? Cakeshine!" declare the Twins. "We just need some picaroos!" They whip out their cell phones and take pictures, saying things like, "We got you, Grampa! Manifest success!"

Herbert is unsure what any of it means but he trusts them. He sees Rebecca nearby and stops the Twins. "Hold on, hold on! Peaches, we're going to need some privacy. Can you get her inside?"

"That's going too far, Herbert."

"Forty meters, max!"

"Not that! You need to get back to your retirement. At Sunset."

"Oh, come now, Lucretia! It's too early for sunset, and we need to get to the bottom of these scams. Plus, I think you'll have a revolt on your hands if we don't all go, as a community."

He indicates his fellow residents holding cruise fliers. Mrs. Pearbottom understands.

"I promise I'll get some rest on board. Just please lead Ms. Holmeslyce away so we can do what we need to out here."

Olivia and the Twins silently appeal with puppy dog eyes. Mrs. Pearbottom finally concedes and approaches Rebecca.

"Ms. Holmeslyce, can your cruise handle an entire boatload of slow but lovable seniors?"

"Definitely!" She lets herself be led inside the building. "How big a commission–I mean community–are we talking about?"

The seniors spread the word with joy as they dance and board their buses. A song like, *Stayin' Alive* by the Bee Gees (1977) kicks up.

Moments later, and with the above song at full volume, Herbert and his family stand waving goodbye to their departing bus.

They then commence a full photo shoot. Herbert strikes various ridiculous poses. First, he looks like he could own a bus. Then, like he could own a whole fleet of buses, and then the Convention Center itself. Probably even the jet airplane passing overhead.

Olivia is quite thrilled and says it. "I am so thrilled by all this teamwork, Dad! What a family we are!"

Herbert smiles weakly. He appears wrinkly and bent over so Woldecott assures him, "Don't worry, Grampa, we can remove all your wrinkles and fix your posture–"

He straightens up, but not to the degree he believes. "What wrinkles? And nothing is wrong with my posture. Children, don't I need to be wearing different outfits?"

"We got all that. It won't look like your empire was built in a day."

"Indeed, Roman times had many parallels to mine."

"Times Ro' fo' sho'! Among other classic fonts." Woldecott keeps shooting as he speaks.

Herbert is delighted. "Great idea! Maybe the *Trevi Fountain*." He had not expected they'd be finishing each other's thoughts. "And how about the *Quattro Fiumi*?"

"Full speed! You'll go from a *Quattro* to a *Lamborghini*, then maybe do a *Lotus*."

"I hate yoga. Should we have a Bentley in the background? Or maybe a Rolls?"

"You got it, *Grahampops*!"

Despite the intergenerational disconnect they are working in sync. If this were a movie, we'd already be seeing a montage of magazine covers being generated that night. Over the course of decades, Herbert seems to have been featured in such world-renowned periodicals as, *Fortunate, Newswick, The Ergonomist, and Consumer Manipulation.* Each cover shows Herbert with a daring hairstyle, outfit, and luxury car from that period.

The first headline reads, *Herbie with His Loved Bugs Employs Thousands* (Stevenson, 1968). It shows a 1970s Herbert in front of an auto plant. Another is from the 1980s and has Herbert in front of the New York skyline then with the title, *Merger She Wrote!* (Fischer et al., 1984-1996). A third one says, *He Gets Knocked Down, But He Gets Up Again!* (Chumbawamba, 1997) and shows Herbert with a surfboard, covered in sand, ready to take on big waves (1990s). A fourth is from the 2000s; a robot service animal called a *Seeing iDog* stands under the headline, *Mr. Big's Vision Is Clearer Than Ever!*

Lastly, a fifth cover has the Twins standing on either side of Herbert, who sits on a gilded throne. The title reads, *There Are No Zeros in This Trillion-Dollar Company.*

Olivia says, "Make it *family.*" They are in Mrs. Pearbottom's office, using her big screen monitors and printer.

Woldecott fixes the last word. *There Are No Zeros in This Trillion-Dollar Family.*

Olivia beams with joy. Mrs. Pearbottom is also impressed.

Herbert appears to be having a sentimental moment and even wipes a tear. Olivia watches with pride as her boys await Herbert's judgment.

He finally renders it. "Well, Boys, if I haven't said it clearly enough already… I love… that you have these skills. You are hired!"

The women are disappointed.

The Twins high-five each other with glee.

Olivia sings to herself, *Oh, no, you can't speed it up. / It will just have to develop over time* (Holland et al., 1966).

Herbert looks for a slot all around the computer. "Ok, where does the disk come out?"

"*Grampops*, everything we've shown you is already everywhere."

"Don't speak gibberish. What do you mean?"

"All over the *world*," clarifies Wayne. "And back in time, too."

Woldecott adds, "If someone doesn't know you, just tell them to *Google* your name."

Herbert can't help a wry smile. "People google up my name all the time, without me asking."

"Cool," answers Woldecott.

Herbert cannot let it go. "Why, *Herbert Bigglesby* is about the worst name anyone could possibly have come up with. That alone almost did me in. Like that Ari Something, once said, I forget his name, *That's me with the coroner / losing all my living.*"

Mrs. Pearbottom and the others ponder his reflection.

Herbert smiles and says, "But tomorrow the tide changes."

This worries Wayne. "I hope the ship can still sail."

Somewhere, a hit song by R.E.M. (1991) plays for the reader's enjoyment while this chapter concludes.

CHAPTER SIXTEEN

The Perp-Driven Life

A luxury cruise liner is docked in a Mediterranean port. A song like Cake's, *Short Skirt/Long Jacket* (2001) kicks in nearby, perhaps on the Reader's device. Lyrics suggest, *She's inspecting the team / and tightening up protocols.*

This matches the energy of Rebecca, who marches along the boarding deck, giving final directions to crew members of various departments. She looks stunning in another cute sailor outfit.

She passes a sharply dressed team of organizers who welcome educators. Their banner reads, *Society for Unprincipled Principals (SFUP!)*. One attendee introduces another saying, "Wait till you see the magic of NEXPEL! You can pass any student, regardless of merit, and keep your funding coming. It even assigns autism and other disorders if you need a few extra million."

"Don't they ever catch on?"

"Are you kidding? I've filled seats with people who overdosed years ago."

"That's so creative!"

"There's more than one way to get a kitchen remodeled."

"Oh, and we've added another book-cooking class!" shares another leader. "It's called, *There's Safety in Numbers!*"

"Backed by lack of reprimand!" adds the first.

If this were a film, the camera operator would now realize she lost Rebecca, who reaches her employer, Mr. Devonheir Le Deuce.

In his mid-60's and with a full set of silver hair, he is the CEO of the healthsharing ministry that is sponsoring Rebecca's recruits.

"Ah, here you are," he greets her. "Just in time." He wears a white suit and waits to greet the seniors who will soon ascend the boarding ramp. "Now, where is that distracted side-hustling… ah!"

"*Zeh* pain! *Zeh* pain!" calls out Danny as he hobbles up the ramp with his cane.

Le Deuce is annoyed to see Danny wearing a similar white suit. He sing-songs, "You're *la-ate*!"

Danny matches his tune. "I had important business to *do-oo*, to make you *zeh mon-ey*." He takes his place next to him, looking like the *Fantasy Island* duo (Spelling & Goldberg, 1977-1984).

Le Deuce complains, "When I was your age, we had to climb rope ladders to get to where we are today."

"Last year?" inquires Danny.

"In dog years, you poodle."

Danny bites his tongue.

"There he is." Rebecca points out Herbert, who makes his way up the ramp with Olivia, Rosie, and the Twins.

Danny is skeptical, "I have seen *zhis Mann* before. He did not seem like a financial wizard."

Rebecca cautions him. "Don't be fooled by the appearance of family. I vetted him thoroughly last night."

Danny is quite alarmed. "*Vetted* him? With what? In *zeh* jacuzzi?"

"No! With water balloons," she mocks.

Le Deuce approves of her sarcasm.

Danny is confused until he realizes, "Oh, *zhis* is joke."

"I don't know how you got to be your ages without hearing of him. He pioneered like so many amazing things."

"Like Steve Jobs?" asks Le Deuce.

"Like, so many jobs! And even after failures and personal disgrace he rebuilt himself into what he is today."

Le Deuce is enticed. "Perhaps he can do more than merely keep us afloat."

Danny clutches the rail. "Why, is *zhere* a problem with *zhis* ship?"

"No, Danny. There is no problem with *zhis* ship."

Herbert and his people approach. "Ah, Mr. Bigglesby, my associates and I are so glad you could join us."

Le Deuce extends a hand and Herbert shakes it. "Thank you! Allow me to introduce my… *daughter* and her boys."

Olivia is thrilled by the public acknowledgment.

Danny, Olivia, and Rosie recognize each other from the conference and smile politely. Rosie covers her nose discreetly.

Herbert is not quite sure what to call her. "And this is…"

"Rosie!" She introduces herself, extending a hand. Le Deuce politely takes it and she unthinkingly crushes it, causing him to *yelp*. Olivia bumps her arm and she releases him. He massages his hand. She looks bashfully at her feet and whispers, "I did a bad thing."

Meanwhile, a bus arrives below. Mrs. Pearbottom, Claire, Olga, Jake, Senior Rita, and the other living Sunset seniors discharge from it. Herbert watches and does not hide his mixed reaction. "Great, the entire Sunset community has arrived."

Le Deuce says, "Mr. Bigglesby, Danny here will help you find your way."

"Are you some kind of guru?" asks Herbert of Danny.

The joke falls short. Danny clarifies, "He meant to your cabin."

"Oh, yes, of course. And I do hope I have my own separate one. We young people do like to do our own thing."

"Of course!" answers Le Deuce.

"You make a lot of *scents*," acknowledges Danny, handing out key cards. "So privacy is very important."

Herbert sniffs his lapel but finds nothing offensive.

"And soon you will be on all fours."

"Excuse me?" asks Herbert, adjusting a hearing aid.

Danny speaks louder, "You will all be on *zeh* deck four."

"Ah," answers Herbert. "And Ms. Holmeslyce? Where will she be, in case I have a burning issue?" He turns and smiles at her.

Olivia fumes.

"Burning like *zeh* U-T-I?" asks Danny.

He receives puzzled looks.

Rebecca answers apologetically, "Mr. Bigglesby, I'm afraid we've overbooked. So, I'll be sharing your cabin."

"Really?" Herbert is delighted.

Olivia mimics him. "Really?" Patricide crosses her mind.

"No, not really," answers Rebecca. "But I'll be around. And I'll be giving our first presentation at ten A.M. sharp tomorrow. Don't be late."

Herbert nods. "No chance of that, Sweetheart. I'd have to be dead or something!"

"Did I miss some good news?" Jake arrives with other seniors.

Rebecca, Le Deuce, and Danny greet them.

Herbert is snapped back to his current reality. "Hello, Jake. I'm so glad you could make it… up the ramp!"

"Nice to see you too, Herbert," answers Jake, hoping to look like the better man.

"Right *zhis* way, Mr. Bigglesby." Danny leads the way, hobbling on his cane. "Ow! Ow! Ow!"

Before he follows, Herbert comments to the Twins, "There's something in the way he moves."

"Like no other brother," says Wayne (cfr. The Beatles, 1969).

Herbert is alarmed. "Why would you say that?" He also asks Olivia, "Why would he say that? Is he on the list?"

"I don't know, what's his name?" she asks.

"Danny something," Herbert recalls.

"Oh, right! *Rysin*, he said at the convention." She flips to the R's.

"You've met him?" he asks.

Rosie answers, "Yes, he was hustling fabrics and a weird toy."

"What kind of weird toy?" asks Herbert, intrigued.

"Never mind!" Olivia holds up the list. "There are no Danny Rysins or Rosens, or anything similar on here."

"That's good," says a relieved Herbert. "No resemblance."

"Sure thing, *Papa*."

In a long corridor, Danny leads Herbert to his door. They enter what is a large luxury suite, with a king-size bed and portraits on the walls. They are of little-known siblings or cousins like the *Mona Liam* and a car mechanic named *Nick Jagger*. Every eyeball in the portraits sparkles with a camera lens.

Herbert is enthused with the portraits. "Ah, I'm in the company of legends." He does not seem to notice specifics.

In a dark room, several video monitors display Herbert as he looks up at the cameras. The monitors are labelled in Sharpie on masking tape: Mona, NickJ, Himmler, and a few others. An empty chair and an open box of Milk Duds sit unattended.

In his cabin, Herbert studies the portrait of Heinrich Himmler. Danny preempts any question with, "No, *zhere* is no relationship. But everyone just assumes. I do not understand it."

Herbert cranes to look through a high porthole. "I didn't realize I'd be under observation."

"Oh, *zhis* is nonsense!" assures Danny. "*Zeh* older people always think *zhat!* Believe me, no one is interested in your private affairs."

"I'm pretty sure that's an Observation Deck up there."

"Oh, *zhat* meaning! Yes. Keep *zeh* curtains drawn."

"They can watch all they want!" answers Herbert. "I have nothing to hide. Fit as a fiddle."

Danny tries to undo the face he just made. "Even so, please do not feel like you must take off all your clothes. Ever."

Herbert moves on. "And where might I find a potent potable?"

"*Zhere.*" Danny points to the lavatory. "And everywhere. All equipped to handle whatever you may have in storage for *zhem.*"

"No, where can I get a drink? Don't tell me this is a dry cruise."

"Oh, *zhere* is a bar one deck up. Take *zeh* elevator to *zeh* left when you exit." He leaves, distracted by his cell phone vibrating. "Goodbye for now!"

As he closes the door, Herbert mutters, "That's *aft*, you nitwit."

Danny re-enters, "What did you say?" He still checks his phone.

"Nothing. There was a *draft*."

"Ah, yes. Sometimes *zeh* Fatherlands must compel *zeh* young men to do *zheir* duty. When *zhey* do not volunteer."

"I see. Do you know if Ms. Holmeslyce frequents the bar?"

"I do not know, *zhere* are five of *zhem*."

"Five Ms. Holmeslyce's?" Herbert is thrilled by the possibilities.

"*Nein*!" Danny checks an irritating text.

"Nine?! I was afraid you might not even have any bars out here."

Danny nods and shakes his phone for emphasis. "Sir, we have five bars! Can you hear me now?!"

"Oh, yes, that's much better."

Danny fears for Rebecca and says, "But please, do not molest my colleague any more *zhan* necessary. She should enjoy her time here when she is not working."

"Oh, I agree," assures Herbert. "I know all about self-care."

"How enlightened of you." Danny turns to leave.

Herbert remembers to ask, "By the way, do you have a last name? And maybe a social security number?"

"*Zhat* is quite intrusive, Sir."

"So it is, so it is. But you don't get to be this healthy, wealthy, and wise without knowing a great deal about people."

"You do not need to know *zhis* thing about Danny Reisenschein, eight, four, seven, Oh no! Five, three, nine—*Schweinhund!* (Call & Keller, 1981). I almost said it all! Here in *zhis* corner!" (R.E.M., 1991).

Herbert ponders his name. "Reisenschein? Don't tell me you're a peppy German in the morning."

"*Nein!* I am from Austria! And I have cramps in *zeh* morning!"

"I see. Where exactly?"

"My stomach, my back, my feet."

"No, I mean, where in Austria?"

"Why do you ask *zhis* thing? I will answer no more personal questions. See you tomorrow at ten A.M. sharp."

"I'll be there early," assures Herbert. "To get a good view of everything Ms. Holmselyce has to offer."

Danny controls his temper and says nothing out loud. He hobbles away on his cane saying, "*Auf Wiedersehen*! Ow! Ow! Ow!"

Not a happy cramper, thinks Herbert.

***

Later in a bar Herbert sits alone at a table, keeping an eye on the entries. Two empty chairs face him. He is freshly bathed and looks as sharp as he can in his old tuxedo. The place is filling up but still no sign of Rebecca.

A song in the background has a refrain, *I Suffer That Emotion* (cfr. Robinson & The Miracles, 1967). Lyrics wonder if, *Perhaps you'll want to shake or hold my hand / But only for one afternoon without recurrence.*

A few tables away, Mrs. Pearbottom chats with two men. She looks far more attractive than before; the exhausted matron stayed ashore. Her gentleman callers are only in their 50s and 40s.

An attractive young waitress approaches Herbert, "Ready?"

"Possibly. I've been waiting for a friend."

She scans the area. "What do they look like?"

"A lot like you. Won't you sit?"

"Oh, that's not allowed. Do you need more time?"

"Is that something you can arrange?"

She doesn't follow.

"Never mind. Vodka martini, shaken not stirred up. And no fruity girly flavors."

"Coming right up." She leaves to get it.

A thin young woman saunters into the bar. She carries a stylish custom-made handbag from an artist the author recommends.

Herbert tries to make eye contact but she doesn't look his way. Then an attractive young man meets her and leads her to a table. Herbert is disappointed.

"Can I buy you a drink?" A woman in her 60s stands across from Herbert's table.

"Do I look like a scientist to you?" he responds.

The woman is taken aback. "I don't know."

"Well, I'm not into carbon dating."

The woman leaves, miffed, while a very young one enters. She scans the bar, looking sexy and confident. When she notices Herbert's leering stare she tears up and runs out crying, "Mommy!!!"

Next, another older woman approaches, ready for a good time. She has already had a few drinks and sits without waiting to be asked. "A charming man like you should not be drinking alone."

"I agree," responds Herbert. "Will your granddaughter be joining us?"

The woman removes herself immediately, bumping into things as she stumbles out, inebriated.

Another woman in her 70s approaches. Herbert puts up a hand, "Madam, I am already hard of hearing. I wouldn't want people to think I'm blind, too."

She shuffles away, offended.

"Is this seat spoken for?" It's Mrs. Pearbottom.

"I'm afraid so, *Peaches.*"

She indicates the other chair. "This one too?"

"I don't mean to be rude, but I think it's best if our relationship remains professional."

Mrs. Pearbottom perseveres. "I am only asking because my friend Greg over there needs a chair." She points to her table, which now has four gentlemen callers. Greg may not even be 30 yet.

Herbert is speechless. "Fine, take it. But promise me you won't fall for some adolescent gold-digger."

"And why exactly would you care?"

"Oh, come now. I might have been sore the other day but we mostly look out for each other."

"Is this forgiveness?"

"I don't know." He shifts uncomfortably. "Does everything need to be formally stated, your Ladyship?"

"I'm sorry, forgive me—I mean, take your time! In forgiving me. Or not. As you wish."

She drags the chair but Greg is suddenly at her side lifting it for her. Herbert can hear him ask, "So, Lucretia, what's your favorite *Minecraft* mod? Or are you more of a Roblox woman?"

Mrs. Pearbottom manages to smile with her lips but can't quite convince her eyes. She looks back at Herbert but his chair is now empty. She sees him shuffling out the door.

The song overhead seems to swell. "*I pick at that erosion…*"

CHAPTER SEVENTEEN

Family Time

Olivia and the Twins knock on Herbert's cabin door. As he rounds the hallway corner coming back from the bar, he sees them and tries to retreat but Olivia spots him.

"Hi Daddy!"

"Oh, goodness," he answers politely. "Is it time for a… family activity of some sort?"

Wayne answers, "No, Sir! We're reporting for duty!"

"Shhhh!" Woldecott cuts him off since other passengers are walking by. "He meant *Call of*, Grandfather! They also have a game called, *Shuffleboard*."

The passersby look back, judging them.

"Oh, I am well acquainted," defends Herbert.

Wayne worries he gave offense. "Oh no, it has nothing to do with how you walk, Grampa."

"I understand! Thank you! I just don't care for it as a pastime."

With strangers no longer in sight, Woldecott whispers, "We want to help you with your mission, Gramps!"

"It's so cool to be here with you!" adds Wayne.

Olivia is proud of them. Herbert is uncomfortable.

"Tonight we should all just get acclimated. Not draw attention."

The boys are disappointed. Olivia urges him.

"Dad, they just want to spend time with you. Show them something you do."

"Yeah! Anything! We're here to help."

Herbert hesitates. It would never have occurred to him to ever share his trade with these people. *And who are they, really? Killers of Bob! And Downright, scary. Me too if they were better at it! But we're family now. Me! A family?*

"Unless you're too rusty," interrupts Woldecott. "No pressure."

Olivia smiles, knowing her father's pride won't allow that.

"Rusty? I'm not the one who lost an old man on a train."

"That was good, Grampa," says Wayne.

"I suppose I'm not above showing off. Would it interest you?"

"Absa-totally!" a Twin exclaims.

Olivia is pleased. "Oh, *Papa*, it's our time together that counts, not any one specific activity."

"Hold on! I don't do filler espionage. This is important stuff."

"Sorry, Papa."

Herbert softens. "Ok, we're going to enter my cabin very quietly and look for what we in the trade call bugs!"

The Twins look at each other and Herbert assumes they're confused. "They're not actual insects. Electronic listening devices."

"No way!" The boys try to look impressed but also sneak peeks at their mom. She conveys for them to be nice.

Herbert continues. "Follow me very quietly and only do what I do." He opens the door and steps inside as stealthily as he can.

Woldecott quietly asks Olivia, "He knows we're not five, right?"

Olivia twists his earlobe. "There will be no disrespecting *Tata*!"

Woldecott rubs his ear where the redness will remain.

From inside his room, Herbert turns back and uses military commando gestures. The Twins pretend to understand but then enter his cabin much more stealthily, using advanced dance moves. They cover for each other as they move.

In the cabin with the monitors, Gunther tries to learn their dance moves. The Twins navigate an invisible array of lasers.

Herbert finds it odd but lets it go. *They're just kids,* he thinks. To impress them after they are done, he turns on a portable *faux* laser array. Gunther and the Twins are impressed. Herbert turns it off and points to a lamp shade.

"Eh-hem! It's a little dark in here!"

"Yeah! Some light would be good, Grampa!" answers Wayne, playing along.

"Come help an old man," he beckons. He positions them in a way that blocks the cameras.

Danny arrives in the surveillance cabin with a soda. "What did I miss?"

Gunther gives up his seat. "They play a dance game. Like Twister but with lights." He lies down for a nap.

"I see. Except, not really." Danny leans over as if it will help him see around the Twins and find Herbert.

Herbert looks under the lampshade but finds nothing. He then turns it on. "There, that's better!"

Next, he repositions the Twins to block him while he checks under his nightstand; again nothing. He then peeks under his writing desk and checks a wall socket too; still nothing.

Danny can't see any of it and is frustrated.

Olivia studies the paintings. On the monitors, her face does not show any reaction other than appreciation of art. She then takes a photo of a portrait with her phone. Danny instinctively combs his hair but then recalls she cannot see him.

Herbert picks up his cabin phone. The mouthpiece is not the old unscrewable type so he has no idea how to open it. He hangs up and it suddenly RINGS, startling him. He answers by speakerphone and winks at his grandsons so they can learn.

"Eh-hem. Mr. Bigglesby's cabin."

"Mr. Bigglesby, are you having an amazing time? This is Ronald with Guessed Services!"

"Oh, I'm so glad you called, but there's no need to guess, Ronald." To the Twins he adds, "They never get it right."

Ronald asks, "What was that? I am calling you today to schedule your completely intrusive free prostate exam!"

"I warned you! That's a terrible guess, Ronald!"

Olivia thinks otherwise but Herbert turns away from her.

"Ronald, perhaps this is too advanced for your management team but you could always *ask* what we want instead of guess!"

"Eh-hem! Sir, I can't really deviate from the script," Ronald confesses. "Our prostate exams are entirely complimentary!"

"Not to me they're not! I can't think of a single thing they go with. Except maybe a man-diaper but thankfully I'm not there yet."

"I think you should get one," opines Olivia.

The Twins look at Herbert's lower half. "He looks dry, Mom."

"Thank you, now excuse me!" Herbert picks up the phone to finish privately.

The Twins get the hint and move away to look at the paintings.

Herbert continues, "The thing is, Ron, I'm still using it." He pauses to let Ron speak, then answers, "I'm sorry, but thank you anyway." He returns the phone to its cradle.

Olivia is disappointed. "Dad, you really should take better care of yourself."

The Twins giggle and Herbert turns to see what they are doing. They snap pictures of each other imitating the poses in the paintings. Danny is offended, even horrified by the irreverence.

"Boys, come on, let's continue," says Herbert.

They stop but Olivia is not finished. "Dad, seriously, your health is important," she insists.

"Daughter, that well may be, but I don't want to be a part of every new fad in healthcare."

"What are you talking about?" she asks.

"What a stupid proud man," says Danny. He pops a Milk Dud into his mouth and chews it.

Herbert rants. "All my life it's been, *Butter*, then, *no butter*! And *milk*, then *no milk*. Oh wait! Milk is back again! Maybe a bunch of dairy heirs got together. Then another group rushes to take the lead out of our paints. It's nonsense! I've had more lead in me than–"

The phone RINGS. Herbert answers on speaker. "I do hope this isn't Ronald again, trying to get a look at my prostate."

Ronald is flustered. "What? No! I'm sorry?"

"Well, thank you for that acknowledgment," answers Herbert. "It means a lot to me. We all make mistakes. But don't worry about it for another second. No enlarged feelings over here."

"Thank you, Sir."

"Dad, get the free test!" pressures Olivia. "You only live once and I've missed most of it!"

Herbert appears determined to resist but finally concedes and picks up the receiver. "Just a second, Ronald." He goes with his gut, using it to cover the mouthpiece. "Daughter, perhaps you and the boys can afford me some privacy?"

"Of course, Daddy! Come on boys! We'll wait in the hall."

They exit the cabin and Herbert waits for the door to click shut. He then speaks quickly and quietly into the phone. Danny leans in to hear better. Olivia does too, in the hallway. Her boys are happily on their phones.

"Ok look, Ron. If you really want to nail this service thing, which I believe you do, how about you send a particularly hot dish to my cabin tonight, say about nine PM?" He looks at the door to confirm it's still closed.

In the hallway Olivia's face darkens as she listens. She gently tries the door but it's locked.

"What sort of dish?" inquires Ronald.

Olivia rattles the door. Herbert turns away and speaks more urgently. "Perhaps Ms. Holmeslyce is available? I have some very important things to discuss with her."

Danny is unfazed. "Yah, good luck with *zhat*." He sips his soda.

Olivia's wrestling with the door grows louder.

Ronald laments, "Sir, I am only able to help you with your health and fitness goals."

"And what a bullseye that would be!" answers Herbert. "It would restore my youth by 30 years!"

The deadbolt retracts and the door opens. Woldecott steps aside with his device and Olivia storms in. She tries to grab the phone but Herbert turns this way and that, keeping it out of her reach.

Olivia tickles Herbert and he laughs, "Ha!"

"I'm sorry?" asks Ronald.

"Hoo… ha!" Herbert squirms away. "Ronald, please follow through—hee hee, stop it!—on this very important preventative healthcare measure. Hoo! And I'll be sure to express my fondest appreciation for your superiors."

Olivia manages to terminate his bad call.

"What is your problem, Daughter!" Herbert barks. "You asked me to take care of my health!"

"I heard you, Dad! I meant get real tests, not that!"

"Seniors have the right to have a say in our healthcare!"

"That girl is a third of your age, Pops! If not a fourth!"

"Yes! A force to be reckoned with! Have you forgotten why we're here?" He suddenly remembers why they are there.

Olivia does too. "*That* is not why we're here!"

"On the contrary!" protests Herbert, hoping to salvage this situation. "I'm here because I have a lot of money to invest if I can only find a worthy cause, and I believe Ms. Holmeslyce is one."

Olivia is disgusted. "Your grandbabies are her age!"

"What is age, anyway? We're not supposed to be so maniacal about those constructs anymore."

"Age is not a construct! And how can you show so little change in 50 years? Aren't you supposed to mature?"

"Indeed, I'm a fine wine! Let others be all piss and vinegar. She is gracious and I'm not going to discriminate against inexperience."

The boys knock and enter without waiting for an answer. "Are you done yet? What is taking so long?"

Olivia continues, "Oh, Papa please! Can't you invest in us for a few days?"

"I am doing that! We're almost done, boys."

Wayne plays on his phone while Woldecott takes an interest in the dolphin painting.

Herbert continues, "You knew I'd be working!"

"I'm so freaked out, Daddy! I almost wish I never found you. If you're going to stay like this."

They have hit an impasse and turn away from each other. After a moment, Woldecott breaks the tense silence.

"Hey Grampa, one of these paintings is not like the others." He gestures at the dolphin.

Herbert is jolted back to the world he knows best. "Don't be silly! Of course it is. It's *avant garde*!"

"I prefer *mocha*."

Herbert assures him, "Every MOCA has works like this." He positions the Twins to block the cameras again.

Danny tries to see around them but cannot.

Herbert feels around the edges of the dolphin painting and calls out, "Bingo!" but regrets it and tries to cover with, "Is a game-oh! That I like to play-oh at the nursing homo…"

Danny stops chewing his Milk Dud mid-Dud.

Herbert senses discomfort and tries to fix it. "I meant nursing home-*though*. Though, of course, *homo sapiens* are my kind of people. Technically."

"Sure, when *zhey* aren't being *zeh Homo Arrogans*," opines Danny.

Somewhere, a chimpanzee wears a t-shirt that says *Homo Arrogans* and has a man in a lab coat playing electric guitar.

Herbert continues, unsure when to stop rhyming or reasoning. "So maybe we could all play bingo, some time-oh!" He peels away a long black wire from the frame. The Twins are genuinely impressed.

"Great idea-O, Daddy-O!" fills in Olivia, trying to help out-O. "I bet they have it here-O. On the ship-O. For after a Hungry, Hungry Hip Replacement."

The Twins look at her, *happy she doesn't post online-O.*

Herbert says, "Oh, goody, let's play that soon. Not that we need to win a lottery! You know, kids, I'm not sure you understand just how much money I have."

He gestures for them to follow him into his bathroom, which they do. "The truth is, I have so much money and so few ideas about what to do with it all. So sometimes you just have to wait for the universe to show you a sign, especially if you're *flush* with cash."

The boys smile as Herbert opens the toilet seat, suspends the mic inside, and flushes.

Danny rips off his headphones in agony. His tinny speakers emit the tail end of a very loud flush. "I hate *zhis* man!" he complains. "He better be filthy stinking rich. Or just rich, no filth, no stink."

Herbert uses the toilet seat to trap the mic mid-bowl. Now every activity there will be communicated to anyone willing to listen. Herbert flushes again.

"And that, kids, is how you deal with unwanted followers."

"Hard stop," says Woldecott. "Why would anyone want to limit their number of followers?"

Wayne agrees. Herbert looks at them with disbelief.

Olivia expresses a concern. "Dad, are you not worried about all the cameras?" She tries not to look out at the portraits.

Herbert shrugs his shoulders. "No, I'm used to it. It comes with being important. And good looking. Plus, without sound, we can throw them off. So please act completely unaware."

The Twins immediately turn to the portraits.

In the surveillance room Danny feels caught, with Devil Dog crumbs all around his mouth. He chews slowly and puts the remainder down. Herbert looks up at a camera as if judging him.

Olivia beseeches Herbert. "Dad, I really need you to do something for me."

Danny puts his earphones back on but can only hear murmurs. He zooms his cameras in on what become the huge lips of Herbert and Olivia. Herbert's teeth are quite yellow and crooked.

Olivia asks, "Boys, can you go back into the hallway for a minute?"

Danny reads her lips. "Good mother."

Wayne asks, "Why?"

"And it's never a minute!" complains Woldecott. "Your minutes take hours!"

"Still, I need to talk to *Granpapi* alone. Go practice some fatal death moves."

"Ok, fine." The Twins resignedly moonwalk out.

When the door closes, Herbert inquires, "Now what am I doing wrong?"

Even Danny feels a tinge of sympathy for the old man.

Olivia softens. "Dad, I know you've lived a certain way all your life. And I realize people don't just change overnight."

"Speak for yourself," reacts Danny. "Only *zeh* weak people lack discipline to change."

"No, they don't," responds Herbert, who can't help a glance at a portrait.

Danny wonders if Herbert somehow heard him; he crumples up his finished Devil Dog wrapper.

Olivia continues. "My boys–your grandsons!–are still very impressionable young men, innocent in so many ways–"

"Apart from the *errands* you've had them do."

"I'm not talking about business! I cannot stand the thought of you and her, or with anyone her age. It's too traumatic for me."

"Traumatic?" Danny is annoyed, like an expert doubted at a Thanksgiving dinner with extended family. "What do *zhese* people know about *zeh* pain of trauma?"

Herbert cannot believe her either. However, before he speaks again, he finds a food menu and covers his mouth like an NFL coach on TV. Danny is frustrated by the cover.

Herbert proceeds, "Daughter, two weeks ago I did not care one whit about seniors being scammed. But it has dawned on me more and more that I can no longer just sit back and ignore it."

Olivia covers her ears. "Stop rationalizing! You remind me of their father! And they shouldn't be my age either," she declares.

"Why are you so hung up on age? There is an evil to be righted, and it's irrelevant that a tool of the ruthless scammers happens to be a young attractive lady." Herbert lowers his menu. "But for the record, Daughter, exactly how young are you?"

Danny leans in, hoping to learn her age as well.

"Fifty-five," she says, her lips huge on the screen.

Danny approves. "Not bad looking, and she likes *zeh* Beetles!"

"But I'll be fifty-six in–"

"Never mind!" interrupts Herbert. "Fifty-five is already quite a big ask you are… asking of me."

"I realize this is new for you, Papa, I really do," she validates. "And I wouldn't think it my business, normally. But then it turns out that the flirting, dirty, unfiltered, old man is my dad! And we're trying to be a wholesome family."

Herbert is saddened by these new demands.

Olivia tries to soften it. "We're making sacrifices too, you know. Not very long ago I wanted to murder and chop you up into little pieces for the rodents in the dumpsters."

Herbert looks aghast. Olivia realizes she may have said too much for the cameras.

Danny is only the more impressed. Who is *zhis* woman?

Olivia continues. "But see? I gave up that hunt." She then covers her mouth with a menu in case it's not too late.

Danny ponders her words. "Who can give up *zeh* hatred so fast?" He blows into his spinning Swapstic8 toy.

Herbert lowers his menu, perhaps soliciting bro-support. "Daughter, I do appreciate your willingness to forgive and forget, but please don't make me seem like such an anomaly. Men have always been older than their mates, historically speaking. It's nature. Many women used to die mid-course, leaving their husbands with no other option but to marry the inexperienced, young, adolescent nanny governess. Whose status would be instantly elevated, no longer rude or impoverished. Men have had to bear that burden, bringing these naive young women up to speed, and with no thanks from society. Only judgment and ill-will, looking back centuries later and out of context."

"How far back are you going, Mr. Dickens? 1855?"

Danny chuckles, "She is feisty!"

"Polio is doing better now, too, Pops. In case you were wondering."

Herbert feels a certain pride. "I can see my own DNA talking."

Olivia is touched by the compliment. She fixes her hair-tie, inadvertently flexing her muscles. Danny is delighted. "Papa, I'm not just all brawn and brute strength."

"I realize that," answers Herbert. "But I am not quite sure how to address all your concerns on the fly. On my fly, in particular. When I welcomed you and the boys–" He suddenly grabs the menu again and blocks his lips. Olivia follows suit.

Danny is annoyed but can't help thinking they're going to order food. "I recommend *zeh* chicken pot pie. It's very good. Not too watery."

Herbert continues behind the menu. "When I invited you and the boys, I did not anticipate you would expect me to so suddenly change all my ways, overnight. It could be disastrous."

Olivia lowers her menu. "Oh blah, blah, blah, Dad!"

Danny is confused.

Herbert lowers his menu too. "I am not saying I won't *ever* change. Just not this week. I need to let it all sink in."

Danny turns to his porthole for reassurance. Then he wonders, "What did she ask him to order?"

Herbert insists, "I think it best to leave this topic alone until we're back on dry land."

Olivia changes her tact. "It's not like I don't understand, Papa."

He becomes hopeful. "It isn't? You do?"

"Of course!" She re-blocks her lips with her menu.

Danny leans to the side but remembers it won't help.

"This Ms. Holmeslyce may have crucial information we need, in order to save seniors from losing their life savings."

"Exactly! I'm so glad you understand!" confirms a relieved Herbert. He covers his mouth. "And I realize I could be wrong. She might not even be part of it, we just don't know yet. She could be anything from a cold-blooded killer, to a scam artist herself, to just an innocent college student doing a summer *fling-ternship* with Mr. Le Deuce. None of it is clear yet."

Olivia is disgusted. Danny is uncomfortable too, based on her reaction. She continues playing up the complex dilemma.

"It must be so hard, Dad, to want to protect not only victims, but also misguided youth. Like me, she may also have had terrible unthinkable experiences as a child that are not yet resolved."

"No, I don't get that vibe," dismisses Herbert. "She seems like a healthy, well-adjusted woman to me, as they say."

"Still!" Olivia counters. "We're a family, and I think we should work together. I can relieve you of the less-than-honorable and even shameful tasks. The things that are frowned upon these days."

"Relieve me?!" The thought is so unwelcome that he forgets to keep his lips covered. "No way, *Jose*! I mean, Olivia. What I mean is, that's a kind offer, but I am not one to shirk my duties."

He re-covers his mouth, which frustrates Danny. "*Schweinhund!* I knew we needed more microphones. And *zhey* are so cheap now!"

Gunther is asleep in the background. Danny opens a drawer and digs out a stethoscope. "Good, I did bring it!" He pops a final Milk Dud and exits the room, hobbling with his cane and muttering his usual, "Ow, ow, ow!"

Olivia continues. "Dad, I think it's wonderful that you want to stop scammers. But please stop creating more tragedies like my life story for countless children."

Herbert realizes he will not get his way.

Olivia offers a proposal. "What I propose is this. That I, myself, take Ms. Holmeslyce down to the engine room, where it's nice and loud, and essentially private. And then with my own tested methods

I will learn everything she knows. Plus, she'll avoid developing any unhealthy attachment to you and thus avoid everything my mother went through. Then she'll probably go on to make better choices for the next 50 years. It's a win-win-win my way."

Not for me, thinks Herbert. "On the contrary, I think a kinder, more uncle-like approach is better. I'll set her on my knee, give her a treat or two, and tell her some stories. Then she'll unveil herself–"

Olivia shuts her eyes and ears. "No! I do not want to picture your methods, Papa!"

"Daughter, the beauty of my softer touch is that she won't even know she's given anything away! She'll be happy. And then only the bad guys will get hurt, while she sees what a thoughtful, mature man can be and not waste any more time on young idiot losers."

Olivia can't bear it. "But Dad, be realistic! Even best-case scenario, you'll break her heart! And then she'll suffer like mama did. Just let me do it my way. I promise I won't leave her permanently disfigured. Everything will heal up nicely, I guarantee it!"

"That's… No!"

As the Twins listen through the door, Danny comes hobbling with his stethoscope.

"What is going on here? Our guests must have absolute privacy!" He steadies the swinging stethoscope.

"Oh, it's just our mom and grandad talking."

"Show *zhem* some respect. Go play in *zeh* pool, perhaps?"

"We did that already," answers Woldecott.

"Well give *zhem* some space." He shoos them.

The Twins move down a few doors but then wait.

Danny wants to put his stethoscope to the door but he can't do it with the Twins so close by. He sighs and limps away, "Ow! Ow! Ow! Don't worry about me!"

The boys smirk at each other.

Herbert tries to end the conversation. "Look, I'm not rejecting your help, Daughter. And by the way, it *would* be helpful if the boys weren't told false things about me. So maybe take *them* down to the engine room and look around. They should have a good time too."

He tries to reach the door but Olivia blocks it. "Papa, please! No more women under seventy!"

"Seventy?! I'm not an embalmer!"

"Fine, sixty-five!"

"Earlier you said fifty-five."

"Deal!" She opens the door, "Boys, we're all done here! You can come in now."

"Hang on kids!" Herbert can't believe she tricked him. He slams the door before the Twins can enter.

"Those numbers are for *after* this cruise."

"No, Daddy. It starts today, here, now."

"You are a difficult child."

"I just don't know what I'll do if you go back to your old ways. It would mean you were fine with what happened to me, and to my mom, and to Danny, and to so many others!"

"Why Danny?" He covers his lips. "You found Reisenschein on the list?"

Olivia covers her mouth too. "No, but he doesn't know who his father was either. He understands my plight."

"I see."

Olivia is bothered. "Are you really ok with all the orphans and widows and broken homes?"

"My goodness, Child, you make me sound like a serial killer."

"Serial something, *Papa*."

Herbert pauses. "This is clearly very important to you."

"It is, Dad."

Herbert's shoulders sag. "Fine. I will agree to… I don't know, *discourage* the young lady–"

"No! You need to stop her! And yourself. No funny business."

Herbert toys with the cyanide compartment on his ring. It's still empty. "Fine, I will not let her have her way with me."

"Nor you with her."

"Oh, very well," he concedes.

"I appreciate it, Papa, I truly do." She gives him a hug. He can only return a modest squeeze. "Papa, you give me hope. You can still be the noble brave Dad I need in my life. Soon I can finally hold my head up high and say, *That's my Papa.*"

Herbert cannot imagine when or where she would ever need to say such a thing. He looks depressed.

Somewhere *Tragedy* by the Bee Gees (1979) begins to play.

Olivia opens the door and Wayne enters. "That took forever!"

Woldecott follows. "So, has Grampa agreed not to bang the beautiful Becca babe?"

Olivia is horrified.

Wayne puts him in his place. "Don't be crude, Bro!"

Olivia is impressed until he adds, "Grampa, do you want one of us to do the deed and find out what she knows?"

Olivia is devastated. "Stop! No! Look what you've done to my poor, innocent lambs!"

"They came this way!"

"Do not go near her, young men. That is an order."

"Yes, Ma'am," the Twins oblige. "Understood."

Danny re-enters his surveillance room. Gunther snores.

Herbert needs this depressing day to end. "Listen, I hate to be a party pooper but I'm a pretty pooped part of this party right now. Can we call it a day?"

"Already?!" Olivia was hoping for more family time. "Don't you want dinner? We can order room service and play board games!"

"I think I'm ready for bed. Alone! Just me sleeping in here."

"Ok, Grampa. Let's go, Mom." The boys lead Olivia out. "See you tomorrow."

When they close the door Herbert looks for something to throw or smash against the wall. He settles for extending his cane and beating his mattress a few times.

Danny notes the aggression. "*Zhis* is not surprising. He is a frustrated old man."

CHAPTER EIGHTEEN

The Pitch

The next day, about 300 baby boomers load up on a buffet breakfast. Among them are Mrs. Pearbottom, Jake, Senior Rita, and other Sunset seniors.

Rebecca stands at the other end of the room, reviewing her talking points on a laptop. She looks amazing again, wearing another stunning outfit. She greets seniors as they sit close to her.

Olivia keeps an eye on her. The Twins wait by a conveyor-belt toaster, bopping to music in their earbuds. Woldecott takes the last two jelly packets from a bowl. (A quick look in women's purses would reveal where the rest all went, stored for who knows when.)

Two pieces of toast drop. Wayne grabs them, steals Woldecott's jelly, and runs.

"Hey, that's my jam!" complains his brother. "Mom!!!"

Olivia resists the urge to intervene. More toast drops out. Woldecott takes them and dashes out of the room, chasing after Wayne. They exit past Le Deuce and Danny, who watch the seniors from the entrance. Once again they are both dressed in white like the *Fantasy Island* duo.

"Good turnout," says Le Deuce. "We might finish early today."

"Good! My chronic ambulatory pain is unbearable."

"You're so dramatic," opines Le Deuce. "It's just life. Anyway, I still don't see Mr. Bigglesby. Would you mind fetching him?"

"He is a grown man, my Boss."

"Yes, who could fund our entire project, so a little effort, please? I'll get us some food." Le Deuce walks to the buffet spread but then turns and calls back. "Danny, what kind of bagel do you want?"

Danny hears his name and comes back into the room but people are in the way. "What?"

Le Deuce tries again but can't quite get a direct line. "What kind of bagel do you want?!"

Danny leans around people. "What are you asking?!"

"Never mind! I'll get you one with everything!"

"No!!!" Danny has finally understood. He points to the bagels he prefers. "*Zeh* plain! *Zeh* plain!"

Le Deuce turns and sees them. "Ah, of course!"

***

Downstairs, Danny arrives and knocks on Herbert's cabin door. "*Herr*–Mr. *Beeglesby*, are you ready for our little talk?"

A female psychologist walks by. She looks aghast but reminds herself she's on vacation and to not get involved. She is practicing her own boundaries and thinks, *Good girl! I mean, Woman!*

Herbert opens his cabin door. "Oh, hello, Dick!"

"It's Danny!"

"Let me guess, time for a *Mai Tai*?" He is mid-tie tying his tie.

"You don't need a tie for *zhis*."

Herbert ignores him, finishes, and dons his jacket. "Say, did anyone ever tell you you look like a cocker spaniel?"

"*Nein*. But I thought you were going to be early today."

"Yes! I plan to be."

"You're too late for *zhat*."

Herbert exits past him. "Nonsense. Your watch must be fast."

"But it is Swiss!" Danny hobbles in the opposite direction. "*Zhis* way please!" he calls out with a smile.

Herbert does a U-turn and quickly overtakes the limping Danny. He overshoots the elevator but Danny stops and pushes the button.

"Eh-hem! Sir Speedy Gone Rabbit."

Herbert returns and primps in a mirror. "Hey Dick, would it be accurate to say Ms. Holmeslyce and Mr. Le Deuce are an item?"

Danny is mortified. "I am Danny. And *zhat* is not correct."

"Too bad. It would make my life easier."

Danny dismisses the comment and checks his appearance as well. He adjusts his tie. "But if you must know, she and I–"

Herbert interrupts. "Though she must have a boyfriend on land somewhere. I can't imagine she's available."

The elevator doors open and they enter. Danny pushes a button.

"*Zeh Fräulein* is understandably drawn to me but I ignore it. I keep our relationship strictly professional."

Herbert does not register anything Danny says. "There must be something going on between them. Would you say she was an overnight success here? Climbed the *Scarlet Ladder*?" (Hawthorne, 1878).

"Mr. Bigglesby, please! I must make something very clear to you. No matter how much money you may have, we take harassment *uber* seriously here."

"I do too. Believe me. I've had a number of trainings on it."

The elevator doors open again and Herbert shuffles out. Danny hobbles behind.

"Yet it would be foolish to underestimate the power of human attraction," continues Herbert. "Compounded with any personal disappointments, stress, and unplanned opportunities, it can catch people off-guard."

"What you are talking about? *Zhere* are only perpetrators and victims. Nothing else."

"Now there's a college education for you," observes Herbert. "Very deep analysis."

"And how much have you paid much in hushy money? For *zeh* indiscretions?" Danny suddenly realizes he might be going too far. "I am, sorry, I must not say *zhese* things to a potential benefactor. Please forgive Danny. Sometimes I am too chummy."

Herbert is surprised at Danny's self-image. "No harm, Dick. And no, I've never hushed a woman. They can boast all they want."

Danny suppresses what feels like a seizure. He runs ahead and blocks the path. "Mr. Bigglesby, do you not realize *zhat zhis* so-called victimless action has consequences? Babies do not just magically appear, *poof!* No! So many come from careless, irresponsible men who produce *zhem* for no other reason *zhan* stimulation, ego, and fun! With a weak, willing, or unwilling woman."

Herbert leans in. "You're trying to tell me something, aren't you? You're against something, is that correct?"

"*Yah! Zeh* children need a stable home! So *zhey* can flourish and grow. How many times have you disappeared from *zheir* lives?"

"You're rather negative, Dick. Have you ever heard the maxim, *It is better to have lived and loved than never to have lived?*"

"I think you misquote *zhis* expression."

"And, *zeh* only risk–" Herbert catches his mimicry. "And the only risk you'll ever regret is the one you didn't take."

"These are terrible sayings! Said by fools, with unbrided lust! Because of *zhem* I was raised by a single mother with terrible boyfriends and low self-esteem. And *zhey* called me less than!" He gasps, worrying he has said too much. "Oh, why do I tell you *zhis*?"

Herbert considers maneuvering around him.

Danny continues. "You see, I also never met my father. Apparently he was also a busy, risk-taking, non-regretting kind of man. *Zeh* world is never enough for such people."

Herbert studies Danny's face. "What was your mother's name?"

"Enough with your nosey questions. I have said too much already. Let us get to *zeh* presentation."

"You're going to present me?"

"Oh, *yah*! Perhaps when *zeh Fuhrer* kisses *zeh* arse of a Marxist feminist Jew sociologist professor! *Zhis* is to say, you will never meet my mother."

Danny hobbles forward with grim determination.

Herbert follows. "I've been making a lot of amends lately. Maybe I owe her from somewhere?"

"Oh, *zhat* is rich!" Danny fakes a laugh. "No, my mother said her sperm donor was an amazing, suave, debonair secret *uberspy* kind of guy. Who visited her hotel at night."

"Was it in Vienna?"

Danny blocks the door. "Oh please, stop! I cannot be laughing in *zhere*. Some of us still need our day jobs until one of our side hustles meets with success." He composes himself. "Mr. Bigglesby, when we go inside, I respectfully ask *zhat* you let Ms. Holmeslyce do her work, unmolested."

"I beg your pardon?"

Danny does not have words. He pretends to read bad news on his phone and becomes sugary sweet. "Oh no! I cannot believe it! *Zhis* event has been cancelled. Too bad! Oh well, our loss. You may go and enjoy *zeh* rest of *zeh* cruise with no further obligation to us."

"Oh, come now, Daniel… Einsenstadt?"

"Not even close."

"Your colleague is in no danger with me. I have committed myself to a life of virtue."

"Don't say nonsense."

"I would not joke about a thing like that. I've learned my lessons. Would you believe I once had to endure nine months of unpaid maturity leave?"

Danny feigns awe. "Nine whole months?"

"For something between two fully conscious undrugged adults. They even had me write an essay."

"How advanced!" Danny would very much like to beat Herbert with his steel-reinforced carbon fiber cane. And then perhaps throw his smelly lifeless body overboard. Instead, he coaches himself with deep breaths and a mantra of, "Breathe. Non-violence. Blessings upon all. Breathe. Non-violence. Blessings upon all."

Herbert is still lost in memories. "I'm reminded of a time I tried to date a yoga instructor. She was surprisingly rude. At dinner she was going on and on about her work and out of nowhere she said I should do breath work. Can you imagine?" He tests his breath by cupping his hand over his mouth; he approves.

Danny backs away a little.

Herbert justifies his life. "Look, I understand. Today's society condemns me. And not just me but any male rock star. It's not our fault people get all googly-eyed and want the fast track. *You auditioned in someone's apartment? Mama mia!* That's not innocence."

"Who demands an audition like *that?*"

"People try things. They don't necessarily expect people to go along with it. Have we already forgotten that Europe had a chance to stop your guy, but every concession created a problem. They fed that beast."

Danny looks shifty-eyed.

"Today kids play with fire and we blame the match company. Even in an equal world, the man will *always* be expected to do all the thinking, for *both* sides. Society will always assume he is the responsible party, there is no *Buyer Beware* anymore. Girls have no idea how dangerous they've become."

"Women."

"Women! They will tease out a pin and be shocked to learn what a grenade is. Why is that excusable? And society rushes to bandage her up while shoving bloodied, ruined men into shallow graves."

Danny cringes. "And writing an essay was supposed to rehabilitate you?"

"Goodness, they didn't ask the impossible. But I did learn to avoid women in the workplace."

"How responsible of you."

"Some are obviously playing games. But the naïve ones are more dangerous. They only stop and figure out how they feel *after* they've ridden a slide. Then the power flips like a switch, with therapists, prosecutors, and judges lecturing the theme park about its mesmerizing attractiveness."

"You poor thing. You should be given a medal of horror."

"O, the ladies hated me when I wizened up. Just like so." He jukes around Danny and enters the presentation room.

Danny grumbles after him. "Ow! I hate you. Ow!"

***

Rebecca is about to begin her presentation and smiles at the sight of Herbert. He turns back to Danny. "See? We're early!"

Danny imagines driving daggers into Herbert's back until he notices Le Deuce holding up his watch with a look of disapproval.

"Good morning, Mr. Bigglesby," says Rebecca.

He is instantly mesmerized by her beauty but tries to curb his natural instincts. "Please forget I'm even here."

Rebecca registers the odd response. Olivia and Rosie wave him over. They are quite far from the front. He passes Maude, Allison, and Dr. Singleton on the way. Maude pretends to read a handout.

When Herbert sits, he blocks Jake's view. The latter shifts his chair noisily to broadcast his annoyance. Today he wears a t-shirt with a wheelchair in the middle that reads, *My grandchild is in law school. Seeking powers of attorney, no doubt.*

"Let's get started, everyone!" says Rebecca. The room hushes. She gazes directly at Herbert. "By a show of hands, how many of you wish you could have your hands all over me right now?"

Herbert is shocked and looks down at his feet. He then gets a second surprise. As he looks up, everyone has a hand in the air; some even hold both up. Olivia and Rosie silently urge him to raise his. Instead, he sits on his hands, determined not to fail this test.

And people think I'm disturbing? he wonders.

"You can put your hands down," Rebecca says. "It was kind of an obvious question, right?" People lower their hands.

"Of course we all want our healthcare provided for!" Rebecca explains. And not just for ourselves but for all our loved ones."

Herbert realizes he must not have heard her correctly.

She continues. "The days of debating about private versus socialized medicine must end. The reality is that we all need care, at various points in our life. We can solve this very solvable problem and make it affordable and available for all."

"I'm skeptical." Jake can't help but share a bad experience. "It took me seven months to get an MRI last year, and that was only approved when my doctor personally got on the phone. But who has time for that?"

Senior Rita jumps in. "My husband died because they would not approve an *upendectomy*. Insurance companies are evil, like the Nazis!"

Danny gasps but fixes his face. *Patience,* he reminds himself.

Other hands go up to share bad experiences but Rebecca nips it in the bud. "So, then I *am* in the right room today! We all know this has to change! And we are changing it! What I represent is for everyone who has ever had a bad experience. No third-party payor should ever be allowed to judge, interfere, delay, or deny what a trained and qualified provider determines is necessary!"

"Lock them up!" chants Senior Rita.

Jake smiles at her with new interest. "But our duly elected *criminals* do nothing about it!"

Rebecca sees Herbert raise his hand. "Yes, Mr. Bigglesby?"

"In all fairness, I think people need to stop overusing the system. I mean, imagine you found yourself in Sub-Saharan Africa with multiple gunshot wounds. Even then you would only really need a lighter, a few rags, and a bottle of native *tequila*."

His Sunset peers roll their eyes, or sigh, or both.

Olivia whispers, "Dad, stop it!"

Rebecca commends him and stares. "That's very resourceful."

Herbert is conflicted, wanting to bask in the light of her smile but regretting even drawing her attention. He soon feels she is undressing him with her eyes so he buttons up his jacket and tries to unimpress her saying, "Though if it were me I would undoubtedly whimper a lot like Jake Kimble at a dental cleaning."

Jake sighs without comment. Rosie becomes self-conscious and closes her mouth.

Rebecca is impressed. "You raise a good point, however. Many of us do try to get by with less, but it's painful and it should not be necessary. Access to quality care should be *normal*, not an exception."

Jake jumps at this. "And it shouldn't take special favors, or a connection, or take six months to a year!"

Herbert prides himself on having a realistic understanding of things. "But that's just supply and demand," he argues. "Are there even enough doctors to go around? With all the nonsense they face? They're leaving in droves and retiring early."

"Insurance rosters are bogus," concurs another senior. "Half the providers say they dropped my plan."

Herbert continues, "I won't even let my grandsons go into healthcare. Law school, maybe."

"Fight liar with liar," quips Jake.

Le Deuce speaks up. "Those are quite a few problems you're all naming. We sincerely hope you'll join our fight!"

Rosie shares her intention. "I plan to!"

Le Deuce gives her a distant fist pump.

Rebecca continues. "That's great! Because some of our best paid analysts have discovered that healthcare is like, really expensive!"

Le Deuce wonders about her intelligence. She proceeds like an attorney general, undaunted. "Plus it's just not fair to have so many denials happening, and the other things happening in the dark." She clarifies, "The bad things, not the good ones."

She glances at Herbert but he looks away, trying not to show weakness. Olivia looks like she may not be done killing people.

Rebecca continues, "We're not even close to achieving the transparency Congress wants."

"Unless you mean good care is nearly invisible," opines Herbert.

"Touché," answers Rebecca.

Danny comments to Le Deuce, "He really gets on my nerves."

"Be patient, *Chihuahua*."

"Why are people always making *zeh* dog references to me?"

Le Deuce gestures for him to heel. He obeys.

Herbert wants to be clear. "My point is that we can't always wait for high-end professionals. We can learn to help each other."

People nod in agreement.

"There are too many taboos coming back. For example, Ladies, I'm too busy myself," he winks at Olivia, "but I'll bet Jake Kimble over here could help you check your lower neck area for lumps, like a *guy-neckologist*."

Jake fake coughs, "*Perbert!* Bigglesby. *Neckologist* my foot!"

"Oh dear," says Herbert. "Maybe others will be less confused about body parts."

Olivia begs him, "Dad, please stop."

Herbert is disheartened; he thought he was behaving. "I'm sorry, Miss, I retract my comments. Please continue."

Rebecca smooths it over saying, "No worries, this is all related! Because, regardless of your past experiences, our goal is to help you, and the whole human family to thrive! We can achieve this! By gifting your entire estate–"

"Did she say, *grifting*?" inquires Herbert of Olivia.

"No! Listen!"

Rebecca is momentarily distracted by them. She repeats, "By grifting your entire legacy to our *bougie bougie* wellness boutique, you and your loved ones, and future generations, will not only be able to access the highest quality care in your own home town, but wherever it's available, with all the costs of travel and lodging included."

Herbert stands up. "That's it! I have heard enough."

Olivia looks down, embarrassed.

Le Deuce moves to intercept him. "Please, Mr. Bigglesby, this free cruise experience requires you to hear out the entire offering."

"But there is no need! I am quite satisfied. She did an excellent job. Wonderful employee. I'll put in a trillion dollars but first I need to go use the facilities."

Rebecca is elated. "How wonderful! Everyone, please give Mr. Bigglesby a round of applause."

"Let's see if my stools cooperate first. They're not always as soft as my heart."

People are no longer sure whether to applaud or not.

Le Deuce offers Herbert his arm. "Let me escort you." As they exit, he adds, "I may have something else for you to consider."

Herbert answers loudly. "Oh, I've tried everything. To be quite open. Down there, I mean."

Faces react with disgust until these two have passed.

Jake gets the meeting back on track with a question. "So, Ma'am, you're saying that by bequeathing our retirement accounts to this healthsharing *what-have-you*, our families will receive free healthcare after we die?"

"Yes! And it's even bigger than that. Your resources will go on to reach far beyond your own kin to the whole human family."

Senior Rita likes what she hears and can't process much more. "I don't have much to leave anybody but I'd like to sign up!"

Others chime in with similar enthusiasm. Rebecca looks at Danny, who smiles with approval. She moves into the sign-up phase and distributes electronic tablets.

"Well, if you believe in what we offer, please take this tablet and enter in all your banking information, retirement, social security, and other sensitive things."

Olga wrestles with doubt. "How can we be sure you won't touch our… *assets* until we're actually dead?" Rosie blushes and looks down, trying not to giggle.

Rebecca answers, "There are laws in place protecting you. Your *assets* will be fully covered." Rosie giggles again. Rebecca is unsure what is funny. "And as with life insurance, if a participant has a suspicious death, or anything looks fishy, then their assets will be frozen—"

Rosie guffaws in disbelief. "Automatically–" continues Rebecca as Rosie tries to compose herself. Rebecca rushes to finish, "Until it gets determined nothing smells funny about it."

Rosie breaks into tears. "It will only stink *if* you unfreeze it! Keep it on ice."

Rebecca continues, "Ok, thank you. Do you all see where to enter your information?"

Noses crinkle. Bifocals are lifted and lowered for comparison as seniors attempt to work the tablets.

Mrs. Pearbottom asks, "Why does this say, Precious Fabrics?"

Rebecca gasps but Danny is nonchalant. "Oh, *that* is just an advertisement. Ignore it and press *continue*."

Jake complains, "I can't see where to type."

Senior Rita has similar difficulties. "Is mine on? I can't see anything."

Danny sing-songs to Rebecca. "O-kay-ay, you were r-i-i-ght."

Rebecca smiles and opens a heavy copier box. "Folks, we're going to simplify this with pen and paper and I'll input it all later."

She produces paper versions of the application and passes them out with pens as well.

Rosie notices "PreciousFabrics.uk" on the pens and smells hers. She winces. She looks for Danny and sees him exit the room.

When Rebecca hands Mrs. Pearbottom the form, the latter says, "Dear, I wonder if we could discuss your precious *outfits* some time."

"Certainly! I can bring samples to your cabin later."

"That would be lovely."

Danny arrives in his surveillance room in time to see Herbert at his cabin door saying goodbye to Le Deuce.

Herbert enters his suite and peruses his small library of books. He selects, *The Once and Future Fling* (White, 1958) and enters the bathroom.

Alarmed, Danny grabs duct tape, cuts a strip, and uses it to block a key part of a monitor as Herbert drops his trousers to his ankles.

Danny is relieved, Herbert not yet.

Herbert strains and pushes like he's giving birth.

Danny removes his headphones and shuts off the monitor altogether.

CHAPTER *NEINTEEN*

Some Assembly Required

Later that day, the Twins splash around in one of the pools. Olivia and Rosie sunbathe on deck chairs. The Twins come running like five-year-olds.

"Mom, when is Grampa joining us?"

"How come he doesn't spend time with us?"

Olivia lowers her sunglasses, sympathy in her eyes. "I'm sorry, Babies. It's just that your grandfather has been a terrible person all his life. Commitment to anyone but himself is still very new to him."

Woldecott understands. "That was cool the other day. I wish we could help him out with his work more."

Somewhere a toilet flushes.

Wayne is also accepting of Herbert. "At least he's not in prison."

"Have I lost you both?" Olivia is quite disturbed by their lack of condemnation. "Where did I go wrong? So far your grandfather has only used you! You made those news stories for him but now he's dropped you until he needs something else."

Woldecott shares a sudden worry. "Hey! What if he's in trouble and needs our help?"

Wayne hadn't thought of that. "Yeah, what if he's trapped doing something he can't handle like before? Isn't that why we're here?"

In hallways above and below them, Herbert's groans resound. People are alarmed as if the ship itself is creaking and cawing.

Rosie turns from her sun worship. "Boys, do you understand who your grandfather is? He can take care of himself."

The Twins smile proudly. "You're right. He even got away from us the other day."

Olivia looks annoyed. "Someone must have tipped him." She closes her eyes. "If you're bored, go do something dangerous. Climb down the side of the ship or something."

"Ok, Mom." They run back to the pool. As they cannonball into it we hear other ploppings and a long toilet flush.

A frustrated Herbert on the toilet rips open a box of patches and attaches one to his abdomen. The logo says EZ-Go and his relief begins almost immediately.

***

On one side of the ship, a repelling line is thrown from a high deck and uncurls beautifully against the sky and the ship.

Up above, the Twins are dressed as window cleaners and act friendly as passengers walk by. This calls momentary attention; they were invisible when just working.

After that rite of passage, Woldecott signals and Wayne jumps over the rail, repelling down with a spray bottle and rag.

Woldecott acts like no one was just there with him, which once again draws suspicious looks from a couple passing by. The woman clutches her purse and the man clutches his partner.

When alone again, Woldecott drops his creepy smile and looks down over the railing. Several decks below, Wayne sprays and wipes a porthole. He then swings himself sideways to another one.

Inside his cabin, Herbert unpacks mundane things like socks and underwear from his duffle bag. The room is momentarily darkened by a shadow crossing his porthole. He turns to look but sees nothing.

Next, he removes his old Chipstick and places it on the counter. He follows that with two pairs of baby-blue diapers with a logo for CyanDieDry. He is puzzled and looks for more. *Did I not pack three?*

He does not find another. The warning label on the diapers is over a meter long and he is unsure what to do with it. Large letters say, "DANGER! ACTIVATED BY URINE." Tiny words shield the manufacturer from liability and stupidity. Little icons forbid wearing them on the head, elbows, or knees. Only a position on the buttocks has a green checkmark.

Herbert thinks it's a rip-off but struggles and can't manage to remove it. *They should use this for seatbelts*, he concludes. *Or parachutes.*

He then takes out his giant survival knife but is careful to hide it from the portraits. It still takes some doing to dispatch them and then he regrets doing so. *You can't leave this sort of thing in the trash.*

He sets them aside and takes out his next gadget, a portable blood pressure monitor. He places it on the counter.

The room is suddenly darkened again by something crossing the porthole. He turns but cannot see what is happening there. Then he realizes someone is cleaning his window.

He uses his body to hide what he is doing. He inserts the labels into the blood pressure cuff. Then he squeezes the inflater till it produces a bright flash in the darkened room, as if gunfire.

Outside, Wayne looks concerned and taps on the glass. Herbert does not hear it. The cuff emits smoke but nothing is on fire. "How retardant," murmurs Herbert. He removes the indestructible labels and studies their makeup. *We could colonize the sun wearing these.*

Wayne uses a throwing star to tap the window and now Herbert hears it. He balls up the labels in his hand and shuffles over to the porthole. He is delighted to recognize *Woldecott. Or Wayne? Whichever one he is.* He opens it.

"Hi Grampa! Are you ok?"

"Yes, perfectly fine. I'm so glad you're here!" He can't quite see the rope or harness too well. "I'm sorry, is that my equipment?"

"Technically you left it behind."

"Did I? Well never mind that. Can you tell your mother to come ASAP?"

"Roger that! Oh, but we only have one rope." He deflates.

Herbert solves the conundrum. "She should use the stairs. Rosie too. But warn them, this assignment is not for the faint of heart. If you can't handle being caught and tortured you should say so now."

"Oh no, Grampa! We're ready to roll!"

Herbert is horrified. "Roll? You must never roll. No matter how slowly they bleed and dismember you, or remove your fingernails, or drill your teeth. Your lips must be absolutely sealed."

Wayne seals his lips but still tries to speak. "Mmm-uhh-uhh-uhhhh, Mmm-mmm. Uhh-uhh-uhh Huhhhh!" which is translated as, "I understand, *Grampa*! These lips are *seal-ified*!"

Herbert feels the breeze and remembers the labels in his hand. "Here, let me get rid of these." He puts his hand through the porthole and releases the long white ribbons to the wind.

"You shouldn't do that, Grampa! The Earth is our friend!"

Herbert points to the label on the latch. *"NO LITTERING. Except for ridiculously long and indestructible product labels."*

"Oh, you got me! And don't worry. We got this!"

Herbert rises on his tippy toes, trying to see whatever Wayne is boasting of. "Got what, window spray?"

"Huh?"

"Never mind. We need to think up an elaborate plan to slowly build trust and draw out the ruthless vultures over time. It could take weeks or months or even years."

"Whatever it takes, Grampa!"

"And even then, it may be nearly impossible to get close to that mastermind Le Deuce."

A loud knock on the door makes them freeze. Herbert gestures for Wayne to stay out of sight. He then leaves, answers the door, and returns, opening a fancy white envelope. He reads the card and holds it up in victory.

"Ah, brilliant. I've been invited to dine with Le Deuce tonight. This is probably all the access we'll need."

"Rock and *not-rolling*, Grampa!"

"Now, what were we talking about?"

Wayne does not remember. "Window spray? Ow! What a jerk!" He looks up. "Woldecott thinks he can just pull my string whenever he wants. But I better give him his turn."

"Right. Well, don't forget. Let's meet at six-thirty tonight, here in my room. Can you convey that message?"

"Of course, Grampa! We'll be here." Wayne crawls up the side of the ship effortlessly.

Herbert calls after him. "And make sure you–Nevermind!" He smiles when he sees Wayne washing portholes as he goes up, so as to look less suspicious. Wayne gives him a *thumbs up*.

***

That evening, in a colorfully lit virtual reality room, several people stand apart. Each wears headgear and is spaced out. Among them are the Twins, Olivia, and Rosie.

In Rosie's virtual world she stands in a newly planted garden with fresh soil. She waters it and beautiful flowers and trees immediately sprout and bear fruit, like slow-motion fireworks.

In Olivia's world she hosts a reunion for hundreds of relatives. She welcomes every hesitant person who asks if they're in the right place. "You sure are, cousin!"

In the Twins' worlds, they each meet an identical young woman with ripped jeans, blue hair, and an *animé* tattoo. Each woman says, "You look nothing like your brother!" which delights each Twin.

Outside the VR room, a sweating, tuxedoed Herbert shuffles to a stop. He considers the various doors and enters the casino.

Mrs. Pearbottom is at a roulette table. She wears a gorgeous new dress that complements her figure. She is happy to see Herbert and doubles her bet.

The croupier spins the wheel and drops the ball in a good way.

Herbert sees Mrs. Pearbottom and shuffles over to her, past the card games. He admires her appearance and stacks of chips. "You've cleaned up nicely."

"I've been dealt a good hand," she answers.

Herbert looks confused as he takes in the roulette wheel. It seems to spin forever. "Have you seen any of my... *family* lately?"

She detects some stress. "No. Is something wrong?"

"Wrong? Why? Not at all!"

Other players look annoyed.

"I just want to spend qualified time with my grandsons."

"You do?"

"Of course! Is that so surprising?"

"Frankly, yes, Herbert. But it's nice to hear."

The ball keeps bouncing about the roulette wheel.

Mrs. Pearbottom continues, "I'm sure they're fine. You should relax and enjoy yourself." She sips her drink.

Over her shoulder Herbert can't help noticing an attractive young woman playing blackjack.

"You should even play a round while you're here," encourages Mrs. Pearbottom.

Herbert does a doubletake at her suggestion. "I'm not really supposed to. But something is different about you today."

"Maybe you were right about some things." She slides a few stacks of chips toward him. "Play a round on me."

It dawns on him that she was being literal. "Oh, no thank you. I need to find them." He pushes her chips back. She is disappointed.

The ball lands and she wins yet again.

A handsome young man across the table smiles and toasts her. She returns the toast but her glass is empty and she smiles.

Herbert notices their exchange and can't help justifying himself. "I didn't mean to be rude. I just don't like rushing roulette."

"What is that supposed to mean?" asks Mrs. Pearbottom. "I am not some moody hothead."

"No, certainly not." Herbert is unsure what he said wrong.

Mrs. Pearbottom places her next bet and catches the good-looking man pointing her out to a waiter, who leaves.

Herbert is annoyed. He speaks in a low, clear voice. "Look, I'm about to have dinner with Le Deuce. I know you're not technically working right now, but if you see Olivia and the boys I would very much appreciate it if you could send them to my room before seven."

The waiter brings her a drink but Herbert takes it and downs it. "I think you can do better," he comments, and then shuffles out.

Mrs. Pearbottom is speechless. She watches him go and also smiles politely at the other man. She then collects her chips and follows after Herbert.

The young man pretends to be a good sport but a bruise is a bruise. He wonders whether he should try to get back with his ex one more time, despite her being married to someone else now.

Moments later, Herbert and Mrs. Pearbottom check activity rooms in the foyer. One promises Stand-Up Comedy. They enter.

A comedian is on stage with a guitar, dressed as an Amish farmer. He parodies Johnny Cash (1968) with, *"I hear the plane a-comin' / Round the hor-i-zon / I ain't had no moonshine since / I don't know where it went / I'm stuck in Wholesome Prison / And planes keep a-flyin' / on down to Rio de Janeiro."*

Mrs. Pearbottom comments, "The potential is there."

Herbert is more skeptical. "Maybe in eight years."

They exit but the comedian yells, "Wait folks, I have more!"

Out in the foyer they next consider whether to give Stand-Up Tragedy a go. They enter into it.

A support group has 20 or so people seated in a circle. Olivia and others nod supportively as Rosie is mid-share.

"Or maybe that's just me," she concludes.

"Not at all!" denies Dr. Singleton. "It's very understandable. But it might be a bit like now doubting all of science just because of a few bad chemists or companies. Sometimes you have to look past the representatives to examine a concoction for yourself. Especially if many people died for spreading such a drink, and attested to its life-changing properties."

Pearbottom whispers, "Should we pull them out?"

"Let's stay for a moment," Herbert answers. Mrs. Pearbottom wonders about him. They find seats but not together.

Rosie continues her testimony. "Well, maybe not *all* men, but I certainly learned early in life not to believe *most* men. Unless I wanted abuse and disappointment. Or a paycheck at best."

Women nod with understanding. "But now I want more. And I finally believe I matter!"

"That's wonderful, Rosie!" says Dr. Singleton. "You do matter! In this life and the next. That's why I call this path an investment."

Herbert gives Pearbottom a knowing look and makes the money gesture with his fingers. She questions his understanding.

Singleton continues. "So please don't ever call me a *believer*. Unless you call Warren Buffet a believer. Or JP Morgan. We are investors, in what lasts forever without any risk of ending. Amen?"

People answer, "Amen!!!"

Olivia suddenly notices Herbert and is touched by his presence. She reads way more into it than is warranted and becomes eager to share. "Hi, my name is Olivia."

"Hi, Olivia!" and, "Welcome!" resound from all.

"I'm still new to this but I really look forward to learning more and doing my steps. I've had so many resentments! For so many years. And I want to let it all go. Because I do agree, life is too short to waste on grudges."

"Crutches? What is she talking about?" Herbert had meant it as a whisper to his neighbor but everyone looks at him.

His neighbor clarifies, "Grudges. Letting go of anger."

"Oh."

Someone calls out, "You're in the right place, Olivia!" Others are also supportive. Mrs. Pearbottom gestures for Herbert to listen.

Olivia is emboldened. "This class teaches me I don't gotta kill nobody when I'm upset."

Listeners assume she is using hyperbole and smile, able to relate.

"I mean, people might have reasons they did what they did. And I don't want to judge anymore. Except the insurance companies. That's a whole other level of bad."

People nod in agreement.

"I mean, if you're gonna string people out till they die, then just cut those companies and we'll do fee-for-service. You don't gotta get elected, then pass a law, just to make so many people suffer."

She catches Dr. Singleton's concerned expression. He makes a mild gesture to tone it down.

She apologizes, "Sorry, ok, no politics. I just want forgiveness. And kindness. This is so powerful and I am happy to be here."

People applaud, pat her, and offer more words of welcome. Mrs. Pearbottom holds up her watch to Herbert. He recalls his dinner appointment with a startle.

"I'm sorry to interrupt," he says. "But I really need to say some things to my daughter."

Olivia beams at her father's interest and acknowledgment. Everyone waits expectantly, ready for a moving confession followed up by a heartwarming reconciliation.

"Of course, Daddy! Tell me anything you want!"

Herbert is caught off-guard. "I mean outside. It's not about this. It's important!"

Frowns appear all around. He tries to smoothen it saying, "I'm sorry, how much longer does this go?"

"Armenians last an hour," he hears Dr. Singleton boast.

"No, they don't!" responds a baffled Herbert.

Olivia is embarrassed. She jumps up to lead him out.

Pearbottom is already in motion, taking Herbert by the arm. She whispers, "He said our *meetings* last an hour. Not Armenians."

"Oh." Herbert lets himself be led outside.

Olivia follows. Dr. Singleton looks at his watch and beckons them to stay. "But folks, it's only 20 more minutes."

Olivia answers, "I'm sorry. Please excuse us. And thank you!"

Rosie is torn but finally follows them as well, politely nodding goodbyes to everyone.

In the foyer Olivia cries, "Dad, how could you do that to me?"

"Didn't the boys tell you? We needed to meet at six-thirty! I'm having dinner with Le Deuce in a few minutes. Where are they?"

Olivia is defensive. "They have ADHD! They must have gotten distracted."

The Twins rush by with tunnel vision, heading for a room offering *Midgitsu*.

Herbert calls out, "Boys! Hold it!"

"You gotta stop, *hijos!*" yells their mother.

They turn and take in the gathering. "Oh, hi everyone!"

Herbert is not sure which Twin to address. "What happened? I told you–or you–that we needed to meet at six thirty!"

"Oh, my bad, Grampa!" says Wayne. "I totally forgot!"

"Well, listen." Herbert draws them closer. "Right now, I am on my way to a private dinner with Le Deuce and his party. I need each of you to do some recon while I'm with them."

Rosie asks, "What sort of reconnaissance?"

However, she and the Twins are distracted by the Midgitsu room. Tall people are periodically carried out on stretchers. Olivia slaps her boys and tells them to pay attention.

Herbert says, "Olivia, I'd like you to go through Le Deuce's quarters and see what dirt you can find."

"Will do, Pops!"

The boys find it odd. Rosie is jealous. "I like finding dirt!"

Herbert ignores her and assigns the Twins next. "As for you two, please figure out where Danny stays. I doubt he'll have anything useful for us but just make sure he's clean."

They are puzzled until Woldecott gets an idea. "I'll check if his towel has ever been used."

"Yeah! And I'll check if he even has a toothbrush," adds Wayne.

Olivia stops Herbert before he can say anything hurtful. He clarifies, "What I mean is, look for things that suggest he might be involved in something sinister. Like taking money from people for no actual services."

"Is that illegal?" asks Wayne. "What if he's a lawyer?"

"What if we find nuclear secrets?" asks Woldecott. "Maybe he has a submarine following us."

"He doesn't strike me as sub-intelligent."

Olivia shows Woldecott the DNA list. "And we still need his real last name if you see it."

"Seriously?" asks Herbert. "Do you see some resemblance?

Woldecott looks uneasy. "Are we even allowed to go there? I mean, isn't he like a protected person or something?"

Herbert is dismissive. "Protected? Even if he is, I think you can each handle a bodyguard or five."

The boys puff up. "*Fo-sho.*"

"I did see one helper," says Rosie. "A big guy. Though I don't agree with his political views."

Woldecott complains. "I wasn't talking about bodyguards! What if some day I'm looking for a job and the People Department says I abused a person of short stature?"

"Oh, microaggression!" says Wayne.

"Ah, now I understand," begins Mrs. Pearbottom, who now understands. "But you're neither hiring nor firing him, so it shouldn't matter. At most an interview, if he should return unexpectedly."

Olivia looks relieved. "Good, maybe just an assault charge."

Herbert is suddenly irate. "Peaches, I don't think you of all people should be commenting on employment ethics."

"What is that supposed to mean?"

Herbert stares her down and makes various head jerks. She finally recalls a recent HR scandal at Sunset. "Oh, I see. But they've turned out to be wonderful additions!" She gestures at his family.

Herbert drops it and gives Olivia and the Twins final instructions. "It's showtime, kids. See what you find and let's meet in my room at midnight."

"Roger that, Gramps!" The boys and Olivia exit.

Rosie is restless. "What can I do? I want to help too."

Herbert ignores her. "Peaches, are you willing to help?"

"It depends. But why don't you send Rosie?"

Herbert hesitates. "Potential conflict of interest."

The women are puzzled. Herbert takes Mrs. Pearbottom aside. "I think we should get a read on that shyster's room too. Can you see to that?"

"Dr. Singleton?!"

So much for leaving Rosie out of it.

"That's a complete waste of time," continues Mrs. Pearbottom. She then sees another side. "But then again, I suppose it can't hurt."

Herbert immediately regrets it. "Actually, maybe Rosie should do it." He calls her over.

"Yes!" answers Rosie with a fist pump.

"No, I can handle it," insists Mrs. Pearbottom.

Herbert grows more uncomfortable. "No, you were right. It was a bad idea. And we have less than 20 minutes."

"Then I better hurry," says Mrs. Pearbottom and starts off.

Herbert looks panicked. "Well, just get a quick look and get right out. There's no need to lie in wait for him."

She turns back, her mouth agape.

He insists, "He shouldn't even know you were there."

Mrs. Pearbottom comes back and tries not to explode. "Oh, and I suppose you'll be the one interrogating Ms. Holmeslyce? For however long it takes, and by whatever means necessary?"

"What are you implying?" asks Herbert innocently.

"Nothing, just the usual double standard! It's alive and well on this ego trip."

Herbert feigns shock, making stupid faces but saying nothing.

Rosie interrupts. "Excuse me? I really want to help too."

Herbert's annoyance flips to enthusiasm. "Thank you, Rosie! Yes! You can help solve a little misunderstanding here. Would you mind checking Ms. Holmeslyce's cabin?"

"Not at all! I definitely think she knows some things." She flexes her muscles. "I'll get it out of her."

Herbert regrets the idea. "No, not like that! Just get in and get out. No *interviews* are necessary at this time." He looks at Mrs. Pearbottom. "By either of you! Are you satisfied?"

"No, I'm annoyed," answers Mrs. Pearbottom.

Rosie asks for some leeway. "Oh, please, Mr. B? It would be fun, like old times. Gosh, I hope I'm not too rusty."

"You'll be fine," says Mrs. Pearbottom supportively.

"No!" responds Herbert. "She mustn't even know you were there. And report back at midnight."

Rosie slumps her body like a sullen teen. "Ok." She moves down the hall, no zip left in her steps.

Herbert turns to Mrs. Pearbottom. "Ma'am, you have less than 15 minutes!"

Mrs. Pearbottom nods. "Consider it done. And for the record, I'm not interested in that monk."

"I see." Herbert does not believe her but wants her to go. She finally heads down the hall and looks back once more before turning a corner. Herbert smiles and waves. The moment she is out of view, he shuffles after Rosie, loud-whispering, "Rosie, wait! I say, wait up!"

Rosie turns and meets him half-way. "What is it, Sir?"

Herbert explains, "While you're in her room you should also collect a few samples of her Precious Fabrics. But make sure it's nothing she would notice missing."

"Ew! Those fabrics stink!"

"Nevertheless, please bring me samples."

"I'll grab a shirt or two," she concedes.

"No!" insists Herbert. "It has to be based on smoothness. You have to feel it out and bring me the best."

Rosie worries. "I don't know if I can do that."

"Why not? They're supposed to be revolutionary. And great investments. If she's innocent I want to see her finest, silkiest, smoothest article. Even if it's something intimate. What's wrong?"

Rosie is nervous. "It's just that…"

"Please, Rosie, time is of the essence."

A door opens 30 feet away. Herbert looks down the hall and sees Le Deuce wave at him. They are ready and waiting.

Rosie continues quietly, "I just don't feel good."

Herbert reacts equally quietly, "Don't you mean *well*?"

"Of course I mean well! I just don't feel good. Is there some other way I can help?"

"But you just *insisted!*"

"I know, but–" She rubs her hands together. "I can't even…"

"Stop with the excuses! You'll be in and out. Just bring me the finest, smoothest article you find. Use a bag if you're embarrassed."

"It's not that!"

"Enough! Go!" Herbert turns and shuffles toward Le Deuce.

"Here he is! Good evening, Mr. Bigglesby." Danny and Rebecca join them at the door.

Rosie turns and resigns herself to doing her best.

Chapter Twenty

Members of the Bored

"Good evening all." Herbert shuffles into Le Deuce's private dining room. He checks his watch and says, "It's wonderful how we could all be here early tonight."

Danny frowns and checks his watch. "It is twelve past *zeh* hour."

"It's fine," assures Le Deuce.

Rebecca extends a hand. "I'm glad you could make it."

Herbert takes her hand as if going to kiss it but he lays his other hand on top of it. She finds it confusing. He does the same with the men's hands and says, "The pleasure is evenly distributed."

They return awkward smiles. Le Deuce takes the chair at the head of the table and gestures for Herbert to sit at his left and for Rebecca to sit on Herbert's left. Instead, Herbert pretends to misunderstand and grabs the chair on Le Deuce's right, which was meant for Danny. Danny pulls it away but Herbert hangs on and they struggle for a bit. Le Deuce nods for Danny to surrender it and he finally obeys and hobbles to the other side.

Rebecca tries to mask her self-doubt with a smile. She discreetly sniffs her own collar but finds nothing offensive.

A waiter enters and presents Le Deuce with a bottle of wine. Le Deuce approves and the waiter pours a glass for each person.

Herbert gets right to business. "Mr. Le Deuce, I'm not one to be beaten around by the Mulberry Bush." His eyes automatically flit to Rebecca and then back to Le Deuce as he tries not to gaze at her. "I simply know a good thing when I seize it."

"You don't waste your time," observes Le Deuce.

"No, just *zeh* other people's," critiques Danny.

Rebecca wonders about Herbert's loss of interest in her. *Perhaps a grey hair?* She checks her reflection in a silver pitcher. It distorts her face dramatically like Bette Davis' in, *What Ever Happened to Baby Jane?* (Aldrich, 1962).

Herbert continues, "I have deduced, Mr. Le Deuce, that you would like me to sit on your Board."

Danny smirks at his rhyme. "If you so… choose!"

His boss ignores Danny. "I can see why you are successful."

"But alas, I am a very busy…" Herbert scans for the right word.

"Goose?" suggests Danny from behind his menu.

The waiter doesn't know if he was ordering so he writes it down.

"Not for me," replies Herbert.

The waiter crosses out goose.

Le Deuce continues. "Ignore Danny. His mind is a little…"

Everyone looks at him, on the edge of their seats. Danny is tempted but resists.

Le Deuce finishes it. "Loose."

"Double standard!" coughs Danny from behind his menu.

Le Deuce proceeds. "Mr. Bigglesby, I want to respect your time. I believe that after some tedious back and forth we can achieve a workable solution."

"Ya! *Zeh* final answer!" declares Danny, instinctively bolting upright and clicking his heels. He becomes self-conscious as people stare at him. "It's chemistry."

Le Deuce continues. "Herbert—may I call you Herbert?"

He hesitates. "Let's see how this first date goes. First."

Le Deuce proceeds, "Very well. Mr. Bigglesby, with your help we could be reaching so many more people, starting at the top of the economic bracket."

"Which would be of much use!" proclaims Danny, eyes on his menu. He ignores disbelieving stares.

Le Deuce glares at him. "In short…" He then shifts to Herbert. "It's obvious that reaching more people with significant resources could be pivotal in spreading quality healthcare farther and wider and faster than ever before."

Danny picks up and butters a slice of bread. He uses broad exaggerated motions. "*Yah*, spread *zeh* healthcare! Anyone can butter *zeh* middle of *zeh* bread, but filling *zeh* edges shows true diligence."

Le Deuce contains his irritation. "We don't need the concept illustrated, Danny."

He shrinks to himself muttering, "See? I try to help and I get yelled at." He nibbles on his bread.

Herbert speaks. "Mr. Le Deuce, I can see you are quite sincere about solving healthcare access. And I do suppose I could speak with a plethora of friends or two around the world."

"*Plethori?*" asks Danny.

Herbert raises his wine glass for a toast. "Perhaps they too can pitch in a trillion here and there."

The others skip a collective breath. *What a contact list that would be!* They raise their glasses but Herbert suddenly lowers his.

"Though I do worry it would be rather taxing for me."

"Not at all!" declares Rebecca, "It's tax exempt!"

Her colleagues lower their heads and glasses in embarrassment.

Herbert can't help asking, "Are you perchance a member of the Air & Space Museum?"

"No," laughs Rebecca. "Who would pay to see those?"

"Good point," answers Herbert. "But any donor list would be a good place to start."

"I once looked into used kidneys," says Rebecca.

Le Deuce tries to prevent further displays of corporate intelligence. "We understand this would add some personal toll, Mr. Bigglesby. What if Ms. Holmeslyce here were to temporarily leave my employ and assume a certain position under you?"

Rebecca is all for it. "Totally! I see this as missionary work." She bites into a chocolate-covered strawberry and juice dribbles down her chin. She wipes it with her finger and eats it. "Anything I can do to help you be you at your best version. Of you."

Danny and Herbert find that troubling. Herbert swallows his own loose saliva and worries he won't have a prayer in keeping his promise to Olivia.

Le Deuce gestures for the waiter, who steps up.

"I'm afraid we're getting way ahead of ourselves."

"I agree," agrees Herbert. "Let's just back it up."

The waiter moves back to the wall. He sees a chair nearby but dares not occupy it.

Herbert studies the menu through his glasses, then over and above them. *The font is ridiculously small and scripty.*

Rebecca tells the waiter, "I'd like something freshly caught." She looks at Herbert, who tries not to look worried.

"We have a blue marlin today," answers the server.

"Perfect."

Herbert says, "I don't go by *Carpe Diem* anymore."

The men don't know if he's kidding. Rebecca looks down at the rug and says, "I don't know. It looks comfy."

Herbert presses his lips shut and breathes deeply through his nose, trying to stay strong.

The waiter asks, "With a side of ...?"

Rebecca looks at Herbert and says, "Potatoes. Mashed. With gravy. And butter. Extra butter."

Herbert hides behind his menu.

Le Deuce is eager to continue. "Mr. Bigglesby, what would you say has been the secret to your success?"

The waiter rolls his eyes and retreats to the wall.

Herbert cocks his head, hoping it's not a trick question. "I think it's simple. I made some very good trades early in life."

"Or trade-offs, perhaps?" blurts out Danny, his mouth full of bread. "Ow!" Under the table he received a kickback from Le Deuce.

Herbert pontificates about the secret of wealth. "You know, once you have a critical mass of money it just grows by itself. A single percent of growth is substantial."

The waiter eyes the comfy chair again. *So close and yet so far.*

"You're very humble," commends Le Deuce. "People today expect to get rich quick. Or they get high and check out. But slow and steady wins the race."

"I don't know about that," replies Herbert. It's unclear if he is commenting on a menu item or Le Deuce's words. "I think both are good." He asks the waiter, "Can you mix the turtle and hare soups?"

"Our turtles have no hair, Sir." He fixates on Herbert's baldness. "No offense."

"I mean, can you mix a turtle soup with a hare soup? I think I'd like both."

"Kind of a win-win," observes Rebecca.

"Or lose-lose," answers Herbert. "From their perspectives."

"Of course. And you, Sir?" The waiter turns to Danny.

"I cannot decide! Duck? Duck? Goose? *Zeh* goose. Well done."

"Thank you, Sir, I've been honing my skills."

Le Deuce also hands back his menu. "I'll have the Carp Sliders."

Rebecca looks down at the rug again.

"Unless you've run out," continues Le Deuce. Then just bring me a chicken salad."

"Very well."

The waiter exits and Le Deuce continues. "Now, Mr. Bigglesby, regardless of how you might downplay your achievements, you obviously planted your resources in remarkably fertile places."

Herbert assumes he knows about the DNA list. "In the past, I certainly did." He catches Rebecca staring at him but he resists eye contact.

Le Deuce continues. "And as I understand it, even when you met with failure, you always bounced back."

"I don't panic, if that's what you mean."

"I trust you've kept your integrity, without compromises."

Herbert is puzzled. "I'm not sure what you mean."

"Mr. Bigglesby, before we can fully accept your generosity, we need to discuss the sensitivity of our image. Healthsharing requires a great deal of public trust."

"What he means is *zhat* our work would be hurt by *zeh* scandals, *zeh* skeletons coming out of *zeh* closets."

Everyone makes a face. "Well, that would be disagreeable," Herbert agrees.

Le Deuces clarifies, "We don't take money from Cartels, for example. Or the politicians they carry in their pockets."

Rebecca adds, "A wrong association could really sink us." *Oops.*

Danny turns to the portholes. "Why are you saying *zhis* thing?"

"Sorry." Rebecca attempts a fix. "It could really rock our boat."

"Still not helpful, Rebecca," whines Danny.

Le Deuce places a comforting hand on Danny's arm. "They're just metaphors. Nothing literal."

Danny breathes deeply and tries to relax.

"Speaking of *syncing*," says Herbert, looking at Danny. "Perhaps we could all synchronize our watches. I know I was early. We were all early, just some earlier than others."

"To be sure," says Le Deuce. "But it doesn't matter. Water under the bridge."

Danny tries not to freak out again.

The waiter brings their food and serves it up.

Herbert finds a hare as he sops up his fabled soup. "It's quite good."

"I'm glad," answers the waiter, who leaves.

Le Deuce presses forward. "Mr. Bigglesby, if you're going to be involved at a leadership level, and we hope you will be, we need to make sure you have no moral or ethical breaches in the public eye."

He is indignant. "My public *I* is no different than my private *I*."

"Why would you need a private eye?" inquires Danny. "For what exactly are you being blackmailed?"

"I'm not being blackmailed." *Oh no!* Herbert fears a mandatory training coming and rushes to correct it. "Or any color mailed. Not that any one hue is better than another." He wipes his chin but misses a clinging wet bread crumb. "For your information, my business is all quite public. Especially the older I get."

Danny wants to nail his coffin. "Have you ever profited from a shady real estate deal?"

Herbert acts as if he has a shameful secret that must finally come to light.

"Be honest with us!" pressures Danny.

Herbert appeals to them all. "Maybe? Once?"

The group loses hope. They look at their watches and wonder how else they could be spending the evening.

"In the 80s I provided backing for a project called, *Pines at Driest Meadows* in Seco, Arizona."

They all look at him, heads nodding with suspicion.

"The value proposition, as they called it, was that its tall trees and broad awnings offered a cool respite from the hot desert sun."

Le Deuce smiles and waits for Danny to get the joke.

"Ah, you are being literal! Not *zhis* kind of shady!"

Herbert smiles. "All in good fun." He raises his glass for the toast they abandoned earlier, but Le Deuce is not ready to go there. Herbert gets serious. He puts his soup aside, wipes his mouth, and leans forward, ready to spill it like a 1950s *film noir* detective. Perhaps in the movie version the room will go black and white, with harsh shadows cast by a streetlight named Desire (Williams, 1947).

"Enough with this side babble, Kids. Let's get to it," he begins.

Everyone responds in character. Rebecca plays with an earring, afraid some dark truth is about to rear its ugly head about her. *It's fine*, she thinks, putting on her best Mrs. Dietrichson face (cfr. Wilder, 1944). *I have nothing to fear. Rock-solid alibis. It wasn't my fault any coaches took me seriously. They chose to ruin their own lives. Oh wait, he's not talking about me*, she realizes.

Herbert has been speaking. "So then I think what you're really asking is whether I ever knowingly trafficked in illegally caged chickens, or free-range women and children?"

"Yes!" demands Danny.

Rebecca doesn't know if she can still do business with Danny.

"Or perhaps you're wondering if I ever grossly underpaid my employees, using slave labor to make whatever it is the Reader is wearing or boycotting these days?"

Le Deuce shifts uncomfortably. "Have you?"

Herbert isn't finished and tells them so. "I'm not finished! Or perhaps you're wondering whether any of my businesses have caused unconscionable, avoidable deaths, with management calculating that lawsuits and settlements would be cheaper than redesigning a whole new engine. Even if it was known to explode and kill families under certain fairly common conditions?"

Le Deuce is interested. "Well, yes, that would certainly be worth knowing."

Herbert is getting worked up. "And you probably want to know if I ever received kickbacks from nonprofits and foreign aid projects, blurring the lines between penicillin and *pistolas?* If that's what you mean, why don't you just come out and say it?"

Danny is equally agitated. "Yes! We are wondering about all *zhese* things and about Marxist Communist leanings too. Or *jihad!*"

Le Deuce raises a hand to stop his inquisition. "That last part is of no importance to me or my business partners. Actually, none of it is. Our bylaws are quite simple."

Rebecca emits a laugh. "Yeah! Gosh. If we asked about all that we'd never achieve our funding goals."

Herbert relaxes. The *film noir* vibe expands back to color. Only soft shadows remain, with no stark accountability remaining. In a movie it won't even look like cinema any more, just home video.

Le Deuce concludes, "Look, all we really need to know about are things like dodging alimony or falling behind on child support. And any incorrect parts of speech in your past. It's perfunctory."

Herbert shows a microflash of concern. *All this preparation and now to be foiled by this?* He tugs at his collar. *Is it warm in here? Have I wet myself?* Out loud he says, "Well, I'm not officially a deadbeat. At least, not knowingly or intentionally!"

The group deflates again.

"Help me understand," says Le Deuce. "You seem like such a family man in everything I read."

"Yes, but… I would not want to mislead you," Herbert answers. "I have not led an exemplary life when it comes to relationships."

"Oh, *zhis* is big surprise," chuckles Danny. "Continue."

Herbert proceeds. "Until a few days ago I didn't even know I had a daughter–or my two grandsons."

"*Zeh* shame!!!" reacts Danny. "You are *zeh* very definition of a deadbeat father!"

"But what about all the articles? The pictures?"

"I had a PR firm predict the kind of family the public expected."

"But they look so accurate!"

"They were good guessers. And now they're here. So, ever since encountering them, I have been doing everything in my power to rectify years of… I'm not sure what to call it."

"Ignorance, irresponsibility, neglect?" suggests Danny.

"Sure," Herbert confirms. "It's true. I was not there for them. But somehow they have forgiven me. It's been quite a reunion and I think we're going to be fine."

"Good," says Le Deuce.

"At least while *zhere* is money in *zeh* bank," comments Danny.

"No, we have deeper reserves than that."

"Oil?"

Herbert nods. "No, for whatever reason, I think they actually want to be with me. They didn't even know I had money when they first found me."

"*Zhis* is touching…" says Danny.

"Truth be told, they had wanted to kill me for a while."

"… touching on insanity!" continues Danny. "So in light of all *zhese* revelations–"

"Hold on there, *Old Yeller*," beckons Le Deuce. "Mr. Bigglesby, I appreciate your honesty and your being so forthright with us."

Danny raises a toast uncontrollably. "*Yah!* Fourth *Reich!*" He notices the glare from Le Deuce and lowers his glass. "Sorry."

Le Deuce continues. "As far as I'm concerned, your family concerns are of no concern among our pivotal concerns."

"Then my money's still good here?"

"Heck, yeah!" declares Rebecca, sensing Le Deuce's approval. "Never better. We can start today! What will my title be?"

"We'll think of something," assures Herbert. He only knows he can never be *Undersecretary*.

Le Deuce raises his glass. "To a long partnership. We welcome your generous help."

"Here, here!" They answer.

And *soon, soon* thinks Danny.

Herbert relaxes. "That's good," he says, "because I have to say, you had me worried for a moment there. I mean, there are a lot worse Baby Boomers out there. I mean, if you're going to start nit picking, in some places they literally strap boomers to babies." He imitates a high-pitched crying infant, "Wahhhh! Wahhhh!" followed by a deep, baritone, "Ka-boom!!!"

Awkward blinking follows.

Herbert continues, oblivious. "I was a strapping lad in my day, but never that kind."

Danny is shocked. "I cannot believe you would say *zhis* thing."

"It's the world we live in!" defends Herbert. "I don't believe in sanitizing it with silence anymore."

Danny stews on his own history. "It is not actual bombs *zhat* do *zeh* most damage. It is fathers missing from *zheir* children."

"Oh, I can agree with that now," answers Herbert. "A little late but not entirely so." He leans toward Le Deuce and asks quietly, "By the way, does your healthplan include therapy? Because that alone could really sink this project."

Danny looks at the porthole.

Rebecca reassures him, "The ship is fine, Danny."

He loosens his shirt collar. "Stop using *zhis* word."

Herbert winks at Le Deuce, wishing he could say, *It's hard to find good help these days.*

CHAPTER TWENTY-ONE

The Fabric of Our Lies

During Herbert's dinner, Olivia picks the lock and enters Le Deuce's cabin. His room and bathroom are spotless. His closet has three suits and five shirts, all the same; he keeps his wardrobe simple.

Photos of a perfect wife and children are on a counter. Olivia will continue to look around and be fascinated, maybe even shed tears about her own life that could have been. She will not find anything of interest to the mission.

The Twins explore Danny's room. This one is more interesting, but not to them; they are oblivious to history. Coasters with swastikas mean nothing to them. Nor does *Hitler Pride* imagery, or insignias for brands no one bothered to change since that war.

Their calls and responses to each other can be summed up as slang versions of, "Hark! Peruse this, my brother!" and, "How splendid indeed!"

They both show interest in a wind-up camel which they race against a wind-up senior with a walker. They take pictures as if spies using microfilm.

In the bathroom Woldecott picks up Danny's Whitey White toothpaste. An image shows shiny white teeth and a tagline reads, *There's a time and a place for white supremacy!*

He shows it to Wayne and they check their teeth in the mirror. Each puts a bit on a finger, sniffs it, and tastes it as if discerning a fine wine.

"Needs more cinnamon," opines Wayne.

He then finds a tiny tube of lip balm called ChapStoppo. He opens it and likes the fragrance, so he applies it to his armpits.

Woldecott declines a hit with, "No thanks, I'm good."

Moving back to the room, Wayne opens a small dresser drawer. Boxes of Milk Duds fill it and Wayne takes a picture. Another drawer has the same; Danny will never run out. A third has a magazine opened to a 1950s advertisement for a wristwatch. In it, a white family is having dinner. An inset shows off an impressive watch on the man's wrist. The headline reads, "He'll never be late again!" The man is wiping his mouth with a napkin and his dialog bubble says, "Well, Honey, off to the racists!"

Wayne comments, "Cool watch!"

Woldecott notices a book on the nightstand, *Adolf on Branding: Fashion Forward Fonts, Fades, and Fascism.* He snaps a picture.

Next, Wayne slides open the closet. It has several white robes with hoodies and eye-holes cut out. Neither Twin is familiar with American history either. One robe is clearly sized for Danny and the rest are longer. Wayne picks out the largest one and tries it on.

In the meantime the hanger itself catches Woldecott's attention. It resembles a noose, molded in hard white plastic. He says, "Bro, this guy is a little odd. How's the robe?"

Wayne returns it. "A little heavy for this time of year."

In another hallway, Mrs. Pearbottom looks both ways and uses a keycard foiling device on a door. She enters Dr. Singleton's cabin. The room is neat, with various pamphlets organized in small stacks on a counter. One title says, *Recover Your Faith in Scientists: Some Are Trustworthy*. Another says *The Unforced Be With You: A Guide to Healthy Relationships.* She takes interest in the latter but soon closes it, not able to change her life just now.

Next, she examines the bathroom; it is very orderly. She samples his cologne and likes it. She then feels his bathrobe. *Such good taste.*

In the foyer area outside the activity rooms, Dr. Singleton says goodnight to his attendees and leaves with his leftover pamphlets.

In his room, Mrs. Pearbottom checks her watch. The countdown reads 11 seconds and dropping. She concludes the room is clean and exits, taking an *Unforced* pamphlet.

Dr. Singleton approaches a corner while Mrs. Pearbottom closes his cabin door. She hurries away and they collide at the intersection. He drops his pamphlets and she ditches hers into the mix.

"Oh, excuse me!" apologizes Singleton.

"The fault was mine, Doctor," replies Mrs. Pearbottom.

They bend to gather pamphlets and their hands touch.

"I'm sorry!" he says again and they stand up.

"Me too. And I'm sorry for disrupting your meeting."

"Not at all," he answers. "Please, take this one on me." He hands her the pamphlet she had taken from his room.

She hesitates, unsure if he knows she had it or simply believes she could use it. "Thanks, but I don't know that I'm ready for anything like that just now."

He understands. "Try putting it in the back of a drawer at home. Then maybe one day when you're looking for something else, some new ideas could be right there waiting for you."

She accepts it. "You're very confident in what you believe. I don't see that a lot."

"Would you like to discuss it some time?"

"Are you allowed to consume alcohol?"

"In moderation."

"Good. Perhaps I'll hear you out some time." She walks away and a song like *Smooth Operator* comes to mind (Sade, 1984).

In the meantime, Rosie explores Rebecca's cabin, a habitat marked by chaos. Disorder. Haste. The bed is unmade. Every surface, chair, and luggage overflows with Precious Fabrics and brochures for Healthsharing. Rosie is stressed.

She opens the closet and finds Rebecca's sailor outfits, spaghetti strap dresses, and other outfits. Drawers are packed with silky pajamas, lingerie, underwear, socks, and bathing suits. Rosie feels them all, trying to discern differences in texture but can't.

She takes out her notebook and pen and scores items from one to five, with five being the smoothest. She second-guesses herself, makes changes, and becomes exasperated. *I have no idea!*

Next, she opens a large drawer. A rough burlap sack is there, filled with stapled paper packets. She takes out a handful and realizes they are the applications completed by seniors. They show bank accounts, social security numbers, and other sensitive information. The not-so-fine tiny tiny print says the accounts will be used for immediate and unlimited donations to *PreciousFabrics.uk* with no mention of healthsharing. *There is something not right about this.*

She feels the fabric of the bag itself again but still cannot tell the difference between burlap and silk. Finally, she takes the whole bag and exits.

CHAPTER TWENTY-TWO

A View from a Roomba

At dinner with Le Deuce, Herbert hears him say, "Mr. Bigglesby, in a few minutes I'd like to show you a really boring documentary that captures the fullness of our vision. Danny and Rebecca have already seen it, I don't know how many times, so I won't require them to attend."

"Eight hundred and fifty six," says Danny. "Plus *zeh* early edits."

Herbert looks at Rebecca. "I suppose there are worse ways to spend an evening."

She is bothered by his seeming imperviousness to her charms.

Later, Herbert and Le Deuce watch the awardless documentary alone; the other two have left. The video is very corporate and polished, with paid actors instead of actual participants. They look excessively sad and bent over, and clearly fake their health problems. It's as if they wouldn't want casting directors to think they might actually have a problem. They are also too young and good-looking beneath the obvious *cakeup*.

In one scene, a toddler runs into the arms of his fake-elderly grandmother, who rises from a wheelchair and scoops him off his little feet. She pretends to be unsteady at first but is vigorous and stands firm.

Yay, there's help for grandma! thinks Herbert, just as the woman's fake daughter uses the same exact words. Herbert looks at his watch and frowns. He holds it to his ear, wondering if it's moving at all.

Le Deuce is immune to Herbert's body language. "It's good, isn't it?"

As they watch, a sexy woman in silky black pajamas and mask searches Herbert's cabin. "Where to even begin?" she asks. "This could take hours." The voice is Rebecca's.

In his surveillance room Danny sips a large soda with a straw. "We don't have hours," he answers her.

"Thanks for the added pressure," she replies. She opens a drawer and it immediately brightens her mood. "Oh, score! Tax returns!" She skims the first, second, and third one. The zeros needed for gross income do not all fit so they are hand-written along the edge. She holds them up to Himmler's eyes.

"*Comrade,* check this out!" she says. "For each year over the past five years he's had like a huge income and zero tax liability."

"So *zhen* he really is rich."

"I told you so!"

"But why did his friend say he was a spy? What if he is part of *zeh* law enforcement somewhere?"

Rebecca guffaws. "Where, *Chuck E. Cheese*?"

"I will do *zeh* witty commentary, *Fräulein.* Excuse one moment, I need to go take—no, leave, a wiz… *vis-a-vis zeh* bathroom."

"Thank you for the play-by-play."

"I will be right back if I survive. With my horrible U.T.I. So painful." He sips his drink a final time and exits.

"So dramatic," she murmurs. In another drawer she finds a silky red, wide-bottomed, fluid-absorbing lingerie by *Victoria's Secretions.* "Shoot me now," she says, expecting to stay one of the young and the rashless for the rest of her life.

In Le Deuce's dining suite they watch a pivotal scene in which a fake-elderly woman uncaps a pen and fills out a form.

"Nice! Anyway, I believe I've given your people ample time to rifle through my belongings." Herbert stands up.

Le Deuce gets to his feet as well. "But that's preposterous!"

"Not really, five minutes would be enough."

"What I mean is, I have no interest in spying on people. That would belie my life's good work."

Herbert looks at him sideways, believing his own life's work has just been judged. "That's rather judgmental of you," he says. "Besides, I would not be offended. Due diligence is a duty."

"Perhaps, but that is not how I operate."

"I hope you thoroughly vetted your staff. Like Ms. Holmeslyce, for example. There's no telling what else she does in her *pre-prosperous* period. Not that I judge her for it. Or you, for that matter."

"Are you implying that she and I… that something has occurred below board?"

"Not if you say it hasn't."

"My honor matters a great deal, Mr. Bigglesby. I adhere to very high standards."

"Yes, but she clearly meets them. An eleven, as they say."

"Will you stop insinuating… sin?"

"Very well. I believe we are mutually reassured. I'd be delighted to serve on your illustrious Board."

"That's wonderful news!" says Le Deuce. He urges Herbert to sit. "Perhaps we can celebrate by finishing the video!"

Herbert shuffles to the door instead. "I think my time is better spent elsewhere. Anywhere. Any other way, really."

"But there's a crucial scene coming up!" Le Deuce fast-forwards, desperate to keep Herbert interested. The screen shows endless shots of people talking and nodding.

"I'm sure it's riveting. To someone. With insomnia, perhaps. But tootles! We'll be in touch." Herbert exits.

"Oh, very well." Le Deuce sits down and continues the video. Tears come to his eyes. He wipes them with a perfectly pressed handkerchief. He simply cannot get enough of his life's work coming to fruition.

Herbert shuffles past the Stand-Up Comedy room and does a double-take. Someone has made it *Stand-By* Comedy with a Sharpie. He can't resist another peek inside.

This time the *faux* Amish performer is singing ala Paula Cole (1996). *"Where have all the milk maids gone? / Oh I know your hands hurt / From churning all the bees wax / I will plow your fields, Wife / You drink lemonade / Where have all the milk maids gone?"*

A woman mans a table with copies of her book for sale. She has a plain face and wears round glasses. The book cover shows the author herself next to a cow. The title says, *The Dairy of Fanny Franklin. How I Went from Self-Harming to Self-Farming.* Herbert buys a copy with Japanese Yen; it's all he finds in his pockets.

Back in Herbert's cabin, Rebecca flips through an album (which is a kind of physical *book*). It holds yellowing pictures in clear plastic sleeves, showing a perfect Bigglesby family from the 1960s to 1980s. A younger Olivia in a bowler hat wears a school uniform and various other outfits at different ages while growing up. In the 1990s she marries a huge tattooed monster. Then she is raising her Twins by herself, the father ripped out of most pictures. In a later image the three visit their dad in a remote state prison. The boys wore t-shirts that said, *Prison Sucks!* and, *My Dad is inmate of the month at UC Lancaster!* (cfr. fernfactor.com). Thanks to photo editing, a younger Herbert has been made present in many of them.

Rebecca asks Danny, "But why did he lie to us? He said he didn't meet his daughter and grandsons till recently."

Silence from the other end. His drink sits there alone.

"Hello? Danny? Are you still not back yet?"

In a hallway, Herbert and Rosie nearly collide. She holds up the burlap bag. "Look, I found something *big*!"

"It's *Mister* Big to you!" He looks at the bag and scowls. "Oh, I can't believe it. Rosie, how can you miss-take something so large? And completely unsmooth? You need to put it back immediately!"

"I know but–"

"That's burlap, about the roughest fabric on the planet. Next to the toilet paper after the last budget cuts."

"I tried to tell you about my feelings!"

"Can't you put those aside when you're working?"

"Please, just look inside!" She holds the bag open.

Herbert smiles politely as other people pass. Then he asks, "Why, is it silky?" he feels the inner lining. "No! Just more burlap!"

"Not that, Sir!" She reaches in and pulls out a few forms. "Look! These are the applications–"

Herbert is done. "I believe they are called *apps* now. I'm older than you and I know that! Please, go put them back." He continues toward his room.

She follows, imploring him. "But this is the scam! We need to stop her!"

Herbert turns. "Rosie, please! I know you want to help but this puts the whole mission at risk. Leave the big thinking to me. You just hurry back and put this bag where it was before it's missed!"

She shakes the bag. "But, Sir! I can make her explain!"

Herbert is horrified to think of Rebecca being interrogated by Rosie, or even shoved into the burlap sack. He tries not to sound too superior in making his point.

"Rosie, I know we were trained a little differently. On my side of the Wall we never stuffed people into laundry bags."

Rosie looks confused.

Herbert continues, "I know, it's shocking. And some people on my side should get sacked. But anyway, please go put it back. Get it back to where it was before" (cfr. The Beatles, 1970). He leaves her.

Rosie resigns herself yet again to submit and obey.

In Herbert's cabin, Rebecca now scans his book collection. If she were not so pressed for time she would want to read some of them. Here are a few:

To Mock a Killingbird: How the Right Missed the Mark with Luigi Mangione and his Exposure of Calls that Kill.

Another is a Southern romance called *Gone with the Wimp.* It's about a Mississippi woman who follows a dream to go fail in LA while leaving a husband, four kids, and her integrity behind.

A third is *The Princess Bright.* She has the smarts to have a great life but small-town pressures urge her to settle for Wendell the unstable boy.

While she peruses, Danny re-enters his surveillance room and takes his seat. Rebecca's voice broadcasts through a tinny speaker. "Hello? Danny-who? Where are you? Still in the loo?"

Danny mutters to himself before he can put on his earpiece. "Everyone thinks *zhey* can rhyme now. It's so easy! At least I bothered to attend *Die Universität Wien* followed by Christ Church College so I know what I am talking about."

He is alarmed to see Herbert shuffling to his room. He puts in his earpiece and yells, "He is coming! *Kamerad,* you need to hide!"

"Wait, what?" she asks.

"Hide! He is at your door!"

Herbert's electronic deadbolt retreats and the door handle turns. He enters his cabin and turns on a light. He ignores the sexy figure in his bed and removes his tie and cufflinks in the mirror.

The world goes black-and-white again. Except for red lipstick on a cigarette, burning on a make-shift ashtray on the nightstand.

Rebecca no longer wears her mask but she is otherwise undercover. Next door, a song resembling, *I'm Looking Through You* (Beatles, 1965) starts up. Herbert hums along with the tune.

Rebecca speaks. "I was getting worried you might not come."

Herbert regards her coolly in the mirror. "That is never my issue. Only people not knowing that know means know-how."

Rebecca wants to answer but has no clever reply just yet.

Herbert applies his Chipstick, wincing due to the poor balm-to-spike ratio. He masks the pain, the blood, and the point. "You know, I see right through that thin cover of yours."

She holds up a corner of the bedspread to the light. "I don't think so. It's pretty solid."

"*Opaque* is the word."

The music stops abruptly. She looks at him askance. "I thought it was *Grease*" (Valli, 1978).

"Is that what you heard?" He listens closely. The 1970s musical now plays next door (Kleiser, 1978). "Ah, yes."

Danny grows impatient. "Enough of *zhis* two-play. You need to woo him."

Rebecca is not enthused.

"Show some pep, *Fräulein!* You said you were a team player. A highly motivated multitasker."

"Fine, I get it!" she says to both men, resigning herself to the role. *It's just a job*, she tells herself. *It doesn't mean anything.* She slithers around under the covers to pique the target male's interest.

Herbert feigns indifference. However, as the music continues next door, he weakens. *What if this is the proper time, the proper space?* he wonders. *She shouldn't have forced me to change so suddenly. And these emotions, why keep reeling? There's not much chance I can shake them. Why throw pleasure away?*

Rebecca foolishly interrupts his dialog with temptation. "So, Mr. Big Bad Wolfie, were you a good boy with Mr. Le Deucey? Did you sign his little form or is that something we will be celebrating here and now?"

She puts her hands behind her head, looking even sexier. Herbert's eyes look to the door, knowing he should flee. His legs and other parts of his body don't agree.

Danny enjoys his waffle. "*Zhat's* good, *Fräulein*! You got *zhis*!"

She tells both men, "No kidding. I have it in the bag."

"Well you don't have to brag," Danny chastises.

Rebecca leans over and grabs her chic backpack, swaying to the music as she slowly unzips it. "So come over here and get it."

Herbert swallows loose spit and wipes his mouth. "Slow down there, Darling."

She slows her dancing to the speed of a robotic street performer and jerkily produces a blank application.

Herbert turns away, throwing off his weakness like a fluffy white bathrobe. "I don't think so, Baby. There would be no meaning in it."

"And what does *that* even mean?"

The philosophical gauntlet is on. The mirror holds a 1940s glamour shot of her as smoke rises from the cigarette.

Herbert addresses her reflection. "Touché! You've answered a big question with another big question."

"I didn't know they came in sizes."

"Oh, yes."

Rebecca puts out the cigarette. "Who even started this?"

"Some say Socrates, but others came even earlier."

"Then you must be exhausted," she says. "I'll keep all those people away in the future."

Danny is embarrassed.

She presses on. "Look, what I represent is such a good Cause." She opens the bed cover for him to join her. "We can have so much fun and *still* think of the children!"

Danny looks alarmed. "*Nein*! Not *zeh* children argument!"

"I've been hearing a lot about kids lately. But look at you." He turns to face her. "Or better not to." He shields his eyes and shuffles to the bathroom. "Do your parents even know you're here?"

Rebecca is baffled by his radical departure. She hears water running in the bathroom and confers with Danny. "I think there's something wrong with him. Maybe he's gay now?"

"Or maybe you need to try harder, *Kamerad*. Have you stopped going to Louisiana Fitness? You put on a few kilos, perhaps?"

She suppresses her anger. "Don't make this about me. Why don't you come give this a try?"

"Me?! Why do you say *zhis* thing? And about *zeh* gay?" Danny runs his hand through his thinning hair. "Please do not start *zeh* rumors!" He sits up taller to look more masculine.

Herbert re-enters from the bathroom, brushing his teeth. "Oh, you're still here. You know, you don't need to be in my bed to get me to sign that thing."

"I don't?" She gets to her feet and fixes up the bed. She finds and pockets her silk mask, hoping Herbert didn't see it.

"Of course not. Like I told Mr. Le Deuce, I believe in your Cause." He looks at her but then away. "Pure and simple."

She blushes. "Not really, but I appreciate the thought," she answers. She grabs her bag and digs out a pen.

Herbert takes it and clicks it a few times, waiting for the application. "I suppose form follows function?"

"What? Oh yeah." She finds the application but then Herbert suddenly turns away.

"I just remembered, I have more to say before I comply with your scheme."

She reacts, wondering if he suspects something is awry.

He continues, "Please listen as if you were my own daughter. If she were a lot younger and prettier. And had your mental issues."

Rebecca contains her various reactions. She sits on the edge of the bed, willing to endure a paternal lecture in exchange for a multimillion-dollar allowance.

"Look, yours is an old story, really. A young beautiful woman–that's not harassment, just a fact. You probably packed it up in some Ruralham one day and headed for the big city, eager to prove yourself. Someone important there probably offered you a break. Except, there's a catch. To be made. You have to reel in a big fish, like me, for some boss-man who promises you shiny things, the right introductions, and all his protection."

Danny listens, worried he might ruin her with knowledge.

Herbert continues, "You probably agreed to it, with no coercion or violence, even though you know the clock is ticking and he's only using you till the next young thing offers more for less. Or more *with* less. Or *less is more* in your trade?" Herbert has confused himself.

Danny reacts with annoyance. "Why does he talk so much? Get back to wooing him, Jo-Jo" (Beatles, 1970).

Rebecca is annoyed with both men. *It's not my first Rodeo Drive.* Aloud she says, "Herbert, Darling, I'm not sure what you think I am. I choose my men for love, with no interior motives."

"Ulterior?"

"Not those either! I don't expect marriage, or divorce! Easy come, easier go." She holds up the application, "It just takes a sec and then, Welcome to Paradise!" (Green Day, 1994).

He looks her over. "No strings, is that it?"

She is unsure but finds her bra straps right where they are supposed to be. "All in good times," she answers, and extends the application. "Say *yes* to love and then no more strings!"

Herbert looks disgusted. "How dumb do you think I am?"

"Why put a number on it? Let's just have fun till we each get what we want out of this. It's a fun world; we should enjoy it!" She stands and takes his hand but he unexpectedly pulls it away.

He even turns away, trying to be the man his daughter and society want him to be. "Baby Doll, can't you see? I am considered a power figure. Ow!" He briefly winces with back pain. "With all my money, reputation, and access to world leaders, you have no choice but to be impressed and overwhelmed. A relationship with me can only be one of exploitation and abuse."

"That's not true! I admire you and it has nothing to do with your money and power and physique."

"That's not even possible! You only think you are free. Dominant alpha males like me are a weakness for you. Under all this imbalance you can only be a victim, and I, a predator. Even if you take my money, my reputation, and my kids. And file unrestrained orders."

Who would want your 60-year-old kids? she wonders.

Herbert continues, "But it doesn't have to be that way! Not for a bright–or at least *young*–lady like you. You don't need to trade your body for security. Or advancement. Here, read this!"

He shows her the book he just bought. She looks it over. "You want me to keep a diary?"

"No, it says, *Dairy*. It's just one example of other things you can milk instead of your feminine wiles."

"While what? My feminine is permanent."

"Is this the life you really want? Always lowering yourself to please some charming man's lowest non-stop appetites?"

Herbert turns away again, lest she hear his thoughts. *Please say no. Do not say yes. Please do not say yes. I'm really trying here.* He lists sideways, much like a man on a ship trying not to tip.

Rebecca is unsure of what to say. Partly because she is not sure what Herbert just said.

Danny pushes her. "Tell him your *yes means yes!* Or *uh-huh!* And *totally!* We need you in his pockets."

She scowls at Danny pressuring her. In contrast she says, "You're very honorable, Mr. Bigglesby."

"I am? I mean, I suppose it can seem that way. But it's important to separate business from pressure. Speaking of which, are you being trafficked? Blink twice if you can't speak openly."

"What? No! I'm not some helpless child. I'm a *disrupter.* I'm powerful too, you know. And this conversation is getting on my nerves. Healthsharing is legit and Le Deuce is legit!"

"That's wonderful news."

"So do you want to be a part of my medical history or not? Even without this." She throws the application aside and climbs into bed, making room for him as well.

Herbert did not expect to still have another opportunity. He resists yet again and grabs the application for review.

"Let's see, you want my bank accounts, social security, mother's maiden name. Nothing too sensitive."

He sits down at the vanity to fill it out. He can't help looking at her reflection. "You know, my mother was a maiden once."

Just fill the darn thing out, she wishes she could say.

Herbert writes but then can't help talking again, his pen idling over the paper. "You do realize I was not criticizing you. There is nothing *shameful* in still having unresolved daddy issues to work through. There's plenty of time to work them out."

He turns to her, no longer avoiding eye contact. "Especially with the right father figure, I might add," which he did just add.

"Go with it *Fräulein!*" coaches Danny. "Let him be your daddy." He opens another box of Milk Duds.

"Are you kidding me right now?" she asks both men.

"Why?" asks Danny.

"Denial is to be expected," says Herbert. "Defense mechanisms in general. But Ms. Holmeslyce, you have nothing to fear. I am not going to indulge in this situation myself, this opportunity."

She looks relieved.

"I will not exploit your gender's weakness for adroit powerful men like me."

"That's so very honorable of you," she says. She makes a writing gesture in the air while pointing to the application.

Herbert shakes the form and says, "I just don't think Mr. Le Deuce should be exploiting you like this. Sending you here to do his work."

"Would you rather a man come?"

"Certainly not!"

"*Kamerad*, tell him it's fine to exploit you! This is his moment!"

Rebecca looks at Himmler. "What ever happened to misogyny?"

Herbert adjusts a hearing aid. "I'm sorry, Miss Who?"

Danny can't believe she is going there. "*Zhis* is no time to argue about principles!"

"Misogyny!" repeats Rebecca.

Herbert racks his brain. "She doesn't ring a bell."

"Liar!" declares Danny loudly, hurting Rebecca's ear. "He has intimate knowledge of *zeh* misogyny. With many trainings on best practices!"

Rebecca closes her eyes and clears her mind for a moment. "Mr. Biggleby, I think you are wrong about all that power talk. I am old enough to know exactly who and what I want."

"I'm on my way!" Herbert is delighted and rushes to join her but she alights from the bed.

"You've convinced me that I shouldn't be here. I'm a living stereotype. It was a terrible life mistake to imply I'd do *anything* for some petty financial gain, even if a good Cause would benefit. It's too shameful. I need to go back to Cincinnati."

She heads for the door as if a Greyhound station. Neither man wants to see her go.

Danny blurts out, "Petty financial gain?! You can *buy* Cincinnati with *zeh* money he has!"

Herbert quickly fills out the form. "Please don't go! I'm almost done. We can stick to the original plan with no funny business."

Rebecca's mind is too clear now. She stops by the door. "I'm sorry, I don't think that's a good idea anymore. Hot young women like me can't be friends with men like you. It's just a fact. There's always something else involved. Mr. Le Deuce can assign me to a female donor and Danny can help you with your needs."

Neither man likes that idea.

"What are you saying, Rebecca? Just get his form, AARP!"

Herbert opines, "That seems like such an extreme unnecessary precaution, I think."

"But *irregardless*," she assures him, "I want you to know I was impressed tonight. I underestimated you. You are much stronger than most men of your persuasion." She kisses him on the cheek.

"Is that right?" He tries for a hug but she doesn't give one. He clasps his hands behind his back to help him stand tall.

Rebecca continues, "I mean, it's crazy, but just moments ago I was ready to throw all caution to the wind, without even a thread of protection between us, but you saved me from that."

"I don't know what came over me."

"That was so noble!"

"It was?" Herbert scrambles to find a new way in. "Or perhaps judgmental, in retrospect? I may have appealed to old taboos. In fact, I'm a little worried we might both be changing too quickly. Which could prove harmful. Like Marcus Aurelius said, *Moderation in all things*. Even in reform!"

"Marcus O'Reilly?" she asks. "Wait, are you back-pedaling?"

"No! Not at all!... Should I be?"

She is disgusted. Danny is thrilled. "You have him! Bring him to his needs! And forget I am even watching *zhis* thing."

Ew! Rebecca is even more turned off now. "You were right, that I should use my mind and not my body to get ahead."

"But your mind is so alluring. It's what I first noticed."

"Don't throw *zhis* all away, *Fräulein*. It's billions!"

Rebecca looks at Herbert's application. It still has too little filled out. She gives up the Cincinnati idea and reconnects with her passion for money. "Herbie-Werbie, you're so smart! We do need to slow down any radical life changes. How about you turn off the lights?"

Danny complains. "What?! Why no lights? Do not be ashamed of *zeh* body, *Kamerad*. *Zhis* is just a job. You are *artiste*!"

Herbert is about to speak.

"Oh, quiet!" Rebecca rips out her earpiece, places it on the nightstand, and gets back into bed. "Just come already!"

Herbert and the room are delighted. But he has a moment of hesitation while in the dark. *It's only fair that I not be rushed. It wasn't fair how Olivia sprang it on me and then tricked me. Plus haste makes waste. I can commit to new ways after this.*

He shuffles toward the bed but knocks over a cart full of food. Platters crash to the floor.

"Are you ok?" asks Rebecca, still in the dark.

"Yes, perfectly fine. Why do you ask?"

"I don't know. I thought I heard something."

"I see. Though not much. But I just remembered something." He goes back and turns on the light. He now holds a gun, fighting against a Parkinsonian tremble. "I can see clearly now," he says.

That song starts up next door (Nash, 1972).

"Oh dear!" gasps Danny.

"You like it a little rough?" asks Rebecca. "I'm game."

"I'm done playing games, Sweetheart. I'll do the talking. Except when I ask a question. Then I'll pause for you to respond."

He pauses. After a moment Rebecca asks, "Wait, was there a question?"

"Quiet! I am still giving my speech. Is that clear? Which is a question. You can answer it now."

"Now? Is that the answer you want?"

"No! Answer if it's clear! That I'm asking the questions."

"I see. I mean, yes, it's clear."

"Good. Let's begin. Before I came in, why were you in here, rifling through my effects?"

She opens her mouth but rethinks what to answer.

"Spill it. Le Deuce is crooked, right? He's scamming seniors without remorse? Will he stop at nothing?"

"That was three questions!" she complains.

"I knew he was law enforcement!" says Danny.

Rebecca looks at the tiny earpiece on the nightstand and then back at Herbert. He does not seem to have noticed it.

"Well? Spill it already!" Herbert insists.

She then reveals her deepest, darkest, life-changing secrets. Actually, in reality she says, "To be honest, Mr. Le Deuce is probably the most naive, honest, and trustworthy person I've ever met."

Herbert is not buying it. "Then why were you buttering me up, offering your body away like a delicious appetizer for his Cause?"

"I told you, I didn't come here for him. I came here for you. That form was just a spare I had in my bag. You captured my heart and soul. I'm fond! Just fond."

Herbert's head tilts as if recalling something. He shakes it off. "That makes sense. But don't expect me to sign anything tonight."

"Of course not! I agree. It's interfering with our relationship. Let's talk about you for a change."

"Me? What do you want to know?"

"Everything!" She points at the photo album. "Why did you lie about not being in your daughter's life?"

Herbert lowers his pistol. "Because I don't always know *who* needs to know *what* or *how* much. Or *when*. That's *why*. Understand?"

She is not sure how many of the five famous *W*'s he just used. She adds her favorite: "Whatever. And are you really who the internet says you are? I mean, is all that money even real?"

"Of course it's real."

"Then why did your friend say you were a spy?"

"My *friend*?" Herbert laughs. "You mean that moron from the senile folks' home? Even if I were the best, foremost—really, topmost—secret agent to ever live—and almost die like three hundred times saving everybody and the planet—do you think I would tell *him*? Seriously, Jake Kimble?"

"Ah, I guess not. Which makes me think you are then."

"A spy? That's rich! For who, Mossad?"

"Ok, but if you're just some rich guy with no government connections, why would you live at that place?"

"First of all, I don't, for one! But yes, I *pretended* to. For research. Because nursing homes are a good racket if they're run right. Meaning wrong. So I was doing my due diligence and I did it so I'm done." Herbert sits on the bed and caresses the bedspread. "I like to get intimate knowledge of things before I make them my own."

"How… diligent," she flatters. "I can see why you succeed in every endeavor you undertake."

They stare at each other for a beat. Herbert suddenly stands up for something. "But it's not adding up!" He re-trains his gun on her. "Who are you really with, Baby? If not Le Deuce then who? CIA? KGB? JDL?" Her confused look makes him clarify, "Jewish Defense League?"

Danny is shocked by possibilities he had never even considered.

Rebecca is dramatic. "I don't know why you still won't believe me! I love Love! And healthsharing. Why can't it be that simple? Are you insecure?"

Herbert almost pistol-whips her. "Sure, Baby, sure! I'm insecure and you seek true love on the high seas. With people twice your age.

Oh, let's be real, three times your age, or four if you go for Jake Kimble! But I'm getting wise. I may not be the quick ticket you think I am. I don't have letters of transit for you, Baby."

"Letters of transit? I don't even know what those are."

"We can't go on like this, Kiddo. I'm falling apart." (Elvis starts up next door; Presley 1969/2002.) "You need to collect your things and get out of here. Go back to Cincinnati. Get out of this racket." He waves the gun toward the door.

She sits up in bed. "What are you saying? I want Love!"

"It's not worth it. A kiss is just a kiss. A banana is just a banana. There's not much more, as time goes bye-bye."

"Please, Love! Be my Daddy and sign that silly paper. Then come celebrate with me!"

"And then what? We live naughtily ever after? Till death do its part? And you take my fortune? Away from my family?"

"Don't say things like that! I'm not some gold-tooth digger."

Herbert thought he was over this temptation but his internal battle is not yet won. "I would love to just shut you up, Baby. And live in the present moment, making wild passionate love to you. But now I know too much. I can't live on this ledge of compromise. Just picture it! After all the fun parts we'll be left with *honeydo's*, except I won't do, and I don't do. And between my virility and your fertility we'd have kids popping out left and right, and then what? It'll be diapers all around for you, Baby! Is that the life you want?"

Rebecca can't hide her obvious, *Nope.* Perhaps she pictures Vilefinger in his own diapers, smearing his feces on a canvas.

"Tell him it's fine!" repeats Danny. Rebecca puts her earpiece back in. "Promise you're ready for whatever *zeh* life brings as long as you are together! Quote *zeh* Pope if you have to and then do whatever you want later."

She tries. "All I know is, our children will be so adorable, Love!"

Herbert shakes her by the shoulders. "Oh, cut the nonsense, Baby! For whom are you working and why?"

"I told you! Le Deuce." She feigns fear which is even more attractive to him.

He slaps the nightstand. "Tell me the truth!"

"Ok, Danny!"

"That midget? Stop lying!"

Herbert slaps the table with every name she names. "Le Deuce!" Slap. "Danny!" Slap. "Le Deuce!" Slap. "Danny!" Slap.

He grabs her lapels. "And you think I should really sink my whole fortune into something this risky, and so unwanted by any government or the powers that keep healthcare so inadequate?"

"Yes, I do!" Rebecca answers, almost in tears. "Why are you so afraid to *win*? And to use your fortune for good? We can be part of this beautiful solution together!"

Herbert still plays tough. "It's not possible! Healthsharing can't be real! It's too good! What is it really all about?"

She nods in disbelief. Then finally laughs. "Ok, wait. You really think healthsharing is a scam?"

"Of course it is! People don't do that for each other. Pay it forward for someone else's care?"

Danny can't believe the irony. "He is so close and yet so blind.

Rebecca takes another tact. "Ok, Mr. Big. You got me."

Danny worries. "What are you saying?"

"I too thought Le Deuce was a scam at first," she explains. "And you're right, I don't really work for him." She smiles innocently.

"I knew it! You're checking up on me! MI-5? MI-6?"

"Emotionally, maybe. But no, you were right. I'm CIA."

"Of course you are!" He includes her team. "Of course she is! I knew it! It was obvious!"

He lowers his gun. The *film noir* look saturates with color.

"And who is he with?" asks Danny. "We still do not know."

"Your cover has been very believable. I had to make sure you hadn't actually defected."

"I always have been a master of disguises," Herbert says.

Danny is all ice. "*Fräulein, zhis* is serious. He cannot leave alive."

She doesn't need his *mansplaining.* "What a relief this is!" she calls out for all her supposed team to hear. "Our joint investigation into Le Deuce is now complete. Please take him into custody, gentlemen, while I sign off and relax for a bit."

Herbert is impressed, and playful. "I'm glad the CIA doesn't make the ladies do the arresting. So what sealed the deal for you? Did it take a little coochy-coochy with Le Doochy? Or, don't tell me you got it from his sidekick Reisenschein?"

"No! Whatever!" She can't hide a brief face of disgust.

Herbert assures her, "No judgment if you did."

Danny fumes, "*Zhat* is not acceptable! Correct him please!"

"Are you kidding?" Rebecca laughs. "Le Deuce made it easy with his family man image. And Danny is, well, gay as fff–*fuchsia*."

"Why do you say *zhis? Zeh* false rumors are hard to undo!"

"To be honest, I was glad they had me work on you instead." She stands and grabs her bag. "It will break Le Deuce's heart to know I was the one spying on him."

"He'll get over it." Herbert does not want her to go.

Rebecca can see it. "Herbert, since we are done so early, maybe we can just relax while my team moves in. You're such a legend! A rock star! Tell me about the old days."

"I'd rather talk about the past instead." He touches her sleeve. "And you can tell me more about these wild fabrics. I'm a big believer in side hustles. I would easily invest in this."

"You would?" She then makes the classic villain mistake of talking too much. "I'm so excited, tomorrow I get to start visiting countries where we'll be sourcing new materials!"

Danny is concerned. "Why are you saying *zhis*?"

DING! Herbert is back in the boxing ring. His vision is blurry as he fights to stay in the present. He pulls himself out of it.

"Are we already in the Suez?" He shuffles to the porthole, gun still in hand.

"Um, yes," she answers. "Why?"

"Change *zeh* subject!" insists Danny.

In the boxing ring, the fighters walk back to their respective corners. One suddenly turns back and attacks the other. Herbert tries to stop him but fails. He has become irrelevant to the forces at play.

"You need to shoot him, Rebecca."

She joins Herbert at the porthole as if eager to see as well.

"How long have we been crossing it?" asks Herbert. He can't help being mesmerized by her fragrance and closeness.

"Not long."

Danny is having a meltdown. "Why are you still talking? Get to *zeh* kissy kissy, bang bang!"

Herbert seems hypnotized but also wants to convey a state of urgency. "Your people need to stop this ship immediately!"

"Why? Le Deuce has been taken into custody by now. We're not letting *him* reach international waters, duh. That would be dumb."

"Good. I'm so glad your people are here. Mine are slow to act."

She touches his collar. "We should celebrate, Rock Star." She gently leads him to the bed.

"What could you possibly want with an old-timer like me?"

"Will you stop deprecating yourself? Any woman who knows your history would be honored to warm your bed." She then climbs in and makes room. "It's so cozy."

He regards her for a moment. "And you're not going to claim abuse later?"

"Of course not!"

She seems so sincere. But he still turns her down. "I'm sorry. I'm supposed to be with my family tonight."

"Why? Let them have some fun! And do they even understand all the pressures you've been under? We both deserve this break." She caresses the bedspread.

"They'll probably come looking for me soon. That would be awkward. I'll go tell them I'm calling it a night." He starts off.

"You promise?"

He looks back. "Are you having self-doubts, Baby?"

"Fine, be quick, then!"

"Only in this matter, I assure you." Herbert shuffles to the door. Before he opens it, Rebecca's silky pajama top lands on his head.

"Just a promissory note," she says, "of things to come."

He inhales her fragrance and looks back. He can see bra straps on bare shoulders but she is otherwise undercover.

"Well done, Princess." Danny sighs with relief.

As Herbert hesitates, Rebecca struggles to remove her pajama bottoms as well. She throws them at Herbert, who stands like a dear in the headlines.

"Come hither, you goose."

Something about that word gives Herbert pause.

"Who's my Papa? Are you my Papa? Wehhh! Feed me!"

Herbert regards her pouty beauty for a minor eternity. "Fine. Let me get naked." He reaches for his buttons.

Except that that is not what actually happens, dear Reader. What he really says is, "I'm sorry, Ms. Holmeslyce. My family would never forgive me a second time."

He opens the door but looks back. "Of course, if your mother or an auntie are ever available, that's a different story."

"No, they won't be. Ever! Can I have those back, and I'll just go back to my CIA friends?"

"Sorry, Sweetheart." He shuffles out into the hallway with her silky black prizes around his neck.

"Stop him! You must stop him!" commands Danny.

"Oh, shut up!" Wrapping the bedcover around herself, Rebecca runs out to the hall but it's too late. Herbert is too far gone, jamming her jammies into his pockets.

A young man approaches the grinning old man. Then he sees the bitter young woman in the background, wrapped in a blanket. "Respect," he says to Herbert.

This time Herbert is turned off by the assumption.

CHAPTER TWENTY-THREE

The Family that Spies Together

In a very large hangar, a fleet of jet skis lines the walls. The Twins sit on two of them, bored and scrolling on their phones. Herbert opens the door and closes it in disappointment. He then realizes he saw something he wanted and opens it again.

"Ah, here you are! I've been looking all over for you."

Wayne responds, "We're so bored, *Grampa*! There was nothing to report from the little guy's cabin."

"Where is your mother? We need to stop this ship!"

The Twins become ecstatic. "Yes! That sounds epic!"

Moments later Herbert rushes into his cabin with Olivia, the Twins, and Rosie. His bedspread is missing.

"Where is your bedspread?" asks Olivia, suspicious.

"An acquaintance needed one. What did you find in Le Deuce's room?"

"Nothing. What kind of acquaintance?" insists Olivia.

"Later. Where is Mrs. Pearbottom?" Herbert checks the hall and closes the door again. "Of course, he's too smart to leave anything lying around. Look, we can't let this ship reach the Red Sea or he'll get away with it. People will lose their savings and our countries cannot prosecute crimes in international waters."

"What are you talking about, *Papa*? People don't just borrow bedspreads!"

"She had one task to do, how is she not here?" Herbert then looks Olivia in the eye. "Please trust me, Daughter! I have honored my commitment to you, and at great personal cost I might add."

"You did add it." Olivia begins to soften. "I appreciate it."

"She better not be with him." Herbert checks the hall again. "They mustn't have their way with people!"

Rosie opines, "I think Mrs. Pearbottom can take care of herself."

"That kind of thinking is when people get hurt."

Olivia asks, "Are you seriously worried about Dr. Singleton?"

"Or Le Deuce?" complains Rosie. "They're not the scammers! It's that little guy and the sexy lady! They're up to something but Healthsharing is good."

"Maybe she needs us." He turns to Olivia, "*Hija*, can I count on you?"

Olivia loves that he called her that. "Of course, *Papi!* I'm with you one hundred percent."

The Twins do fist-pulls. "Yes! We are too!"

Olivia continues, "It's not that I trust your judgment, *Papi*. Or your limited perspectives. But I do trust your heart now."

Herbert keeps it real. "And I trust your hat, and your boys' skills. But we need a plan."

Rosie does not want to be left out. "I'm not saying I won't help. I just have some reservations."

From the surveillance room, Danny and Rebecca watch Herbert's secret secret meeting. Gunther sleeps in the background, a large volume on his lap like Churchill's, *History of the English-Speaking Peoples*. Rebecca wears a beige track suit and sneakers.

"I do not know if I have ever seen a bigger fool," says Danny.

Rebecca defends Herbert. "I admired his tries at self-control. It was cute. A little confusing at first."

Danny continues. "I was worried Precious Fabrics might be too obvious a scam. Not healthsharing. Sharing *zeh* cost of health is only a some-brainer, like preventing crime and sewer backups."

Rebecca clears her throat in a particularly loud and attention-drawing manner. Gunther is startled awake for a moment.

In another cabin, Le Deuce and three CIA agents in flowery shirts perk up, listening to Rebecca's conversation with Danny.

"Goodness, you are a master scammer!" she continues. "As you heard, Mr. B does not even suspect our Precious Fabrics might be crooked. He even wants to invest in it."

"Good!" answers Danny. He notices a wire sticking out of Rebecca's top and reaches for it. She startles, unsure if she has been discovered or if he is being inappropriate. He tucks the wire back into her top as if it's just a loose thread. Then he caresses her cheek with the back of his hand.

"You know I could have you, right? If I wasn't so gay?"

"Of course, my Boss Man. And I appreciate the delay. Later it will be an honor to have our excellent working relationship capitulate into an ill-fated romantic one. But please explain it all to me again. What is it we are really doing here, since I am a girl and cannot possibly understand the full genius of your plan?"

"Do you still not see? Nazi *zeh* point?" He smiles at his own joke. Her eyes idle in vacancy. "Come *Fräulein*! You even passed out *zeh* forms! We have their bank accounts! And 401k's! Everything! Without us sharing a single truffle with *zeh* health or Le Deuce!"

She plays along. "Such stupid people. They all deserve to be scammed and bamboozled!"

"Soon *zhey* will all part with their money and *Nazi* it again, ha-ha! It will all be given to Precious Fabrics, not to *zeh* Mr. I'm-So-Smart-and-Tall-But-Can't-Even-Deduce-Le Deuce!"

"Oh, wow! You really are a criminal genius like no other!"

Danny gloats. "After so many years of being called less than, it is nice to finally be *recognize-ed*."

In the room with the CIA agents, the summer intern asks, "Who is she talking to again?"

The Lead ignores him. "Well, that about wraps up our work here. Like a gluten-free turkey wrap, no mayo. Thank you so much, Mr. Le Deuce, for cooperating with our infestation."

"My pleasure," answers Le Deuce. "I didn't realize Danny was the one giving my free cruise a bad name. The most trusted person, right under my nose."

"More like your nipples," suggests the Lead. "Geographically." He also shares a theory he's been working on. "I'm guessing his mother let him have coffee as a child. Ok, let's go nab him and then grab ourselves some cucumber water."

No one thinks the latter sounds appealing. They slowly suit up with bullet-proof vests, ripping endless straps of Velcro.

Back in Herbert's room, Wayne has an idea. "Hey, how about this? To keep this ship from reaching *inter-racial* waters, what if we start a reality show? And we get a million views and subscribers!"

Only Woldecott sees the potential. "Yeah! A dance contest!" He busts a move. "Then they'll have to stop and wait for all the big names who come by helicopter!"

The others share looks. *What are they talking about?* Herbert offers an alternative.

"I was thinking something more like taking over the control room and hitting the brakes."

Danny suddenly points at the monitor with Herbert's huge lips. His watch goes flying from his wrist. "Did you see that?"

"Was that your watch?" asks Rebecca, looking for it.

"*Zhey* want to take over *zeh* control room!" Danny leans forward to find his wristwatch. He accidentally runs it over with his chair and it makes a loud CRUNCH. "No! Not on my *vatch*!" He collects the broken pieces. "Oh, yes on my *vatch.* I loved *zhis vatch.* Swiss *vatch, zhis vatch.* I did *Nazi* it *zhere*." He stands, cocks his gun, and puts on a long dark raincoat. "*Goonter!* Let's go!"

"Muscle worker," Gunther corrects. He gets up, prepares a large gun, and also dons a long dark coat to conceal his weapon.

"Be safe, Comrades!" encourages Rebecca, wringing her hands as they go. She stays behind as expected, too helpless a female for the manly tasks of defending hearth and homestead.

***

Herbert shuffles down a hallway followed by Olivia, the Twins, and Rosie.

"Why are we going this way?" asks Olivia.

Herbert stops and knocks on a cabin door. No answer.

Olivia urges again, "Dad, we need to move!"

"I'm worried about Mrs. Pearbottom." Herbert bangs on the door again.

Neighbors crack their doors before Dr. Singleton finally opens his. He wears cheap PJs and ties his bathrobe. "Can I help you?"

Herbert insists on trying to see through him. "Is *Mrs.* Lucretia Pearbottom here, per certainty?"

Rosie smells a familiar fragrance and is embarrassed. Quietly she says to Herbert, "I don't think we should be here, Mr. B. She's a grown woman."

Olivia hunches down behind her boys, also embarrassed.

Dr. Singleton opens his door wider, eager to display or dispel any scandal. "I don't keep such late company. And certainly not mixed company."

"Oh, spare me your hypocrisy!" chides Herbert. He nods for the Twins to enter. They don't understand so he gives them a nudge and they go in. "Bring her out, please."

"Did you try her room?" asks Dr. Singleton, logically.

Herbert is disgusted. "Wouldn't that be convenient!"

The Twins check his closet, bathroom, and under the bed. "She's not here, Grampa."

Rosie is relieved. She detects the scent went down the hall.

Herbert says, "I'm onto you, Doctor."

"Good," answers Singleton. "I hope you soon find your way."

Olivia smiles with the same hope.

In another hallway they stop at Mrs. Pearbottom's door. Herbert knocks forcefully and again several neighbors open to watch. She finally opens in a silky bathrobe.

"Herbert? Why are you waking everybody?"

Herbert is annoyed. "Why didn't you report back to basecamp?"

"Wait." She looks at their audience and brings her people inside. "Are you serious? There was nothing to report so I went to bed."

"Whose?"

"What business is that of yours?"

Olivia and Rosie are impressed. They take in her nice décor.

Herbert continues, "Get dressed. We're stopping this ship."

"Oh, now you have lost it, Herbert. And it's no longer harmless. This requires an intervention." She pulls for family support but they all turn away. Even Rosie.

Herbert insists, "Peaches, trust me for once. This isn't paranoia. We're living in a particular moment-in-crime and we need to act. We can't let down a whole lot of seniors who have a lot to lose!"

"You're saving seniors now? Are you insane?"

"Is that term acceptable again? Maybe there's hope."

"It's better than hijacking! And piracy! You're talking about committing a clear violation of international maritime law, Section... I don't recall which one just now."

"You missed the boat once, Lucretia! Don't do it again. Something nefarious is going on and we're going to stop it."

"Herbert, please! Even your daughter knows Mr. Le Deuce is a legitimate harmless do-gooder. So is Dr. Singleton."

Olivia looks away. "I didn't say they were harmless."

Mrs. Pearbottom asks Rosie. "Do you think they're crooked?"

Rosie lowers her head. "I doubt it. But we can still stop the ship and ask questions later."

"That's correct," says Herbert. "Suit yourself, Sleeping Beauty."

Herbert turns but Mrs. Pearbottom blocks the door. "Ok, fine. Just this once. Let me change into something less comfortable." She enters her closet.

"That's my Peach! Ok, everyone, gear up."

He shuffles to what looks like a portable dresser. He feels around for a hidden button and presses it. The cabinet opens into a display of heavy and light weapons.

The fellowship is impressed.

***

The flowery-shirt CIA guys burst into Danny's surveillance room but find no one. The Lead Agent acknowledges their failure. "We're too late. He seems to have eluded us."

Another agent expands on his despair. "He's probably halfway to the Caveman Islands by now in some untraceable vehicle."

"Unless he just went to the bathroom." This comes from the intern, who clearly does not know his place.

The Lead makes an allowance for his youth. "It's theoretically possible. But unlikely. Let's just wait a little."

He looks around, eventually noticing names written on the monitors. "Is that the same Himmler?"

Outside, the sun is edging over the horizon into a new day. Danny and Gunther are stationed on each side of the ship's bridge. Weapons bulge under their coats.

Around a corner, Herbert and his team discuss options. "We could just use brute force, but then several people could end up hurt or even dead."

"Do we foresee any problems?" asks Wayne.

Herbert can't help a dismissive look.

"Excuse me?" Rosie has a suggestion but is shy about presenting it. She clears her throat. "Eh-hem. Whenever I'm in a situation like this, rather than attack directly, I look for some way to get ahead of the problem."

Everyone looks at her, wondering what she means.

Moments later, Team Herbert is skimming the Suez Canal on jet skis. For some readers, an accompanying song might play on a personal device (E.g., AC/DC's 1988, *That's the Way I Wanna Rock 'n' Roll*). They look like bad-rumpus commandos.

Claire notices them from a deck and points them out to Olga. "Hey, look! Maybe Mr. B wasn't kidding about being a secret agent."

Olga watches with longing. "I never doubted him. He had such strong boundaries."

Herbert's team reaches a cargo ship and launches steel hooks from tubes. They establish rope ladders and scale up the side.

The ship's crew is curious but nonchalant, either taking videos or playing games on their phones.

When the team reaches the main deck they aim weapons at the crew. "This could get ugly fast," declares Herbert. "Or you can stay on your phones while we conduct our business."

"Works for me," answers a part-time influencer.

His fellow crew members sit and relax. Several laugh at a video one shares on his screen. The Twins move to join them but Herbert intervenes.

"Sorry, kids, no time for that."

"Oh yeah, sorry," says Wayne. He and Woldecott pull away from their new almost-friends. "We're working."

"Right on." The crew members totally understand.

Herbert looks up the steel ladder to the bridge. Mrs. Pearbottom requests a sidebar. "Herbert, may I speak with you a moment?"

"What is it?" he asks.

She gestures to the crew. "As a precaution, shouldn't they all strip naked till you-all are done up there?"

"We-all?" Herbert regards the all-male crew. They are ripped, tanned, good looking young men. Some are checking out Mrs. Pearbottom. "Certainly not. Rosie will handle them. Just as they are."

"Again with the double standards!" complains Mrs. Pearbottom. "It just never stops."

She grabs the ladder and begins her ascent. The men watch her, hoping for a chance viewing. Brash ones even hold up their phones, recording. She is flattered but pulls her sporty skirt closer.

Herbert is alarmed and tries to block their view. He motions for Rosie to step forward. "Gentlemen, Rosie here will guard you all at gunpoint. I expect full cooperation, no funny business, or she'll have to take lethal action. Which she enjoys."

Rosie smiles and looks away, embarrassed by his accuracy.

The crew is disappointed. One didn't understand why Mrs. Pearbottom couldn't be assigned. "Why can't she watch us?"

She looks down, amused.

"Because I said so," answers Herbert. "Let's go!" He gestures for the Twins and Olivia to make their way up.

Olivia follows the Twins but first kisses Herbert's cheek. "You did the right thing, Papa."

Herbert appreciates the warm glow. He brings up his rear and says, "No gawking, please!"

The men turn away as he climbs. Some lean over to vomit.

Moments later Herbert's team bursts into the wheelhouse of the cargo ship. Crew members put their hands up except one who is too busy on a call to notice. He is the Captain and has a nasal voice.

"I know we said the green ones, Babe, but I just don't think they're working."

The Officer of the Watch pulls his attention to the intruders.

"Oh sorry, hang on, Dear." The Captain presses his phone to his abundant stomach. "Can I help you?"

Herbert waves for Woldecott to speak for them.

"Me?" He is caught off guard but smiles at the honor. "We need—" His voice cracks. He clears his throat. "We need to take over the helm?" He looks at Herbert who confirms it with a nod.

Wayne jokes with a Compton accent, "Oh helm, no!"

The Captain ends his call. "Hey, I'm going to have to call you back, Hon." To Herbert's team he says, "You do realize this is a violation of international maritime code? Article one-oh-one, section alpha point one, to be exact."

"That's right!" confirms Mrs. Pearbottom. "I couldn't remember the exact statute."

"Come on, people! It's piracy 101."

Herbert holds up his revolver. "Well, today we're going to supersede alpha point one with point three five seven, among others."

"And we're not statues," adds Wayne. They show off their weapons for the crew to admire.

"Those are good ones," a crew member admits.

"Very well," responds the Captain. "Look, we're all just employees here, no stock options or anything. So, what is it you need to accomplish?"

Herbert picks up the ship's announcement system and makes an impassioned speech about the glory his team will soon memorialize from this day forward. Actually, he simply announces, "Folks, this is your Pirate speaking. We apologize for the inconvenience. It's about to get a little rocky so please hang onto your soups and teas."

Olivia whispers an important omission. Herbert adds it over the intercom. "And your coffees too, if that is your drink of choice."

The Twins agree with their mom. "Right on."

Herbert waves away the Helmsman with his gun. He then suddenly and forcefully spins the steering wheel non-stop.

The ship turns abruptly; its thick metal hull creaks, caws, and moans loudly. Teas, coffees, and soups spill throughout various rooms. (If a movie is made, one particular brand of travel mug does not seem to budge at all, or if it tips and rolls nothing spills out. A crew member picks it up and takes a satisfying gulp. "Best Secret Santa ever.")

On the bridge the Twins maintain their balance like the righteous skateboarders that they are. They barely feel the torque as others fall over and grab desperately for handrails.

The turbulence suddenly ends, *a bit too abruptly* in Wayne's opinion. A little bird leaves a lamppost and flies to a position high up above. From that vantage point it sees the cargo ship wedged perpendicular to, and blocking, the entire Suez Canal.

Le Deuce's cruise liner and other ships hit their brakes, turn, and slightly crumple into each other as they attempt to stop. Many emit high pitched braking sounds despite being in water.

As the cruise liner leans hard, some passengers are flipped over the rails and into lawsuits. Danny and Gunther struggle to hang on as they guard the wheelhouse from outside.

"*Vhat* is happening?" asks Danny.

On the cargo ship, Herbert surveys his impact. "People are really going to wonder what happened here today."

Woldecott jokes, in radio announcer voice, "Today's traffic sponsored by Team Bigglesby."

Mrs. Pearbottom quips, "The official versions will be quite amusing to read.

The Captain grows annoyed. "They'll probably say it was due to intoxication."

"Or a flock of endangered ducks swimming by," complains the Helmsman. "They'll say all were spared when the brave Captain put nature above commerce and took evasive action."

Mrs. Pearbottom wishes she could offer the Helmsman a job. "My agency could use a spinner like you."

Herbert nixes it. "They have enough fact-skippers."

***

Back on the cruise ship, Rebecca and many passengers emerge onto the decks to see what happened. All are in awe as they see so many ships piled together.

Rebecca notices Danny and Gunther, hurrying down from the bridge. She runs inside and they do so as well. Gunther, however, only fakes it for Danny and immediately returns outside.

Under a stairwell, he snaps off his outer clothes like an NBA player ready to go in. He wears a t-shirt that says, *I LOVE EXERCISING... MY RIGHT TO A HIDEOUS CORPUS.* He wraps his discarded coat around his weapons and throws them overboard. He then tries to blend in with confused passengers.

Moments later Danny bursts into Rebecca's cabin and into her closet. He opens drawers till he finds and grabs the large burlap sack with the completed applications. As he turns around, and for the rest of his life, he will wonder how he failed to notice the CIA agents pressed against the wall behind him. Perhaps the flowery shirts look too much like wallpaper. The Lead Agent startles him.

"I do hope you like to bathe, Sir."

Danny drops his shoulders and his sad sack of overwhelming evidence. The other agents look equally perplexed at their boss.

"What does *zhis* mean? I wash myself every day."

"Because you're all washed up," he explains, annoyed that nobody got it. "Does nobody get it?"

Only the intern feels obliged to smile. The other two nod and think, *just give me a raise already*. They hold Danny.

The Lead defends his joke. "That used to be a thing. *You're all washed up, Bub!* Remember? Hygiene was frowned upon."

The door bumps him in the back. He stumbles forward against the agents holding Danny. It's Rebecca.

She plays even dumber. "Oh my! What is going on? Danny, is something wrong?"

"Grab her! Appropriately!" commands the Lead to the intern.

The intern keeps his hands in full view and only grabs her arms. He keeps his elbows up, in full view like chicken wings.

"She had nothing to do with *zhis*!" insists Danny, hoping to save her life. "I put *zhis* bag myself in her *ghoom*!"

"Her womb?" asks the Lead.

"*Zhis* room, *zhis* cabin!" clarifies Danny.

"Oh!" answers the Lead. He instructs his men, "Get him out of here so I can deal with my likes of her personally."

Glances are exchanged but no one corrects him.

Danny insists, "I insist, I acted alone!"

The two subordinate agents drag him to the hallway but he holds onto the door frame. "Don't worry, Baby. *Zhey* know you had nothing to do with *zhis*. I am sorry I had to hide all *zhis* from you. It's my dark side as a provider. I am entirely to blame." He winks for her to play along, fearing she might be too stupid to understand.

Rebecca keeps up her innocence. "What are you talking about, Danny? Did you do something… not allowed?" Her dough-liking eyes appear very sincere. The intern holds her back, still keeping his limbs where everyone can see them.

Danny says a final goodbye. "In case you never see me again, *Fräulein*, just remember my mother was wrong. I was never *zeh* less than." He releases the door frame and gets taken away.

"Um, Ok," she answers.

The Lead Agent takes hold of Rebecca and tells the intern, "I'll take it from here. Go with them and learn a few things."

"I doubt the second part will happen," he mutters to himself.

"Please take him," answers the Lead.

They exit and the Lead closes the door. "And, scene! Ok, good job!" He releases Rebecca. "Though I do have to ask, why did you give him up? This bag must contain access to millions of dollars."

Rebecca feigns internal struggle. "I just couldn't see myself going through with it. Something inside me woke up."

"Your conscience, maybe? That keeps some people up at night."

"Oh no, not me. It was more that I realized I had been *groomed!* Into something I'm *not*. He used a lot of *confidence bombing*. And told me to believe in myself!"

"Goodness, I hope you didn't pay tuition."

"No. But he was just so cocky, with his plans to redistribute the wealth to the very few. Luckily, I was able to break away and return to the masses."

"That's quite a testimony. Have you ever thought of teaching?"

"You think I should?"

"Absolutely! Colleagues–I mean, colleges–would love to get their hands on you. Even offer you a well-endowed chair."

"Thank you!" She looks at herself in the mirror and stands taller, pleased with her appearance. "Though it's my mind I would want to be known for."

"Of course! That's what first drew me to you. I needed help with this case." The mirror frames them as a couple. The Lead places his hand on the small of her back. "I couldn't have done it without you and I'm so glad you made the right choice. We were about to rain down so hard like an insurance claim denial."

Rebecca looks at his lips as if about to kiss them. "I appreciate all the guidance I was given, to see the error of my ways. And to be given this chance to help with a society at large."

The Lead hoists the burlap bag over his shoulder. "Say, would you like to grab a bite later? Celebrate this victory of the people?"

"I'd love to!" she says. Eyeing the bag, she asks, "Um, I think I have some personal things in there. Can I just…?"

"Oh." He puts it down and opens it for her. "Sure. Take a look."

She feigns embarrassment. "I mean girlie stuff. Would you mind stepping outside? I'll just be a moment."

"Oh, right! I'll wait out…" he points to the door and exits. He even calls through the door. "Take your time!"

Rebecca rushes the bag to her closet. She dumps it out and fills it with blank applications instead. She then carries it back and surrenders it to the agent. He looks nervous.

"Hey, I hope I didn't creep you out or anything. I mean, we can invite colleagues if you want. Except yours that we just locked up."

"No worries. I'd be happy to meet alone with you later. Just the two of us, undisturbed."

He is relieved and pleased.

"That way you can totally be suspended if I don't like how things go."

He worries again but she softens it. "Just kidding! Meet at 8:00?"

"Sure." He leaves, thrilled to have a date.

She calls out to him, "Um, you forgot something!"

"Oh, sorry." He returns, lunging in for a kiss. She dodges it and points at the bag. "Oh, right." He heaves it onto his shoulder and realizes he must look like Santa. "Till then, ho, ho, ho!"

"Oh no, I prefer Rebecca!" She closes the door and rushes back to her closet. She finds an extremely gaudy top and bottom, a large beach bag, and running shoes.

CHAPTER TWENTY-FOUR

Chasing Dreams

On the observation deck of the cruise liner, Claire and Olga watch as Herbert and his team make their way back from the cargo ship. They climb over rails and move from ship to ship. Herbert struggles but slaps away the Twins when they try to help.

"Suit yourself, Grampa."

Claire looks in the other direction. "I wonder what country that is over there."

Olga ignores her.

Something catches Claire's eye: A female tourist with a heavy beach bag rushes out onto the deck and climbs over a far rail. She hops from ship to ship, headed for land. Claire does not realize it's Rebecca in those awful clothes.

"I bet there are some good deals to be had over there."

Olga keeps her eyes on Herbert. "Where, in Egypt?"

"Is that Egypt?" asks Claire, suddenly enthused. "I've always wondered if I might have some important destiny there."

"I know! We all know!" Olga turns and sees the tourist with the heavy bag. "That's not good for her lumbar."

"Something is not right," Claire declares. She checks on Herbert's progress; it's slow and he's wiping sweat from his face. "I think that woman needs to be stopped."

Olga is dismissive. "No, she'll make it. This will take days."

"I'm not letting her out of my sight!" says Claire. "Look, when Mr. Bigglesby gets here, please give him your cell phone so he can call me and catch up."

"What?! You've never wanted him to call you!"

"I think she's the one they want to stop. But she's getting away!"

"What, you're an expert in the spy business too?"

Claire worries about losing more time. "I need to go! I need to keep an eye on her!"

"Then I will go and Mr. Herbert will have to call *me!*"

"But you have a bad knee! Here look, I have an idea." She grabs Olga's cell phone and shoves it into Olga's own bra.

"Excuse me! What are you doing?" she complains.

"Olga! Make. Him. Find. It!" suggests Claire. "Any way you like. But I gotta go!" She runs and starts jumping handrails.

Olga has an *aha!* moment. "Oh, I see!" She turns and prepares for Herbert's arrival. They are getting closer. She shifts her shoulders sexily. "Mr. Bigglesby! I have information you might find very important, but I won't share it easily." She strikes a defiant pose.

After a few such rehearsals, Herbert and his team arrive and catch their breath. He turns his back to Olga, who moves around to face him. "Mr. Bigglesby, I have valuable information–"

Herbert waves her away. "I'm sorry, Olga. It's not a good time."

Olivia and Mrs. Pearbottom exchange looks, bothered by his dismissal of her.

Herbert continues. "Ok, team, we need to find Le Deuce, Singleton, and the contracts the seniors filled out."

Mrs. Pearbottom and Olivia are skeptical.

The Twins notice Claire following Rebecca, both climbing over rails and crossing decks on their way to land.

"Is that Rebecca?" asks Woldecott.

The women look. Herbert neither hears them nor turns around.

Olga tries again. "Sir, I believe you'll find something very valuable hidden on my person."

Herbert ignores her again. "Now, the culprits are probably going to be almost impossible to find at this point. Think of it like a chess match. Between masterminds. Some of the most ruthless, cunning, uncaring, *users* are involved, who think life is cheap and disposable."

Wayne asks, "And what is their side like?"

Herbert is disturbed by the question.

"Herbert Sherbert, everything you need is right here." Olga holds the flagpole, leaning away as if held by a dance partner.

Mrs. Pearbottom is disgusted. "Olga, please, have some dignity!"

"That is easy for you to say!" she protests. "Is dinner and a movie too much, in exchange for the information I hold?" She turns to Herbert. "I know who has the contracts, Handsome."

This stops Herbert short. His shoulders drop. He understands when a chore simply must be done. "I see. Shall we go to my cabin?"

Olga smiles and claps giddily.

Olivia and Mrs. Pearbottom cry out, "What? No!" They are not ok with an unveiled suggestive transaction. Rosie is more conflicted.

Herbert tells his daughter, "She's clearly way over the minimum age you imposed."

Olga does not like the sound of that.

Olivia answers, "That may be, but what about the whole not-using-people idea? And then throwing them away?"

With that possibility stated so bluntly, Olga is embarrassed. She realizes it makes her seem quite desperate.

Herbert is frustrated. "And who is using whom, exactly? Am I the only one serious about stopping this theft on the high seas?" He looks around at his accusers. "She clearly knows something. What are we supposed to do, rough her up instead until she talks?"

"Yes!" resounds from Olivia and Mrs. Pearbottom alike. They grab hold of Olga, who falls and writhes on the deck.

"Nooo! Not fair!!!" she shrieks like a demon being cast out. "Why should Olga be treated like this?"

Rosie watches with mixed emotions. She hesitates to lay a hand on Olga after the freezer incident.

During the struggle, Olga's phone suddenly pops out of her blouse and slides across the deck. "Darn it!" she laments and cries. "More than that can come out if you give me a chance!"

"A phone?" asks Mrs. Pearbottom. She picks it up and wipes it clean with a towelette. "What is Herbert supposed to do with this?"

Olga turns away like an angry child. "I'm done talking!"

"Oh dear," says Mrs. Pearbottom. She worries this will take a long time and makes a suggestion. "Herbert, given the urgency of this situation, and her being an adult, and the willingness and consent of each party, I believe your former ever-deplorable ways might be warranted this one last time. As an exception."

Olivia is horrified. "Gross! Mrs. Pearbottom, no!" She shakes Olga violently. "Why does my Pops need your phone?"

Rosie can no longer stay neutral. "Stop it! Leave her alone! This is no way to treat a fellow lady! Woman! Olga, I am still so sorry I stuffed you into that freezer."

Olga is touched. "Thank you, Rosie."

Mrs. Pearbottom is annoyed.

Rosie continues her support. "If you ever need to talk to someone, I'm all earbuds." She indicates her own phone in hand and earpiece in her ear.

Olivia tightens her grip. "Ok, Olga, spill it already! We don't have time for this!"

"You are all just no fun!" Olga complains. "I endure so much and then the one day fate puts fortune into my hand you take it away and shame me! Fine! I will not fight this evil destiny." She points at Claire, who has almost disappeared from view.

"You are to call Claire."

Herbert jumps forward. "Claire wants me to call her?"

"See? I just can't win! You could have everything with me but instead you choose to be a terrible superficial man!"

Olivia wants to defend him but gets hushed by Rosie.

Olga cannot hear anything just now. She wishes Herbert's lively, happy look could be for her. For once. *Why can't he just see me for who*

I am, and make passionate love to me? How good I would take care of him! He would be the happiest man ever, even in diapers! But I know this is not possible, and never will be, not for me.

Olga explains. "She is following the crooked lady from the presentation. She ran away with a bag full of something, probably the contracts, distressing her lumbar vertebrae like a fool. Your favorite little *I'm-so-perfect-PT* will keep up with her until you arrive."

Mrs. Pearbottom searches the phone. "Let me get her number."

Herbert sees the great distance between himself and Claire, and all the climbing required.

Woldecott makes a suggestion. "Grampa, why don't you let us handle this one? We can go and be right back with her."

Wayne agrees. "Yeah, you older people can give it a rest."

A desolate Olga cries out, fearing she has ruined her chances. "I didn't mean it, Mr. Herbert! I will still be here for you when all these people leave you and you change your mind."

Everyone ignores her except Rosie, who pats her shoulder.

The Twins hop the rail and wait for the order to give chase.

Mrs. Pearbottom supports their plan. "Herbert, your grandsons can easily handle this. Let these young people do the legwork." She extends the phone to Woldecott.

Herbert reaches to intercept the phone but has a back spasm. "Ow! Oh… Ok, just bring her back in a one-piece." The women let the slip go unchallenged but he corrects himself. "I mean alive, not dead, for example."

Woldecott presses buttons. "Yo, this battery is dead."

Mrs. Pearbottom takes it back but can't get it to work.

Wayne is quickest to intuit the root of the problem. "Ms. Olga, when was the last time you charged it?"

She looks embarrassed, helpless, and ready to break down again. "We're on a cruise! I didn't think I needed it!"

Rosie steps up. "It's not a problem. Just give me something that belongs to her."

"To Claire?" asks Olga.

"Or Ms. Holmeslyce. I need a sock or something."

Herbert turns away, as if unable to help with that.

"What room was she in?" asks Mrs. Pearbottom, ready to go fetch an article.

"I feel like her essence is still here," says Rosie. A scent leads her to Herbert, whose jacket pockets bulge. "There! I need that, Sir." She points and everyone turns to see.

"What do you mean?" asks Herbert, as if genuinely unaware.

"What's in your pockets? You have something of hers."

Without hesitation, Olivia reaches in and takes out Rebecca's pajamas. "Oh, Pops, no!!!" she wails.

The Twins are further impressed by the old man.

Olivia nips that. "This is not something to be proud of!"

Herbert defends himself. "I was trying to slow her down."

"How?" asks Olivia. "Wait, no! Never mind!"

"We're wasting time," Rosie reminds them. She takes the pajama bottoms and sniffs them. Others are disgusted. "Follow me!" she instructs the Twins, and climbs over the rail. They follow her at full gallop across various ships, hunters led by a bloodhound.

Olivia holds up the other half of the pajamas and glares.

Herbert does his best to explain. "I didn't even ask for those. I was leaving my room when suddenly I felt something come over me. What was I supposed to do? For your sake I didn't even look."

"Dad, stop! We had an agreement!"

Mrs. Pearbottom has an idea to help everyone cool off. "How about we go find some Jello?"

"I need coffee!" barks Olivia. She rushes indoors.

Mrs. Pearbottom follows. "I second that devotion."

"I need a nap," announces Herbert. He shuffles indoors too.

Olga follows him. "Mr. Bigglesby, I really didn't mean those awful things I said. Would you like a massage? I can be very gentle."

Herbert waves her off. "I'm sorry, Olga."

Left alone, Olga punches a wall in frustration. "Very intelligent, you idiot woman!"

CHAPTER TWENTY-FIVE

Threads Unraveled

We now come to the final stages of our story. Claire stealthily tracks Rebecca in Ismailia, Egypt, and repeatedly calls Olga's phone but only reaches her voicemail.

This leads to Claire's insecurities bubbling up. She begins to imagine the others are laughing at her while sipping mimosas on the ship together. She even chides herself for having actually believed she might have some great destiny here, whereas perhaps all she has been doing is stalking some innocent fellow tourist.

To regulate her spiraling mood, she considers leaving her post and getting a massage. As if a sign from heaven, a placard offers a low, low price for a luxury reflexology experience, right across from where Rebecca browses indigenous pottery. A massage seems like a healthy alternative to dousing herself in chocolate.

Just then Rosie and the Twins arrive at the nearby corner. Claire is ecstatic to see them and runs over. She is nearly hit by a Rick Shaw, a college student pulling people in a cart. He does not stop.

"I'm so glad you came!" Claire whispers loudly to her friends, wiping away tears. She is too ecstatic to talk. They do their best to wait for her while keeping a low profile. Locals point at them and whisper. Meanwhile, Rebecca exits one shop and ducks into another.

The group uses unnecessary signals to communicate and they rush over to that shop. Rosie gets distracted by the must-have Persian carpet in the window, ON SALE 70% OFF. The Twins look at each other with mischief in their eyes.

"We'll go in from the back," says Woldecott.

They make their way down the alley. Mothers pull children inside. Men offer toaster-ovens and cappuccino machines saying, "For you, good price!"

The unbelievable rug sale turns out to be legit and Rebecca finds herself carried away. The Twins do the carrying, triumphantly marching the lumpy roll through crowded streets in what looks more like *Casablanca* (Curtiz, 1942) than modern day Ismailia.

Rosie and Claire follow, eating ice pops. They comment on how low these former empires have fallen in the world.

"If you think this is bad, you should see Athens," Rosie says.

Claire answers, "Still, they should make Egypt great again."

"That would be MEGA!" adds Wayne.

"Maybe I'll move here and help," says Claire. "Like Cleopatra."

When they reach their ship they haul their rug and themselves over the final rail and onto the deck.

"What's this I see?" asks the Lead CIA Agent.

He and his men are sunbathing. They jump to their feet and draw guns and badges from who knows where. "Stop! CIA!"

The Twins obey and stand idling, trying to recall if they are ok or will need to eliminate these men.

The Lead continues, "Out for a little human trafficking are we, during this unexpected hangover?"

Rosie answers, "If you're CIA then we just did you a favor."

He ignores her. "You brigands are messing with the wrong country! Put down your contraband and back away. *Ponlo bajo*!" he adds in Spanish. Then "*Fàngxià tā*!" in Mandarin.

Rosie wonders about the big gaps in intelligence. "You know these are the Wrong Boys, right?"

"It's Agent Wright to you!" he barks. He holds up his badge. "I'm in charge here."

Rosie squints and reads aloud, "Claudius M. Wright. Central Intelligence Agency. USA."

The Twins are impressed and put down the carpet.

"At your service," offers Woldecott.

The agent, now accepted as being Wright, says, "Something very wrong is going on here."

The Twins smile. "That's good! Something Very Wrong *is* going on, right here and right now!"

"Stop using my name like that! Unroll the carpet, please."

His agents flex their muscles to encourage cooperation.

"Let me do it." Rosie steps up and the Twins move aside. She grabs hold of the edge and unfurls it harshly, as if shaking out vermin. Rebecca rolls out, dazed.

Agent Wright is astonished. "Hey! Be gentle with her!"

"Sorry. That's how I unroll." Rosie is not actually apologizing.

Agent Wright takes a knee. "Rebecca?" As she becomes more oriented, she suddenly scrambles behind him for protection. He savors her touch and fragrance.

"What is going on here?" he asks.

"They kidnapped me at the market!"

"Bazaar," clarifies Rosie.

"Very!" opines Wright.

"Save me, Darling, please!" begs Rebecca.

Wright feels more manly than usual. "This is unconscionable! Unthinkable!"

"Thank you!" agrees Rosie, proud to help capture a true villain for once. "Claire, show him what you got on her."

The men perk up. Claire steps forward with Rebecca's beach bag and holds out applications.

"What are those?" asks Wright. He takes a handful, concerned.

Rebecca pretends to faint. Wright catches on, irritated.

Rosie isn't having it either. "She's fine. Let her do drama club in prison. If I'm right, these forms have the bank accounts of hundreds of seniors who thought they were signing up for healthcare. She was making a break for it and we caught up with her in town for a dialog."

"No way!" exclaims Wright. He holds Rebecca by the shoulders but she still pretends to be fainty. He orders his men, "Stand her up boys! And somebody go get Daniels."

His three agents and both Twins all step forward to help with Rebecca. The Twins realize he probably didn't mean them so they step back. The agents sweep Rebecca to her feet, somewhat roughly.

"Ow!" she complains.

"Oh, did that hurt?" asks Wright. "Well, I didn't like being stood up either. We said eight o'clock, did we not?"

"Wait, did you meant AM?" asks Rebecca. "I meant dinner!"

Claire and the intern look at each other. Wright hesitates; perhaps he misunderstood. He holds up an application.

"Miss Holmeslyce, did you take these and give me blanks?"

"No! What do you think I am?" she defends. "I found more so I was keeping them safe while I went shopping. For our dinner tonight. At eight PM."

Only Claire and the intern seem to question their socializing. "Is that allowed in your field?" asks Claire.

The intern does not want to answer in front of his boss.

His boss answers, "It's never an issue unless it doesn't work out. Then it's abuse, of course."

Rosie adds, "But if it works out you get a *Mrs.* not a *Misconduct*?"

"Correct. But you have to live in secret like in other advanced countries."

A door opens and Olivia rushes out onto the deck with Herbert and Mrs. Pearbottom in tow.

"See? I told you they were back, *Papi*!"

Rebecca resumes her cutesy sales *persona*. "Mr. Big! I'm so glad you're here! There's been like, a giant misunderstanding. Ha! My CIA colleagues actually think I went rogue or something. But you know how complicated our work can be, and what I was really doing!"

The agents turn to Herbert, not expecting much.

Mrs. Pearbottom is surprised to learn of the CIA presence. "Yes, Mr. Big, what is she talking about?"

Herbert is delighted to have Rebecca call on him to explain things. He addresses all the agents, unsure who is in charge. "Oh yes, well, let's see. When a woman is this young and beautiful—that's not harassment, just a fact. She is able to elicit the attention of powerful adroit men, and it can be difficult for her to prioritize her *intellectual* development—"

"No, not that nonsense!" barks Rebecca.

Herbert is startled. The men were all following without question.

Olivia jumps forward to protect him. "Watch it, Bimbo!"

Agent Wright wants to be able to say he has heard it all. "Please, let him continue."

Herbert obliges. "Thank you. So instead of developing their minds, many girls will trade on their looks. It's simple, and ancient, really. They hope to latch onto some brilliant successful man like myself, who can put them ahead, if only they're willing to hold off on thinking and dignity. They just do whatever he says at first."

Most of the women are disgusted but the men nod, waiting for something new and unexpected to be said.

Rebecca tests that wind. "It's true! I didn't want to believe it, but he's right. Complying became my identity, Officer. That Danny took advantage of me! I was so powerless over his… power over me."

The other women do not buy it.

Agent Wright picks up on the threat. "I think I see where this is going. But let's wait. My agent is bringing up her partner. She betrayed him for her own survival, but he does not know it yet. We can all see how he takes it. Please don't give it away."

"I'm a hero, not a villain!" insists Rebecca. "I did my civic duty!"

Mrs. Pearbottom asks, "Agent, who exactly are you?"

Rosie is a bit surprised. "You haven't met Mr. Wright?"

Mrs. Pearbottom blushes. "There's no need to get personal."

Agent Wright produces his badge. Mrs. Pearbottom can't tell if her glasses are helping or making it worse. She finally sees the tiny font, "Oh, *you're* Mr. Wright."

Each feels a tingle of interest but pretends not to.

Herbert becomes protective. "Agent, why are you wasting time with mere underlings? Have you rounded up Le Deuce? And that Singleton? They are the real masterminds of nefarious conduct."

"He's right, Agent Wright!" says Rebecca. "I was *groomed!* By Lester the molester! It's like I'm coming out of a trance now."

Other female faces wrinkle with fatigue but the experts dare not question it.

Mrs. Pearbottom asks, "And who is Lester?"

A door flings open and bangs the wall. "I told you, she had nothing to do with *zhis!"* cries Danny.

They all look. He fights to stay inside, his cuffed hands clinging to the door post. The agent wrestles him through the doorway. "Baby, *zhis* nightmare will all be over soon!"

Rebecca hams it up. "I won't leave you, Friend! No matter what they do to us! We'll get through this! Then, when you've served your time, we'll be together, Les!"

"*Nein!"* yells Danny, upset. "Never *zeh* Les! *Fräulein*, I am Danny! Danny the *Ubermann*!"

"*Ubermann*?" Olivia flips to the U's on the DNA list. *Nothing.*

Rebecca tries to fix her slip. "Of course! I'm so sorry! You've never been Les Dan. To me you will always be Greater Dan!"

"*Nein! Zhat* is my brother!"

Everyone is quite confused, trying to follow.

Rebecca continues as if in agony for him. "I'm so sorry your mother called you that, Danny! It was a cruel joke, but it was not aimed at you. It was aimed at your awful, absent, runaway father!"

Mr. Wright shares an insight. "Ah, family dynamics. You can't live with 'em, you can't live without 'em. It's no wonder you ended up on this path, Daniels!"

Olivia hadn't thought of that as a last name. She turns to the D's.

Herbert grows frustrated. "Mrs. Pearbottom, if the CIA will not arrest their employers, perhaps you can do the honors?"

Danny grovels in a spasm of contempt, fury, and disbelief. "Our employers? Why can't I be the mastermind of all of *zhis*? Why must it always be *zeh* big tall men who are in charge?"

"I knew it!" declares Olivia. "Look, Lester Daniels!" She shows Herbert the list.

"*Nein!* Never call me *zhat*!" begs Danny. "Only my mother calls me *zhat*!"

Herbert struggles to recall something distant and vague but important from his past. "Daniels? Your mother… Did she feel trapped and complain about being in Lockenhaus?"

Danny lies. "No, we were in Vienna."

Agent Wright has heard enough. "What is this, 23 & You?"

"Way more than 23!" boasts Olivia. "According to DNA, Mr. Daniels is my half-brother."

Danny feels conflicted. Mostly disbelief and distaste, yet with some longing for family.

Olivia continues, "Oh, and meet your little nephews!"

The tall Twins smile and wave but Danny can't process it all just now, least of all their size and non-European side.

"It's never going to be all-white, is it?" he asks himself.

Olivia comforts him. "We're gonna be fine, Brother!"

Danny is tapped out. Numb. He sees the young agents and then the Lead. "I am exhausted. Can I go to prison now?"

Agent Wright answers, "Sure, we can make that happen."

"Yo! You can meet up with our dad!" says Wayne.

Danny ignores him, unable to absorb any more. He still believes Rebecca to be innocent, or at worst, coerced. "I'm sorry, *Fräulein*."

Olivia protests, "Don't be, Bro! She's a criminal! She said you brainwashed her!"

"Of course I brainwashed her!" confirms Danny, unlawyered, and blind to his own powerlessness. "She could not resist me. It's understandable. My every wish was her command."

Agent Wright is bothered by accidental critical thinking. "Wait, why did you have her wear our wiretap?"

Danny nearly has a stroke. He chokes it down. "She had a wire?"

"I had a wire?" ask Rebecca.

The agents realize this is a hard moment for Danny. He doesn't wait to be asked. "Per chance, is *zhere* someone else who would like to sucker punch Danny in *zeh* testicles? *Dad*, maybe?"

Herbert pities his neglected and overwhelmed child. "This whole thing seems bananas." To the CIA agents he says, "Can we stop this sham of an investigation? You need to arrest Le Deuce and Singleton! This is not the work of some supermodel and a midget!"

People take offense all around. But keep reading.

"Ouch!" declares Mrs. Pearbottom. "Herbert, we need to leave all this to the slightly competent authorities."

"No you don't!" Rebecca advocates.

Just then Mr. Le Deuce and Dr. Singleton stroll outside chatting about a vision or plan.

Rebecca yells, "I demand to be released at once! Mr. Le Deuce, they have me all wrong! Tell them what a good employee I am! They think I'm some kind of master villain or something. I even helped with their investigation and this is how they repay me!"

Yeah, you spied on me too, he believes. Le Deuce takes in the crowd and asks, "Are you in some kind of trouble, Dear?"

Danny stands as tall as he can. "That is a very stupid question my former employer! She has betrayed you! And me! She tried to run off with your money!"

"Oh my, that is very, very bad, Rebecca," confirms Mr. Le Deuce. "I thought you had worked alone, Danny. Or with that henchman of yours."

"Muscle worker," corrects Danny. He turns, wondering where Gunther went. "Where is *zhat* mercenary traitor?"

Olga is inspired and leaves to look for him. "I'll find him."

Woldecott feels a rush of loyalty toward Danny and another of disgust for Rebecca. "This isn't fair, Grampa. Lady, you messed with the Wrong family! He's our uncle!"

Wayne chimes in, "Yeah, you're the mole-ster, not him! Get her out of here before I do something unbecoming!"

Rebecca tries another tactic. "Oh, Herbie Werbie, did I mention I'm pregnant?"

Before Olivia can react, Herbert says, "Don't believe her, Daughter! Besides, I chose *you* over *her* last night."

Various eyes shift, faces wrinkle.

Olivia takes a breath and centers herself. "I believe you, Dad. Our bond is tight!" To Rebecca she says, "Oh, is there no one left to help you? Looks like you're having an out-of-buddies experience."

"That's pretty bad," judges Rebecca.

"Not in my family," answers Olivia.

"Take her away," commands Agent Wright.

His men do so and leave Danny with the intern. Rebecca growls and strains against her captors.

"This is not the last you've heard of me!" she cries.

After she's gone, Olivia smiles. "What a good day this is turning out to be! I even got to see her arrested bitch face." (In a film we'll likely cut to a photo shoot for her mug shot. She tries to melt the camera and seduce the photographer, who ideally looks like Holly Hunter (cfr. Coen, 1987). We eventually get a good exhausted look.)

Olivia assures Danny, "Don't worry, Brother! You won't be alone for long, right, Pops? We'll visit a lot!"

"I'm so *fruct*," concludes Danny.

"You most certainly are, from what I gather," says Dr. Singleton. "Just don't let it go to waste."

"I don't want to talk about it." Danny walks away, followed by the intern.

Herbert adjusts a hearing aid and asks Olivia, "Did he ever say who his mother was?"

"Not yet, Papa. In time he will."

Mrs. Pearbottom addresses Agent Wright. "We've been making quite a scene out here. How do we end this?"

Agent Wright looks around. Passengers watch from all sides. "I suppose we could neutralize the crowd. And call it something else."

Herbert is open to the idea. "I didn't see anything." He shuffles inside. "I have to go work on my gratitude movements."

Agent Wright invites Mrs. Pearbottom, "Say, maybe we can celebrate our interagency achievement with some breakfast?"

"I'm down!" says Wayne.

"Me too!" agrees Woldecott.

Neither of whom were invited. Wright clarifies, "Ma'am?"

"I'm afraid I have a prior non-commitment to attend to." She catches up to Herbert and walks with him.

"Very well." Agent Wright looks to Claire. "Join us?"

"Sorry." She leaves.

"I'll come," agrees Rosie. "Unless we should all do a big dance number first."

"Yeah!" The Twins love this idea and start grooving.

"Let's keep it to breakfast," prefers Wright. He picks up the bag of applications and gives it to Le Deuce. "I believe these are yours. Though we'll need to photograph them as evidence."

"Of course," agrees Mr. Le Deuce. After Wright and the others leave, he turns to Dr Singleton. "It's a shame this cruise had to be soiled by such unprincipled people."

Dr. Singleton answers, "They must all need our prayers. I've seen quite a bit of heart disease and corroded arteries."

Behind them, the educators pose for a group photo. Their photographer calls out, "Say, long live property taxes!!!"

The unprincipled obey and hold up their hands in glee.

CHAPTER TWENTY-SIX

Four Eyes Only

Outside a small airport, a shuttle from Sunset View picks up Herbert, Mrs. Pearbottom, Olivia, the Twins, Rosie, and seniors from the home. The driver opens the door and is immediately recognized by Mrs. Pearbottom.

"Dr. Bentiron! What a surprise!"

He leans toward her and confides, "I'm not really allowed to go by *Doctor* just now. But welcome back!"

Herbert dead-stares at Mrs. Pearbottom as seniors board. "You sure know how to pick 'em." She avoids his gaze.

At Sunset View, Herbert shuffles into his room accompanied by Olivia, who carries a few weeks' worth of mail. She reads some of the envelopes and oversized postcards.

The first one says, "*You may have already died! Open for a chance to win an all-expense paid funeral for you or a tolerated one!*" She looks at him. "Should we open it, Papa?"

"I don't think so."

She reads another. "*Mrs. Bigbuttsbee*—why do they always assume there's a Mrs.? *Is your husband making even less sense than before?* So rude. We should visit these companies. Unofficially."

"Now, now."

A third one says, "*Leave your legs to charity! Our biocarbon technologies cut the pathetic and supply the prosthetic!* Low budget cuts, Papi."

A final one offers, "*Discount caskets! All sizes and models! Grab one now before you're all gone!* Ok, this one makes sense," she opines. "To be ready at least."

***

Down in the PT office, Rosie and the Twins clean up. They pick up equipment and broken cabinets and glass. Claire and Olga direct the efforts.

In the kitchen, wearing yellow hardhats, Mrs. Pearbottom tours the damage with a team estimating the costs of a remodel. They are led by Delilah Culpa, formerly Ms. Fourchin.

A cell phone rings. Mrs. Pearbottom bristles at the caller ID. "Excuse me."

She soon enters Herbert's room followed by Rosie and the Twins. Herbert and Olivia perk up.

"What's going on?" asks Olivia.

"Ok, P, we're all here." Mrs. Pearbottom places her phone on the table and all gather around it.

P begins, "Herbert, I'm afraid we cannot let you retire just yet."

Olivia is annoyed. The Twins are disappointed by her reaction, ever-eager for adventure.

Herbert placates Olivia. "Oh, I don't know, Percy. My daughter begs to differ."

P continues, "Mrs. Pearbottom, are you sitting down? I only jest. But in all seriousness, we are re-assigning you to another facility."

She and Herbert try to hide a certain sadness from each other.

P continues, "We are confident Herbert will also fit in as well."

Now the old spies hide their joy behind feigned indifference.

Olivia is concerned. "What are you talking about, Mr. Percival?"

P continues. "We need Herbert and Mrs. Pearbottom to begin the work of unravelling what appears to be a deeply embedded cell directing subversive activities with international import."

"What sort of imports?" asks Herbert, intrigued.

"No! This is Wrong!" begins Olivia.

"My daughter," clarifies Herbert.

"Nice to meet you."

"You might not be, Mr. Percival! Because what my dad needs, and which no one seems to understand, is that we can't trust you for what is in his best interest, or for his family."

Herbert supports her. "You did put me out to pasture, Percy."

"But you're still so capable!" insists P. "Look, the assignment comes with full benefits for you and all your dependents, which I understand are quite a few."

Olivia warms up. "What sort of benefits?"

P continues, "Healthcare and all that. Free museum passes. And global pardons for most of your relatives. Though I'm sorry, Herbert, I was not able to get colorectal screenings waived."

Herbert is not pleased. "Oh, I don't think I'm up for this kind of assignment, *per se*."

"Not true! He'll be there!" answers Olivia. "We just had a few questions, which you answered. What do we need to do?"

P smiles. "Good! It shall all be revealed in due time. In the next few days, Mrs. Pearbottom will be sent ahead to set up shop as the new director of a facility. Then Herbert will be sent as a patient."

Olivia wants more details. "What kind of place is it?"

P is dodgy. "A rose is a rose is a flower. What's in a name? It's important to focus on the big picture."

Herbert grows suspicious. "What facility, Percy?"

Olivia is more practical. "And will we have an expense account?"

"Yes, but no vehicle allowance."

"Why not?" asks Herbert.

"Well, it's a kind of penal institution."

"A prison? At my age?"

"A hospital. Forensic. For the criminally insane. It's called, The Sentimental Mental Center."

"The Sentinel what?" asks Herbert.

"Your cover is having killed someone while delusional and hearing voices."

"Is that a prophecy, *per se*?"

"Herbert, do you want to serve your country or not?"

His daughter pushes for more. "We have to be able to visit, Sir. Ideally, we'll also work there. Including Rosie."

The latter appreciates the inclusion.

P assures them, "You'll all play a role. In fact, I'm emailing your sons right now with some work to get started on."

The Twins pull out their phones.

"Welcome back, Mr. Bigglesby," finishes P.

Herbert stays non-committal. "I don't know, P. But we'll give it due consideration."

"Mrs. Pearbottom, will you work on him? It could be his last assignment."

"Yes, of course, Percival. Tootles." She hangs up the phone.

"I need a nap," declares Herbert. "Can you people get out?"

"Sure thing, Papa!" Olivia kisses him on the cheek and the group files out. "I'm so glad we'll be working together as a family."

"I didn't say I'd do it, Daughter."

"No, but you should think about the benefits."

Once they're out Herbert closes the door and breathes. A tiny smile cracks on his face, with a twinkle in his eye.

The End

References

AC/DC. (1977). Whole lotta Rosie [Song]. On *Let There Be Rock* [Album]. Albert Productions.

AC/DC. (1988). That's the way I wanna rock 'n' roll [Song]. On *Blow Up Your Video.* Atlantic Records.

Alan Parsons Project, The. (1982). *Eye in the Sky* [Album]. Arista Records.

Aldrich, R. (Director). (1962). *What Ever Happened to Baby Jane?* [Film]. Seven Arts Productions; Warner Bros.

Arlen, H., & Harburg, E. Y. (1939). We're off to see the wizard [Recorded by Various Artists]. On *The Wizard of Oz* [Film]. Metro-Goldwyn-Mayer.

Astley, R. (1987). Never gonna give you up [Song]. On *Whenever You Need Somebody* [Album]. RCA Records.

Bee Gees. (1977). Stayin' alive [Song]. On *Saturday Night Fever* [Album]. Capitol Music Group.

Bee Gees. (1979). Tragedy [Song]. On *Spirits Having Flown.* RSO Records.

Berlin. (1986). Take my breath away [Song]. On *Top Gun: Motion Picture Soundtrack.* Columbia Records.

Blue Swede. (1974). Hooked on a feeling [Song] On *Hooked on a Feeling.* EMI

Cake. (1996). I will survive [Song]. On *Fashion Nugget* [Album]. Capricorn.

Cake. (1998). Never there [Song]. On Pro*longing the Magic* [Album]. Capricorn Records.

Cake. (2001). Comfort eagle. On *Comfort Eagle* [Album]. Columbia Records.

Cake. (2001). Short skirt/long jacket. On *Comfort Eagle* [Album]. Columbia Records.

Call, A., & Keller, J. (1981). 867-5309/Jenny [Song]. On *Tommy Tutone 2* [Album]. Columbia.

Carter Family. (1935). Can the circle be unbroken (by and by) [Song]. On *Can the Circle Be Unbroken: Country Music's First Family.* Banner Records.

Cash, J. (1968). Folsom prison blues [Song]. On *At Folsom Prison* [Album]. Columbia.

Christie, A. (1934). *Murder on the Orient Express.* Collins Crime Club.

Chumbawamba. (1997). Tubthumping [Song]. On *Tubthumper* [Album]. EMI Records.

Coen, J. (Director). (1987). *Raising Arizona* [Film]. Circle Films; 20th Century Fox.

Coldplay. (2008). Viva la vida [Song]. On *Viva la Vida or Death and All His Friends.* Parlophone; Capitol Records.

Cole, P. (1996). Where have all the cowboys gone? [Song]. On *This Fire* [Album]. Warner Bros.

Columbus, C. (Director). (2002). *Harry Potter and the Chamber of Secrets* [Film]. Warner Bros.

Coppola, F. F. (Director). (1972). *The Godfather* [Motion picture]. Paramount Pictures.

Curtiz, M. (Director). (1942). *Casablanca* [Film]. Warner Bros.

David, L., & Seinfeld, J. (Writers). (1995). The soup nazi [Television series episode]. In *Seinfeld.* NY: NBC.

Demme, J. (Director). (1991). *The Silence of the Lambs* [Film]. Orion Pictures.

Dostoyevsky, F. (2006). *Crime and Punishment* (S. Monas, Trans.). Signet Classic. (Original work published 1866)

Fischer, P. S., Levinson, R., & Link, W. (Executive Producers). (1984-1996). *Murder, She Wrote* [TV series]. Universal Television.

Flack, R. (1973). Killing me softly with his song [Song]. On *Killing Me Softly.* Atlantic.

Forman, M. (Director). (1975). *One Flew Over the Cuckoo's Nest* [Film]. United Artists.

Frank, A. (1995). *The Diary of a Young Girl: The Definitive Edition* (B.M. Mooyaart-Doubleday, Trans.). Doubleday.

Gaynor, G. (1978). I will survive [Song]. On *Love Tracks* [Album]. Polydor.

Goldman, W. (1973). *The Princess Bride: S. Morgenstern's Classic Tale of True Love and High Adventure.* Harcourt Brace.

Gordon, R. W. (1926). *Come By Here* [Audio recording by H. Wylie]. Library of Congress, American Folklife Center, Robert Winslow Gordon Cylinder Collection (AFC 1928/002). Retrieved from www.loc.gov/item/ihas.200197143/

Green Day. (1994). Welcome to paradise [Song]. On *Dookie.* Reprise.

Hanna, W., & Barbera, J. (Executive Producers). (1960–1966). *The Flintstones* [TV series]. Hanna-Barbera Productions.

Hawthorne, N. (1878) *The Scarlet Letter.* J.R. Osgood and Company.

Hitchcock, A. (1945). *Spellbound* [Film]. Selznick International Pictures.

Hitchcock, A. (Director). (1946). *Notorious* [Film]. RKO Radio Pictures; Vanguard Films.

Hitchcock, A. (Director). (1958). *Vertigo* [Film]. Paramount Pictures.

Holland, E., Dozier, B., & Holland, B. (1966). You can't hurry love [Song]. On *The Supremes A' Go-Go* [Album]. Motown Records.

Ivory, J. (Director). (1993). *The Remains of the Day* [Film]. Columbia Pictures.

Jackson, P. (Director). (2001). *The Lord of the Rings: The Fellowship of the Ring* [Film; four-disc special extended ed. on DVD]. WingNut Films; The Saul Zaentz Company.

Joel, B. (1978). My life [Song]. On *52nd Street* [Album]. Columbia Records.

Joel, B. (1980). You may be right [Song]. On *Glass Houses.* Columbia.

Kleiser, R. (1978). *Grease* [Film]. Paramount Pictures.

Kool & the Gang. (1980). Celebration [Song]. On *Celebrate!* De-Lite.

Kubrick, S. (Director). (1980). *The Shining* [Film]. Warner.

Lean, D. (Director). (1968). *Oliver!* [Film]. Columbia Pictures.

McTiernan, J. (Director). (1988). *Die Hard* [Film]. Twentieth Century Fox.

Nash, J. (1972). I can see clearly now [Song]. *On I Can See Clearly Now.* Epic Records.

Presley, E. (2002). Suspicious minds [Song]. On *Elvis 30 #1 Hits* [Album]. RCA Records. (Original work by James, M. (1969).

R.E.M. (1991). Losing my religion [Song]. On *Out of Time* [Album]. Warner Bros.

Reiner, R. (Director). (1987). *The Princess Bride* [Film]. Twentieth Century Fox.

Robinson, S. & The Miracles. (1967). I second that emotion [Song]. On *I Second That Emotion.* Tamla/Motown.

Rogers, K., & Parton, D. (1983). Islands in the stream [Song] On *Eyes That See in the Dark.* RCA Records.

Rowling, J. K. (1997). *Harry Potter and the Sorcerer's Stone.* Scholastic.

Run-DMC. (1986). Peter piper [Song]. On *Raising Hell* [Album]. Profile Records.

Sade. (1984). Smooth operator [Song]. On *Diamond Life.* Epic.

Simon, P. (1986). You can call me Al [Song]. On *Graceland.* Warner Bros.

Spelling, A., & Goldberg, L. (Executive Producers). (1977–1984). *Fantasy Island* [TV series]. Created By Gene Levitt. Spelling-Goldberg Productions; Columbia Pictures TV.

Steinbeck, J. (2000/1937). *Of Mice and Men.* Penguin Classics.

Stevenson, R. (Director). (1968). *The Love Bug* [Film]. Walt Disney.

T-shirts donated by fernfactor.com.

The Beatles. (1965). I'm looking through you [Song]. On *Rubber Soul* [Album]. Parlophone.

The Beatles. (1969). Something [Song]. On *Abbey Road.* Apple Records.

The Beatles. (1970). Get back [Song]. On *Let It Be* [Album]. Apple Records.

Tolkien, J. R. R. (1993). *The Lord of the Rings.* 2nd ed. Houghton Mifflin Co.

Tolstoy, L. (1993). *War and Peace* (L. Maude & A. Maude, Trans.). Wordsworth Editions.

Traditional folk song (n.d.). *She'll Be Coming 'Round the Mountain* [Song].

Train. (2009). Hey, soul sister [Song]. On *Save Me, San Francisco* [Album]. Columbia/Sony.

Valli, F. (1978). Grease [Song]. On *Grease: The Original Soundtrack from the Motion Picture* [Album]. RSO Records.

Van Halen. (1984). Panama [Song]. On *1984* [Album]. Warner Bros. Records.

Warren, D. (1997). How do I live [Recorded by T. Yearwood]. On *Songbook: A Collection Of Hits* [CD]. MCA Nashville.

Wham!. (1984). Wake me up before you go-go [Song]. On *Make it Big.* Columbia; Epic.

White, T. H. (1958). *The Once and Future King.* G. P. Putnam's Sons.

Wilder, B. (Director). (1944). *Double Indemnity* [Motion picture]. Paramount Pictures.

Williams, T. (1947). *A Streetcar Named Desire.* Signet.

Witt, P., Thomas, T., & Harris, S. (Executive Producers). (1985-1992). *The Golden Girls* [TV series]. Touchstone Television.

Wittliff, W. D. (Writer), & Wincer, S. (Director). (1989, February 5–8). Lonesome Dove [TV miniseries]. Motown Productions; Pangaea; Qintex Entertainment.

Work, J. W., Ryder, N. W., King, A. G., Fisk University Jubilee Singers & Myers, J. A. (1909) *There is a balm in Gilead.* [Audio] Retrieved from the Library of Congress, https://www.loc.gov/item/ jukebox-128181

About the Author

James P. Rochester Jr. III is a very private, reclusive person. He was last known to be raising alpacas in Uruguay. He is a man of naturally mean talents and is pained in disposition or that. His relatives deny any resemblance and he has little time to spare.

Our Sponsors

www.fernfactor.com

Incapables.org
Hey Big Felon.org
Saints of Restraint.org
Comedic Relief Line.org
SnapBackApp.org

I hope you enjoyed this book.
Please keep in touch!
www.jamesprochester.com

Made in the USA
Coppell, TX
15 May 2026

77526221R00184